PRAISE FOR

ANNE HOLT

'Step aside, Stieg Larsson, Holt is the queen of Scandinavian crime thrillers' *Red*

'Holt writes with the command we have come to expect from the top Scandinavian writers' *The Times*

'If you haven't heard of Anne Holt, you soon will' *Daily Mail*

'It's easy to see why Anne Holt, the former Minister of Justice in Norway and currently its bestselling female crime writer, is rapturously received in the rest of Europe' *Guardian*

'Holt deftly marshals her perplexing narrative … clichés are resolutely seen off by the sheer energy and vitality of her writing' *Independent*

'Her peculiar blend of off-beat police procedural and social commentary makes her stories particularly Norwegian, yet also entertaining and enlightening … reads a bit like a mash-up of Stieg Larsson, Jeffery Deaver and Agatha Christie' *Daily Mirror*

Also by Anne Holt

THE SELMA FALCK SERIES:

A Grave for Two

THE HANNE WILHELMSEN SERIES:

Blind Goddess

Blessed Are Those Who Thirst

Death of the Demon

The Lion's Mouth

Dead Joker

No Echo

Beyond the Truth

1222

Offline

In Dust and Ashes

THE VIK/STUBO SERIES:

Punishment

The Final Murder

Death in Oslo

Fear Not

What Dark Clouds Hide

ANNE HOLT

A NECESSARY DEATH

Translated from the Norwegian
by Anne Bruce

CORVUS

First published in Great Britain in 2021 by Corvus,
an imprint of Atlantic Books Ltd.

Originally published in Norwegian as *Furet/værbitt*. Published by
agreement with the Salomonsson Agency.

10 9 8 7 6 5 4 3 2 1

A CIP catalogue record for this book is available from the British Library.

Hardback ISBN: 978 1 78649 867 0
Trade paperback ISBN: 978 1 78649 853 3
E-book ISBN: 978 1 78649 855 7

Printed in Great Britain.

Corvus
An imprint of Atlantic Books Ltd
Ormond House
26–27 Boswell Street
London
WC1N 3JZ

www.corvus-books.co.uk

Yes, we love with fond devotion
This our land that looms
Rugged, storm-scarred o'er the ocean
With her thousand homes.

(Norwegian national anthem, Bjørnstjerne Bjørnson)

It is a paradox that liberal democracy's greatest strength
is also its greatest weakness: tolerance of those who wish to
destroy it.

(Bård Larsen, *Democracy in Trouble*. Civita, 2019)

Previously, we politicians were made to pay if we did
something wrong. Nowadays we're met with malice,
contempt and hate when we do the right thing.

(Minister of Justice Tryggve Mejer, *A Necessary Death*)

AUTUMN 2018

Selma Falck

S omeone shouts.

What she hears is her own voice, but she can't make out the words. She can't force her eyes open and her brain is empty. Nothing but pitch-blackness, thick and sticky, or maybe soft, as if it's stuffed with cotton wool. Cotton is a word she remembers.

She searches inside for her own name. For who she is and where she is now. Seconds, minutes, pass, it's impossible to know how long, all she notices is that time exists. It passes. Time passes, and she is freezing, even though she is aware of the crackling of a fire.

Still in the dark, she turns her head, and through her eyelids she can make out something red and flickering. Something is burning, and she can smell it now, a whiff of scorched pinewood.

Panic strikes her, pitching up from her diaphragm. Adrenaline pumps through her body. She touches her crotch and realizes she is naked, she is shivering, something is burning, and she simply can't open her eyes, it is just impossible.

Selma, she suddenly whispers. I am Selma Falck.

The Meeting

'It's time. It's our solemn duty!'

Tryggve Mejer was the one who broke in. He ran both hands through his hair and slammed his palms on the table. The slap was muted, as if he had regretted his outburst at the very last second.

'No,' a voice piped up. 'Not yet. Probably never.'

The old man sat at the end of the table. He weighed half of what he had during the war. Soon he would have put a whole century on earth behind him, and his voice was barely audible as he cleared his throat and continued: 'This was not what we had in mind at all. This is not our battle.'

The four others around the table, three men and one woman, said nothing.

Oppressive, stuffy silence.

The old man placed his hands on the casket in front of him. His fingers were skinny, and the yellow nails scraped on the wood when he finally drew it towards him and, with an almost imperceptible sigh, lifted it on to his knee. The cedar-wood casket was scarcely bigger than a shoebox, and everyone present knew approximately what it contained. It certainly was not heavy. Nevertheless, a grimace crossed the man's wrinkled face, as if the exertion was too much for him. The man raised his eyes again, and let them flit around the table.

At one time his eyes had been sky-blue. Now a cataract had consumed the one on the right and the entire eyeball was grey. The colour of the iris on his left eye had also faded with the years, as if most of the blue pigment had been used up. All the same, there was still strength in his gaze, and he was well aware that he was the one whose decision was final. The others seated around the highly polished table were his to command for as long as he retained the power of thought.

And he did.

Ellev Trasop was the man's name, and he had been born on 11 November 1918.

The baby boy had arrived with the peace.

At five o'clock in the morning, as he was fighting his way out into the world in the National Hospital in Norway, a ceasefire agreement was signed in a railway carriage in the French town of Compiègne. Six hours later, at eleven minutes past eleven a.m. on the eleventh day of the eleventh month, the most dreadful war in the history of the world until then was over.

'Peace,' Ellev said quietly. 'It is peace we must protect.'

'Peace,' Tryggve repeated, nodding his head. 'Exactly. Peace, freedom and democracy. That is what we must ensure.'

He grabbed the edge of the table with both hands.

'Don't you see what's happening, Ellev? Can't you see that everything is falling apart? Don't you appreciate that respect for everything that's the very foundation of—'

'The meeting is over,' the old man interrupted. 'The decision has been taken. You are the Minister of Justice, Tryggve. You, of all people, ought to know the rules we are bound by. It was not this threat that we were to vanquish. Not all ... this. This is just ...'

His hand waved the rest of the sentence away. At the same time, the signal caused the till-now almost invisible woman dressed in black who stood by the door to tread soundlessly across the floor towards him. With practised movements, she unlocked the brakes on his wheelchair and pushed the casket further down on Ellev's lap.

'You'll hear from me by summer,' he mumbled as he was wheeled towards the double doors leading into the detested bedroom in which he was forced to spend more and more of his time. 'If I'm spared.'

He knew that no one could hear this final remark.

Mina Mejer Selmer

'You really can't go on like this.'

Dad was standing in the doorway. Mina glanced up; he looked exhausted. He raked his hand through his hair in a gesture of despair, just like when Mum was at her most unreasonable.

'I can well understand that this has been difficult,' he said.

Mina did not answer.

'Ingeborg was ill, sweetheart. Extremely ill.'

'She was exactly the same age as me, Dad.'

Crossing his arms, her father leaned his shoulder against the doorframe. He had put on weight, she noticed. His stomach was hanging over his belt, which was too tight, and his face was pale, even though the weather had been bright and sunny for the past fortnight.

There was not much sunshine inside his office, of course. Or in those black limousines. Or in the Parliament building, or on planes or in meetings. Or in bed, for that matter, into which he usually collapsed long before it had even crossed her mind to call it a night.

'Teenagers get ill too,' he said softly. 'Even small children get cancer and die. Accidents happen. That's life. Unfortunately.'

Mina ran her thumb over the display on her mobile. 'She didn't have cancer,' she muttered.

'No.'

'Ingeborg was healthy a year ago.'

'Yes. And then she became ill. These things happen.'

'She was driven to death by bullies.'

His eyes narrowed. 'Now you're being melodramatic.'

'You know nothing about it.'

'Yes, I do. The police have looked into the case, and Ingeborg was not subjected to anything more serious than what every teenager in this country sadly—'

'Ingeborg just couldn't stand it,' she broke in. 'Were you the one who knew her, or what? Were you the one who had to comfort her?'

'Yes, I knew Ingeborg. Not the way you did, of course, but she was your very best friend. Naturally I knew her. It was terribly sad that she died, but six weeks have gone by since the funeral, and you must somehow—'

'Get over it? Get over Ingeborg, is that what you're saying?'

She shouldn't cry. Shouldn't. She bowed her head and covered her eyes with one hand, quick as a flash – a magic invocation to ward off the tears. She forced a smile and looked up again.

Dad looked so worn out. Even more so than when he had come in only a few minutes ago.

He nodded his head slightly in the direction of the living room. 'Shall we play a game? Chess? Cards?'

Mina shook her head and placed her thumb on her phone. 'Tryggve Mejer is a traitor,' she read aloud. 'He'll be first in the queue when the People ...' She glanced up. 'They've started to write "people" with a capital P. As if they were a tribe or something.'

5

'Give over,' he said, taking one step inside the room. 'You need to stop that. Put it away.'

She threw the phone down on the quilt. Her father came closer and sat down on the edge of the bed. Mina drew up her feet and clasped her hands around her knees. Her father smelled of evening time. Day-old stress, and a little of the hair gel he combed through his hair every single morning and that turned a bit rancid in the course of a working day.

'You're sixteen,' he said. 'You shouldn't be bothering about such comments.'

'They're threatening to kill you.'

'Don't visit those websites. Don't give a damn about them. Their bark is worse than their bite. Far worse. Tough as nails behind a keyboard, but spineless cowards the minute they're confronted with that filth.'

'Every day, Dad. Everywhere. All the time. And not just ...'

No.

Dad should not know. He most certainly did not need to know any more. Dad was thirty-four years older than her, but sometimes she got the feeling she had to look after him all the same.

That she was actually the only one who *could* look after him.

'It's just a transition stage,' he said quietly. 'Humanity must get acclimatized to the internet. Your generation is going to fix it. You're the ones who've grown up with all these opportunities.'

His gaze shifted from the MacBook on the desk to the iPad on the bedside table, finishing up at her mobile.

'I trust you and your peers,' he said in an undertone, placing a hand on her back. 'You'll learn the limitations. The norms. Acceptable rules will be arrived at eventually.'

Mina did not respond.

'Come on,' he whispered, touching her neck. 'Let's find

6

something to do. And then we'll go to bed. We have to be up early in the morning.'

'Not me,' Mina said.

'Aren't you coming? It's the seventeenth of May! Our National Day! I'm going to make a speech at ...'

Mina lifted her face and looked at him. For a long time and in total silence. If she did not give up, and held eye contact, he would give way. As he always did. The way she could always, for some reason she had never before been able to fathom, employ a lingering look to force him to nod and leave.

Dad nodded and left.

AUTUMN

The Fire

Selma Falck could now remember her own name, but it was still impossible to open her eyes.

The smell of the fire was even more acrid now.

She was still frozen, but maybe only on one side. She tried to turn over towards the source of the heat. Her entire body was aching, and she changed her mind. She had to see it first.

Her eyes had to open, but they simply refused.

She stretched her body as much as she possibly could. Raised her right arm. It lifted. She guided her hand towards one eye and forced it open between her thumb and forefinger. It was swollen and sore, but it did remain open. She repeated the procedure on the other eye.

Stared straight up. The ceiling was untreated pine. Old and yellowed, with a flickering red glow from something that must be a fireplace. Slowly she sat up, at the same time trying to ascertain whether all this terrible pain was a result of serious injury. Whether she had broken something. Or was badly burnt; the smoke from the fire was stinging her nose more and more. She sat up straight when she finally managed to turn her head. Nothing in her body seemed grievously damaged. She had just been beaten up, and felt tender and bruised, exactly like after a never-ending handball match in hell, and she failed to comprehend why she was naked.

The fire was not burning in a fireplace. The whole wall was engulfed in flames.

She was sitting in a spartanly equipped cabin, in the living room, measuring barely twenty square metres. The furnishings could not have been renewed since the sixties. Pine everywhere, and dilapidated tartan upholstery. For some reason, the windows had no curtains. On the other side, it was pitch dark. The flames licked up the wall only three metres away from her, and she leapt to her feet faster than her aches and pains would actually allow. She groaned once she was upright, staggering and unsteady, as she struggled to force her brain to take in her surroundings.

And why she was there.

That would have to wait.

In the middle of the blazing wall she could see a fireplace. A fire had burnt down to a mound of red-hot coals in the deep, open hearth. The cinders were not inside the wrought-iron grate as they should be. The entire hearth was full to the brim and a broad trail of logs, still alight, had been built out from the fireplace and along the walls on either side. The flames had caught the wall panelling and already climbed a couple of metres up the timber. When Selma raised her eyes, she realized that it would be only a matter of seconds before the ceiling was also consumed by the flames. An ice-cold pain shot up through her thighs into the small of her back when she stepped back.

Fire extinguisher, she thought.

She tottered towards the only door in the room. Although closed, it was not locked, and led out into a long, narrow hallway. It smelled of age and dust, and she had to make do with the light from the fire in the adjacent room.

No light switches. A paraffin lamp with a glass globe was suspended from the ceiling above what she assumed to be the front door, right at the end of the hallway.

The cabin had no electricity.

The thought of a fire extinguisher occurred to her again, and she felt yet another jolt of fear when she recalled that cabins without electricity also usually had no plumbed-in water.

Selma could not remember what date it was. Not even what year it was.

On the main wall to the left were two small doors and she opened the first of these. The kitchen. Tiny, with a worktop, two cupboards and a washtub perched on a stool. Immediately inside the door was a black woodstove.

Cold.

No fire extinguisher here.

The fire had begun to crackle, and the noise grew louder and louder. She ran out of the ancient kitchen to open the next door. This room was slightly larger and bunk beds took up most of the space. The lower bunk was made up; Selma thought she could make this out in the almost total darkness. The upper mattress had no bed linen. There was a cupboard behind the door, but it was empty, as she discovered when she opened it and thrust her hand inside the inky blackness.

The fire in the living room was now roaring.

It dawned on Selma that she was not going to find a fire extinguisher. On the spur of the moment, she grabbed the quilt from the bunk bed, dragged it with her and rushed back to confront the flames.

The ceiling had caught fire. The other walls too. Pungent black smoke billowed up from the stuffing on a two-seater settee near the fireplace.

It was too late. The fire could not be extinguished, at least not with a quilt. She had to get out. The moment she made up her mind, she spotted her bag, the bright yellow North Face duffle bag. Well, she had one like that, at least. She now saw that her clothes were slung over it. Holding the quilt up in front of her as a shield from the flames, she only managed to stagger a couple of steps before the wall collapsed. Cinders and heat surged towards her. Automatically, she threw off the quilt, forward, to ward off the heat that was now so intense that, unthinking, she lurched towards the hallway. At the door she turned one last time.

Her clothes were on fire. Her bag was on fire.

The whole cabin would soon be ablaze, and she was still naked.

She could not remember spotting anything useful in the kitchen, and had no time to check more closely. She tore the sheet from the bunk in the bedroom before grabbing the front door handle. Heavier than the others, it was made of brass that still felt cold to the touch.

The door did not budge.

She wrenched the metal hard, rattling it repeatedly, and suddenly the door sprang open: it had not been locked after all.

She was out.

Panting violently, she pushed her feet into a pair of enormous wellington boots she found on the stone steps and fled from the burning cabin.

Once she was at a safe distance, she wheeled around to see the little house blazing ferociously.

Outdoors, it was icy cold: night or evening or crack of dawn. A half moon, glimpsed behind scudding clouds, showed that she was completely alone.

The mountain plateau stretched out around her in every direction. She was far above the tree line, and maybe not even in Norway.

There was no light to be seen from other cabins. No diffused light from distant settlements. Only grey-black sky, the occasional star, craggy knolls, barren ridges and heather.

Her body ached all over.

Her legs and back, her stomach and arms and hands. When she tried to wrap the sheet around her and ran her fingers through her tangled hair, even her scalp felt sore and painful to touch. Selma's teeth were chattering and she moved closer to the fire to get some heat at least. She still had no idea where she was. Her headache was almost unbearable. Her thoughts were not even spinning: her mind was quite simply dark and blank.

'Selma Falck,' she whispered over and over again with every step she took into the frosty heather. 'I am Selma Falck.'

She stumbled on, zigzagging across the ground, and stopped suddenly as the flames broke through the turf roof. For a split second, a tremendous shower of sparks shed light on her surroundings.

That was when she saw it.

The car.

Selma's red Volvo Amazon 123 GT from 1966 was parked close to the front cabin wall. The sight brought her to a sudden halt. Soot and flakes of burning timber drizzled down from the sky and it struck her that the car could burst into flames at any moment.

She had obviously driven to this godforsaken place. After all, her car was here, it had climbed high into the mountains, and so she must be able to make the journey home.

Selma broke into a run. The sheet slid from her body as she rushed on, stark naked, as fast as the pair of ancient boots that were far too big for her would allow. She stumbled, kicking off her footwear, and ran on. Yet another rumble, a small explosion, and the rest of the roof collapsed.

Selma kept running. She had to rescue the car. If she didn't save the car, she would most likely die out here.

SPRING

The Casket

It was high summer in the middle of May.

At night, it was still only eight to ten degrees Celsius, but on this day too the temperature had soared to well over twenty degrees even before noon. From the living-room window of the old villa in Terneveien in Hasle, Tryggve Meyer could see the Oslo Fjord glittering below, behind a city that had settled down for a rest on the day after a successful, exhausting National Day. The hum of traffic on Grenseveien, usually steady and distinct even with the windows closed, was now muffled, almost absent; only now and then did a lorry rumble past and make the crystals on the huge chandelier jingle. It was the Friday between a public holiday and the weekend, a day off taken by those who were brazen enough.

Tryggve had his hands clasped behind his back. He stood with his legs apart, squinting at the bright light. In the courtyard outside, the black limousine's chauffeur had stepped out to stand in the shade of an enormous chestnut tree. When he glanced up and caught sight of the Justice Minister, he gave a crooked smile, patted his pocket and decided against it.

'Did the day go well?' a voice squeaked from the wheelchair behind him. 'Would you like some coffee?'

Tryggve turned around with a smile. 'No, thanks. I'd prefer some Farris. And yes, the day turned out well. Apart from Mina being at the age when …'

He gave a slight shrug. Crossed to the settee of midnight-blue brocade and sat down. Ellev Trasop waved to his carer, and was immediately trundled across the room. Another wave of his skinny hand and she disappeared as surprisingly soundlessly as always. Tryggve Mejer poured some Farris mineral water from a bottle into a crystal glass before raising it with a questioning gesture towards the old man.

'Yes, please. She's sixteen now, isn't she? Mina?'

'Almost seventeen. And a sworn anti-nationalist. The celebration of our national constitution has become an abomination for her. It's the first time since the age of two that she hasn't worn her national costume for the occasion.'

The sunlight etched sharp geometric outlines in white against the dark interior. Tryggve screwed up his eyes as he peered at the old man who sat in the midst of the pool of light, and without asking, the Justice Minister abruptly got to his feet and returned to the large casement window. The curtains were heavy and the fabric felt almost greasy on his fingers as he drew them shut. The living room was suddenly bathed in semi-darkness, considerably more comfortable.

'Thanks,' Ellev Trasop said, with a sigh. 'These carers insist on light and fresh air. I call all this airing nothing but a draught. And we old folk should beware of draughts, as you know. The sunlight nowadays wipes out what little sight I have left, into the bargain.'

A trembling hand rubbed beneath his nose, where a little droplet had been threatening to fall ever since Tryggve's arrival.

'Political commitment in teenagers is nearly always a good thing,' he said. 'No matter what. Is she still as clever?'

'If by clever you mean clever at school, then yes. She's taken advanced classes in Maths and English for a few years now. She plays handball, though not at a particularly high level. Dancing on Thursdays. She also has a job at weekends, clearing tables in a restaurant. I can't fathom how she finds time for it all. But that's how it is at that age. Can't miss out on anything.'

'And politics? Is she still as keen a member of the party's youth wing?'

Tryggve refrained from answering. 'How was *your* seventeenth of May?' he asked instead.

'Berit called in.'

'The Major?'

'Yes, she's a nice girl, Berit. A very nice girl.'

'She's older than me. Anything else? What did you do?'

'I'm too old now to celebrate. Too old to live, to be honest.'

Ellev sighed and seemed to shrink into his chair. His shoulders were so narrow and angular that it was no longer possible to find clothes to fit properly. At least the kind of clothes he insisted upon: immaculate white shirts with starched collars under a dark blazer for meetings and other occasions when he met people, and blue checked flannel shirts to wear at home. Both options made him resemble a wrecked scarecrow. Ellev Trasop's clothes were clean and, judging by appearances, received excellent care, but he gave off a cloying smell all the same. Not only from his less than fresh breath. It was as if he had already started to die from the inside out. A faint smell of decay seemed to seep out through his yellow, porous skin.

'I'm going to die,' he said, sighing.

'We all are.'

'Don't put on an act.'

'I didn't mean it like that.'

'It means you'll have to take over. And that you have promises to give me.'

Tryggve inhaled a deep breath through his mouth and let it leak out slowly through his nose.

'We've talked it all over,' he said quietly. 'A long time ago.'

'No, not entirely. You can't initiate this ...' His slender claw of a hand waved in mid-air. '... Rugged/Storm-scarred operation of yours. You simply can't.'

Tryggve studied the old man and said: 'We're living in dangerous times.'

Ellev looked up. 'I know that,' he replied.

His eyes were terrifying. Tryggve always tried to fix his gaze on the still functional part. It was now so lacklustre that the old man most of all resembled a Roman marble statue, with blind eyes missing an iris.

'We are nonetheless a liberal democracy,' Ellev continued. 'Paradoxical, I know. The greatest strength of liberal democracy is also our greatest weakness: we have to tolerate those who wish to destroy it.'

'Exactly. A paradox. A dilemma. That we will soon be forced to resolve.'

'If we resolve it, we cease to exist.'

'If we don't resolve it, we go to the dogs.'

'No!'

Ellev's voice cracked in a rasping falsetto. As he began to cough, he grabbed the glass of mineral water and drank deeply and slowly. Returned his glass to the coffee table with hands that were shaking even more.

'I'm going to die soon,' he insisted, 'probably in the next few days. That's why I asked you to come.'

A grandfather clock struck three in an adjacent room. Tryggve suddenly felt a jolt of unpleasant nausea. A bouquet of lilies in a tall vase by the window exuded a sickly-sweet, heavy scent of putrid water. He swallowed audibly and opened his mouth to say something.

'In other words, you have to take over the casket,' the old man said, stealing a march on him. 'And everything that goes along with that.'

'But ... you ...'

'I really think it would be better if Berit takes over. Far better. Her background is in the military and she demonstrates better judgement than you do.'

'Better judgement? What do you know about—'

'I know everything that's worth knowing,' the old man interrupted sharply. 'But giving the casket to Berit would mean breaking a pact between your father and myself. I can't do that. It's sitting over there. Fetch it, please.'

Tryggve glanced across at an imposing, dark oak sideboard. The little cedar-wood casket sat on one side of it. He remained stubbornly in his seat.

'That was the agreement,' Ellev said, a touch more gently this time. 'You've known of it since before he died.'

This was correct. Tryggve Mejer was fifty years old, and for the past twenty of these he had been aware that he would at some point or other take over this responsibility. He shared this knowledge with three other men and one woman.

No one else.

For all his adult life he had juggled the roles of politician and lawyer, father, husband and bearer of national secrets in precisely the same way as his own father had done. His existence was compartmentalized. Some of the compartments were connected: many were bright and clear, others lay closed and locked in a far corner of his soul. There was a great deal he was able to talk about, but other things he could only share with a very few. Certain secrets were his, and his alone.

Such as that for the past six months he had been looking forward to Ellev Trasop's death.

'Are you ill?' he asked.

The hoarse laughter changed into a feeble coughing fit. 'I've been ill since I was eighty,' Ellev enlightened him when he recovered his breath. 'But yes, I'm even *more* ill now.'

His hand tentatively tapped his chest. 'My heart. It doesn't want to go on. I don't either, to be honest. You know, when my peers began to drop dead around me, it was sad. When their children began to peg out, it moved me even more deeply. I've no wish to go on living until it's their grandchildren's turn to grow old and die. Fetch the casket, please.'

Tryggve rose from his seat. He almost stumbled on the thick carpet, but managed to regain his balance. For a moment he stood in front of the sideboard staring at the box that he had never seen without the lid being closed and locked.

It was not necessary anyway. He knew what it contained. It had existed since 1948 and been opened now and again, including by his own father. No doubt some items had been removed and others added by a number of men in consecutive succession, of whom all except Ellev Trasop were now deceased.

'Bring it here,' Tryggve heard behind him.

He used both hands to carry the casket and set it down in front of Ellev. The old man reached out his hand. Tryggve noticed a little key and moved to take it, but Ellev closed his fingers around it, preventing him.

'You must promise me you won't do it.'

'I can promise not to do anything rash. Nothing out of keeping with the remit.'

'We weren't established for that purpose, Tryggve.'

'Yes, we were, we were constituted to protect democracy.'

'In case of a possible occupation.'

'In a sense we are already occupied.'

'We are not.'

18

Tryggve Mejer calmly took the old man's hand. He forced the fingers open, and found barely any resistance in them. Took the key. It was small and unassuming, almost like the keys for the diaries young girls wrote in when he was young himself. He stood up to his full height and tucked it inside his pocket.

'We're at war with lies,' he said. 'With evil, ignorance, unreason, smear campaigns and hatred. And we're in the process of losing. A living democracy implies not only free debate. Someone must also be willing to take them on.'

The old man's breathing had become laboured and shallow.

'Increasingly, people hang back,' Tryggve said. 'Locally. Regionally. And most definitely at national level. Take Elisabeth Bakke, for instance. She's not even forty, and has been involved in politics all her life. Former leader of the Young Conservatives. A Member of Parliament before she was thirty. An obvious future leader of the party. Amazingly competent. She had only one fault, Ellev. Only one. She speaks about immigration the way I do. As if immigrants are human beings. As if they actually mean something. She doesn't stand for anything revolutionary, not for anything ...'

His hand moved quickly through his hair before he leaned forward with his palm flat on the table.

'Not even anything radical. She's exactly as realistic as I am, and knows that we have to set boundaries. Quite literally. It's just a matter of rhetoric. Of decency.'

'She stepped down for family reasons,' the old man said. 'That's still permitted.'

'She stepped down because she couldn't stand it any longer!' Tryggve said, raising his voice. 'She couldn't bear the messages, the hatred. The comments on social media. Elisabeth gave up politics because she quite simply couldn't take any more. And she's not alone, Ellev. Sadly, she's not alone in being unable to take

19

any more of it. Or in losing the taste for entering politics altogether. There are local elections next year, and we can no longer persuade the best candidates to stand.'

All of a sudden he got to his feet again. This time he ran both hands through his thick hair.

'We can't lose the best candidates,' he said, with a sigh. 'A democracy needs its most capable women and men. Being a politician has always entailed hardship. It should do. You're placed under a magnifying glass, my father said to me when I embarked on it myself. That was fine. You're held accountable for every smallest action, he said. Inside and outside the party. That was fine too. Now, however …'

For a fleeting second, he hesitated. Cocked his head and took a deep breath before he ploughed on: 'Now the situation is such that real misconduct has hardly any consequences. A rap on the knuckles and a fortnight's media storm, and then things are back to normal. Those of us who still try to stand for something, to hold opinions, to stick to the occasional principle, have to wade through a morass of savagery and malice. We are losing the best people, Ellev, and that's dangerous.'

He thrust his hands into his pockets and hovered over him so that Ellev was forced to meet his eye.

'In the past, we politicians were made to pay if we did something wrong,' he said. 'Nowadays we're met with malice, contempt and hate when we do the right thing.'

Someone knocked on the door. Without waiting for an answer, a woman in black entered, carrying a tray. 'Tea,' she said briskly, and superfluously, as she put down two cups, a sugar bowl and a pot of tea on the coffee table.

The two men remained silent until she picked up the tray and disappeared again.

'Mina has given up the AUF.'

'What?'

The old man appeared befuddled for a moment. Then he leaned forward towards the teapot.

'Here,' Tryggve said, beating him to it. He poured out a cup, dropped in two sugar lumps and stirred it with an engraved teaspoon.

'What a shame,' Ellev mumbled. 'I had great expectations of that young girl. She could have become Prime Minister, Mina.'

Tryggve gave a guarded smile for the first time since he arrived. 'You were the one who manipulated her into the ranks of the social democrats,' he said. 'But now all that's at an end.'

'Why?'

'What do you think?'

He fished out his smartphone from his trouser pocket. 'The broken climate of debate. The many hate-filled arenas. All the hatred and abuse. Her best friend took her own life a while back. Absolutely tragic. The girl was mentally ill, of course, and according to what I've heard, wasn't subjected to any more than many others. But for some people that's enough, Ellev, and it certainly doesn't help the most sensitive among us that these ...'

The tea sat untouched. Tryggve lifted the saucer and held it out to the man in the wheelchair. He grabbed it with both hands; the cup rattled and the tea sloshed over.

'... shenanigans are allowed to continue.' He cast a glance at the display before returning the mobile to his pocket.

'Hatred towards individuals. Fake news. Lies and conspiracy theories. Twelve per cent of the American population still believe that Hillary Clinton is the leader of a murderous group of paedophiles! Even now! Some people believe ... some believe that the earth is flat, Ellev!'

'Some people have always thought that.'

'Yes. But they haven't had the opportunity to spread their idiocy in the same way. The conspiracy theories out there are totally out of control. They're spreading like a plague, helped along by extremist websites that make themselves look like "online newspapers". The comments sections there are like—'

'I don't know very much about that kind of thing,' Ellev cut in, raising his teacup with a shaky hand.

No, Tryggve thought. You know nothing of this at all.

'A liberal democracy can only survive as exactly that,' Ellev said, lowering his cup. 'To intervene, taking action against opinions, no matter how crazy they might be, would be democratic suicide. We're meant to protect the country from the communists, Tryggve. Not from people's strange opinions.'

'They aren't strange. They are downright dangerous. Mortally dangerous. And they're approaching a critical mass. An explosive, ignorant and highly critical mass that will destroy our country. The whole of the Western world, in fact.'

The teacup was about to topple. Tryggve took careful hold of it and put it back on the table.

'The Russians,' Ellev muttered. 'It was the Russians we were meant to protect ourselves from.'

'Exactly. The Russians.'

The old man stared up at him. Another droplet now hung from his nose, and his mouth quivered.

'The Russians are still working to destabilize other countries,' Tryggve said, lifting the casket. 'As they always have. Here, there and everywhere. They have destroyed the USA, possibly beyond all chance of setting everything to rights again. They're definitely not getting the opportunity to destroy us. Not as long as I'm able to put a stop to it.'

He moved to the door, towards the hallway, and placed one hand on the doorknob before turning around.

The man in the wheelchair was his godfather. He had once

been an impressive figure, at the full height of his powers. Ellev had taught him to ski and to cycle. He had been more of a father to him than his own father had been, a better support, despite the difference in their party allegiances.

Now he was nothing but a dry husk in a wheelchair.

That same night Ellev Trasop died, only six months short of his hundredth birthday.

AUTUMN

The Car

The fire was everywhere.

The flames soared over the supporting beam that held the roof ridge aloft, and that still stretched between the gable walls. It would not be long until it collapsed. The front and back walls had caved in a long time ago, each making a separate, noisy rectangular bonfire. The hearth and chimneystack stood black and threatening in the midst of it all, surrounded by a sea of fire.

Selma came to a sudden halt five metres from the car.

Burning wall panels had fallen on the bonnet. Even the huge lump of turf that now covered almost the entire car roof was ablaze. The acrid dark smoke surged towards her.

Despite all this, it would still be possible to save the car, but the heat was so intense that her body refused to go on.

She must.

She retreated further from the fire. Using both hands, with no thought for how much pain she was suffering, she uprooted icy heather from the ground. She rubbed it on her face, over her breasts, her thighs, over her whole body; it cooled her down, and the night frost wet her skin as it melted on her.

It was dry and unbearably hot before she had advanced even three metres. She grabbed the damp sheet and held it in front of her like a gigantic shield as she once again attempted to move closer to the car.

The sheet caught fire before she reached the vehicle.

She backed away, stumbling, sobbing, falling, with the heat in pursuit, searing her skin. Her mouth was sore. Her throat too, the mere effort of breathing must have singed her windpipe. She scrambled up again, half crawling, half running onwards. Not until she found herself one hundred metres from the fire and the cabin did she turn around and look back at the catastrophe.

The car was now engulfed in flames.

Selma had not heard any loud bangs. No dramatic explosion, like in films, when the petrol caught fire and the tank blew up. All she heard was creaking and crackling, and little thuds from falling firewood. The gable wall had also succumbed now and it was almost impossible to see the car.

All of a sudden, there was an almighty boom.

Selma jumped, crashing back into a large boulder. A ferocious pain shot up from the small of her back, making her scream.

It was the front windscreen cracking open, and the interior caught fire at once. Once again the smoke thickened into an almost impenetrable fog, and a few seconds later she was aware of the stench of burning plastic.

Slowly, as all the different pains decided to coalesce, making life totally intolerable, she got to her feet. Looked around. Nothing new had appeared. No people. No cars, or anything miraculous; no vehicle of any kind to bring her a sliver of hope of getting away from here.

Home.

Sagene, it dawned on her.

She lived in Sagene.

And suddenly she remembered a wedding.

The Wedding

Selma Falck was seated beside the toilet door at her only daughter's wedding reception.

As early as in the church, she should have realized that it was a bad move to have come. The first pew was reserved for the family and Selma arrived in good time. As she approached the people already seated there, they spread themselves out, taking only a few seconds to ensure there was no longer room for the bride's mother.

She should have turned on her heel and gone home.

Instead, and for reasons she was later at a loss to explain, she had followed the marriage ceremony from the second-back row. She had smiled afterwards as she boarded the bus laid on to convey the reception guests to the restaurant. She had amiably refused the offer of champagne during the waiting period while the bridal couple were being photographed on the Opera House roof. She had become bloated and slightly nauseated by the alcohol-free cider, which she had nevertheless had to continue drinking because the weather was so insufferably hot. Since other guests had buttonholed her from the moment she stepped on the bus in her dark-red dress until a bell rang to summon them to the tables, she had neglected to check the table plan.

When she finally reached the huge poster at the foot of the stone staircase, she had made up her mind.

She turned around to leave as discreetly as possible. In the stream of people making their way up, this was difficult. A stranger in his sixties with far too many teeth grabbed her arm and loudly announced that he was honoured to be her escort for the evening. Selma Falck, no less, he grinned as he dragged her, quite literally and rather roughly, with him up the stairs and towards the table in the corner beside the door marked with a blue and white pictogram. He pulled out her chair – it would move only so far – and Selma no longer had any choice. Behind her back, right on the other side of the terrace, past the almost two hundred guests who were all ranked more highly than her, sat the best man and chief bridesmaid, the bride and groom and the newlyweds' parents. Selma had been replaced by her ex-husband's new live-in partner, barely five years older than the bride herself. By now Jesso had already delivered his speech, in the interval between the starter and the fish course. Selma's back was aching from twisting round. Eventually she gave up and fixed her gaze on the door sign.

Not a breath of air reached the interior walls of the building.

The summer of 2018 was the hottest in living memory.

At least since 1947, declared the oldest man at the table, conjuring images of a post-war summer when fish were hauled ready-cooked out of the sea. 2018 was nothing compared to 1947, in his opinion, as he wiped the sweat from his forehead with a handkerchief so sodden that it had turned as grey as his complexion.

He was one of the lucky ones who had been invited to the wedding as early as February.

As for Selma, she had received a text message from her future son-in-law only ten days earlier:

Dear Selma Falck. If you would like to come to our wedding, I think it would be really nice. Anine too, I think. She does really. You most certainly belong at the celebrations on our big day. Best wishes from Sjalg Petterson.

It had been Sjalg who had made contact. She had not heard a single word from Anine.

The guests had offered Selma warm congratulations on the occasion, remarking on her daughter's obvious happiness; they hugged and clapped and exclaimed about the beautiful ceremony in the cathedral, the fantastic refreshments that awaited them on the terrace up here and not least the weather, this blessed, perpetual sunshine that had rolled across the entire country since early May.

Selma must be so proud, they all thought, and so incredibly happy.

She had smiled and made small talk for more than two excruciating hours. The heat was so extreme that the restaurant had run out of ice cubes long ago, and Selma was compelled to drink lukewarm Mozell, a soft drink made of apple and grape juice.

All the same, it was better than water at almost body temperature.

The man with the teeth had clearly not followed very much of the headline news in the past six months. As early as the starter, Selma could feel an unwelcome hand on her thigh. She firmly lifted it off. Seconds later, it was back again.

Selma could not take any more.

She rose from her chair, thrust her clutch bag under her right arm, smiled vaguely into thin air and made to leave. A short shriek made her wheel around.

In the days to follow, Selma would rerun the scene in her mind's eye, image by image, slowly and carefully. Sjalg Petterson was on his feet with the speech to his bride in his hand. He let it go and clutched his throat, his chest, he grew red in the face, then blue, before turning pale and tumbling down on to his chair. He tugged at his shirt collar, his bow tie, he tore and scratched until his grip slackened and both arms fell limply to his sides. The bridegroom's face took on a look of astonishment, his eyes became vacant, and he slumped slowly forward on to the table.

Anine let out another scream, more piercing this time, she called for a doctor, for Sjalg's EpiPen, for the adrenaline that could save him – it should be there, as it always was. Or maybe it was somewhere else.

Her husband's face hit the plate with a smack.

After a marriage lasting two hours and forty-nine minutes, Selma Falck's daughter was already a widow.

Anine was no longer the only one who was screaming.

The Assignment

Four days had elapsed since the wedding, and Sjalg Petterson's tragic death had already been cleared up. From both the descriptions provided by the many eyewitnesses and the preliminary post mortem, it was easy to conclude that the thirty-six-year-old man had died of anaphylactic shock.

He was extremely allergic to macadamia nuts.

'We knew that, of course,' Jesper Jørgensen said. 'The kitchen, the cool room, the crockery, the cutlery, the terrace … everything was washed down before we moved in. Absolutely everything. Virtually sterilized! Macadamia nuts are not exactly a food item that's difficult to avoid. I've hardly ever used such a nut in my entire career.'

The man flung out his arms in consternation.

Selma Falck knew that the career he was talking about had not been lengthy, though it had been considerably more successful.

Jesper Jørgensen was only twenty-seven years old, but was already considered one of the indisputably best chefs in the land. Four years earlier, he had won the Bocuse d'Or, the unofficial world championships of the culinary arts, as the youngest ever winner. Since then, he had built up his restaurant Ellevilt in Dronning Eufemias gate, in the midst of the Barcode Project, with the Opera House, the angled design of Lambda, the new Munch Museum, and all the other buildings that were slowly but surely progressing into some kind of modern urban quarter of Oslo of which Selma for one found it difficult to understand very much. Already, after eleven months in business, Ellevilt had been rewarded with a Michelin star. The following year it gained two. Only the world-renowned Maemo was one notch higher with its three.

'Christ, I really regret it,' the young man said in dismay. 'Of course I shouldn't have gone along with the idea of doing the food. I wanted to be in my own kitchen, but we don't have space for so many guests. Sjalg Petterson is a persistent guy, and he was paying fucking good money, and I ...'

Once again he spread out his arms.

Jesper Jørgensen sat in an armchair in Selma Falck's combined home and office. The apartment was not large, two rooms and a kitchen, but it was practical and ideally situated in a newly built block in Sagene. It was only a short distance to the city centre, and fairly anonymous into the bargain. On the doorbell below it said only SF, and the actual entrance door was not marked at all. In the course of the six months or so that she had lived here, the neighbourhood had nevertheless become well acquainted with her. In the first few weeks it had been tiresome dealing with all the requests for autographs and selfies, and also inquisitive questions about her rather modest abode.

But she soon got used to it. Selma Falck was happy with her circumstances.

Since she had salvaged her freedom and finances by proving a skier's innocence of a doping charge prior to Christmas, she had burnt most of the bridges in her life. Her licence to practise law had been handed in to the appropriate authorities some time ago. Of the thirteen million she had received in ready cash for her efforts in that case, she had given her ex-husband three. A penance of sorts, in all likelihood, as by that point she owed him nothing. Most of all it had been an attempt to persuade her children to forgive her, she had to admit each time she gave it any real thought. Something she did more and more infrequently. It had not helped much either. Anine was still borderline hostile on the rare occasions when they had to be in touch. Her brother seemed completely indifferent – at the wedding Selma had seen her son Johannes for the first time in four months.

The sixty-two square metres of newly built apartment had cost almost five million and could be furnished for next to nothing. The basement parking space was included in the price. Taking into consideration that her unfortunate penchant for gambling had bankrupted her and nearly led to her imprisonment, she had soon made up her mind to put the rest of the money in the bank. A buffer for more difficult times. The account was opened at a different bank from the one she normally used. She had taken care not to learn the new account number. Both the papers for the five million kroner and the plastic card that came with the bank account were in safekeeping at Einar Falsen's residence. He had no idea what it was for, but knew that it had to be kept secure.

If Einar was still strange and sometimes completely off his rocker, she had at least managed to persuade the former policeman indoors. The Poker Turk, Selma's old client, housing shark and manager of a number of illegal gambling dens in Oslo, had allowed Einar to move into the run-down, smelly bedsit in Vogts gate where Selma herself had lived during a bleak Advent.

Surprisingly enough, after many years of being homeless, Einar thoroughly enjoyed having a fixed abode. He was weird, and sometimes extremely unwell. All the same, he was the only person Selma really trusted. Even the annoying cat Darius that Selma had been forced to take with her when she left her broken marriage had stayed with him in Grünerløkka. Together, the cat and the madman looked after Selma's money, pigging out on cheese puffs and reading newspapers that Einar went around stealing at the crack of dawn, up with the lark and ready to catch a worm or two.

Now it was Selma who had a visitor.

The master chef was in despair.

'We've already had cancellations,' he complained. 'Loads of them. People think it must be my fault. *Our* fault. Ellevilt's fault, even though we weren't even in our restaurant. Every chef's worst nightmare is poisoning someone. And that guy, he just ... dropped dead, for heaven's sake! For some reason that I can't fathom we had anything to do with. Because of some fucking ingredient that I've hardly ever used. My food is Norwegian. Macadamia is from Brazil. A bloody Christmas nut, something that ...'

It was as if all the air went out of him. He slumped on the chair, deflated, and massaged his forehead. Eyes blinking, making it look as if he was struggling to stop himself from bursting into tears.

'What does the Food Safety Authority say?' Selma asked. 'I assume they've been brought into the picture?'

'Yes, of course. The whole place has been examined. They haven't found any trace of nuts anywhere. Not until now, at least. They've been crawling all over the place. Looking into every-thing. Everything that was used, the plates, the serving platters, the casseroles ... every last utensil. It'll be a while until they issue a final report, not until these ...'

He took a deep breath and shifted slightly in his seat.

'... investigations. Tests. Are completed. It takes a while. But if there were macadamia nuts in that food, then it must have been only microscopic quantities. Invisible traces, I would claim.'

'These things happen. Some people are extremely hyper-allergic. It could even have been in a room where someone ate nuts a while ago so that someone ends up terribly ill.'

'But then he shouldn't have been eating in a restaurant at all,' Jesper Jørgensen snarled angrily. 'No one can entirely and consistently monitor food. Anyway, it was incredibly idiotic that he had given that syringe, that pipe-pen or whatever it's called ...'

'EpiPen. Adrenaline.'

'Yes. To his best man! So that he didn't have a bulge in his pockets in the photographs, for goodness' sake! And his best man just stood there, like a moron, and watched the bridegroom die without lifting a finger.'

'He was probably in shock. These things happen. What are the police saying?'

'The police?'

The young man now had a half-taken aback, half-sceptical, frown on his forehead.

'Why would the police have anything to do with this?'

Selma, who was sitting on the settee with a bottle of Pepsi Max in her hand, gave a slight shrug. 'Sjalg Petterson was far from uncontroversial,' she said.

'Uncontro ... what do you mean?'

'You do know who he was?'

'Some kind of celebrity? In politics, isn't that right? I don't follow politics. I don't give a fuck. I'm only concerned with food.'

'Food can be political too,' she said with a smile. 'And it must have been hard work avoiding all the newspaper articles about his death.'

'Whatever. I stay away from newspapers. Especially now. With every fucking headline we lose our reputation and business.'

Now he looked most of all like a defiant teenager. He had slid forward on the chair, his thighs spread, and was fiddling with a ring on his thumb. From one sleeve of his T-shirt, a snake crept out, tattooed in winding circles all the way down to his wrist. The head, raised to strike, was terrifyingly realistic.

'Anyway,' Selma sighed and put down the bottle, 'I don't entirely understand what you want me to do about it.'

'Help me.'

'How?'

'By demonstrating that neither me nor my brainchild is to blame for that guy's death. I ...'

His phone was obviously in his back pocket, and a half-smothered double ping resulted in him groping his right buttock.

'Bloo. Dy. Hell.'

'What is it?'

'More cancellations. We'll probably have to close this weekend. No point in staying open without any customers. Fuck it.'

'This will blow over. It'll all be forgotten in a couple of weeks.'

He stared at her as if she had suggested a spur-of-the-moment trip to the moon. 'You understand all about marketing, I see?' The sarcasm was reinforced by a slight roll of the eyes. He sat up straight in the chair and leaned forward.

'No one forgets in my line of business. I've got two Michelin stars. I can wave goodbye to them if people continue to believe that I'm slapdash in my work. Sjalg Petterson had a serious nut allergy. It was public knowledge, according to a couple of the boys in the kitchen. He was involved in some kind of information campaign for Norway's Asthma and Allergy Association. The boys follow these things better than me. Besides, he was so adamant about keeping himself safe. That bloody nut allergy was not only brought up every fucking time I spoke to him or his bride ...'

He raised his thumb with the silver ring. '... it was also mentioned in all the email exchanges.' His forefinger popped up in the air before he also lifted his middle finger. 'And thirdly there was a warning in the contract. Written in red!'

Unruffled, Selma nodded. 'OK. You know best, of course. But there's little I can do. The Food Safety Authority will probably get to the bottom of it.'

'Food Safety!' Jesper spat out. 'They're going to find out all about it, yes! But if they find a single piece of damn macadamia nut in that kitchen or any of the food, then I'm seriously fucked. Seriously! The Food Safety Authority doesn't give a shit for Ellevilt. Or for me. Anyway, I'm the one who carries the can.'

Selma darted a quick but obvious glance at her watch. She had no plans for the day, but was tired of listening to this young man. The trendy sleeve-tattoo on his right arm was painstakingly executed, but the three-day-old stubble, the silver ring on his thumb and the fact that he was wearing a baseball cap indoors gave him a ten-a-penny appearance. He was probably a genius with food. But he was certainly not good with people.

'I can't help you,' she said, getting to her feet. 'Sorry.'

'You must! The boys in the kitchen say you're the best!'

'It's true, I am the best. But I can't help you, and you can't afford me.'

'How much ... how much an hour do you cost?'

Selma flashed a broad smile and tucked her hair behind her ear. 'That's not how it works. I only bet.'

'Bet?'

'Yes. I only take cases in which the client is willing to enter into a bet with me. If I solve the case, then I want a considerable slice of the cake. If I don't, then they don't need to pay.'

'Oh.'

Now all the air had oozed out of him again. He sat on the chair like a sack of potatoes. He had taken off his cap and was twirling it round and round in his hands.

'Just like American lawyers,' he mumbled. 'In the movies. No win, no fee.'

Selma tilted her head to one side. 'Well, yes. Something like that. A bet brings a certain flexibility to the situation. Something has to be at risk, you might say. It suits my ... nature. And since your case doesn't revolve around money, then it's not to my taste. Despite the steep prices, I understand it's not exactly lucrative to run a restaurant at your level.'

He still made no move to leave.

'I'm a bit busy,' Selma said.

Jesper Jørgensen remained seated.

'I must really—'

'I don't have cash,' he interrupted her. 'But I do have the restaurant. If you get me out of this jam, then you can eat for free.'

Selma scrutinized him. Now he looked up. His eyes were the only part of the whole guy worthy of attention. They were large, dark-brown, and with the longest lashes Selma had ever seen on a man. He looked like a bewildered toddler.

'What is it that's required here?' she finally asked. 'I mean ... what would it take for Sjalg's death not to tarnish you and Ellevilt?'

'That I couldn't have prevented it,' Jesper answered quickly. 'That it's not my fault. None of us, sort of thing. Us in the kitchen. That it must have been someone else, someone who ...'

He obviously had difficulty imagining who, apart from the people who had prepared the food, could possibly have added the nuts, because his mouth snapped shut.

'So someone else must have done it, then?'

'I don't know,' he replied, increasingly frantic.

'That would mean that someone wanted to injure him. Or kill him. If you have the slightest suspicion about that kind of thing, then you ought to tell the police. At once.'

It struck her with an intensity that surprised her: if Sjalg Petterson had really been murdered, then this could be the perfect crime. He had died of an illness, the police were scarcely interested, and the case was only one dry report from the Food Safety Authority away from being dropped.

She became lost in thought.

Jesper's mobile, now lying on the table in front of him, roused her when it pinged again. He touched the display.

'We're closing for the weekend,' he said.

Selma thought she could hear that his voice was on the verge of breaking.

'Ever since I was ten years old,' he said softly without looking at her, 'I've worked hard to become the best chef in the world. And I did it. I was a fucking child-welfare kid. Mum was dead and Dad was a scumbag. I was no good at school, and I was fat. A real lard-arse. All I did was hang around the kitchen. Making food. Reading. Getting better. Running a restaurant of the standard of Ellevilt is the worst job in the world. And the very best. It's all I can do. All I want to do.'

Selma sat down again. Reconsidered.

The boy was verging on sweet now. His mouth was trembling, and the fact that his cap was not in shreds as a result of his febrile fiddling was evidence of its quality.

At the moment she had no assignments on the go.

After the spectacular case of the sabotaged cross-country skier, she had exploited her position to the fullest. Accepted everything that offered the opportunity to advance her new position as a private investigator. She had guested on all the breakfast programmes in existence, both radio and TV. Talk shows and debates. In-depth interviews, which actually were not particularly truthful, but which were given even more coverage. As far as she knew, no one else in history had managed to be the main guest on both Skavlan and Lindmo on the same weekend.

At least she liked to think so.

It was all done with a finesse that had allowed Selma's gambling addiction and the resulting bankruptcy, moral as well as financial, to remain a secret shared with only a very few.

Before Christmas 2017 was over, there was hardly a Norwegian over the age of five who did not know that Selma Falck, A-list celebrity and winner of *Shall We Dance?*, double Olympic silver medal winner in handball and a star lawyer into the bargain, from then on intended to dedicate her time to being an investigator in the private sector.

The cases she was offered were numerous. The ones she had accepted, however, were few. On the other hand, they were sensational, and she had solved all three. Her new, small company, called Falck Solutions AS, so far had a turnover of four million kroner in only six months. Three of them came from the same client, a jeweller who had failed to discover a disloyal employee until the thief was in the Cayman Islands, in possession of valuables worth around thirty million.

Three weeks later, both the robber and the diamonds were returned to Norway, the former extremely unwillingly.

With tiny overheads, the operating profit margin of Falck Solutions was impressive. Ten thousand kroner went each month to Einar Falsen for 'consultancy services'. To a separate account, every month Selma transferred a similar amount for personal use on online poker. She had scaled down the habit, shown discipline, and managed to restrict herself to two nights a week. Her new life had done her good in every way.

At present, the poker account was running a comfortable surplus.

Her now-controlled gambling brought her the tranquillity she needed. At the times she had attempted to cut it out altogether, she had become restless and lacking in concentration, and she could not see in any way that it was wrong to find some balance in her life.

Even if she could not tell anyone about it.

Right now she had thought of taking a holiday, but nothing had been decided. The weather in Norway was still at its record-breaking best, she had her daily swimming sessions at the new public swimming complex in Sørenga, and she had acquired a better tan than at any time since childhood.

The young chef seemed completely crushed.

'So you think that a dinner at Ellevilt is worth my efforts for what might possibly take a few weeks?' she said at last.

'Not one dinner,' was his fast reaction. 'Once a month.'

'Once a month?' Selma laughed. 'For how long, then?'

Jesper thought for a few seconds. 'One year. You can have a permanent table.'

'I'm not so terribly interested in food. Fishcakes with vegetables are really enough for me.'

'After one meal at my restaurant, you'll appreciate the meaning of food. The deeper meaning in what we eat. I promise.'

An idea occurred to her. Being able to shove Einar into the shower and then take him to Oslo's second-best restaurant once a week would be an adventure. Besides, with such an arrangement, she might even have somewhere to impress clients, free dinner at one of the very best restaurants in the country.

'Not enough,' she said. 'But if you make it once a week for a whole year, then I'll agree to think it over.'

'Once a week? Are you mad?'

Selma shook her head and gave a Gallic shrug. Jesper hesitated for a few seconds.

'OK,' he said. 'But if you don't succeed, then you get nothing. That's the deal, isn't it? Will you take it on, then?'

'Sjalg Petterson was my son-in-law.'

'Eh … what?'

'For two hours and forty-nine minutes.'

Jesper stared at her in incomprehension. 'What?' he repeated.

'Which means,' Selma went on, 'that as a matter of form I must ask my daughter if it's acceptable for me to delve into this case.'

'Yes, of course! Thank you!'

Now he sprang up. For a moment it looked as if he was going to come round the table and hug her. Fortunately he did not.

'Your daughter is sure to want the same thing as me,' he said eagerly. 'It'll be great for her to find out what really happened too!'

'I'm not promising anything.'

Selma motioned with her hand towards the door, inviting him to leave. He finally took the hint and began to move.

'When will I hear back from you?' he asked.

'I don't know. But fairly soon, I'd think.'

At the front door, he stopped, still with his baseball cap in his hand. He curled the brim and put it on his head.

'It might not be OK to say it,' he said.

'What?'

'You looking fucking amazing. For your age.'

Selma smiled.

'I mean … not for your age, I mean … you're great, really. Your looks, I mean. You look a bit like that woman … the one in the TV series, you know.'

'Yes. I didn't think that chefs in your league watched crime series.'

'Binge watch sometimes. You do look really like her.'

He glanced down, his face hidden by the visor on his cap. 'Maybe a bit #MeToo?' he grinned sheepishly.

'Not at all. Thank you very much. Nice of you to say so. But now you really must go.'

Without another word, he stepped out into the stairwell. Even though the elevator door opened at that very moment, he took to his heels. Selma watched as he left, and decided that if you ignored the youthful uniform of hippy clothes and the creepy snake, he certainly did not look too bad himself.

Especially from behind, it crossed her mind, but she made no comment.

SPRING

The Setback

The group of six was reduced in size.

Ellev Trasop was now six feet under, after a ceremony in a packed church and subsequent wake at the Folkets Hus restaurant. He had been the leader of LO, the Norwegian Confederation of Trade Unions, for fourteen years, and the funeral service had borne the stamp of this. The trade union movement had exploited the occasion to demonstrate its strength, and had formed an impressive phalanx of banners in the square at Youngstorget. An enormous trough filled with red roses had looked beautiful for twenty-four hours, and thereafter became an embarrassment to the local authority. Politicians of varying affiliations had gathered to show their last respects to the old champion of the labouring classes.

At one time seven, and then six in number, now only five sat around the table in the Frogner apartment belonging to the only woman in their midst. In her mid-fifties, she had reached the rank of major in the Norwegian Army before being recruited as the Director of Human Resources at Norway's largest bank. Her name was Berit Ullern, but nevertheless she was never called anything but 'the Major'.

One of those present was the Deputy Chief of Police. Another called himself a wholesale greengrocer, but in reality owned something most resembling a fruit empire. The last and youngest of them all was a middle manager in the Norwegian Tax Administration.

All were steady, stalwart Norwegians.

Tryggve Mejer sat for the first time at the head of the table.

It felt uncomfortable, convening so soon after their previous meeting. Normally years might pass between each occasion, and their communications protocol ensured that they had good contact without seeing one another in person. The security and secrecy surrounding the small group, which they called simply 'the Council', was total, and had been ever since it had been finally established in 1991. In the first few years, a few new members had joined after a couple of the old ones had died. Since 1998, when Tryggve gained entry, only two had passed away: Peder Mejer ten years ago, followed by Ellev in his hundredth year.

According to the statutes, neither of them should be replaced.

'We cannot do this.'

The Major was speaking. She conducted herself as if she were still in the military. Her well-groomed hair was kept short. Her nails too, though they were carefully manicured with clear polish. Of them all around the table, she was the only one who did not use the backrest of her chair. She sat bolt upright with her knees close together and her hands placed symmetrically on her lap.

'Ellev was right,' she continued. 'This is beyond our remit.'

'Is it really, though?' Tryggve asked.

'Yes. It would be extremely undemocratic.'

Tryggve let his eyes run around the table. His pulse was far too high, and he was struggling to breathe quietly. They were not on his side. At least three of them anyway. When Ellev had still been alive, none of them had spoken much. Especially not the Major, whose voice Tryggve could barely recall having heard more than a handful of times in the twenty years he had known her.

Now her mind was set.

'We are living in a more polarized society than ever before in the modern history of our country,' Tryggve insisted. 'A journalist used the expression "the political epoch of extreme weather". It is a telling description. We can no longer use the traditional right–left axis to place people's opinions. Instead, the outer edges are located at the far end of the spokes from a hub, and support for them is on the increase both here at home and in the countries surrounding us. The hub …'

He paused and took a deep breath before continuing: 'We are the hub. The sensible ones. The ones oriented towards consensus. The decent people! And there are fewer and fewer of us. The hub is shrinking. The hub provides the strength for everything, Berit! It's the hub that keeps every wheel going. It has to be strong. And in the midst of all this misery we have these damn …'

He was growing agitated. The heat was rising in his cheeks.

'This social media,' he went on in a calmer tone. 'The internet. And so-called online newspapers, they're becoming more professional in proportion to their own extremism. The storm is turning into a raging hurricane. If you look at the papers I've given you …'

A couple of the others began to leaf through them while the Major sat motionless.

'… then you'll see that we are on the point of proving that both default.no and wrongs.no are partly financed by the Russians. These websites spew out stories that are as full of hatred and bile as of lies and misleading allegations. Stories that every single week are some of the most shared on social media. And that increasing numbers of people believe.'

'In that case, why don't the Police Security Service do anything?' the Major asked. 'Or you? As the Justice Minister, I mean? If the Russians are really behind it? Why do we have to intervene?'

'I said "on the point of proving". The Security Service works hard every single day to monitor undue Russian influence. Every single day. All the same, it is getting worse. The Security Service has to concentrate more on regular, blatant intelligence activity rather than the manipulation of social media, for example. They simply lack the capacity. And also they're constrained by procedural rules that we do not require to take into account. We can, for instance, use the press in a completely different manner from them.'

He paused again. Breathed, and moistened his lips.

'We are being destabilized,' he eventually added. 'By progressively larger groups here at home, and above all: by foreign powers.'

He put extra emphasis on the last two words.

'Foreign powers,' he repeated. 'We must protect ourselves from these foreign powers. We've gone off the rails. As a nation and a democracy. By relatively simple, but absolutely precise means, we can put the train back on track again. In the USA, things are worse. There, all the carriages are lying smashed in the gully.'

Silence fell. The three men were thumbing through the papers. The document had been written on an old IBM golf-ball typewriter and the ribbon subsequently destroyed by fire.

'The operation is relatively comprehensive,' one of them said at last. 'Do we have the means for all this?'

'Yes,' Tryggve nodded. 'Means, capacity and opportunity.'

'Hm.' The man hesitated. 'I have to agree with the Major here. The situation is troubling, but we are not under occupation.'

'We are on the way to that!' Tryggve said, far too loudly. 'By the kind of chaos that makes it impossible to move democracy on. Earlier, these barbaric forces confined themselves to the arena of immigration, but now the contagion has spread. For example ...'

He took a deep breath before continuing: 'When cooperation on energy was put on a firm footing almost a decade ago, hardly anyone bothered about it. No one at all! Last winter, all of a sudden our affiliation to ACER became a question of Norwegian sovereignty. It was debated with the kind of hysteria more appropriate to the idea of moving Norway to Africa. ACER! A practical, unified agreement on energy supply that ...'

He broke off and placed both palms flat on the table.

'We must do something now,' he said, with a note of resignation in his voice. 'Before we're all lying in the gully. Before we reach the stage when no one is any longer willing to move this democracy on. Before the price gets too high.'

Once again there was total silence in the room. Outside the closed windows they could hear children's laughter and a tram rattling past. The sun was baking the windows, and it was far too hot inside the room.

'You say something completely different out there,' the Major pointed out. 'This ...'

Her eyes narrowed slightly. It crossed Tryggve's mind that even her wrinkles were symmetrical.

'Sjalg Petterson?' she said. 'Petterson. That politician, he—'

'Sjalg Petterson isn't a politician,' Tryggve interrupted. 'He doesn't have a seat in either parliament or government. He's never been anywhere near City Hall either.'

'He calls himself a political influencer,' said the man from the tax authority, who now appeared to have finished reading the document. 'The guy writes some kind of blog. But in reality he works at the university.'

'Good Lord,' Tryggve groaned, putting his face in his hands. 'Influencer.'

'He likes to go for the jugular with you,' the Major said. 'And if I remember correctly, you said in here only a couple of weeks ago that we lived in a liberal democracy, and that it was entirely legitimate to criticise the Justice Minister. You were extremely calm about it, and even smiled.'

She looked at him with eyebrows raised.

'Out there, I'm a liberal democrat,' Tryggve said heatedly. 'Democrat, Justice Minister, and Dad. In here, I'm a soldier in the service of democracy. As are we all.'

'We should put it to a vote.'

He stared at her in amazement. 'Vote? But we've never put anything to a vote.'

As a rule, their rare meetings consisted of a discussion in which they all had their say before Ellev Trasop came to a decision.

The Major shook her head slightly. 'No. But then we've never before initiated an operation like this ...' She squinted at the cover of the closed document. 'Rugged/Storm-scarred. "Operation Rugged/Storm-scarred". Never. And besides, you're not Ellev. We'll vote on it.'

Tryggve felt backed into a corner. He had not envisioned this. As far as he could recollect, the Council had never ever had to take a vote on anything whatsoever. He had certainly anticipated that the others would be difficult to persuade, especially the Major, and maybe the Deputy Chief of Police, but he had not counted on an outright mutiny.

'OK then,' he said doubtfully. 'Who is for?'

His own arm shot into the air. One of the other men raised his hand ever so slightly, but let it drop again.

'And who votes against?' the Major asked briskly when the Council leader remained silent.

Four hands in the air.

'Then it's decided,' the Major said calmly, as she started to gather up the documents. 'I'll see to the destruction of these.'

She got to her feet, tucked the bundle of documents under her arm and said in conclusion: 'You know the routines for each of us exiting the premises. Goodbye.'

The Quarrel

Mum and Dad were arguing again.

For as long as she could remember, they had quarrelled. All the time, even when they were really friends. Mum had a certain tone of voice with the crack of a whip in it, no matter what she was talking about. If Dad stacked the glasses the wrong way in the dishwasher, for example. After all, it wasn't really the greatest catastrophe in the world, and anyway he was just using his own method. Not actually wrong, simply different from the way someone like Mum did it. She seemed to snap at him. Cutting and beastly. By force of habit, as if she had long ago found a voice to use against Dad that was almost impossible to change.

Now they were having a serious quarrel.

For some reason they did not appreciate that she could hear them. When she was little, she had sometimes lain awake the whole time until they went to bed. In those days, Dad used to check if she was asleep, but she learned very early to pretend. Even though the bedrooms were on the upper level, they never closed the kitchen door. Yet another of Mum's hang-ups. The door was held open with a block of wood: Mum said that it got so stuffy in there if it wasn't left open.

Worst of all was when they were actually afraid that she would hear.

Like now.

They were talking so quietly that only fragments of sentences reached all the way up to her. Mum managed to be angry even when she was whispering. Almost like cats hissing. Dad's voice just grew deeper, but he too was raging. They interrupted each other the entire time, and at one point a glass shattered. An accident, most likely. Mina had never witnessed either of them become physically violent.

But it set the mood, that broken glass.

'... for all these years,' she heard Mum say. 'Two years! You promised, two years ...'

Dad groaned. Mina envisaged him putting his face in his hands at that moment, more or less like a disconsolate child.

The Progress Party had been granted the Justice Minister post when the new government came to power five years ago. In the course of the first twenty-two months, three of the post holders had made fools of themselves and had to resign, one after the other, and the Conservatives had appointed their own man. Dad had been really reluctant to accept. Mum was furious. The Prime Minister had won.

Only until the next election, both the Prime Minister and Dad had promised.

Two years.

Mina well understood that the Prime Minister needed him. He was clever. A safe pair of hands, in a sense, in the way that only people who have been involved in politics since their teenage years can be. He had been a cabinet minister before that too, when Mina was little. At that time Mum had thought it perfectly OK. In fact, she had been quite proud. Mina could see that in the photos in her childhood album. Mum looked happy in them, and there was one of all three of them inside Dad's office. The window glass was pale green and bulletproof, so Mum looked as if she was ill in the photograph. But she was smiling. The look she gave Dad was filled with love, and Mina wished she could remember all that.

Since then, Dad's office had been blown sky high by a fascist extremist and the internet had metamorphosed into something entirely different.

That was what troubled Mum.

All the smears. All the unrest.

Mum liked peace and quiet, so it was odd that she continually created such a rumpus around herself. Everything stressed her out. Loud and complaining, sometimes she drove Mina completely crazy. She had asked to be allowed to follow Mina on all her social media. Since Mina mainly used only Instagram and Snapchat, it was fine that her mother had access to Facebook and Twitter. Next to nothing happened there. Insta and Snap, on the other hand, were the most important channels Mina used to keep in touch with her friends. At the same time, it was on Instagram that the horrible messages ticked in. Mum had seen a couple of them and gone ballistic. Mina had been forced to delete her account while Mum sat and watched. As her mother used social media so seldom herself, she knew precious little about it. Mina had just temporarily deactivated her account and logged in again three days later. Then she had blocked her mother and prayed to higher powers that her Mum would not check again.

All the same, it was virtually certain that she would not.

Mum understood next to nothing, in particular that it was absolutely impossible for a soon-to-be-seventeen-year-old girl not to be on Instagram. Fortunately, her mother could not get the hang of Snapchat at all. Since she never received any messages from Mina on that platform, she thought it was inactive.

Now everything was almost silent down there. In a way, that was even scarier.

Suddenly Dad was standing at the door. He hadn't even knocked, but Mina managed to slip her mobile under the quilt anyway and look tired as she squinted at him over the edge of the bedcovers.

'Are you OK?' he asked, switching on the small lamp beside the wardrobe.

'You woke me,' she moaned, turning round in bed. 'It's late. You don't usually stay up so late.'

He came into the room and sat on her bed. Mina lay with her back turned and shoved the phone in between her thighs. Luckily the sound was off, since she had received four messages in only the last minute.

'Mum says you're getting hate messages,' he said. 'Because of me. Is that true?'

'No.'

'She's seen a couple of them. On Instagram. Surely she's not lying?'

'They weren't exactly about you, though.'

'What were they about, then?'

He put his hand on her back. A few seconds passed, and she began to feel the heat from his hand through the quilt.

'Nothing. Nothing to be bothered about. You said so yourself a couple of weeks ago. They're tough as nails behind a keyboard, but cowards in real life. You said that I shouldn't bother about them.'

'I also said that you should stay away from websites like that.'

'It's Instagram, Dad. Not a website. You can't stay away from Instagram.'

Mina could almost hear him smile. When she suddenly sat up and pulled the quilt to her chin, she saw that the smile was joyless. His eyes were sad.

'Mum wants me to resign,' he said.

'It's not up to her.'

'What do you think?'

Mina drew up her knees and hugged them. The bedroom was cold and she noticed goose pimples on her arms below the T-shirt from the Øya Festival that was far too big for her.

'I think you should continue. And I also think that you and Mum should get a divorce.'

'We're not going to do that.'

51

'You should. You argue all the time. She doesn't pay any atten-tion to you.'

Now his smile took on more warmth.

'She does, you know. In her own way. That's why she wants me to give it up. To escape from all these smears.'

'I don't get it.'

'What?'

'Why they're so angry with you. You're a Conservative, Dad. On default.no they call you a left-wing extremist. Just because you refuse to go along with all that ... hatred of Muslims. Because you sit on that religious liaison body. Because you ... because you're decent, really. And talk sense. There was someone on there who thought you were definitely a paedophile too. Since you only had me, sort of thing, a home-grown girl, you could ...'

Dad interrupted her. 'Don't read those web pages, I've told you. They're extremists. A bunch of idiots.'

'That guy Sjalg Petterson isn't an idiot. He's a professor of history, even though he's not very old. He's after you the whole time. Have you seen this?'

She leaned towards the bedside table.

'Are you charging up your iPad overnight again?' he asked, annoyed. 'It's dangerous, Mina. It could catch fire.'

Instead of answering, she keyed her way into a blog.

'*Tryggve Mejer is a typical example of politicians who lack backbone,*' she read aloud. '*Instead of heading up the confron-tation with Islamic culture and negative developments in our society that is necessary in order to begin a dialogue about Norway's future, he panders to the current trends that are reduc-ing it to rubble. Instead of reading up on Islamic—*'

'Stop it.' His voice was unusually sharp, and he tried to grab the iPad from her. She was faster than him, though, and pushed it under the quilt, where her mobile was already hidden.

'That man got mad with me years ago,' her father said. 'Long before I became Justice Minister for the second time.'

'Why?'

He scratched his head and stifled a yawn.

'I thought the immigration balance sheet was a bad idea. Not because it wouldn't be interesting. There is never reason to fear statistics in themselves. I just find it strange to pick out one part of the population to see what they cost. People *do* cost money, Mina. The sick. The old. Slobs. Children. You, for instance.'

He smiled. 'You've cost Mum, me and society millions up till now. A real loss-making business.'

Now it was Mina's turn to give a smile, but it quickly vanished.

'Do you never get tired of it, Dad? That guy there seems pretty factual sometimes, and he can certainly write, but he gets all the others worked up. The ones with permanent caps lock and far too much time on their hands. The really nasty ones. We all thought that things would improve after the twenty-second of July. Don't you remember that?'

'You were only nine then, sweetheart.'

'I remember it really well! We were to answer hate with love, to get more democracy and blah blah blah. Then it just got worse. Not only on the very far right, but the crazies on the left wing too. Increasing hatred of Jews and bonkers conspiracy theories. Opposition to pure science and truth. Vaccinations, for example. Hatred and smear campaigns and everything that got so difficult for ...'

She caught herself in time.

'Ingeborg,' her father completed the sentence.

'Yes. Don't you get ... don't you get really fed up with it?'

He stood up. He looked tired and stiff, and had continued putting on weight. Mina had noticed that he had started to eat chocolate in the evenings. They hadn't been in the habit of having that sort of thing in the house, as Mum was strict about everything to do with sugar. She often said that Dad had an 'incorrigible sweet tooth', and if it weren't for her 'dietary regime', Dad would be as fat as when they had first met. In the last few weeks, however, there had constantly been revealing wrappers in the rubbish bin. Mum had discovered them. She had ranted and raved. It did not make him stop, though, he had just made sure to put the wrappers further down inside the bin.

Slowly he crossed to the window. He placed his hands on the small of his back and stretched. Standing with his legs together, he began to move up and down on his toes. He stood there for such a long time without saying anything that Mina got up out of bed and walked towards him.

Oslo lay like a jewel before them.

It was no longer completely dark at night. The sky was a deep-blue, almost indigo, arch soaring across the horizon. They could see from the silhouette of the spherical military installation at Lutvann lake in the east, almost all the way to the Maridalsvann lake in the north-west. The black slope of the Holmenkollen ski jump rose at the top of the western hill. The city itself was a shimmering, glittering belt of light, and the furthest reaches of the dark fjord disappeared past Bærum all the way out to Hurumland.

The flashing blue lights of a police car were visible on Ringeveien.

'Can you keep a secret, Mina?'

His hand encircled her waist. Letting him draw her closer, she laid her head on his shoulder.

'Yes, of course. You know I can.'

'I sometimes get really sick and tired of it all.' He was whispering. 'I get so fed up that I want to puke. I get scared. I think of what this is doing to us, all this hatred. All this rage. The polarization.

The internet. Mum is afraid too. We probably quarrel too much about the small things, but that's more of a routine.'

'A routine?'

'A habit. Stupid. The point is ...'

He let her go and began to massage his neck with his right hand. .

'Sometimes I get fed up. So fed up and scared and angry that I could kill someone.'

The police car down below turned off at the Sinsenkrysset interchange and raced on towards Carl Berners plass.

'Not in real life, though?'

'No, Mina. Not in real life. Of course not in real life. Now you must go to sleep. So must I.'

She crept back to bed and he tucked the quilt around her and gave her a kiss on the forehead. Again she noticed that smell from him, the sickly sweet odour of stress. Really she wanted to tell him everything. About the actual import of those messages.

But it was impossible. Dad had enough to think about. It was so long since he had said goodnight like this. In the first place, he often went to bed before she did. And also, he had changed so much.

So unhappy, sort of. Totally different from the secure, self-assured man she saw on TV almost every week. Out there he seemed larger somehow. Here at home he was submissive, even when he was arguing with Mum.

It was as if Dad were two different people.

He switched off the light and was about to close the door behind him.

'Dad?'

'Yes, sweetie?'

'I've decided what I'm going to be.'

He took a couple of steps back into the room again. Silhouetted against the bright light in the hallway, his figure became dark and faceless.

'What's that, then?'

'A lawyer. Just like you.'

Dad laughed. Genuinely laughed, and for a long time. It was ages since she had heard that laughter, amazingly light and bubbling with happiness, exactly like Grandma's had been.

'That would mean throwing away a talent such as yours,' he said finally. 'You ought to be a realist, my friend. Norway and the world need realists. Scholars. Seekers of knowledge and truth. You're far smarter than I am. Just as smart as Mum. What the world absolutely doesn't need, is yet another nit-picker.'

'I want to study law.'

'As you wish. You've more than two years ahead of you, plenty of time to change your mind.'

Now that her eyes had grown accustomed to the darkness and the door was half closed behind him, she could see that he was smiling.

'Goodnight, sweetheart. Sleep well.'

'Sleep well, Dad.'

The door closed silently. Mina checked her mobile for messages, and put it, too, on the bedside table to charge. She lay awake for a long time, until it was just starting to grow light outside the window.

The birds had begun to sing when her eyes finally slid shut again.

The Run

It was far too long since he had taken any exercise.

Tryggve Mejer had just arrived at Akebakkeskogen, but he was already exhausted. From the house in Lofthus terrasse up to the edge of the Marka recreational area was barely two hundred metres, but it was an upward slope and the final stretch was steep. He stood for a while with his hands on his knees, gasping for breath. He had deliberately risen far too early. It was not yet five a.m., but if he waited another hour, Oslo's well-used city forest would be swarming with both runners and sleepy dog walkers.

Security was the reason he was up with the lark.

Usually he had next to no personal protection as a private citizen. The Police Security Service assessed the threat level from day to day, for him as well as all the others for whom they had responsibility. Only on three occasions in the last three years had they found it necessary to provide him with a twenty-four-hour bodyguard. Once this had lasted for three weeks, and both he and his family had been driven crazy. Especially his wife Cathrine.

He had no desire for security guards, but even less wish to be spotted. He was out of condition and had put on weight. His tracksuit was far too tight and his belly wobbled. Never before had it been necessary for him to stop as soon as this, but then it was also at least two months since he had last moved further than the distance between black government limousines and offices or conference rooms.

May would soon be over. At this time of day, before the sun had warmed the air and the thermal turbulence increased, the birdsong was at its most beautiful. The cool remains of the night still lingered between the trees when he broke into a run again.

She was standing two hundred metres along the forest track.

She too was wearing a tracksuit, but looked better in it than he did. Despite the eight years difference in their ages. Red, tightly fitting trousers and a light-as-air anorak. Her shoes were white and looked brand new.

'Hello,' she said tersely as he stopped.

'What are you doing here?'

'Waiting for you.'

'How did you know I would be out running?'

'I needed to talk to you,' the Major said.

'But ...'

She pointed up the hillside, and he realized he would not be given any explanation as to how she had located him. All the same, he slinked obediently off the track and into the precipitous forest on the left-hand side.

They continued up until they could barely make out the track below. The Major sat down on a tree stump. He remained on his feet, leaning his shoulder against a spruce trunk.

'I have to assure myself that you won't do anything,' she said in an undertone.

'Straight to the point as ever,' he replied brusquely.

'Yes. Straight to the point. You were caught napping by the vote. I must have your assurance that you will respect it.'

He blew away the hair that had fallen into his eyes as he scratched his neck. 'Of course,' he said. 'But you were all wrong.'

'No. Rugged/Storm-scarred would be sheer madness. I absolutely share your concern about the developments in our society. All the same, that won't help. Our remit doesn't cover anything of that nature. That's quite simply not why we're in existence.'

When he refrained from answering, she added: 'Besides, I don't see how such an action would be of any use. Even if we could fairly effectively stop some of the worst offenders, it would be like pissing into the wind. Mushrooms just spring up again, Tryggve. If you pick out a few, it's just a question of time before new ones appear where they had been. It would be a Sisyphean task. Futile.'

'Then you have to keep going. Start over again after a while.'

She stared at him with a look he struggled to interpret. Apprehension, perhaps. Alarm? Contempt, he concluded.

'Are you aware of what you're saying?' she asked, raising her voice a notch, before she restrained herself once again and went on:

'That we should conduct some kind of purge, based on opinions and convictions, for the unforeseeable future here in this country?'

'Not a purge. Weeding out. The democratic flowerbed is in need of some weeding, nothing more, nothing less. In the end there will be no one left to do what's needed, the work of democracy.'

Now she too got to her feet. 'You're forcing me to speak out,' she said.

'What?'

'I must raise the alarm.'

'Who are you going to tell?'

'The Prime Minister. The Security Service. Bloody hell, Tryggve ...'

Never before had he heard her swear. There was a bright pink flush on her cheeks, and the pulse on the right side of her throat had become plainly visible.

'... I'm going to expose the Council. Rather that than ...'

Tryggve smiled. He ran his finger under his nose, sniffed, and smiled even more broadly.

'Raise the alarm,' he repeated. 'And of course you've thought over the consequences of something like that?'

'Right now I don't give a damn about the consequences. I'm far more petrified of the possibility of you refusing to respect the decision of the majority. Everyone apart from you, Tryggve. All of us said no.'

He licked his lips and crossed his arms.

The Major was tall, but her shoulders were narrow. Slim and sinewy; she probably weighed less than half his weight. Her features were now marred by the fact that the corners of her mouth were turned down.

By exactly the same amount on either side.

'What are you going to tell them?' Tryggve asked, unperturbed. 'That the former leader of Norway's Employers' Association and ditto of the Confederation of Trade Unions have upheld an organization with formidable powers, means and resources, entirely beyond democratic control? For thirty years, Berit? Is that what you're going to tell them?'

She did not respond. In the distance a dog, grouchy at this time of the morning, was barking. A pair of magpies chattered unnervingly above their heads, obviously keen for them to leave. They stood their ground. He simply did not believe her.

She would never decide to expose either the Council or the huge, invisible organization it ruled over.

'Or that you've participated in this?' Tryggve added, suddenly whispering. 'That a former major in the Norwegian armed forces for a number of years has taken part in a network that was denounced as early as the 1980s? In that case, you can safely kiss goodbye to your life as a respectable citizen.'

'And yours.'

He nodded. 'Yes, and mine. And the others.'

'You're the Minister of Justice. It will be worst for you. Your fall from grace will be from the greatest height.'

'Yes. Most likely. The problem is ...'

His tracksuit trousers had slipped down, and his stomach looked extra large above the tight elastic of the waistband. He pulled the tracksuit top out of his trousers and took a step towards her.

'The problem is that to begin with I wanted to be the Justice Minister. Like a whole lot of others, I expect. It's a purposeful job. It's exciting. Exhausting and time-consuming and sometimes stressful, of course ...'

He shrugged.

'... but actually overall, very satisfying. Until recently many people have wanted to take it on. To take part in politics. In what democracy itself is based upon: people discussing a way forward to beneficial solutions. For everyone.'

'I'll raise the alarm,' she said softly. 'If you don't give me your word of honour.'

'Did you know that nearly half of all local politicians in this country have received threats? Real threats! Local politicians! What kind of democracy does a society become when people are scared into silence?'

'Shh.' She placed a slim index finger on her lips and looked around.

'You've no idea what it's like,' he said just as loudly. 'You sit in a fucking bank behind high ramparts and solid firewalls. You're invisible. That doesn't apply to me or anyone else with opinions to advance in this society of ours. My wife ...'

His voice cracked, and he swallowed before continuing.

'Very soon I'll have to resign from the government,' he said. 'Not because I'm not up to the task. Not because anyone else will perform better. Not even because I no longer actually want to do it. I'm going to resign this summer because my wife can't sleep at night. I'm giving up because Cathrine doesn't want me to go on doing it. She can't take any more of all the crap.'

The Major looked at him. The ill-tempered expression around her mouth was supplanted by a look of determination. Saying nothing, she adjusted her anorak, clicked her heels and let her arms fall straight down at her sides with her hands lightly closed. Her thumb touched what would have been the seam of a normal pair of trousers, in the military style of standing to attention.

She breathed deeply in and out a couple of times before turning on her heel and starting to pick her way down to the forest track.

'Wait,' he said sharply.

She stopped. Without turning around, she spoke into thin air: 'You should never enter into a war you know you're destined to lose. Never.'

'Imagine if Winston Churchill had thought like that,' Tryggve answered.

Now she did turn around.

'Then the world would have looked very different,' he went on.

'That's an absurd comparison.'

'Is it? Is it really?'

'The Second World War was a battle against evil. Against an aggressive, totalitarian dictatorship. Against Nazism, maybe the worst and most inhumane ideology of them all. It was a battle that had to be fought. No matter what.'

He strode towards her. She took a couple of steps back, as if she suddenly felt afraid of him.

'Don't you follow what's going on?' he roared. 'Don't you see what's happening? Here at home, out there ... Russia, Poland, Hungary, Brexit ... the USA! This time the wickedness isn't storming towards us in awful helmets, doing the goose step, Berit. The leader is not a loud-mouthed midget with a moustache and a dog. Not this time. Now the filth comes sneaking in, spreading out like a plague. In our time nationalism, hatred, anti-Semitism, contempt for politicians, fear of foreigners and standardization ...'

He gazed up at the sky in desperation.

'... through the internet! Social media. Lies don't need to be bellowed out in front of blinded masses to be effective.'

'No one can stop the internet.'

'No. But we can put the brakes on the flood of sewage in there.'

'It's not possible. Rugged/Storm-scarred is an anti-democratic operation, Tryggve. Ellev said no. Your father would have too. They were both true democrats. A democracy is never stronger than the load it can tolerate. Than the opposition it has the strength to meet. I want you to give your word that you will submit to the will of the majority. If not, I'll raise the alarm at the Security Service. And then what comes of that will just have to come.'

'You have my word.'

'Do I?'

'Yes. You're wrong, but you're in the majority. I give you my word of honour. I won't initiate Rugged/Storm-scarred.'

Her eyes changed colour. They were normally blue, but now they were grey, almost colourless. Poker-faced, she held out her hand. He gripped it and held it firmly.

'I want to take charge of the casket,' she said decisively.

'The casket is mine,' he said, even more resolutely. 'My word of honour is enough.'

With a brief nod after a momentary pause, she released his hand and continued down towards the track with Tryggve following on her heels. At the foot of the hill, he asked: 'How did you find me here?'

'I didn't find you here. I wanted to catch you before you were picked up to go to the office. To make it look as credible as possible, I dressed for a run. When it turned out that you also wanted some exercise, I ran after you for some distance. It didn't take long to understand where you were going, and it was easy to take a shortcut and get here first. You're in really bad shape, Tryggve.'

For the first time he saw the suggestion of a smile on her tense face.

'Why did you come so early?' he asked.

'The early bird catches the worm, doesn't it? So I have your word?'

'You have.'

Without another word, she began to run on into the recreational area. As for Tryggve, he glanced at his watch before walking back to the barrier at Akebakkeskogen.

The Major had given up the idea of the casket. Far too easily, it occurred to him on reflection, but that was probably because she trusted his word.

And right now the casket was the most important thing of all.

The Mailbox

She had felt unwell for several days. Nauseous and out of sorts, tired, and with a terrible tension headache. Almost like being pregnant. Her age and a hysterectomy some time ago made her wonder if she had cancer.

She always thought it must be cancer whenever anything was wrong with her. Which was a rare occurrence. Cathrine Selmer had hardly taken a single sick day off since completing her studies. Nevertheless, the sight of the sausage stew in the canteen at lunchtime had forced her to turn and flee. And head for home.

The others told her there was a bug going around, and she took a taxi.

The mailbox at the gate trumpeted that Tryggve Mejer, Cathrine Selmer and Mina Mejer Selmer lived here. A green box with a bright yellow-and-black sign because Tryggve supported the Lillestrøm SK football team. Cathrine had longed to change it for a more discreet version, since it was surely unnecessary to make it a target for potential vandals. Tryggve protested. He had been compelled to accept an unlisted phone number when he became a cabinet minister for the second time, but insisted that his address should be freely available. Nothing to be scared of, he always said; after all, they lived in Norway, the safest land in the world.

According to Mina, the post was normally delivered around two p.m., but Cathrine opened the lid anyway.

Although it was not yet half past twelve, she could see a package inside.

A PostPak box, the cartons you can buy at the post office in different sizes and the simplest way to send items larger than a letter. It was addressed to them all.

The Selmer/Mejer family. The correct address. But unfranked, she noticed. Very odd.

The package was not particularly heavy, not even one kilo. Cathrine shook it. A hollow sound of something sliding from side to side indicated that the standard box contained another package. For a second she tried to think whether any of them had an impending birthday. Some kind of special occasion? But no.

Despite the nausea that came and went, she grew inquisitive. She would tear open the outer container at least so that she could dispose of it in the paper-recycling bin at the end of the driveway. Cathrine put down her handbag and opened the package.

A food container, she saw in surprise as she got rid of the cardboard box. It felt heavy in her hand; it was dark-blue and filled to the brim with something.

Of course she should not have opened the clips on one side and lifted the lid. She should have informed someone. The Police Security Service should have been told, at least; it was stated in the instructions that all kinds of threat, even minor unpleasantness, should be reported. Evidence should be secured, and this was far beyond what she should expect to cope with. Tryggve should certainly be told: he really had to see this, to be convinced; he had to give up this confounded job of his. She should phone him. The sooner the better, and the box of shit accompanied by a repugnant message might well be the very thing to convince him.

She told no one, and instead opened the lid. It must have already smelled foul when the cardboard wrapper was removed and she stood with this jam-packed food container in her left hand as she clicked it open with her right.

The stench was actually unmistakeable. On top of a close-packed heap of human excrement lay a note.

Traitors.

She let go of the box and it crashed to the ground, the note still stuck to all the brown mess. Cathrine staggered back a couple of steps before bending over and throwing up.

She wiped her mouth with the sleeve of her blouse, kicked the food container into her neighbour's rose bushes, grabbed her handbag and raced to her own front door. She dropped her keys twice, but finally got inside. On the way to the bathroom, she tore off her clothes. After a shower lasting quarter of an hour, the water so hot that the skin on her breasts turned dark red and so forceful that the drain was almost clogged with the dark-blonde hair she scrubbed from her scalp, she got dressed. She found a pair of single-use gloves in a kitchen drawer and two large plastic bags in another. Retracing her own steps to the bathroom, she stuffed every single item of clothing into one of them, tied a hard knot at the top when she had finished and went outside again. She lifted the lid of the rubbish bin, took out three of the bags already inside, dropped in the bag of clothes and covered it with the others.

She looked around.

The early-day silence of suburbia surrounded her as always. No vehicles in the small cul-de-sac. No people. Not even a dad on paternity leave, aimlessly pushing a pram. Quickly, she ran to her neighbour's rose hedge. She could smell the foul odour from several metres away. Breathing through her mouth, she crouched down and flipped the empty plastic bag over the food container. She jiggled it into the bag, like an enormous dog turd, and put it all into number 7's rubbish bin. The house had stood empty for six months following an inheritance dispute that showed no sign of resolution.

Wrenching off the rubber gloves, she let them follow the bag. After slamming the lid shut, Cathrine returned to her own house, where she boiled her keys for ten whole minutes. The pot she used was the oldest one she possessed, and after the keys had been disinfected, she laid them down to dry on a kitchen towel and put the pot in the garage.

It would be thrown out at the earliest opportunity.

Cathrine Selmer gasped for breath as she fought the urge to throw up again. Just like the time when she was nineteen and about which she had never let a word escape her lips either.

She was a civil engineer, a graduate of the Norwegian University of Science and Technology, with a PhD from the Massachusetts Institute of Technology. She was a chief executive and had a 2nd Dan in Tae Kwon Do. Despite all that, as she stood there clinging to the kitchen sink while she let the water run so that she had a clean sound to listen to, she burst into floods of tears.

She could not breathe a word of this to Tryggve. It struck her with a force that made her sob all the more that she did not want to tell him. The thought of yet another round of endless argument that led nowhere was more than she could bear. There was no point. There was nothing more to be gained from Tryggve – he had politics in the marrow of his bones, and would never manage to extricate himself completely. She was alone, as she had always been, in the strictest sense of the word.

Cathrine sobbed until she had made the decisions that had really already been taken the minute she opened the dark-blue food container.

First of all: no one would get to know of this. Never, exactly like that time when she was nineteen. She alone had carried the secret of a rape for more than half her life, and would have to cope with this as well.

Secondly, she wanted a divorce.

Haakon VII

Two days had elapsed since the Major had taken Tryggve Mejer by surprise in the woods. Since then, he had not heard anything from her. He hadn't expected anything else either. He had given his word of honour, and his word was still believed implicitly.

The safe in the basement was capacious: one and a half metres in height and built into the wall. He himself had never understood the point of the secure cupboard, but it had been there when they bought the house in 2002. And it was virtually empty. The title deeds to the house were stored there together with some jewellery that Cathrine never wore. And his certificate from the University of Bergen, where he had graduated in law because when he left high school he had fallen in love with a girl from that city. Cathrine's diplomas from NTNU and MIT in Boston were also there, along with Mina's birth certificate. It could all have been easily accommodated in a small safe-deposit box.

Without Cathrine's knowledge, he had changed the code on the safe cupboard, even though she never came down here. Tryggve was not even sure that she remembered the old code. The last time she had needed to open the safe, she had had to ask him. That must have been three years ago.

The cedar-wood casket had plenty of space: a shelf all to itself. Tryggve took it out carefully and carried it across to the workbench he had received for Christmas six years earlier, and that had stood untouched ever since. The key was already in the lock. It was so tiny that it was difficult to hold it firmly, but after some fumbling he heard a click.

Even though, for many years, Tryggve had had a clear idea of what was in the casket, he could feel his pulse race. The lid was fashioned from a piece of wood with a frame around it. The carpenter had painstakingly engraved King Haakon's monogram in the middle, a large H enclosing the number seven, beneath a stylized royal crown. The symbol was surrounded by an awe-inspiring relief of spring flowers. Coltsfoot and Siberian squill, snowdrops and something that could be blue or white wood anemones. The casket had been made by a resistance fighter while held captive in Grini Prison Camp from November 1944 to the end of the war.

How on earth he had got hold of cedar wood and intricate tools while in the custody of the Nazi regime was a mystery not even Ellev Trasop could explain.

The symbolism was overstated, anyway.

King Haakon's monogram gave Tryggve goose pimples.

Every single time he saw it. In the succession of countless rules introduced by the Nazis during their occupation of Norway, from banning the wearing of red Santa hats to ordering the surrender of wellington boots from size 41 upwards and all dogs more than 40 centimetres in height at the withers to the wartime military powers, the prohibition of propaganda in support of the Norwegian royal family was brought in as early as the late autumn of 1940.

The monogram became the war's most defiant graffiti.

Tryggve himself remembered an enormous version of it in a childish scrawl under his grandparents' dining table. His father's little brother, only four years old when the war began, had been sitting under the table at Christmas Eve, half hidden by a white tablecloth, and used up the little he had left of pencils to mark his irate opposition to the occupying forces. The old dining table now had pride of place in his uncle's living room, and the monogram was still visible for anyone who could be bothered searching for it.

The spring flowers conveyed the hope of better times.

He carefully opened the lid.

A white envelope lay on top. His own name was written on it in a hand so shaky it was almost illegible. An attempt had been made to seal the envelope, but a simple flick of the thumb was enough to open it. The paper did not even tear.

Dear Tryggve,

In this casket lies great power that must not be misused. I hope you will allow yourself to be influenced by what has always been

the guiding spirit of our organization: Norwegian freedom, inde-
pendence, welfare and democracy.

Best wishes to you and yours from your old friend and mentor,
Ellev

Tryggve had to blink back tears. He cleared his throat and stuffed the letter back inside the envelope, folded it and tucked it into his back pocket. It was to be burnt that same evening. Then he lifted a little booklet. It was printed, but obviously not dupli- cated. It bore the name of neither the author nor the publisher. It had no title either, and on the front cover was nothing but a roughly sketched map of Norway.

He opened the booklet. The paper was dry and it squeaked slightly when he folded the pages out far enough to read it. His eyes skimmed the closely written contents, and he leafed back and forth, taking in fragments of text, stopping for a moment and then continuing to browse.

The pamphlet dealt with the history of Norwegian resilience arrangements for possible occupation after the Second World War. The allied countries' fear of Soviet invasion after the victors had finished chopping up countries from the ruins of Europe had authorized the establishment of Stay Behind groups in the non- communist states. These groups were, as the name suggested, to stay behind in their home countries after the Russians had arrived. By fighting behind enemy lines, they would obstruct the work of the occupying forces.

And set their nation free once again.

From just after the war until 1953, networks were set up throughout Norway. Blue Mix was to handle evacuation. Lindus was in charge of intelligence. Rocambole had responsibility for sabotage and liquidation. From the outset, they were all led by prominent figures from the resistance movement.

Tryggve Mejer was well informed about this history, having

been steeped in it since he was old enough for his father to take him seriously.

The organizations that together comprised the Norwegian Stay Behind network were beyond political control. He knew it had all been organized with so many partitions between the participants that there would be no more than a handful of men who understood the group's full scope.

And knew the identities of its members.

Tryggve was also aware that the participants recruited to service in the system often had no knowledge of anyone other than their immediate superior. Six years of world war, five of those as an occupied nation, had taught the members of the resistance the necessity for secrecy. No one should know more than absolutely necessary. Stay Behind was composed of organizations born of a blazing-hot war and had grown up in the icy freeze between the two great powers in the world.

But the Russians had never arrived.

Society made new rules as time went on. Modern demands for transparency and political oversight. Slowly but surely, norms were changed and the Second World War grew increasingly distant. Men began to die of old age. If they took most of their secrets with them to the grave, there were still sufficient numbers of them left that it all began to unravel. A few random events, a couple of serious blunders, several persistent investigative journalists and certain revelations later, and then the Berlin Wall also fell.

The era of Soviet power was over.

Stay Behind was disbanded after around forty years of existence. Throughout Europe, and also in Norway.

Tryggve Mejer was of course well aware that the Norwegian intelligence services still harboured secrets. That was only to be expected. Bit by bit, all the same, the control mechanisms were improved, most importantly through the establishment of the Parliament's committee for control of the intelligence, surveillance and security services. EOS, the Norwegian Parliamentary Oversight Committee, became the eyes of the people's elected representatives on the secret side of Norway.

But not on the little organization that, under wraps, lived on.

Peder Mejer and Ellev Trasop did not trust the Russians. In reality, Communism collapsed with the Berlin Wall, but the Russian mentality would never die. Gorbachev's days were numbered, and when the alcoholic, unpredictable Boris Yeltsin became the first democratically elected leader of Russia in the summer of 1991, Peder and Ellev received all the confirmation they needed.

They had done the right thing.

Russia would always be a threat, as the country had been for generations, and every nation had both the right and the duty to make preparations to repel foreign aggression.

The money for the original Stay Behind groups had come partly from the USA and the UK. From the CIA and MI6. The Allies had every possible interest in supporting their European friends with capital and equipment to increase their resilience against communism. In 1990, Tryggve's father and Ellev Trasop, both participants ever since the groups had been established, had long ensured that large parts of their resources were transferred to Switzerland. They perceived the direction of travel as early as the mid-eighties, and everything had to be done very discreetly from then on. The Alpine land's outstanding secrecy and fortunate hand in money matters had led to the situation where Tryggve Mejer now had considerable resources at his command.

He put the booklet down on the workbench.

The casket also contained two memory sticks and a satellite telephone with a charger. He switched it on. As it was fully charged, he turned it off again and returned it to the casket. The USBs were wrapped in plastic bags, which he opened. Each bag also contained a note.

'Personnel' was written on one of these, and the other said 'Accounts'.

Tryggve went back to the safe and took out the brand new, simple laptop he had placed there himself that same day. It was air-gapped, and therefore had never been linked to any network. It could not be hacked. He inserted one of the memory sticks in the USB port, scrolled through the image that appeared on the screen and gave a little nod before removing the memory stick and inserting the other one.

Personnel, cash and communications would present no problem.

It took him five minutes to tidy up. When everything was back in the safe, on a whim he changed the code yet again before heading upstairs and out into the garden.

The sound of a TV programme could be heard outside, shrill voices talking over one another. A debate of some kind, he thought, even though it was not the right time of day. Maybe Cathrine had switched on the TV set. She was so strange today. So abnormally quiet. He glanced up at Mina's window, where the light curtains were fluttering in the breeze. It was already ten past eleven at night, but for once he did not feel tired.

Instead, he felt uplifted. Confirmed in his belief. He puffed his chest out a little. He was about to break his word of honour. He had never ever done that before now. But he had been forced into it. The way the world now appeared, he had to do what he could.

The way Norway now appeared, this was a matter of self-defence.

The night air was warm. The last remnants of light hovered above the hillside at Holmenkollen, after the sunset of only an hour earlier. A pink sheen overlaid on the clear mid-blue that grew darker and darker the closer the sky came towards him. A scent of newly mown grass hung between the hedges and the slender pines on his neighbour's property.

It was 31 May and in fifty minutes' time, spring would be over. Summer had really arrived.

AUTUMN

The Stone Shelter

After the fire had petered out, Selma Falck moved steadily nearer to the cabin and the wrecked car. Despite the gigantic blaze, it was difficult to keep warm. The front of her body was far too hot, but her back was still ice-cold. For the last couple of hours she had pivoted around slowly, as if she were being cooked on a humungous rotisserie. She had slid the boots off and on a few times. They were damp and frozen, but they protected her feet from the jagged ridges of rock and the bristly heather. The last time she had wrenched them off, she had noticed that the soles of her feet were bleeding.

She had no idea how long she had been awake and no idea where she was.

She was Selma Falck, lived in Sagene in Oslo, and had taken on an assignment she could not remember anything about.

Right now, when the colossal fire was starting to peter out, she did not know what frightened her more: that she was going to freeze to death, or that she had lost her wits. Her brain was full of words and knowledge spinning around like a tumble drier, but it held no clear memories. No faces, just jumbled words. Selma could remember expressions such as *negotiorum gestio*. Unauthorized administration. *Ex officio*. By virtue of office. *De lege ferenda*.

What the law ought to be. *Retrograd amnesi*. Memory loss dating from a brain injury.

The term came to her. She had no idea where from, but that was probably the correct diagnosis. It was as if large parts of her brain had switched themselves off and she struggled to concentrate without arriving at anything but staring into a huge, black void. Something like being senile, she imagined.

Senile. That was a word she remembered. Dementia.

She continued to mumble foreign words and convoluted legal terms, explaining them to herself.

Everything was in place.

An intense feeling of loneliness overwhelmed her. An intense feeling of abandonment. A sudden memory surfaced in her groggy brain.

Woodstock.

A music festival, and she was just a little girl, her brother even younger. He was a baby, in fact, and had a name. Selma had a brother. They were sitting in a green bathroom, crying. The bathroom was not green. The bathtub was green. And the toilet. The basin too, and the strange lady wore a pale-green dress.

The Woodstock festival was held in Bethel, New York, not in Woodstock. It was in 1969, and she was three years old.

It was impossible to remember anything from when you were three years old.

The fire had collapsed into a glowing pile of cinders, still giving off heat, and she moved closer and closer, while turning around slowly to avoid one side of her body freezing.

Until now, her fear and the acute danger of the situation had enabled her to shut out all the pain. Now, when it was too late to save anything, and it could only be a matter of a couple of hours before there was no more heat to be gained from the remains of the cabin, it came back. More agonizing than ever before.

She had been thoroughly knocked up, beaten black and blue.
Her head felt worst.

A shooting pain was rooted somewhere deep inside her
brain, sending out pulsating, ferocious stabs in every direction.
She massaged her temples, but it did not help in the least. She
closed her eyes, and the pain grew worse. Opened them, and
the jabbing pains grew unbearable. Only now did she notice
that it was not merely her scalp that felt sore. She had a long
gash on the back of her head. Using her fingers, black with soot,
she tentatively probed it. The wound must be nearly ten centimetres long, and fairly deep. She did not dare to examine it
more closely; a scab had begun to form, and she did not want it
to start bleeding again.

She stopped her perpetual rotation.

A couple of hours must have passed since she woke surrounded
by fire. Or three. Or maybe just half an hour. It was impossible to
say, since her sense of time was as bad as her memory. Through
the chaos in her brain, one thing was absolutely clear: she must
do something.

'Think,' she fulminated, balling both fists. 'Think!'

Dawn was breaking. A narrow strip of paler grey was outlined
behind the mountain plateau on the other side of the burnt-out
ruins. The cloud cover was low, and Selma tried to check what
the temperature might be.

'East,' she pointed towards the light with her arm outstretched.

She turned ninety degrees three times over.

'North. West. South.'

It was bitterly cold. The ferocious heat had melted the frost in
a huge circle around the cabin, but outside this, the heather was
frozen. Now she could also see that the landscape was not quite
as flat as she had thought earlier. A chain of lower peaks came
into sight in the west. A fine layer of snow drew a sprinkling of

icing sugar over the mountaintops. Here and there, clumps of dwarf birch grew, she noticed, and when she sat down to take a closer look at the heather, she discovered that there were different types of plants. She could only guess at their names, but thought she recognized them.

Selma was in Norway. And she was on a mountain plateau.

Her teeth were chattering now that she had moved so far away from the cabin, and she veered back. Now she had the brainwave of balancing the wet boots on a stone near the embers with the legs turned inwards. Maybe the heat would make its way inside and dry them out. This meant she had to walk barefoot for a while, but a little more or less pain could hardly make much difference to the possibility of survival.

It must be autumn.

While the firmament grew gradually brighter and the ruins of the cabin darker, she became even surer that she was not abroad. The cabin interior, or what she had been able to see of it before she had hurried out, was also typical of a spartan Norwegian hunting cabin.

A movement in the distance caught her attention so suddenly that she turned round too quickly. The pain caused by the jolt to her muscles made everything go black all at once. She staggered for a moment, but regained her balance and tried to focus on what she had seen.

Something moving.

Far away, where the plateau rose to a peak, three shapes were walking slowly towards what Selma now knew to be north. She began to shout, but realized that her voice was in no condition to make much impression. Besides, the movements were too far away for anyone to be able to hear her.

One stopped.

Reindeer, Selma could now make out.

Not just three of them; from a depression in the terrain, a whole herd moved into sight.

Wild reindeer? Domesticated reindeer?

Selma struggled to prick up her ears. Domesticated reindeer had bells round their necks. Some of them, at least.

All she could hear were crackles and soft thuds from the burnt-out ruins, and the wind sweeping over the plateau. It had picked up now, and here and there, tiny fires flared up again amidst the cinders.

She could be in Finnmark.

'Idiot,' she whispered.

There were any number of mountain plateaus in Norway. Several of them had herds of both domesticated and wild reindeer. There were southern Samis and northern Samis and hunters and reindeer everywhere, and her headache was now so painful that she passed out.

She must have been unconscious for a while.

The frost woke her. Never had she experienced such pain. It was as if the outer layer of her skin no longer existed. Inside, it was neither warm nor cold, just terribly painful. Except for her feet. She could almost no longer feel them, they had grown numb, deadened appendages to a broken body. It was a pleasant sensation, and for a second she closed her eyes just to feel her feet. She couldn't care less about the rest of her body, but her feet were starting to feel warm.

She remembered Woodstock, a green bathroom and a dreadful feeling of loneliness.

'Get up.'

She got up.

Snow had started falling. Light, white flakes whirled around her.

Sluggish and limping, she skirted around what was left of the cabin, looking for things in the ruins of the fire. Something to use, something to wear, something to give her some warmth. But everything looked black and charred and useless.

Once again she turned to face the peak where she had spotted the reindeer. They might still be there, but now the snow was falling so heavily that she could only see a few metres in front of her.

She was crying, she realized. It was stupid and unnecessary. Anyway, she couldn't shed tears, she was firmly convinced of that, even though she could not recollect why.

But she was sobbing.

And then she noticed a stone shelter some distance away, she could only just make it out. Someone had painstakingly laid one stone on top of another in some kind of circle: it was a low igloo of stone, covered in moss. Slowly, she came closer to the mound. It was only a cairn, she figured out, but all the same she went to the bother of walking around to the other side.

A door. Low and plain, roughly hewn, and with hinges that looked ancient.

No lock. The door was simply closed with a slide bar. She lifted the bar, even though she barely had the strength. Opened the door, despite it being far too stiff. She had to duck to go inside, and let the heavy bar drop again behind her.

It was dark in there. But it was not snowing.

Selma screwed up her eyes as much as she could despite the pain. When she opened them again, she could make out the contours of a bed.

A bed.

She collapsed on to it. The mattress was a sizeable sack stuffed with straw or heather or something else that felt prickly, but it did not matter. Two blankets lay at one end. Woollen blankets. Selma tucked them around her with stiff, frozen fingers. Grabbed hold of an animal skin – she thought it must be a reindeer hide – and used it to cover her huddled body.

The wind whistled outside. She could smell urine in here. Her pains intensified.

A human being could not remember anything from the age of only three.

Nevertheless she was overwhelmed by the endless sorrow of being abandoned.

All at once, she remembered a man. Jesper Jørgensen was his name, and he had given her an assignment. It dawned on her that she had a daughter, Anine, who had never really been hers. There was a son as well, but it was impossible to remember what he was called.

There was something about nuts, and Anine had never been easy to deal with.

The pain was suffocating her.

But she was no longer freezing, and she soon fell asleep.

SUMMER

The Showdown

'Anine absolutely won't have it,' Selma said, discouraged, as she sat down on the settee. 'She's totally against me trying to exonerate Jesper Jørgensen. It's out of the question.'

'Well, you couldn't really expect anything else,' Einar Falsen told her. 'Have you and your daughter ever actually been on the same wavelength?'

Selma did not reply. Darius, the cat she had had to bring with her from Ormøya when, penniless, she had moved out of her former life, stared accusingly at her from the coffee table. Its tail swept aggressively from side to side.

'You've taken the pussycat's place,' Einar said. 'You never learn.'

Selma moved across to an armchair. It was worn, but useable, and quite comfortable to sit in. On the whole, Einar's bedsit looked better than when she had been compelled to live there for several weeks prior to Christmas. Selma had splashed out on new glass for the windows and persuaded the Poker Turk to replace the flooring. The old settee with the obscure smell had been deposited at the dump, and for twenty thousand of Selma's kroner, Einar had furnished the entire little apartment with second-hand purchases made here and there. This was still one of the worst addresses in Oslo. Gloomy inside, with a stream of heavy traffic and tramcars only a metre and a half from the windows, but Einar had at least come indoors. He would scarcely have survived yet another winter sleeping rough under the Sinsenkrysset flyover.

Also, he had become more mindful of taking his pills. And more willing.

'Did she give you any reason?' he asked.

'N... yes. In the first place, she was offended because I left the wedding after Sjalg died. But what else was I supposed to do? There were plenty of people there, if I can put it that way. Anine would not have anything to do with me anyway, so why she's upset that I didn't stay is a mystery to me.'

'If I beat or if I'm beaten,' Einar muttered.

'And secondly, she was pretty indignant that I might take it into my head to do anything at all that might clear Jesper Jørgensen and his crew of Sjalg's death. If I know Jesso, and I do, then he's almost certainly already planning to sue on behalf of his daughter. Our daughter. I don't think Jesper has even considered the possibility of that. He's only concerned about his reputation.'

She took a swig from the Pepsi Max bottle.

'Anine was furious about everything. That I had raised this before the funeral. And that I even showed up, I think. And that I had never exhibited any interest in either her or Sjalg. That I hadn't come up with any money for the wedding, which really takes the biscuit. Considering that I was hardly invited, I mean. A text message with some half-hearted information that arrived just before the wedding and that came from Sjalg, anyway, and not from Anine. And to top it all, she was raging because—'

'I get it,' Einar broke in. 'She was angry.'

'Yes. More angry than sorry, even though I could see that she'd been crying a lot. Surprisingly enough, I think she really and truly was in love with that guy.'

'Scumbag.'

'Anine or Sjalg?'

Einar let Darius jump on to his lap. The cat purred content-edly, treading three times around his legs before settling down.

'I've never met Anine. Nor Sjalg Petterson for that matter, but I have read about him. As I said: a scumbag. I read an article about him in *Morgenbladet* not long ago. Charismatic – a bit like these American demagogues. He has followers, you know. That's always scary.'

'We all have followers in these #SoMe times. There's nothing wrong with that.'

She herself had more than 120,000 followers on Instagram, probably a record for someone her age.

'I mean disciples like the ones Jesus had. Like the evangel-ists. Like Hitler, for that matter. People who regard a person as something greater than themselves. Someone with a message bordering on a religion. Fanatics.'

Selma drank the rest of her soft drink and put the empty bottle down on the coffee table.

'He surely wasn't as bad as that? Not one of the worst, at least.'

'You're not interested in politics, and don't understand it either.'

'You don't know anything about that.'

'Yes, I do.'

Unusually, Selma felt a growing irritation. Other people often irritated her, though she almost never showed it. Einar was the only person she always made allowances for, but now she felt the need to put him in his place.

'I keep up with it really well,' she said. 'And I *am* interested. The fact that my job and … my position in society has made it expedient not to flag up my political standpoint, is another matter entirely.'

'Coward,' Einar said. 'Your position as a celebrity, you mean? As a talk show guest and participant in a reality show? As a super lawyer in the past and Norway's most famous private investigator now?'

'Cut it out. Help me instead.'

'If you've been following things, you'd know how dangerous people like Sjalg Petterson are. Or were, now that he's dead.'

Einar grinned as Darius rolled over on to his back. 'Good riddance, isn't that what they say?'

'He was my son-in-law.'

'For all of two minutes.'

Selma stood up abruptly. 'I can't be bothered with this.'

'With what?'

'Sitting here and ...'

'Sit down.'

Einar heaved the cat down on to the floor and padded out to the kitchen. Selma sat down hesitantly. She was aware of clattering cutlery in there, and she heard the fridge being opened and closed.

'You must define your assignment,' Einar said when he returned with a yogurt carton and a spoon. 'What does it involve, really?'

'Finding out how Sjalg Petterson could possibly have ingested macadamia nuts when so many people realized he had an allergy, and every precaution was followed to the letter.'

'No.'

'No?'

'Your task is to demonstrate that Jesper Jørgensen is not to blame for Sjalg Petterson ingesting macadamia nuts. You're just as much his representative as when you were a lawyer.'

'But I know that!'

'But you haven't drawn any conclusions.'

'Of course I haven't. I've hardly started on the assignment.'

'You must start at the right end, Mariska.'

For many reasons, Einar Falsen had not watched much TV in the past fifteen years. The few times he had managed to stay put in a shelter for a day or two, he had however ventured into the common room. Keeping as far as possible from the TV set, he had been glued to *Law and Order: Special Victims Unit* as soon as he could find someone to help him select the right channel.

Mystified, he had been convinced for a couple of months that Selma played the main role in that series. She looked so like Mariska Hargitay. He still used the old nickname, even though moving indoors had normalized him to such a degree that he occasionally called her Selma.

Especially when he was exasperated. 'You must start at the right end,' he repeated.

'Which is?'

'What are the alternative answers as to how Sjalg might have consumed those damned nuts?'

'Eaten them?'

Einar rolled his eyes and took a deep breath. 'There's no point in this. Why did you actually take on this assignment?'

She realized she was blushing. Selma Falck never blushed. She grabbed the empty bottle to hide her face. It seemed idiotic, and she put it down again, shaking her mid-length hair ever so slightly to cover as much of her face as possible.

'I felt sorry for him,' she said, knowing that this was half true.

'But have you considered what this assignment involves?'

'Yes. If I succeed, you and I will be able to eat well. Often.'

'If you can prove that the nuts weren't in the food because someone in the kitchen was sloppy, then Sjalg Petterson was murdered.'

'What?'

'Maris … Selma.'

Einar got to his feet. His knees would never be able to support him properly; both hamstrings had been permanently damaged by bitterly cold winters and severe intoxication. He shuffled around the table and stood immediately in front of her.

'Sjalg's death was due either to an accident or a deliberate act. Taking into account that the police, as far as I understand, are not particularly in the picture, then the prevailing view must be that it was all a macabre accident.'

'Eh ... so?'

'Selma Falck.'

'That's me.'

She glanced up at him. He seemed completely normal, apart from the fact that his beard had been trimmed in a comical zigzag shape from ear to ear, and his hair was sticking out in every direction and could scarcely have been washed for the past month.

And that he couldn't straighten his knees.

'You're intoxicated,' he said.

'Intoxicated? I never drink alcohol. You know that.'

'You're high on yourself. It doesn't suit you.'

'Me? High on myself?'

Even more surprisingly, her anger was rising. Einar Falsen was the one person she never lost her temper with. Who never lost his temper with her. He was exclusively hers, the one who was always on her side. She had taken care of him when he had become a killer, with the best reason in the world. She had saved him from prison, moved him into an involuntary psychiatric health-care facility and out again as quickly as possible. In all the years he had spent between being slightly barmy and stark staring mad, increasingly distanced from reality and the people who had once been concerned about him, it was Selma who had never let him down. She had searched for him, in the woods and on the city streets and even one time, abroad. Looked after him when he had been at his most ill. Had him admitted for a day or two when, every once in a while, he was on the verge of dying. It was impossible to say how much money and time she had spent on this man, and now an unfamiliar fury was about to engulf her.

87

'Cut it out,' she said sharply. 'Seriously. Just cut it out, Einar.'

'The past six months or so have been good for you. Strictly speaking, all the same, you're in direr straits than you were when you'd stolen millions of kroner from a client and were just a hair's breadth ...'

He let his thumb touch his forefinger with no discernible space between them, and squinted intently at the absent distance.

'... from landing in jail. But you saved yourself. Thanks to your competence, good luck and the grateful father of a young woman whose innocence you proved. It was a one-per-center, Selma. You could have been sitting in prison right now. There was approximately ninety-nine per cent chance of it. In prison because of your own weakness. Your own mistakes. Your own deception.'

He was towering over her, closing in, with a junkie-like buckling of his knees and a foul stink of rotten teeth.

'When all is said and done, you're extremely alone,' Einar told her. 'And you're starting to get too old to take that.'

Selma placed the empty plastic bottle on her face. She began to tap it lightly on her forehead, in a regular beat.

'It's a shame, of course,' Einar went on. 'But loneliness is not to be blamed. Loneliness is the worst excuse on earth for not seizing life.'

Selma swallowed audibly. Fortunately, she could not cry. She had damaged her eyes at a handball match a couple of lifetimes ago.

A gift, she had always thought later. She thought so now too.

Einar ran his skinny hands over his knees as he continued: 'You're suffering from the most pitiful loneliness of all: the anxious kind. The cowardly kind, if I can speak plainly. You move around in this society of ours like a star, and you enjoy it. Many people feel they know you, but no one really does. Not because they don't want to. Not because they're not concerned about you. Bloody hell, Selma, you've got more friends than I ever had when I was fit and well. And I had lots. Your problem is that they are friends with you. You're not friends with them. Because you don't dare.'

'I have to go,' Selma said. 'And I think this medicine you're on just now is making you a bit over-excited.'

She stood up. Darius hissed when she almost trod on the end of his tail. She had not noticed him lying on the floor between them. She resisted the temptation to kick the brute. Snatching up her bag, she slung it over her shoulder and headed for the front door.

'Photographs,' Einar said in a loud voice.

'What?'

She turned before she had reached the door.

'We live in times of photographic moments,' he said. 'Everyone takes pictures. All the time. And when do we take them most? At parties. There must be hundreds of photographs from that wedding, Selma. Maybe thousands. Taken by more than two hundred guests, almost all with mobile phones. It was good weather and the bride and groom were beautiful, a dozen or so celebrities present and no doubt a whole pile of selfies taken. Start to collect in the photographs, Selma. You'll be able to reconstruct the entire wedding reception.'

He had sat down on the settee. Slurping down the last of the yogurt, and spilling some on his absurdly shaped beard. Darius sprang up from his lap at once and settled down again after circling around several times in succession. Einar put down the carton and cradled the cat's head in his hands, scratching behind its ears, and running his hand slowly and firmly across its well-groomed fur.

Then he looked up.

'By the way, don't forget what I remind you of in every case that gives you grief,' he said. 'Qui bono?'

'For whose benefit?' Selma Falck answered, and left for home.

Sjalg Petterson

Selma's balcony was not large, but it was favourably situated all the same. As the only one in the building, it hung like a wart angled towards the south-west. The architect must have had the idea that a sudden break in the smooth façade would look dramatic. From the outside, it looked idiotic, to Selma's mind, but for her it functioned perfectly. No neighbours nearby, at least not in close proximity, and an unrestricted view all the way down the green sweep where the Akerselva river divided the city in two. Children playing, summer and winter, busy people and dogs everywhere. Selma could see them all, but no one saw Selma.

Perfect.

On the balcony, she had set out a coffee table and a simple IKEA office chair, small enough to ensure there was also room for a sunbed. Selma had sunbathed on it for a couple of hours every day since the middle of May. She looked as if she had been on a sailing trip in the Caribbean all winter.

The sun initially made it impossible to see anything on the computer screen. However, she had come upon an announcement on Facebook. More correctly, the announcement had come upon her, but anyway, she now had a handy little tent attached to the table, shutting out the light, and covering the MacBook sufficiently well for her to work outdoors. For a long time Selma had as good as lived on the balcony. Barely four square metres was tiny in comparison to the extensive property with shoreline and bathing hut where she came from, but this was hers and hers alone.

And far, far better.

She pulled the skip cap down over her forehead as she logged on to the machine.

Sjalg Petterson was of course not unknown to her.

She had never met him, apart from his polite enough greeting at the wedding, in contrast to Anine. Just after the bridal couple had arrived from the Opera House roof in a veteran car, Selma recalled. He had caught sight of his famous mother-in-law, nodded and smiled, before going on to force his way through the crowd of happy, congratulatory guests. The two of them had barely exchanged a string of polite phrases before he allowed himself to be dragged away by his best man.

The guy was better looking in reality than in photographs. More handsome than on TV too – he was unusually tall and broad-shouldered. His gaze was direct and friendly; his handshake had been firm and lasted just long enough. With an almost imperceptible toss of the head, Sjalg Petterson had conveyed to Selma that he found Anine's hostility towards her own mother pretty idiotic. The laughter lines had told her that this would soon be sorted out, and that he at least was pleased that she had come.

Selma had liked the guy there and then. Despite everything, he had invited her, and he seemed genuinely interested in having her there.

She didn't like him now.

Politics had never really interested Selma Falck. When her ex-husband, Jesso Mork, was elected to parliament some years earlier, the tiny scrap of interest she had taken in national government had vanished. The dinners, which had already been fairly boring, were now dominated by insufferable conversation about support schemes for small businesses, patients' rights and suitable early-years teaching.

She herself had voted for the Labour Party at every election from the time she had the right to vote, but no one else knew that. The choice she had made in her youth was based on pragmatism rather than ideology: Selma Falck was in the main satisfied with how things ran. The Labour Party was well situated in the middle of everything that was solidly Norwegian, and stood for the same priorities as she did. The welfare state. Distribution of wealth. Equality and the rule of law. A public school system and health care for all. Respectful treatment of refugees. Despite the Labour Party becoming almost identical to the far-right Progress Party as far as the final point was concerned.

Sjalg Petterson voted for the Progress Party. No one had known about that either until a couple of years ago.

The man was a historian, and was appointed professor at an unusually young age. His special area of expertise was Norwegian post-war history. For a time he positioned himself as a frequently used analyst and commentator in both old and new media outlets. Eventually he started writing his own blog, exceptionally popular for one associated with an academic. To begin with, he was uncontroversial. Following a conflict in which he took the side of a colleague against senior management at the university, however, it grew increasingly clear to all the world that Sjalg Petterson had an agenda far beyond becoming known for his ability as a professional historian. His colleague had written an article in the *Klassekampen* newspaper in which he postulated that he could demonstrate a link between immigration from foreign cultures and academic decline at universities and colleges. Sjalg Petterson managed at one and the same time to both offend his colleague and humiliate the senior management of the university in his defence of the guy. The article was badly written and furthermore, marred by the misuse of data, he pointed out. Nevertheless, it was even worse that the University of Oslo had completely misunderstood the meaning of freedom of speech.

Sjalg Petterson set them straight, to the obvious delight of quite a few people.

Six weeks later, another article was published in *Klassekampen*, this one written by him. It discussed the connection between increased social differences in Oslo schools and the city council's unsuccessful housing and immigration policies. From a factual point of view, it was relatively unassailable. All the data was correct, and nothing of what he wrote was untrue. From a political standpoint, on the other hand, it provoked furious debate, and gave him a symbolic twentieth place on the Progress Party's list of candidates for the parliamentary elections in 2017. If he had wanted, he could have been far higher on the list. Sjalg Petterson, however, was more interested in trumpeting from his ivory tower in Blindern rather than becoming tied up in parliamentary duties for at least four years.

Around this time, he had met the much younger law student Anine Falck-Mork. Jesso had been far from pleased when they fell in love. Selma had shrugged, and when their engagement was announced after only three months, she had lost interest in the professor.

The Facebook tent had begun to collapse.

Selma fiddled with the flimsy supporting legs. The patent was certainly not as idiot-proof as the advert had promised, but after a bit of back and forth she was again able to read the screen.

Anine no longer used the name Falck, she noted from the strapline beneath a photograph of the pair on their way to a film premiere only a couple of months earlier.

The increasingly popular and controversial Sjalg Petterson also made an appearance on the red carpet. Here accompanied by his fiancée Anine Mork.

Quick as a flash, Selma moved on to the next article.

Now her daughter might be called Anine Petterson, even though the duration of the marriage had been rather skimpy. Or Anine Mork Petterson. Falck had disappeared altogether. Since

Selma had insisted on a hyphen between the children's surnames, her daughter must have had to apply officially to make the change.

Actively seeking to get rid of her mother.

Selma stood up so abruptly that the little coffee table almost toppled. She snatched up the laptop and fled into the living room, leaving the balcony door open, and slammed the machine down too hard on the dining table. She fetched herself a Pepsi Max and an apple from the kitchen.

She should turn down this assignment. It just didn't make any sense.

The police had shown no urgent interest in the case. That at least was clear from her conversation with Anine. A sudden death like Sjalg's would in all probability be recorded in a folder lying somewhere at police headquarters, but would hardly be the subject of comprehensive inquiries. The cause of death was already as good as self-evident. And logical. A hyper-allergy to a relatively common food item would always involve an element of risk. Unless the Food Safety Authority found anything out of the ordinary with regard to the badly mistimed death, the case would be shelved.

Which was strange, in fact, when she gave this closer thought.

She pushed the MacBook carefully aside. Then drew it towards her again.

Her fingers raced over the keyboard, and a portrait photo of Sjalg Petterson appeared, the Asthma Association's blue logo stamped on his chest. The brief accompanying text spoke of the seriousness of food allergies and encouraged everyone to show understanding for invisible disabilities.

Like his, which was his allergy to macadamia nuts.

Selma thought she recalled the case that had given rise to the advertising campaign. The parents at a primary school in Bergen had protested against the consequences of a pupil's nut allergy. They had been requested not to let their children bring any kind of nuts to school. Not even peanut-butter sandwiches. Their solidarity did not stretch as far as packed lunches, and the boy had become extremely ill as a result. He survived, but for a few days there had been a public debate about who should give ground: the allergic child or his classmates who could not for all the world forgo having nuts in their schoolbags.

'Good Lord,' Selma mumbled, bending towards the screen.

She was on the side of the little boy's parents, and could well understand why they had taken part in the discussion. It was more difficult to fathom why Sjalg Petterson was happy to come forward and publicize such a condition.

It left him wide open if someone wanted to harm him, but that had obviously not entered his head. Probably because he had not believed that anyone would wish him harm.

Or quite simply because no one *did* wish misfortune upon the young professor. Norway was not like that. Norwegians did not kill one other for their views.

22 July crossed her mind.

Benjamin Hermansen, the fifteen-year-old boy with a dark-skinned father who was stabbed to death by racists in 2001.

The Hadeland murders. A case in the eighties when two young men were shot and killed, described as an out-and-out execution, and the moment when Norway lost its innocence.

Sweden, the country so very similar to Norway in language and culture that the two nations should really have been one, had lost both Anna Lindh and Olof Palme to cold-blooded killers. Or madmen.

It was one and the same thing.

Selma opened Word, located a little document and pressed the print icon. The printer in her bedroom clicked and hummed.

Heading in, she picked up the sheet of paper and placed it in front of her on the table when she came back.

Qui bono? Einar had reminded her.

Who gained? Selma had written at the top of the printout.

The obvious candidate was Anine, unless they had entered into a prenuptial agreement that disinherited her. Sjalg had no children from before their marriage, and Selma assumed that it would therefore be Anine who was left whatever there was of an estate. There was no reason to believe that there was much more than the apartment in Tåsen, which was perfectly ordinary, a car and possibly an inherited holiday cabin somewhere. University staff did not earn serious money, and the man was relatively young.

Of course Anine had not killed her husband less than three hours into their marriage. Her daughter was difficult and unreasonable, but not dangerous.

Not stupid.

Selma crossed out her name with a black marker pen.

After opening a Google search, there was still no reason to believe that there was any financial motive to be found if this were indeed a case of murder.

Below Anine's name, Selma had written 'Chefs in competition'.

Sjalg's death had the potential to damage Jesper Jørgensen. Rivalry was probably just as common a phenomenon in that profession as anywhere else.

She took a bite of the apple. Chewed. Swallowed and gave a heavy sigh.

There had to be countless easier methods of discrediting a competitor than this. Selma raised the marker pen, took off the lid, and after reconsidering for a few more seconds, also crossed the chefs off her list.

The names that followed were far more numerous: the politicians whose throats Sjalg Petterson had gone for.

Although in actual fact he had not gone for anyone's throat. He was crass, and his pen was sharp. After spending almost four hours reading up on Sjalg's life, conduct and public statements, it struck her all the same that he had never been directly offensive. He did not use the tone to be found in the comments sections of the newspapers. The contempt, smears and conspiracy theories of Default.no, Wrong.no and all the magnificent adjoining right-wing extremism were absent. He took the crudest bias expressed in the comments on his own articles to task, and obviously carefully moderated anything that bordered on, or was, actionable. But that was all.

Selma opened the Pepsi Max bottle and drank deeply. This was the third she had resorted to that day. She had just read an article about the deleterious effects of soft drinks, and put the lid back on. Pushed the bottle to the far end of the table. Took another bite of the apple.

The most problematic aspect of the Progress Party was that it was no longer true to say that all cats were grey.

Not even in the dark.

Previously, things had been simpler. Then the adherents of the Progress Party came in only one type, as Selma saw it. Blindly hostile to immigrants, ultra populists, and a bit stupid. At least after the frenzied, bloody civil war leading up to their national conference in 1994 was done and dusted. The populist wing won, and the time of the charming liberals in the party was at an end. The Progress Party found its place as the most extreme party of the right. Strong in numbers, admittedly, but all the same enough of a political pariah for Selma, in common with most others of her ilk, to see no way that the party would achieve a place in government.

Until they did. And something had happened.

There were still plenty of simple souls in the Progress Party. But some of them were smart. Razor sharp. Downright pleasant. The party was still plagued by scandals. Prominent representatives were from time to time caught in various tricks and mischief, even crimes, and the #MeToo wave had forced both old and brand new skeletons out of the cupboard.

Be that as it may.

Some of them were like Sjalg Petterson. Especially Sjalg Petterson.

His sphere of interest was extensive. He was an anti-globalist and climate sceptic. Critical of the elite and opposed to the EU. He had picked apart the EEA agreement on energy policy and claimed it was not fit for purpose, and he was still among the last of those prepared on occasion to defend President Donald Trump.

The immigration question was however the subject closest to his heart.

He had picked them off one by one, the people he considered responsible for welcoming an irresponsibly large flood of refugees into Norway. All the Labour Party prime ministers since the start of the seventies. Most of the justice ministers in the same time frame. In the past year, however, he had particularly attacked two of the Progress Party's colleagues in coalition government, members of the Conservative Party, surprisingly enough.

The Prime Minister was one. The criticism of her was something Selma quite simply found difficult to understand. She could not bring herself to try, either.

The main cannon fire from his bunker in Blindern was aimed at Justice Minister Tryggve Mejer.

In the past six months, hardly a month had gone by between the occasions on which Sjalg Petterson had issued a blog post about the Conservative Minister of Justice. They were always trenchant in style, but nevertheless always remained within the boundaries of respectable debate.

The comments that followed were not.

The cheers came from an abyss that Selma felt queasy at having looked into. It made her think of a story from the Brothers Grimm she had read as a child. In one of the illustrations, the beautiful, harlequin-clad Rat Catcher danced and played the pipe, leading an endless stream of vermin, each more repulsive than the next. The picture had fascinated her, and she recalled that as a six-year-old she had roamed around all summer trying to catch rats, playing a tuneless recorder.

Sjalg Petterson was the Pied Piper of Hamelin.

Well-dressed, with fine words. But the rats followed him.

Whereas Sjalg used words such as irresponsible and unhistorical, his supporters let rip with accusations of treason and threats of capital punishment. When Sjalg talked of consequences, and obviously meant political ones, his fans screamed about hanging opponents from lamp posts as soon as the popular Norwegian revolution became a reality.

The professor did not employ the language of the masses. He was well read, knowledgeable and smart, and also had a pleasant manner between the battles.

Selma herself had experienced that at the wedding.

She wondered what he had really wanted.

The man did not seek power, but had great influence. He did not wish for any position other than the one he had, but he could have become a cabinet minister had he wanted to. He had a body of followers that seemed to expand exponentially.

The man was the guru of the extreme right, and now he was dead.

Most likely as the result of an accident. One of life's tragic, sudden reverses, the kind that sometimes occurred and which human beings were never really prepared for all the same. The bereaved were left searching for scapegoats, as Anine was doing right now. Not only would she insist that Jesper Jørgensen was to blame for the death, but to her mind he should also pay for it. Things could not just happen, randomly and casually, according to common wisdom.

Though that was exactly what they did, Selma thought.

And for once she was reluctant to follow Einar Falsen's advice. Qui bono? was not relevant. Not in this case. It was quite simply unthinkable that someone had deliberately killed him by somehow making him ingest nuts during his own wedding reception.

She got to her feet and returned to the balcony. Snapping shut the shadow tent, she pushed the office chair into the living room and set up the sunbed. Tugging off her blouse, she placed a towel on the bed and lay down.

Closed her eyes.

Of course someone was secretly glad that Sjalg Petterson was dead. The man was an increasingly troublesome irritant in the politics of Norway to the left of the Progress Party. No matter how Selma twisted it and turned it, it still remained impossible to imagine that anyone had deliberately taken his life.

Just an accident. She had no case. Jesper Jørgensen would have to fight his own battles.

Lifting her mobile from the little table, she ran her fingers through her mid-length hair, drew her sunglasses on to her head, adjusted the top of her new bikini, gave a broad smile and took a selfie. She posted it on both Instagram and Facebook, accompanied by a whole screed of hashtags with nothing in the least to do with how she was or what she was doing.

It could mean that Jesper would go bankrupt.

The boy had seemed really shattered. Moreover, he was sweet, somehow. A combination of street urchin and modern man. Velvet eyes and aggressive tattoos. Broad-shouldered and fit, but still thrusting out his bottom lip when he was upset.

Selma had taken a liking to Jesper Jørgensen.

It struck her that one possibility remained. She could listen to another piece of Einar's advice. Her irritation grew when she thought of him, but his suggestion might have something in it. Probably it would be a far-reaching task. Once again she hesitated, but then finally decided to give it a try.

The display on her phone lit up constantly. She grabbed the phone and saw that she already had more than 100 likes on Instagram, and 49 hearts and thumbs-up on Facebook. Plus an invitation to a barbecue at Vanja and Kristina's: at last they were starting to live again after their son's tragic death just before Christmas.

She tapped in a thank-you, a thumbs-up and a heart before switching off her phone and lying back on the sunbed.

Tomorrow she would begin to gather in the photographs from Anine and Sjalg's wedding. She even knew where she would make a start.

AUTUMN

Water

Her body was screaming. Selma was screaming.
And outside, the wind howled.

As she opened her eyes, she knew more about herself.

'Selma Falck,' she said in a voice that barely carried. 'I am Selma. Anine is my daughter. Johannes is my son, and at one time I was a lawyer.'

There was warmth deep down inside her core. She lay curled up, wrapped in two woollen blankets, on top of a mattress filled with something prickly. A reindeer skin she remembered covering herself with had fallen down on the earth floor. The heat inside, deep below her skin, somewhere in her intestinal system, was like a match flame. It could blow out at any minute. She curled up even more tightly, and folded herself around the tiny ember that had kept her alive throughout the sleep that might have lasted an hour. Or two days.

She had no idea.

Her headache was still ghastly. But a bit better. Or no, not exactly better, just different. The pain was more constant, and it was easier to deal with a regular pain than the sudden stabs that pierced her nerves and forced her to brace herself all the time.

She was suffering from a terrible concussion.

Ought not to have gone to sleep.

It was dangerous to fall asleep with concussion. She clearly recollected that she was no longer freezing when she had fallen asleep, which was also a bad sign.

But at least she had woken up.

She remembered that she had found this place. She remembered the difficult bar on the door. The heavy door. The pitch darkness.

Now her night sight had improved.

And she was thirsty. Heart-wrenchingly, terrifyingly thirsty. Hungry too, but above all else she felt her tongue like a huge, dry lump inside her mouth. She tried to force out some saliva, but there was no moisture left in her glands.

To hell with food, it was water she needed.

Water and warmth.

Selma scrambled up into a sitting position. Her body was sore and protested with each movement she made. When she was finally upright, with her back to the ice-cold stones that comprised the walls in this little, round shelter, she realized that it was better equipped than she had realized before she fell asleep.

Probably this stone shelter was ancient. It could have been Samis who had built it several hundred years ago. Or trappers. The old stone refuge was not large. Almost completely circular, and probably two metres in diameter. She had seen pictures of such tiny dens made of stone before. They were not usually round, but square, and were normally situated on a slope and fashioned in such a way that they became almost impossible to detect with their turf roofs and grey walls.

This one was round.

Maybe she was not in Norway after all.

The bed she had collapsed into was nailed together from rough, unplaned wooden boards, and it was not long enough for her, not for any adult in fact. It could scarcely be more than a metre and a half from one end to the other. However, that was of no consequence to Selma. It was broad enough to lie curled up.

From a crack halfway up the dome that formed the roof, a narrow strip of grey light trickled through. Not enough to prevent the room from being shrouded in deep darkness, but Selma could at least see that the stone shelter must also have been used in modern times. A small black stove sat on the opposite side of the bed. The chimney was just a pipe, but it looked intact and disappeared up through the stones. Someone had used mortar for insulation around the simple smoke outlet.

Beside the stove there was a plastic bucket filled with firewood.

Wood!

Selma stood up as fast as she could, still with one blanket wrapped around her body. Where there was firewood, there must also be matches. There must be.

Must be.

Now she caught sight of a simple cupboard above the low door. It was more a kind of shelf, she saw when she moved closer, with unusually high-lipped edges. Lipped edges belonged on a boat. Selma was none the wiser and thought she might as well tear down the whole caboodle.

It was actually a wooden box, hung up on rusty nails that had been hammered into the gaps between the rough, flat stones.

Inside the box there were two short, thick candles. A large box of matches of the kind they kept beside the fireplace on Ormøya island – long and with an extra helping of sulphur. Two tins of tomato soup. A small saucepan. A ball of coarse string and a knife so blunt that it did not cut her skin when she ran it over her finger. A crime novel by Kim Småge, read so many times that it was falling apart.

Her hands were not trembling, they were shaking.

After emptying the box, she put it upside down on the bed, to use as a little table. She tried to light one of the candles, but it was futile. She was too thirsty, she was too weak, and maybe the matches were damp. She had already broken three of them, right beside the sulphur head, when she laid aside the box and collapsed on to the bed.

Tomato soup. Food and liquid at one and the same time.

She had no tin opener.

Really she just wanted to sleep.

It was difficult to say which was worse, the pain or the thirst. They reinforced each other in all likelihood, the headache had deteriorated now, and her throat was so dry that it felt clogged.

Her feet, though, were no longer cold. She could hardly feel them at all.

'Handball,' she tried to say. 'I used to play handball.'

Selma Falck was scarcely an outdoors kind of person. From the age of ten, and for two decades after that, she had spent most of her free time in handball arenas. She remembered that now. The smell in these places, the rank smell of perspiration, rubber and adhesive. A foul odour that in some strange way was safe and reassuring, just like the stink of rot, wet earth and tar in this cavity that was protecting her from the murderous storm raging outside.

Selma knew little of survival skills. Admittedly, she had, like everyone else, been on the occasional trip to a cabin somewhere, but she had never moved more than a few kilometres away from a shower and a functional kitchen. She had never gone to a gym. She ran forty kilometres a week, but seldom in the forest. She had trainers for running on pavements, and preferred to do her running among other people. The network of walking trails in Oslo was now so good that she had never seen the point of anything other than jogging in the middle of the city.

She knew next to nothing about mountains.

Eating snow when thirsty was not a good idea.

She did know that. The energy it would take for her body to melt the snow, would drain her of strength she no longer possessed. Make her even colder. She must have lukewarm water. Preferably hot.

There were about ten matches left.

Selma clambered up again and grabbed one of the ones she had already spoiled. It was just possible to hold the wood without touching the rust-red primer. Concentrating all the strength she still had in her grip, she placed the red top on the striking paper and pushed. Not too hard, not too gentle. Struck it, fast and firmly.

The flame flared up.

It burnt her fingers, but she refused to let go. She lowered her hand towards the candle. The wick might be damp too. It fizzled. She dropped the match, and it landed beside the black stub of cotton thread in the middle of the chubby candle. It did not go out. Selma held her breath.

The candle was burning.

A clear, bright flame flickered up towards her face. She cupped the candle in her hands. A tiny puddle of melted wax gathered around the wick, and after a couple of minutes, Selma dared to look up.

Behind the bucket of wood beside the stove there was even more firewood. A couple of old newspapers were tucked down behind the stack. The low, heavy door on the opposite side of the shelter was slightly pressed into the space, she saw: a lot of snow must have fallen outside. She moved the box with the candle on it all the way to the foot of the bed before taking hold of the saucepan and with one more burst of exertion, she moved to the door.

It was difficult to budge.

She was locked in. The blanket had slid off her and naked, she put her shoulder to the door and shoved as hard as she could. It still did not move much. Panic rose within Selma: she was all alone in the world, and locked inside an ice-cold stone shelter. Maybe it was completely covered in snow. Maybe even the air would run out, this could be like being caught in an avalanche, and a slow death being steadily suffocated was all that awaited her.

Her breathing was already shallow from sheer terror.

She picked up the blanket from the earth floor, and wrapped it around her like a towel, with a tight fold over her breasts. Her arms and shoulders were bare now, and her sore feet were numb on the ground. Automatically, as if her consciousness was already beginning to fail her, she held the saucepan to the gap between the simple doorframe and the partly damaged door, scrabbling her fingers into all the ice-cold snow packed solid outside.

Snow did not pack solid. It was light as a feather.

Feather-light snow was full of air, her mind told her. She would not be smothered immediately. Maybe she was simply too weak to open the door. Yet. There could be a great deal of snow out there, but it was airy and light, and she dug and scraped. The saucepan was filled in the blink of an eye, even though it weighed no more than when it was empty. Selma tamped the snow down as firmly as she could, using the knuckles of her right hand. Filled some more, and then even more.

She had to light that stove.

Like an automaton, she walked across and grabbed the newspapers. They felt quite dry. Her eyes caught the logo and date.

The *Hallingdølen.*

7 July 2006.

The Hardangervidda sprang to mind, but it did not matter, not now, the most important thing was to get the fire going, get water into her body; she no longer felt thirsty, and realized with a mind-blowing glimmer of insight that she was on the verge of dying from dehydration. Somewhere in the middle of her headache lay a thought that suggested her blood was starting to thicken. It would soon become unable to flow around her body in order to do its job. Waste matter was accumulating. Her blood pressure was sinking, her pulse racing, and she could hear her heart's extreme exertions in her eardrums as she opened the door on the small black stove that could save her life.

Placing the paper on the bottom, and the kindling on top.

It caught fire.

She could not resist the temptation to put the pot on the stove while she crawled back to the door and filled her mouth with ice-cold snow, light as down.

The fire was crackling behind the black stove door.

The snow melted, but it yielded hardly any water. She filled it again. Then filled it again. And again and again. Her hands grew numb with cold as she scraped out more snow and dropped it into the pot.

She saw steam and lifted the hot saucepan.

The water burnt her lips. A blessing. She lapped up the liquid, slurped and drank, it was impossible to get enough of it.

Her pulse was sinking.

Without being able to either feel or think, she stuffed the stove so full of wood that it might even be dangerous.

Everything was dangerous at the moment.

She drank the rest of the water before refilling the pot with snow. It melted at once now, and she drank even more, as she put another three sticks of wood into the stove. She closed the door that was now black with soot. Wrapped the blankets around her. Lay down on the bed with her head nearest the fire and plucked the reindeer pelt from the floor. Instead of laying it on top of her, she tucked it behind her back to protect her from the ice-cold wall.

Before she fell asleep again, she remembered that there was a deadline.

It was a deadline she had to meet, a deadline that was fast running out, but it was impossible not to fall asleep.

Not even the thought that she had not peed for ages and that her kidneys might fail could keep her awake. A blessed darkness settled around her while the candle went on burning.

The Conversation

'We'll have to use a drone.'

'So you've not been out there?'

'No. The storm took us by surprise. It's not often that it snows as early as this in September. We didn't want to leave tracks. Whoever finds her must be the first person on the scene. I expect she'll soon be reported missing, and the digital trace will fairly easily lead the search party to the cabin. It was let in her name. Paid for with her money. Her car is up there, presumably burnt out too. We thought there was a cart track all the way up, but the maps lied. The last five or six hundred metres were hard going, over stony ground. We parked as close to the wall as possible and left the nearest window open. Relax. The woman's dead.'

'How can you know that for sure?'

'She was dead when we left, for fuck's sake! Besides, the cabin is burnt down to the ground. You can see nothing but ruins under the snow, apart from the chimney and hearth that are still standing. Everything's white. No sign of life, neither human footsteps nor animal tracks.'

'So you're absolutely one hundred per cent certain that she's dead? And that all her belongings are destroyed?'

'Yes. She's dead several times over. Beaten up, suffocated and burnt to a crisp.'

'OK. Thanks. You can go.'

Soup

Selma was not dead.

It felt like it, but after having been awake for a few seconds, she noticed that her teeth were no longer chattering. Not because she was freezing to death, something she had once read could be fairly pleasant towards the end, when the cold releases its grip and a lethargic, phantom heat disengages you from life.

It was quite simply that the temperature in the stone shelter had risen.

Not by much, but she understood this when she leaned over the edge of the bed and cast about for the saucepan. There was still some water left at the bottom. Not ice.

She squinted at the stove.

Through the air vent in the door, a faint orange light was visible. It did not flicker. The fire had burnt down, but the remnants were still glowing. The candle had dwindled, but not too much. She could not have slept for long. Slowly she sat up and, remarkably enough, felt better. Stronger. She drank the rest of the water from the pan and tucked the blankets more snugly around her. Warily, she ran her fingers over the deep cut in the back of her head. Held them out in the glimmer of light. No blood, she thought. Not so sore now either.

Underneath her was wet. In the bed, on the straw mattress. She lowered her head towards her crotch and sniffed. Pee. She had peed herself in her sleep. From the dark patch she saw when she got up, it was difficult to tell whether her urine was bloody. She grabbed the paperback and tore out the last page. Pressed it down on the wet patch. Lifted up the paper and held it to the candle flame. The stain was yellowish-brown. Mostly yellow, rather less brown. She hoped the dark tinge was the result of too little liquid, and not of damaged kidneys.

She turned the mattress over and dragged herself across to the stove. The bucket was empty, but there was still quite a lot left of the stack of wood behind it. She pushed two new logs into the embers, closed the sooty door and went back to sit on the bed.

It was peculiar to feel so hungry.

She knew it was her blood sugar level sinking, and that the low blood glucose was causing her brain to send messages about eating. Many messages, continually, and the dizziness was a result not only of the blow to her head, but also of her lack of energy. Normally Selma never used to allow herself to become really ravenous, and very rarely ate so much that she was absolutely replete. A long life that included a great deal of exercise had taught her to maintain a balance in her metabolism.

These were not the usual hunger pangs.

There was some kind of rodent gnawing at her insides and eating her up.

The two tins of tomato soup sat in front of her. She had to find an opener, and looked around for one. There was no shelf other than the one she had already torn down. No hiding places apart from the bucket of firewood, which she knew was empty. She began to fantasize about ripping out a stone from the wall and attempting to hammer a hole in the tin, but was unsure if she had the strength. She picked up one of the tins. It was upside down, she now noticed in the gloom, and when she upended it, she felt a surge of relief so intense that her headache let go of her skull for a single fleeting moment.

The tin was fitted with a ring pull.

Her fingers fumbled with the metal loop. As she took hold, she froze. It was possible to tear the ring off without bringing the lid with it. She tried to remember the best way to avoid that, but her brain refused to cooperate. She was sick with anticipation. Soup, the inside of her head was telling her.

'Soup,' Selma whispered.

Carefully, but at the same time firmly, she pulled the ring while using the knuckle of her middle finger to apply pressure to the metal below.

Deep-red, thick soup revealed itself. Almost like porridge.

It was a Heinz tin, and for some reason she recalled that this, unlike Campbell's, should be diluted with water. It should also be heated up, that would help to heat her up, there was heat to be had from hot soup and the stove was already blazing.

Selma put her lips to the sharp edge and drank.

The soup filled her mouth. It tasted salty and metallic with a hint of old, sweet tomatoes. The rodent in her stomach was desperate for her to swallow, but the queasiness would not ease off. She chewed the soup, over and over again, but her throat refused to cooperate. She twisted the tin to find a sell-by date. Without success.

She must swallow.

She needed food.

Salt and energy. There was very little energy in tomato soup, maybe 150 calories in a tin, possibly only 100, but it was far better than nothing. Maybe the soup would be poisonous. Too old. Full of lead or whatever it was that gave the sweet taste of iron to the porridge she could not manage to swallow.

All of a sudden she sat bolt upright, took a deep breath through her nose and held it for a second. Swallowed. Slowly the soup ran down her gullet, it opened, it was forced to give in, she took another slurp, she drank and swallowed, and before she had time to think of saving some, the tin was empty. She pulled the lid right off the tin, thrust her forefinger inside and scraped out the remains, finally licking her fingers. Over and over again. She grabbed the other tin, and was about to open it too, but stopped herself just in time.

This at least should be saved.

She was remembering such strange things. That point about the difference between the two soups, for example. But she couldn't think of a single friend.

Yes. Einar. Einar Falsen was a friend, and he looked after Darius. He took care of her money. Selma took care of him.

She put two fingers on each temple. The pain in her head had returned, just as severe as ever, but the chaos inside was settling down. The darkness was lifting. She no longer recollected only words, definitions and specific things, but also people. Memories. Not distinctly, and in a far from sensible order, but her ability to remember was on its way back.

Selma knew many people. In her mind's eye, she saw faces in rapid succession and mumbled their names aloud in the smoky space. She was separated. She liked Indian food and had embezzled from a client who nevertheless had not sent her to jail. Jan Morell was his name, and Selma slumped back against the reindeer skin.

The animal in her stomach had dozed off.

An unsuccessful wedding and a successful funeral, Selma remembered.

An assignment and a guy called Jesper who was far too young for her.

The stove consumed wood at an alarming rate. She would have to put on more, and at the same time tried to calculate how long the little pile would last.

She could not do it.

Once again she stuffed the black stove full of firewood and refused to remember anything more. She collapsed on to the bed. She really did not want to remember.

She had had sex with Jesper. Whose surname was Jørgensen. Who was a chef. Who had given her an assignment.

She had slept with a client who was quarter of a century younger than her. Selma screwed up her eyes to keep out all the unwelcome memories that suddenly jostled their way through. It took an uncomfortably long time before she fell asleep again, shutting out all the pain, cold and everything she had no wish to remember.

Absolutely no wish to remember.

The Decision

In and out of sleep.

Out and in.

At some time she must have crawled into a corner to take a shit. Selma did not remember it. The stench was probably what woke her for something other than tossing more wood on the fire or merely turning over and sleeping on. In one corner, beside the hatch that served as a door, she could see a glistening pile of excrement. Not large, but the stink was unbearable. At first she considered bringing in more snow from the crack beside the door to cover the disgusting mess, but realized in time that it would all just melt and go from bad to worse.

There was no more firewood.

The fire in the stove was still burning, but she had nothing more to put on it.

Sitting up, she twisted her head from side to side. Backwards and forwards. Her headache felt a bit better. Maybe she had simply grown accustomed to it. It was no longer so difficult to move. Sensation had returned to her feet. They were aching, but she had managed to get some heat into them under the blankets. She threw the reindeer pelt on the ground to avoid planting her bare feet on the earth floor, and stood up, stretching to her full height.

She could do it.

The pains in her back were tolerable. Her eyes were no longer so difficult to open. She held her hands up in front of them and opened and closed her fingers. Everything was whole, and everything was possible.

Selma needed to get out of here. Away. She had to find her way back to civilization, and she knew it was urgent. There was a deadline she had to meet.

It was important, extraordinarily important, and she walked to the door. Knelt down and pushed. Snow still blocked the door outside, but she had regained more of her strength. Maybe the stone shelter had grown tired of her. Wanted her to leave. In any case, she felt the snow give a little. Soon she had created an opening of about thirty centimetres. It was daylight outside. Light, at least.

It had started raining.

A quiet, almost soundless rain was falling vertically from the sky and had made the snow collapse. A final little push of the door and the shelter filled with fresh air. Selma drew the blanket more tightly around her, pushed the reindeer pelt out to stand on, and stepped outside.

The first snow never lay for long.

Not this time either. Now it was barely ten centimetres deep, compact and sodden, and could disappear entirely in the course of a few hours. She stood taking in the scent of the wet mountain plateau for a couple of minutes before moving back inside and closing the door. She snatched up the paperback and muttered an apology to the author before ripping it to shreds and flinging it on the fire. By smacking the wooden box against the wall a few times, she had harvested enough wood for another half-hour. It would remain habitable in here for a couple of hours. Or so.

Two hours was all she had to force down another tin of ancient tomato soup and fashion some clothes and footwear out of two blankets and one reindeer skin. The tools she had at her disposal were a ball of coarse string and a blunt knife. She gathered together everything she had, sat down and drew the last candle closer. It sat on the floor now, and she had to be careful not to knock it over.

Selma Falck had no idea how long she had been on this mountain. She should have followed the alternation of light and dark out here, but much of the time she had been slipping in and out of something that most resembled unconsciousness. It must have been a matter of several days at least.

She still had far more questions than answers.

But she was not going to die.

At least not today.

SUMMER

Runhild

Selma Falck had expected to meet an older woman.

Sjalg Petterson was thirty-six years of age when he died. His mother was therefore in her early fifties at least, even if she had given birth as a teenager. During the wedding, Selma had noticed that Runhild Petterson was slim and well groomed, but she had only seen her from a distance then.

It appeared that the woman had given birth when she was only a child herself.

It must have taken considerable doses of Restylane, and two or three surgical procedures into the bargain, to look like this. Her cheekbones were high, but not as sharp as her real age would suggest. Her lips had clearly been enhanced, but without producing the tragic duck-beak-effect that younger and more enthusiastic women end up with after this kind of treatment.

'Come in,' Runhild Petterson said, waving her hand invitingly before retreating further into the apartment.

Selma followed her obediently. The vast living room was situated to the left of the hallway and had picture windows facing south and west. The external venetian blinds began to lower without Selma having seen the other woman press anything. The light gradually grew more comfortable. The room was rectangular, with a south-facing terrace that Selma glimpsed before the blinds were down. A pergola covered a third of the space outside and the ivy was obviously old as it spread like a solid roof and cast cooling shade on the seating area below. A kitchen zone with sink and permanent barbecue dominated the east-facing end, and in the centre of the roof terrace there were three large deckchairs in fancy wood with small tables in between. A Turkish towel lay folded on one of the sunbeds. There was still a damp patch beneath the outdoor shower in the corner, and a half-full jug of water with added lemon slices sat on one of the tables.

Runhild Petterson had spent the morning basking in the roasting city sunshine.

She looked as if she had just come straight from a fridge.

Her skin was brown, but not sunburnt. Dry, almost matte, probably powdered. Her eyes were deep-blue and her ash-blonde hair fell youthfully around her narrow face. Her make-up was discreet, and so professionally applied that Selma caught herself listening out for someone else in the apartment. It was thirty-two degrees Celsius in Oslo city centre right now, and on the roof terrace it must be at least forty.

Her handshake had been cool and dry.

'Can I offer you anything?' Runhild Petterson asked. 'I understand you like Pepsi Max?'

'Yes, please,' Selma replied.

The other woman moved soundlessly across the floor. Only now did Selma notice that the room was not actually a rectangle at all, but a large L. A folding door separated the living room from the kitchen, into which Runhild disappeared. Selma heard the clinking of ice cubes in a glass and a fridge door open and close.

The furniture here must be worth several million.

At least many hundreds of thousands. Selma recognized the settee she sat on. Poltrona Frau. The coffee table was made of glass, and probably also Italian. The dining-room furniture, logically placed outside the folding doors into the kitchen, looked Norwegian. And extremely expensive. Selma did not recognize them, but noticed the meticulous detail where the tabletop met the frame underneath, and the seamlessly joined wood. The chairs were of the same light oak as the table and upholstered in anthracite-grey wool.

'The dining room was custom made by a cabinet maker,' Runhild said, as she floated back with a glass in each hand.

One was filled with Pepsi Max, the other with water.

'If you were wondering, I mean. You were staring. And yes, the Munch lithographs are genuine. The lamps hanging in the dining room were actually prototypes of Enigma by Shoichi Uchiyama. He made them himself, you see. By hand.'

She passed a glass to Selma and sat down.

'You're a … detective. You have an alert eye, I assume. You're probably wondering how I can afford to live like this. A divorced woman on a professor's salary.'

'Not at all,' Selma said, unfazed, and raised her glass. 'I came to speak to you about Sjalg. And to offer my condolences, of course. Thanks for taking time to see me.'

The other woman was studying her over the rim of her glass. Selma stared back. The make-up could not completely conceal the fact that Runhild's eyes were slightly red-rimmed. Not much. At each corner of her mouth, a sad frown sliced into the pricey complexion. Only just.

'It's quiet at work now that it's summer,' she said, obviously no longer feeling the need to explain her luxurious apartment. 'I haven't taken a holiday yet, but it's easy to work from home. It suits me fine now, before the funeral.'

Selma found it remarkable that she was apologizing for being at home in the morning two days before her son was to be ·

119

cremated. She wanted to say something, but failed to come up with anything as Runhild sniffed quietly and put down her glass.

'How can I help you?' she asked.

'As I said, I wanted first and foremost to express my condolences. We haven't met before, but ...'

'I thought it was outrageous to seat you like that at the wedding. Both in the church and at the reception.'

'Oh?'

'I said so to Sjalg as well. I don't concern myself with how other families live, but that placement was over the top. It would really have been better not to invite you.'

Selma opened her eyes wide and took another swig of cola. 'Well, you might think so, but ...'

'Anine's a pretty immature woman. She has a defiance about her that doesn't really suit her. It doesn't really suit anyone over eight years old. Not that it's any of my business, as far as that goes, and I don't mean to offend you.'

Selma said nothing. She did not feel particularly offended either. More taken aback, to tell the truth – she had expected to find a woman immersed in deep sorrow.

'She was far too young for Sjalg,' Runhild continued. 'Of course I don't have anything to do with that either, he's a ...'

Once again that little sniff, almost inaudible, but made all the more obvious by the pucker of her mouth and the vibration at the sides of her nose.

'... he was a grown man. As I said, I've never interfered in any way, but that relationship was bound to come to grief. Sjalg needed someone to take care of him. Instead he took on someone to take care of. That would never have worked. And so it didn't.'

She raised her hand in a deprecating gesture, as if she thought Selma would protest.

'Of course, I don't mean that women should take care of their husbands,' she added quickly. 'A relationship is a two-way thing, and I was born in 1962, not 1862. What I mean, but what I never breathed a word about, of course, is that Sjalg depends on someone looking out for him. That's quite simply what he's like. Or was like. Not only these allergies of his, which we knew could be life threatening, but also his vehemence. It could get the better of him. That's how he's always been.'

'Do you mean it's Anine's fault that he died? That she didn't look out for him?'

'Well, as long as Sjalg was living at home, and he did that until he was twenty-six, I always made sure he had the necessary medication close at hand. We've known about his allergy since he was five years old. He was on the point of death. On Christmas Eve, of course, as inconvenient a time as it possibly could be. I mean ...'

Once again she took hold of her glass. Raised it to her mouth, changed her mind and put it back with a thud that was rather too loud.

'In a smaller place it could be fatal. In the past, everything closed down for the holidays. We lived three minutes away from Ullevål Hospital at that time, so Sjalg survived. Only just. He should have done this time too. If only Anine had given him that injection. I've taught her to do it. Myself. I've explained to her how crucial it is to have it really close by at all times.'

'It was his best man who had the EpiPen, as far as I understand. Not Anine.'

'Yes, just so.'

She sighed in resignation and shook her head gently.

'If only Sjalg had had the good sense to choose Njål as his best man.'

Runhild must have noticed Selma's confusion, because she added immediately: 'My younger son. Sjalg's brother, Njål. He has lived around Sjalg all his life, and would have done what was required. But no, Sjalg was obstinate in his insistence on choosing this Kolbein Fagernes. That ...'

The ethereal appearance had vanished. The living room was cool, and the hum of the air conditioning suggested that it was on too high. Nevertheless, Runhild Petterson's upper lip was moist. She twirled a diamond ring round and round on her right hand.

'That party colleague of his,' she said in the end. 'They hadn't known each other for more than a couple of years. A friend of Anine's, I believe. As a matter of fact.'

'A student friend of hers,' Selma replied, with a nod. 'But more Sjalg's age than Anine's.'

'He just stood there. Like a wimp.'

Now she was staring expressionlessly into the room. The ring was being rotated round her finger at ever-increasing speed.

'He just stood there,' she repeated tonelessly. 'If I had known that he was the one who had the adrenaline, I would have been able to save Sjalg. Instead I screamed at Anine. She just screamed back at me. That she didn't have the pen. That she didn't know ...'

Runhild dissolved into tears, in total silence.

Selma leaned forward and let her elbows rest on her knees. 'Who is accompanying you to the funeral?' she asked quietly.

'Njål. And my ex-husband, of course. Bo. His name is Bo, and he will pick us both up from here in good time.'

'Fine. I think we'll draw a line here. We can have a chat later. After the funeral. In a few days' time.'

'No.'

Instantly and deftly, Runhild dried her tears, straightened her back and forced out a smile.

'No,' she repeated. 'What was it about? You said on the phone that you needed help.'

Selma hesitated.

'I was thinking of making a little photo album,' she said finally. 'Of the wedding. For Anine. She would appreciate it once things had calmed down, I thought. Even though the marriage was brief, they had lived together for almost two years. She might well think ...'

'I'll do the same. For myself. And for Njål too. If he wants one. I've already collected a whole host of photographs. From relatives and friends.'

She moistened her lips and straightened her back even more.

'Are you going to make something like that for Anine? You're not exactly on good terms, so won't that be a bit ... unwelcome?'

Selma gave a warm smile and tilted her head.

'I'm doing what I can to repair our relationship,' she said. 'You know, Anine will always be my daughter.'

Runhild nodded, but still seemed sceptical.

'You don't have daughters yourself,' Selma said, showing her palms in what she hoped would seem to convey that she was slightly crestfallen.

'No. That's probably something quite different. Why don't you ask someone you know? There must have been lots of them at the wedding.'

Selma stole some time by taking a drink. She used her thumb and index finger to wipe around her mouth before saying: 'I wanted this is to be a surprise. Anine has friends around her all the time now, and they would most likely let the cat out of the bag. So that's why I thought of you ...'

She left the rest of the sentence hanging in the air.

Runhild stared at her for a few seconds. Then she nodded briefly and picked up her mobile phone from the glass table.

'I've created a huge file,' she said. 'What's your email address?'

Selma spelled it out, and a few seconds later noticed that her iPad was growling from her bag on the floor.

'You've quite a task ahead of you,' Runhild Petterson said. 'There are over 800 pictures there. And I keep getting more photos sent to me as well. If any of them are good, I can send them on to you.'

Selma managed to restrain a smile. 'That would be very kind,' she said softly instead. 'Is there anything I can do for you before I go? Or afterwards, for that matter?'

'No thanks. Or … you're a lawyer, aren't you?'

'Yes.'

'I've received a provisional post-mortem report. And a preliminary report from the Food Safety Authority. Of course, I understand most of what they say, but could you take a look at them and tell me if there's anything to pursue? Naturally I don't have anything to do with it, and I certainly don't want to get mixed up in it, but Anine seems so eager to prosecute that poor chef. Summons him to court, I mean. Her father believes that …'

Her hands were rotating, as if she was trying to make herself talk faster.

'Jesso is overly trigger happy,' Selma said when the other woman seemed unable to continue. 'He always wants to find a reason for everything. Someone to blame. Always wants someone to pay. To be held to account.'

'I do too, really,' Runhild said, so softly that Selma was not entirely sure that she had heard correctly. 'I reproach both Anine and Kolbein. And myself, I suppose. If we had just taken better care of that damnable EpiPen … One moment.'

She stood up in a single smooth movement and moved towards the hallway.

And disappeared.

Selma looked around yet again. There was something formal about the room. Something stylishly impersonal, like a terribly expensive hotel. Everything matched. There were no personal possessions on display, no photographs or things that children had made when they were little. No bookshelves, despite Sjalg's mother being a professor of Scandinavian literature. Three deluxe editions lay on the glass table, but they looked as if they had never been opened.

A distant, scraping noise could suddenly be heard above the regular hum of the air conditioning. A couple of faint clicks followed. A few seconds later, Runhild returned.

'Here,' she said, handing Selma a small bundle of papers. 'I made copies for you. If you'd be so kind as to read them, and maybe get back to me when it's all over and done with? The funeral, I mean. Plus a few more days. That would be really good of you. I don't entirely trust Anine, if you can forgive me for that.'

'Absolutely,' Selma said with all the warmth she could muster. 'Could you go to the bother of giving me a copy of the guest list for the wedding as well? If you have one, I mean?'

'Yes ... but ... why?'

'It would be so practical to know exactly who was there. In connection with this photo album, I mean.'

Runhild hesitated momentarily before giving a shrug and heading back to what must be some kind of home office.

Selma could hardly believe her own luck.

Almost a thousand photographs and copies of the provisional reports. All the result of a half-hour visit and a couple of tiny white lies. She had not even had to do anything wrong, and now sat with the information that would otherwise have taken her days to scrape together.

Runhild returned and handed her a three-page document.

Selma took it and got to her feet. 'Thanks a million,' she said. 'You'll hear from me.'

'We'll see you the day after tomorrow, won't we?'

Selma hesitated. She had not yet decided whether to attend the funeral.

'I'll be sitting at the very back,' she said sympathetically. 'To avoid causing any unnecessary drama. I'm not sure you'll see me. You said so yourself: Anine and I are not exactly on the best of terms. Just old grudges from her teenage years, but she's not very adult, as you already pointed out. Not particularly mature.'

Runhild nodded. Selma picked up her bag from the floor, folded the documents and placed them inside. She moved out to the hallway.

'Thanks for coming,' Runhild said.

She sounded sincere. And somewhat at a loss. Her shoulders were no longer so straight, and her spine not nearly so upright as when Selma had arrived. Her lilac silk blouse bore the suggestion of dark rings under the armpits.

It must take hard work to look like that, Selma thought.

All for the sake of appearances. She herself spent no more than ten minutes in front of the mirror every morning, and she had never resorted to any external help to hold back her almost fifty-two years, other than exercise and some face cream.

'You're so beautiful,' Runhild said out of the blue. 'So ... fresh. Anine really doesn't look like you at all.'

'Eh ... Thank you?'

Selma heard that she had placed a question mark after her thanks for the ambiguous compliment.

'Likewise,' she added quickly. 'And I'd like to tell you that it was ...'

She hesitated, smiled and wet her lips before continuing: 'It was Sjalg who invited me to the wedding. Not my own daughter. I thought it was really nice of him. Polite and kind.'

The other woman's eyes were brimming with tears. Selma rushed to add: 'Hope you'll be OK. As soon as it's possible to be, I mean. See you.'

126

A handshake would be too formal. A hug too intimate. Selma raised her hand in farewell instead, and stepped out into the stairwell outside.

As soon as the door closed behind her, she ran down all seven flights of stairs. By the time she alighted from the bus at Sagene church half an hour later, she had read the reports from both the Food Safety Authority and the pathologists twice over.

And was astonished.

The Reports

'What would you have done if such a case had landed on your desk when you were in the police?' Selma Falck asked.

Einar Falsen did not answer. He sat on the settee studying the report from the Food Safety Authority. Literally with a magnifying glass. Selma had frequently offered to accompany him to an optician's, but there were too many electronics there, he doggedly insisted. Even when she had persuaded Krogh's in the Storo shopping centre to promise to use only the old methods, a frame round the head with interchangeable glasses in front of the eyes, he had refused point blank.

At his craziest, Einar Falsen had been convinced that the CIA was everywhere. And the Security Service. In addition to Mossad, MI6 and a secret remnant of the Soviet KGB that few apart from him knew about, and which he feared most of all. Every electronic device presented a threat, even a small travel radio. He not only believed that he was under surveillance – the worst thing was that they were torturing him with high-frequency noise. Selma would have heard it too, he asserted obstinately, if she had not already been so brainwashed.

Moving from the stony desert under the Sinsenkrysset flyover to the bedsit in Vogts gate made his life simpler. Some aspects of personal hygiene were still lacking, however. The condition of his teeth was even worse than his body odour, and Selma wondered occasionally if he was actually walking around with constant toothache. The greatest change was in his spirit. He was calmer. The anxiety attacks and total delirium seized him far less often than before. In January he had been willing to be reassessed, even though that had involved a week in the madhouse, as he himself called it. His medications had not only become more accurate, he had also become better at following the regime recommended by the doctors.

Also, he loved Darius. He lavished affection on the poor creature, which had a better life as an indoor cat in Oslo's most disgusting apartment than when it had lived in luxury with around an acre of hunting ground on Ormøya island. The cat's fur had not looked more luxuriant since it was a kitten. Daily grooming and a teaspoon of cod liver oil mixed into tuna fish for breakfast made the animal shine and always look ready for a cat show.

Darius was no longer his name, but Pussycat.

Pussycat had worked wonders with Einar, and he didn't worry so much about everything electrical.

He tolerated living indoors. Electric plugs, light bulbs, cooker and water heater notwithstanding. He did shower, once a week anyway. He had learned to use the washing machine in the bathroom, even though it was mostly Pussycat's blankets that were kept spotlessly clean. Selma had left the 52-inch TV set when she moved out. Before Christmas she had announced that the electron grid, which was actually ordinary chicken wire she had bought at the Clas Ohlson store and used to cover the screen, would protect him from all forms of radiation. He had accepted this without much persuasion, and still used the TV set, with the chicken wire attached.

Sometimes Selma wondered if he was in fact recovering his health.

Hardly. It was far too late for Einar Falsen, but at least he had some kind of life now.

'What would you have done?' she repeated. 'Isn't this really odd?'

Einar still did not answer. Pussycat tried to push away the papers he was reading. Einar gave the cat a little nudge in return. From where Selma was sitting, in the chair on the other side of the rickety coffee table, Einar's right eye looked gigantic through the old-fashioned magnifying glass.

'Well, more than this at least,' he said finally, putting down the magnifier. 'I agree with you, Mariska.'

'In what?'

'In that, taking all things into consideration, Sjalg Petterson's death should have been investigated thoroughly.'

'Shouldn't it?'

Einar let Pussycat settle on his lap. His rough hands stroked the animal's fur, lightly and repeatedly.

'The post-mortem report is unambiguous,' he said. 'And really contains only three things of interest. Firstly that the man died of anaphylactic shock, entirely compatible with his previously established extreme nut allergy. Secondly, no sign of the presence of nuts was found in the contents of his stomach and intestines. The pathologist expresses the reservation that the absence does not mean that there cannot have been microscopic traces of nuts in his digestive system immediately prior to his death. And thirdly ...'

'How can they actually come to that conclusion, though?'

'Wait a minute now. Thirdly there are no injection marks, wounds or other skin damage to indicate that Sjalg might have ingested nuts in a different way from via his mouth.'

He grabbed the paper again, held it at arm's length and squinted. Then cast it aside again.

'Hm,' he said emphatically. 'Suspicious. Especially when the Food Authority's preliminary conclusions are also that there was no trace of nuts anywhere. Not in the food. Not in the kitchen. No nuts of any kind, and certainly not that maca … that Christmas nut. Which police lawyer has responsibility for the case?'

Selma shrugged.

'I'll find that out tomorrow,' she said. 'It'll probably be someone I know. If I'm lucky. The only thing I know at the moment is that they're showing zero interest in the case. Anine has not even been interviewed. She received a phone call from an investigator, she said, but it lasted less than five minutes. Runhild Petterson seemed as if it hadn't even entered her head that this could be a police matter. Jesso, as far as I understand, is exclusively interested in the civil side of the case. He's after money for Anine.'

'Strange behaviour from the police. So strange that it could even look like dereliction of duty.'

'What do you mean?'

Einar did not respond. He lifted Pussycat from his lap and held the cat close to his chest. Pushed his whole face down into the fur. The cat purred. It sounded as if Einar did too.

'What did you say?' Selma asked.

Einar put Pussycat down on the floor.

'It's almost like a locked-room mystery,' he said, with a lopsided smile. 'The guy died of ingesting nuts, but he hasn't ingested nuts. All the orifices of the body are locked. There is no trace of nuts anywhere. But those bloody macadamia nuts must have got into his body somehow. A bit like Sherlock Holmes, really. Are you staying to watch the news round-up on TV?'

Not really, Selma thought. It was far too hot in this cramped bedsit. Opening the window was scarcely advisable, as the room would be filled with exhaust fumes and so much dust, becoming unbearable. Besides, it was almost as uncomfortably hot outside. Once bitten twice shy, she was sitting in only a vest, shorts and trainers. And was sweating profusely.

She had run here the long way round, and would run straight home again. It would take no more than ten minutes.

'We can watch the start of the broadcast together,' she said. 'Have you anything more to drink?'

He switched on the TV with the remote control, which he had wrapped in aluminium foil and secured with gaffer tape in such a way that only three buttons were available. On-off, volume and *NRK*, which was on button number one. He shuffled out to the kitchen and returned with a glass of water. Selma accepted it diffidently.

'Water? I don't drink water. Only Farris in emergencies.'

'Mariska, you should read up on how dangerous that shit you pour down your throat really is. Water is the nectar of the gods.'

Selma raised the glass tentatively towards her mouth. Took a sip. Made a face and put the water down.

The *Dagsrevy* logo appeared on the screen.

The headline story was about forest fires. There were many of them, the length and breadth of the country, and the exceptional summer was of course given the blame. Everything was dry, and according to the exhausted fire fighters, the wind was blowing in every direction at one and the same time. The next story dealt with old fogeys at sea. They had not taken a boat-handling test, even though they were the most dangerous sailors on the water. After a piece about summer being high season for eating disorders, Selma was ready to leave. Watching the news with Einar meant putting up with a soundtrack of complaints and occasional bizarre comments. Now he was excoriating the bikini as a concept, and calling for the return of the buxom female ideal of the sixties.

'Marilyn Monroe,' he said dreamily.

'You were born in 1960,' Selma pointed out. 'It must be your mother you're remembering.'

It was reported that a house had burnt to the ground in Randaberg, the final item of news before the sports review. The cause of the fire was unclear at present, but the two residents, a married couple, had both been arrested and charged with cultivating marijuana. Plants had been found in their basement, but the business must have been relatively new, according to the far too young police lawyer whose eyes flitted around nervously as he said far too much. It was already obvious that the electricity consumption in the detached house had increased markedly in the last few weeks.

'Wonder if cultivating hash would pay,' Einar said, scratching his hair. 'After this summer, electricity prices will be hellish when the cold sets in. And hash needs a lot of heat. Heat and moisture. Not exactly what you want inside a house.'

Selma looked around, thinking that the indoor climate in Einar's apartment would be very suitable.

'We could still have a wet late summer,' she said, getting to her feet. 'And autumn.'

'... the man is a Norwegian citizen. His wife is Russian, but has lived in Norway for a number of years.'

'That police lawyer really ought to go on a course,' Selma said, reaching her arms over her head before swaying slowly from side to side. 'Day one of an investigation and he stands there telling us everything they know.'

'Don't you want to see the sport?' Einar asked.

'No. I need to go home.'

On her way out, she nearly tripped over the huge piles of old newspapers by the door. Selma was worried that he might soon be caught for these thefts. Admittedly, he tried to take a fairly extensive morning walk, so that no one would lose a news-paper more than once a month or so, but all the same it was highly risky.

'Bye,' she shouted over her shoulder but received no reply.

It must be possible somehow to persuade Einar to use a laptop. Not only for his sake, but also for hers. He had seriously started to become an important conversation partner. He could be a great help if he had faster access to information than through stolen copies of newspapers.

When she closed the door behind her, however, it dawned on her that, deep down, she really missed the old Einar.

The one who was a raving lunatic, who never made any demands, and who, from within his distorted world, loved her absolutely and unconditionally.

Tears

Mina sat in her room staring at the wall.

She was wearing unusually heavy make-up, even though she had no intention of going anywhere. Soon Dad would come home, and he would see that she had been weeping. Weeping and weeping and weeping. If Ingeborg were still alive, Mina would have had someone to talk to. About everything that was so dreadful and secret and impossible to bear on her own. But Ingeborg was ashes in an urn that had still not been scattered on the earth – there wasn't even a grave to visit.

Mina had always wanted a dog. A dog that was large enough, a springer spaniel, maybe, to sprawl on your bed and also go long walks with you. The dog would be called Sara, and there would have been someone here to talk to, but Mum refused to counten-ance a dog.

Maybe Mina should just start walking.

She could do that now. Put on her running shoes, fill a bottle with water and just keep walking. Northwards. She could start at the barrier at Akebakkeskogen, continue through Nordmarka, venture into the mountains and through the valleys all the way to Trondheim. As a matter of fact, she could walk even further than that. Norway was about two thousand kilometres in length, and she could travel on foot all the way to the North Cape if she wanted to.

And maybe start swimming.

Dad no longer noticed anything. He was not quite so tired in the evenings, but he was distant. Distracted, somehow. He never came to her room to say goodnight.

Neither of them had noticed that Mina had given up her part-time job. That she had cut her hair. Not very much, but enough that Mum at least should have spotted it.

Mum had not even discovered that Mina was back on Instagram.

There were still quite a few horrible comments ticking in, but they were far fewer in number. Previously, Mina's profile had been open. As the deputy leader of the Nordre Aker branch of the AUF, the youth wing of the Labour Party, and what's more as leader of the Pupil Council even though she was only in her first year at upper high school, social media provided a welcome speaker's platform. The unfortunate negative messages were part and parcel of transparency. At the time when she had deactivated her account in the spring with her mother's eyes upon her, she had almost four thousand followers. When she had sneaked back a few days later, she had resigned from the AUF and decided that her career in the Pupil Council was over. She had made her profile private. With every nasty comment she received, she blocked the sender. Now she was down to about eight hundred followers, and felt safe.

But still messages of hate and malice came in. Today it had been awful.

Three messages, all from people she did not know. She blocked them immediately, but a sense of resignation was spoiling everything. She should just have deleted the account. Deleted everything.

Deleted herself, if she could.

She should talk to Dad. Once upon a time he had been the best father in the world. Patient and kind and loving, and he always used to say that no problem was so bad that he would not be able to sort it out for her.

She just couldn't talk to him. He couldn't sort this out.

He wasn't even taking a holiday this year. Mum had not been angry, as she usually was every time Dad's job got in the way of something. Just accepting, sort of thing. Resigned. A bit fed up, perhaps. He had so much to do, Dad had said at dinner one time in June, and he wanted to use the peace and quiet of the summer to catch up with things in the office. Mum had booked a trip with a friend and her daughter, and was keen for Mina to come with her.

Mina said no.

Mum became grumpy, but Mina did not want to go on holiday.

She just wanted to walk. She would march off and not think of anything other than how to find food in the forest. Now and again she could venture into a town. She had plenty of money in her account since her confirmation. If she left after Dad had fallen asleep, no one would miss her until the next day. Maybe not even then. It was the school holidays and Dad went to the office before Mina woke up. At least before he thought she was awake.

She could walk and walk, until she was completely gone.

Mina could get lost. That would probably be the best thing for everyone.

AUTUMN

Clothes

Selma had fashioned boots from the reindeer skin.

At least something resembling them. The knife she had found in the wooden box was so blunt that she had attempted to sharpen it on a stone she had coaxed out from the wall. It was no use, probably because Selma did not have the faintest idea how to sharpen knives. In the end she had managed to tear the pelt into two pieces of similar size with the help of the blunt steel, her teeth and all the brute strength she could still muster from her hands and arms. She placed a foot in the middle of each piece, folded the rest up around her legs, and tied it tightly with string just below her knees.

The black stove was dead. The last of the candles had burnt down. It had turned cold inside the stone shelter, but the water in the saucepan she had made sure to fill while there was still some heat in the fire, was still liquid. The mild weather had come to stay for a while, and she drank what water she had.

The woollen blankets had become a top and trousers.

The trousers were very simple. One of the blankets was ripped in two. Selma had wound the rectangular strips of cloth around each of her legs. The design would make it easy to relieve herself, since she had nothing to sew the crotch together with. In the middle of the second blanket she had torn a hole for her head. A poncho, no less. It was too airy to let it hang free, so she had made openings for her forearms, far down near the hips, so that she would not lose the protection over her shoulders and upper arms. Then she tied a belt of braided string all the way round the makeshift garment. The rough fabric chafed her skin. It was especially uncomfortable on her nipples, which were already painful enough after the beating she had received, and who knew what length of exposure to frost and horrendous hygiene.

The body odour no longer bothered her too much. In the beginning, after a day or two, she had hardly been able to bear her own stink. A mixture of perspiration, urine, anxiety, fire and soot had made her queasy. After she had, in her befuddlement, taken a shit beside the door, the situation had improved, paradoxically enough. Compared to the grotesque droppings of brown slime, she was perfumed with lavender.

And now she was going to leave this place.

She lingered for a moment at the door before opening it.

The stone shelter had saved her life. With the protection its walls had afforded against both storm and freezing temperatures, and with the important small items left by a Good Samaritan.

A proffered hand from a stranger Selma would never meet.

Now the stone shelter was empty. The firewood burnt. The crime novel and the box on the wall also consumed by the black stove. An hour ago, Selma had forced down the last of the inedible tomato soup. She had destroyed the reindeer pelt to make a pair of boots, and she was taking the blankets with her.

A tiny candle stub and a few matches were all that was left.

At a guess, she had been there for three days. It might have been five, but now that her ability to reason was improving, she doubted whether the limited amount of firewood could really have lasted so long.

At least her body was not aching as much as it had a few days ago. She was stiff as a board, and from time to time she felt a stab of pain behind her eyes. But not so often now. She had drunk as much water as possible in the past few days. The hunger pangs had abated too. The tomato soup, this time diluted and heated in the saucepan, had done her good.

Her memory was also on the way back. Selma's life still appeared as an unfinished jigsaw puzzle, with too many white patches in the picture. It was exhausting to try to fill the gaps, but increasingly many of the missing pieces were dropping into place by themselves. Especially if she did not exert herself too much. When she slept. When she was concentrating on something else, such as swallowing down some soup or making clothes out of old rags.

How she had come to be in the mountains, who had assaulted her, and what had happened in the weeks leading up to the fire, these were details that were still completely unclear.

It was time to go.

She turned one last time. Applied her shoulder to the door, and it gave easily. Fresh air surged towards her and she took deep breaths of it, like after a dive. She placed one tentative foot into the wet, melting snow. Heather and dwarf bushes were dotted around everywhere. She trudged all the way out and let the door swing shut behind her.

Everything was grey and wet.

A heavy layer of cloud obscured the northern mountain peak. It was not really raining, and the mist was not too thick for her to see a couple of hundred metres ahead. All the same Selma felt soaked through already, as the air was full of moisture. It was like standing in a cloud of rain that had not yet begun to fall. She took a few faltering steps towards the site of the fire, almost bare now. The chimney stack towered black and threatening against

138

the sky, but otherwise everything was burnt to the ground. The Volvo, which had once been red and the most beautiful car Selma had ever owned, was now a cadaver of black steel and charred plastic. The tyres had melted in the blaze, making the chassis look as if it had lain down to die.

There might be something useful among the ruins. Maybe it would be sensible to root around for anything that could be used somehow. Or eaten. Even though she recalled that the kitchen had seemed empty, she could easily have overlooked a store of tinned food. Under the sink, perhaps, or at the top of the cupboard she had quickly decided was empty, but had not really had time to search properly.

Tins of food would have exploded in a fire.

Knives, perhaps. She could make use of a knife.

She did not need a knife. Selma had to reach people, that was what she needed to do. Access to a phone, in order to warn someone about something that was about to happen, even though she could not remember what it was.

It was so silent. All she could hear was her own breathing and the sound of her feet on the heather as she tramped closer to the wrecked car.

'The Hardangervidda,' she whispered, and stopped.

She could not be certain. The fact that there had been a copy of a newspaper from Hallingdal in the stone shelter did not have to mean anything at all. But she could hope.

Finnmarksvidda would have been worse. More desolate.

Gietnjojávrrit was the name that came to mind. The most desolate place in Norway, she thought she remembered, without knowing why. In the middle of the mountain plateau between Kautokeino and Karasjok, almost thirty kilometres from the nearest anthropogenic point.

Anthropogenic. Made by humans.

Selma could not fathom how she could bring such words and facts to mind, but still not have any idea how she had ended up on the mountain plateau.

She could walk for thirty kilometres. Without a doubt she could trudge for thirty kilometres almost without clothes and with animal skins on her feet, she was sure of that, as long as there was no frost. No snow or strong winds either: thirty kilometres was manageable in this weather, and she certainly was not in Gietnjojávrrit, the most desolate spot in the whole of Norway. She was on the Hardangervidda, the largest mountain plateau in Europe, one and a half times bigger than the Finnmarksvidda. Maybe she was in the national park.

Maybe not.

'Let this be the Hardangervidda!' she shouted all of a sudden. 'Dear God! Let this be the Hardangervidda!'

The area was popular. Much visited. She would be able to find people on the Hardangervidda. Everyone went to the Hardangervidda at some point, there was hardly anyone in the whole country who did not go there now and again, and some paid frequent visits. Selma would be able to find cabins, modern cabins, even though the area was vast. There were hiking paths criss-crossing the terrain, marked ski trails everywhere, areas with signs that would show her the way home. The tourist organization had enticed people to come up here, exactly in this spot, for generations, she might even encounter some hunters with hot coffee in their flasks, there was grouse shooting, and probably reindeer hunting, in the autumn.

It was autumn. It could be September, it might be October; Selma was crying and could not comprehend where the tears were coming from.

'Dear God,' she sobbed. 'Dear God. Please let me be on the Hardangervidda. Then there will be other people here.'

She had to walk. It was time to set off, and she chose her direction at random. A few metres south, she changed her mind. She remembered the compass points from the position of the cabin, and turned east instead. Oslo lay to the east. To the south-east. And long before Oslo, she would find people. In cabins, proper cabins, with people and heat and food and mobile phones.

The string beneath her left knee was already starting to loosen.

Selma untied the knots and tightened them all over again. So forcefully that it was physically painful. When she stood up, she could not recollect which way was east, but she plodded on regardless. The mist grew thicker, and the mountain plateau was flat. Slightly up, slightly down, and surprisingly quickly up again. She wanted to go down, she knew, to lower terrain, she had to keep on walking until she could feel that the ground was sloping down towards a valley and taller trees.

It was impossible to know how long she had been walking.

The rain-filled clouds eventually released their moisture, and a light drizzle began to fall. The mist had cleared a little when she stopped yet again to tighten the animal skin covering her legs.

When she stood up, she caught sight of the wolf.

Grey and scrawny, with head lowered, standing less than fifty metres from her. She was paralysed with fear. The wolf approached, still keeping its head down, but its eyes were locked on hers. Now the beast was so close that Selma thought she could smell the scent of its ravenous spirit.

The wolf stopped.

Its gaze was pale blue, and just as Selma thought her heart would explode, it dawned on her who the wolf's eyes reminded her of.

Tryggve Mejer, it struck her, and she could not breathe.

Everything went black. Her legs buckled beneath her.

Once again Selma had collapsed into a blessed, empty darkness.

SUMMER

The Photo Wall

Selma had roughly sorted Runhild Petterson's photos on her laptop and then printed out about 400 of them. It had taken all morning.

The advantage of having obtained photographs from Sjalg's side of the crowd of friends and family was that he was in nearly all the pictures. During the wedding, Selma had seen her own friends snap endlessly in Anine's direction, more preoccupied by the dazzling bride than the man she had married.

Now all the photos were pinned up on three of the bedroom walls, almost from floor to ceiling. The drawing pins would leave marks, but nothing that she could not tart up and paint over some spare afternoon.

The photographs were of varying quality, both technically and aesthetically, and about forty of them had been taken by the professional wedding photographer. Selma had printed out only a couple of the photos from the Opera House roof. The rest were from the restaurant, both before and during the meal. These were sharp, taken by an expensive camera and displayed in A4-size.

As of now, they told her nothing.

The rest of the photos had been taken with mobiles. Selma had printed them out in postcard format to ensure that she had enough space on the walls. If any of them proved of particular interest, she could always make new, larger copies later.

Only four of the pictures had been taken after the groom had stood up to give his speech. Three of those showed a smiling, self-confident Sjalg Petterson, already with his jacket off, and with his tie loose like a pigtail around his neck. In one of them he had lifted a glass of water to clear his throat: the sunlight hit the glass and radiated a beautiful spectrum of rainbow colours.

In the last photo, he was dying.

It crossed Selma's mind that this was a remarkable picture to send to the victim's mother. The sender could not have studied the images, and had probably sent off the whole collection in eagerness to comply with a pious request from a grieving mother.

Sjalg's mouth was open and he looked astonished. Terrified, almost: his eyes were wide. His hand had moved halfway up to his throat. Selma herself remembered him clawing his neck as his breath grew increasingly shallow and his blood pressure plummeted.

There was no unauthorized person anywhere near him. No authorized person either: no one serving him or replenishing his glass.

Anine was sitting on his right-hand side. She had just let go of her glass of white wine, at that very second; it was balanced on the edge of the base of the stem, and about to topple. She looked up at Sjalg in bewilderment and had raised her other arm to grab his hand. Since someone at a different table had taken the picture, the outlines of out-of-focus heads were visible at the bottom of the photograph.

Selma took the picture down from the wall and perched on the edge of the bed.

Anine looked really scared. Selma's eyes had not been on her daughter when it all happened. It was Sjalg she had been watching, as he scratched and gurgled and keeled over before he died with his face planted in the remains of a halibut hors d'oeuvre.

The man was far too young, of course, but he had succumbed to a quick, if not exactly pain-free, death. From that point of view, his death was worse for Anine. And for Sjalg's parents and younger brother.

Selma found the picture taken the second before and placed the photos side by side on the bed. One was lighter and a tad more indistinct than the other: they must have been taken by different phones.

One second. Maybe two. At one moment a proud bridegroom, admired by his smiling bride, was standing with his glass of water raised in the sunshine on a wonderful summer's day. In the next, everything had fallen apart.

'These things happen,' Selma said.

No nuts. Nowhere to be seen.

A man in the prime of life, allergic, but otherwise fit as a fiddle, dies instantaneously at his own wedding. Of a nut that isn't there. Wasn't there. That cannot be found anywhere. There was scarcely an experienced policeman in the world whose curiosity would not be piqued by such a case.

Because things like that do not happen. Not really. Not without some kind of explanation. You do not simply die because you've been exposed to something that doesn't exist.

Her mobile phone peeped. Selma tapped into a text message.

Hi Selma – what a shame about your son-in-law. Condolences. I've checked, and it's Sandra Bjerke who is the police lawyer responsible in this case. Hugs from Sophie (Are you in the city this summer? I'll be around until the beginning of August. Meet up some day?)

Selma had never heard of any Sandra Bjerke.

She keyed in a response: *Who is Sandra Bjerke? New? Young? S*

The workload at the Oslo offices of the public prosecutor was obviously not overly onerous in the middle of summer, because Sophie's answer pinged back at lightning speed.

Brand new. Just a temporary post. Holiday cover, you know. Haven't met her. What about tomorrow? Dinner?

Selma gave this some thought. *Thanks for the info. Can't manage tomorrow. Funeral. I'll call you.*

A heart and a crying face came by return. Then all went quiet.

Selma glanced yet again at the two photographs before replacing them and heading back to the living room. She grabbed her little bag, let herself out of the apartment and walked down the stairs as she wrote another text message.

It was time for a trip to police headquarters, and she was keen to make sure that the young lawyer would not be expecting her.

Surprises were powerful.

The Fly

A fly was buzzing around in Oslo.

This particular housefly, a musca domestica, was of noble birth: she had hatched out in a wastepaper bin in the parliament building. A bread roll, left behind after an evening meeting before summer had really set in, provided nourishment throughout the larval stages for both her and the almost one hundred siblings she was blessed with. Sixteen days had elapsed since she had forced her way out of the reddish-brown chrysalis and embarked on the last phase of her metamorphic life. Which in this heat would soon be over. Heavy and sluggish from heat and age, she flitted about from one place to the next, close to the floor, where food was to be found.

A door opened. People streamed in from the street, and the mortally exhausted fly let herself be carried along by the undercurrent of animated voices and perspiring backs.

One of them belonged to Lars Winther.

He had been a journalist in the *Dagens Gang* newspaper for six years. In that time he had transformed the *DG* sports pages from running classic, narrative sports coverage to being unsurpassed at critical journalism about sport. Sport was all about power, money and culture, and Lars Winther took all these aspects extremely seriously. After a couple of SKUP press awards and finally the prestigious Journalist of the Year prize for his efforts, things followed their natural course.

He grew just as tired of sport as sport was of him, and he was headhunted by *Aftenavisen* as a news reporter.

It was the quiet summer period, and he had tagged along with the only political commentator on the newspaper who was not on holiday.

'Just an hour and a half's notice,' someone said.

'Something big,' said another.

'A #MeToo story, don't you think?'

'A press conference in the middle of the trades holiday fortnight? With Siv Jensen present? Bound to be fraud. Something fucking serious, anyway.'

People were talking in voices both loud and soft. Someone was whispering, others were shouting so piercingly that the confused fly had to take a break on someone's shoulder. Just for a second, until a quick hand slap landed on the spot where she had been sitting, only a moment too late.

Lars Winther said nothing and found a seat in the first row.

The leader of the Progress Party entered the room. She was tanned and her short hair was almost white. Nervous, Lars Winther thought. For once the Progress Party's leader seemed nervous. Worried, maybe even scared. Her mascara had run a little under one eye. A fly buzzed around her head and landed on her cheekbone, Lars noticed, but the woman swiftly ran her finger under her eyelashes. The mascara smear did not vanish, but the fly took off again.

'Welcome,' boomed briefly from the loudspeaker, and silence fell.

A door opened again and a man came into the room.

'Pål Poulsen has informed me that he wishes to resign as first vice-chairman of the party,' the woman said. 'This wish has been ...'

A buzz of voices surged through the room. Someone whispered. The photographers clicked and jostled forward.

'This wish has been discussed by the rest of senior management, of course,' the party leader continued in a louder, stronger voice. 'We have asked Pål to consider remaining in post until our spring national conference, but that is unfortunately impossible. A decision has been taken that until then the party will function with only one vice-chairman, who will be the present second vice-chair, Knut Solstad.'

Clearing her throat, she glanced at her notes.

'Naturally, the only course of action open to us is to accept Pål's decision. He has been a major resource for the party ever since he was voted on to the national committee more than twenty years ago, and it is a great loss for us to lose him now. He won't be entirely gone, of course, because he will continue to sit in parliament for another three years. At his own request, he will withdraw as parliamentary leader and move from the justice committee to the local government and public administration committee. With heartfelt thanks from the party for many years of outstanding contribution to his country and party, I now give the floor to Pål himself.'

The woman handed the microphone to the man. She herself stepped down from the podium. She stood with her hands folded on her stomach beside the door through which she had entered.

147

'Thanks for your kind words,' the man said, tapping his finger on the mic he had taken over. 'This is still on, isn't it?'

He coughed into his fist.

'It's true that I've decided to withdraw from my party office,' he said. 'This is because I would like to spend more time with my family, who have paid the price for my political work for so many years. It has been an honour to serve the party, both as an elected representative and in parliament. Especially my many journeys the length and breadth of the country, to workplaces and in—'

'When do we get to know the real reason?'

It was a young man from *DG* who interrupted him.

'I expect you to take me at my word,' the man on the podium replied. 'My wife and children have been unusually patient, and everything has its time. Everything comes to an end. My role in the party is now—'

'Your children are eighteen and twenty-four years old, aren't they? One has already left home, isn't that right? And the youngest actually lives with her mother in Molde?'

Pål Poulsen raised a plump, flat hand.

'I won't have my intentions called into question,' he said. 'And besides, no one in this room knows my family and their needs. However, I do.'

'But moving from an important committee to one as boring as the local government and public—'

'Local politics are not boring!'

'You've made your mark as an opponent of immigration! For more than two decades!'

'And law and order. You are chiefly known as—'

Now everyone was piling in with questions.

'Will you continue to spearhead the party's immigration policies? Will you—'

'I'm drawing a line here,' the man shouted.

Now he had raised both hands and bowed his head.

'I've made my decision. Thank you for listening.'

He approached the woman and they exited together through a different door from the one the journalists had used.

The noise in the room exploded.

'Must be something else.'

'A scandal.'

'... the right is weakening ...'

'He looked as if someone had died!'

'Siv Jensen is furious, that much is ...'

Lars Winther said nothing. He glanced down at his notepad, which was blank. He had his own thoughts, but absolutely no need to share them with anyone. He stuffed the pad into his jacket pocket and strode out through the door, which was now wide open.

The room emptied, and all the doors were shut again.

The fly was left on its own. She dropped to the floor, where she scuttled around on her six legs for a while, until she found an apple core someone had thrown away. She settled down to eat some of it. She had entered this world nobly, born on a bread roll in the parliament building, and she died nobly too, on a rotting apple in the Progress Party's largest conference room.

The Substitute Police Lawyer

'Hello,' Selma said, flashing her broadest smile.

The woman in the small office at Grønlandsleiret 44 stared up from the work in hand. Her surprise grew steadily more obvious in the ensuing seconds before she finally stuttered: 'Eh ... Sel ... Hm ... Selma Falck?'

'The one and only,' Selma said. 'Can I come in?'

The woman did not answer. She might be about thirty years

old, and was almost certainly a sharp young lady. She did not look like that at this particular moment, however. Selma approached the gawping creature and held out her hand.

'Sandra Bjerke, I assume?'

Sandra Bjerke leapt out of her chair. 'Eh … yes. Hi. Pleased to meet you.'

It did not really appear so, and it was precisely this effect caused by her sudden proximity that Selma had sought. Instead of phoning ahead to make an appointment with the substitute lawyer, she had contacted one of her countless acquaintances in the enormous, crescent-shaped police headquarters in Oslo. Her friend had willingly led her through the security doors, shared a cup of coffee with her in the canteen while gossiping about the biggest police corruption case in Norway's history, and then happily accompanied her to the office where Sandra Bjerke had recently launched her career as a representative of the police prosecution service.

'What are you doing here?' she blurted out. 'And how did you manage to …'

'I was visiting a friend,' Selma replied disarmingly. 'And then I thought I might just have a chat with you since I was here.'

'About what?'

Her confusion was wearing off. There was a glint in her brown eyes, and for the first time she made steady eye contact with Selma.

'A case I understand you're responsible for,' Selma said. 'It has to do with my son-in-law. From a legal point of view, he only managed to be so for two or three hours.'

'Sjalg Petterson.'

'Spot on.'

The other woman spoke not a word.

'The whole thing's a tragedy,' Selma went on. 'For my daughter, of course, but also for all his family.'

Sandra Bjerke nodded, but still said nothing.

'Sjalg's mother has asked me to take a closer look at the case,' Selma said.

'Petterson's mother? Not your daughter?'

'Well, we could say the family,' Selma said. 'I'm investigating the case more closely on behalf of the family.'

'I see. Then perhaps you should have made an appointment. So that I could have prepared.'

'For goodness' sake!'

Selma stood up and, remaining on her feet, looked down at Sandra Bjerke.

'If you need to make preparations to answer a couple of simple questions from the family about a case you're responsible for and that's hardly part of an especially arduous portfolio ...'

Selma shot a glance at the in-tray on the pale desk. There were two slim case folders in it. The out-tray was empty. It was years since she had seen such a state of affairs on a desk in police headquarters.

'... then I'm happy to come back another time. How long do you think you'll need? You're young and inexperienced, so I really appreciate that ...'

'What's it about, then?'

'Can I sit down again?'

Sandra nodded. She had begun to sweat.

'Paper documents?' Selma asked, as she resumed her seat.

She leaned forward and peered at the old-fashioned green folder.

'Interesting,' she commented. 'Very old school.'

'I like paper. Easier to follow. What were you wondering?'

'What are you doing?'

'Doing?'

'Yes. What stage is the inquiry at, then? What's happening? What steps have you initiated in the investigation?'

Sandra Bjerke stared down at the papers in front of her.

'Is that the case folder?' Selma asked, nodding in the direction of the document.

'Yes.'

The police lawyer snapped the folder shut, but left it lying.

'I'm examining it now,' she said, swallowing audibly.

'Only now? It's more than a week since he died.'

'Well, yes, of course some action has been taken. The scene investigation took place on the same day, and ...'

'But you've released the body for cremation. Isn't that a bit early?'

Silence.

A detainee was refusing to budge in the corridor outside. Loud complaints combined with brusque orders, and someone came running.

'What has happened since the forensic examination of the scene?' Selma asked, attempting to take the edge off her increasing annoyance with a smile.

'Yes. No. We've received the Food Safety Authority's report, of course.'

Her fingers, well manicured with pink nail varnish, tapped the closed document folder.

Selma nodded. 'Yes. I've seen that myself. Is there anything in it that might take you further forward?'

'I don't exactly know what you mean,' Sandra said. 'This is a routine case, really. The victim was allergic. Hyper-allergic. We've also received the provisional post-mortem report ...'

Again her nails clicked on the green cover.

'... and according to it we're dealing here with anaphylactic shock. Extremely regrettable, of course, but it's the sort of thing that can unfortunately happen when you suffer from hyper-allergy.'

'Mmm. But don't you think …' Selma raised one hand and held it open edgeways. 'When the post-mortem report says that he died of ingesting nuts …'

Now she raised her other hand, as if she was about to describe the fish that got away.

'… and you have a report from the Food Authority that says there was no trace of those nuts anywhere …'

Her arms sank down again.

'Don't you feel a little curious? Strictly speaking, we're talking about a missing weapon here, aren't we?'

'Weapon? We're not talking about a weapon at all. This is about nuts, and the post-mortem report makes certain reservations about …'

'Yes it does,' Selma cut in, closing her eyes for a moment before forcing yet another smile. 'Who is the investigator assigned to the case?'

'Bengt-Ola Syversen. He's on holiday just now, but we—'

'On holiday? An investigator on holiday? Doesn't he work in the proceeds of crime section, anyway? Tell me …'

She cleared her throat. Smacked her lips a little, and looked out of the window. The sun leached colour from the view towards the old Oslo Prison, which stood grey and imposing beside the swathes of lawn, scorched brown now, on either side of the famous avenue.

Bengt-Ola Syversen was the worst slacker in the whole of police headquarters. If it had not been for the fact that he was approaching pension age, she would have personally ensured that he got the sack for the hopeless job he had made of the diamond theft that Selma had solved, despite him. It might be that the top brass shared her opinion, and were shuffling him around from department to department, in anticipation of his impending retirement on full pension.

'Were you the one allocated to this case initially?' she went on after some thought.

'Why do you ask?'

'Well, I was just wondering. Didn't you feel inquisitive yourself?'

'Inquisitive? Eh … No? I don't usually get terribly inquisitive about my cases, to be honest, I think more about …'

The sentence was left hanging in the air.

Sandra Bjerke had most likely been involved in no more than this one case and the other two enclosed in the folders in her in-tray.

'I won't trouble you any further,' she said. 'Thanks for taking the time. I'll find my own way out.'

Selma got to her feet and tucked her bag under her arm.

'It was originally Amir Resaae's case,' Sandra volunteered. 'The police lawyer.'

'I know Amir,' Selma said.

Amir Resaae had taken his masters in jurisprudence in record time, and had gone straight into the police after his exams and been there for eight years now. He was a slugger.

Amir would never have dropped this case.

'What happened?'

'I'm not entirely sure, there was some talk of a redistribution of cases. I'm new, and I don't have very much …'

She glanced at her in-tray.

'Who made the decision?' Selma asked. 'And when?'

'I … As I said, I'm not very sure. But you can of course—'

'Good luck,' Selma cut in, this time only managing to sound ever so slightly encouraging. 'If I can help you with anything, then I'm very easy to get in touch with. Just ring.'

This was the place where police cases were sent to die.

Here, to this greenhorn behind the desk, in partnership with the laziest policeman as her only assistant. That was bad enough, but it was made worse by having the appearance of someone keen to have it so. Someone in the police force, far higher up the system than poor Sandra Bjerke, may well have sent the case here to be shelved, quite deliberately. The idea kindled a vague sense of disquiet in Selma.

A kind of anxiety that would not really let go.

The Tip-Off

'You have to see this. You just have to see this.'

Lars Winther had opened the door of the news editor's office without knocking. In his hand he was carrying a forty-eight-page document, printed out exactly as long ago as it had taken him to read it.

'Is it about Pål Poulsen?'

'No.'

'Then I'm not interested.'

'Take a look, won't you!'

'Pål Poulsen, I said!'

The news editor pointed irritably at the door and roared: 'There's a dog buried somewhere in this story, and it stinks to high heaven. That guy hasn't resigned out of consideration for his family. Not Pål Poulsen, the greatest fighter in the Progress Party. Get out and look. Turn every stone. You. Just like everyone else here. Two sections, in fact. Both understaffed because of the holidays. Now!'

'Take a look!'

Lars Winther placed the document on the desk. The editor adjusted his glasses and read the first page. Pushing his glasses further up to the bridge of his nose, he started to riffle through it.

'Sit down,' he murmured after a couple of minutes. And read on. After ten to twelve pages he lifted his gaze.

'Where the hell did you get this?'

'In an email. From a totally insignificant address. I just managed to get hold of one of the IT boys to see if they can find out where it came from.'

'This can't be true.'

'Yes, it can!'

'That Russian sources are transferring considerable sums of money to Default.no? That in reality they are financing this ...'

His grimace tripled his double chin and, pulling a face, he continued: '... so-called online newspaper?'

Default.no was a relatively recent bloom in the increasingly rich variety of burgeoning online newspapers taking a stance on the outermost wings of the political spectrum, on both right and left. Most of these were something between blogs and pure propaganda channels. They were all remarkably alike, both the dark blue and the dark red: hostile to immigration, with a strong affinity to conspiracy theories, combined with a lenient approach to press ethics, truth and the good name and reputation of other people, to put it mildly.

Some of these webpages were old. Some, like Wrong.no, had originally had some merit. A couple of enthusiastic feminists, as early as the nineties, had taken the side of immigrant women against the antiquated, patriarchal culture. This led to them eventually receiving government support as deserving contributors to the work of integration. A considerable sum of money had been left hanging in the permanently repeated entries of the government's budget, to annual, increasingly voluble, protests. There was not much left of the original feminism in Wrong.no, but far more undisguised contempt for everything that might have anything to do with Islam.

Default.no had made a more sudden appearance. Three multi-millionaires in the financial markets had splashed a couple of million each to establish what they called a 'politically independent media channel critical of the powers-that-be'. Within a few months, the website had distinguished itself by hosting the country's most insane comments section.

Lars Winther had himself felt the discomfort of coming under suspicion in Default.no. In an update on Facebook, he had pointed out that it could scarcely be true that NATO's general secretary, Jens Stoltenberg, was the leader of a Jewish global conspiracy, the object of which was to Islamize the whole of Western Europe. The reasoning was illogical and completely absurd, and Default.no should therefore refrain from suggesting anything of the sort, Lars Winther had risked saying.

The shit storm had lasted for three weeks. Default.no's method was simple. A dubious headline accompanied a huge image of whatever should be called to account. The body of text that followed then identified the person in question as an enemy of free speech and diversity of opinion, and furthermore the relevant person was a member of the despised elite. Then the hordes were let loose. Lars could subsequently read in the comments that he was a corrupt, perhaps gay, certainly gay, horrible, anorexic guy with filthy contempt for true Norwegians. He was a traitor, a message boy for the powers-that-be and what's more – and this became increasingly unequivocal the further down you came in the list of comments – a paedophile.

'It's certainly not news that the Russians are attempting to destabilize nations in the West,' Lars Winther said. 'Especially via the internet. What's the difference between the troll factories they've been incontrovertibly shown to be running and making sure that the people there ...'

He motioned with his hand towards the papers his editor was still leafing through.

'... can be kept busy with such madness? It's fucking horrible to be left exposed to them, Knut-Ola. My wife got pretty put out when it was at its worst. The kids are still too small to pick up on things like that, but I had to promise Sissel not to put my head above the parapet once they're a couple of years older. Bloody hell, they even published my home address. And phone number. Had to get a new one after a day or two of constant crap. It'll be a long time before I mention that rag again. It's a bad day when people hang back from taking part in ordinary public debate, Knut-Ola. To put it mildly. If it had just been the rubbish in the comments you had to endure, then you could shut your eyes to it. Just not read them. But the sewer is overflowing. Spilling over the edges, in a way. When they give out an address, a phone number ... yes, even *the names of your children!* Then it becomes impossible to shut your eyes to it.'

The editor glanced up.

'It takes a really determined kind of person to tolerate this life,' he said, nodding. 'And we're in a bad way if it's only the most thick-skinned of us that can bear to have anything to do with politics. Or even worse: if politics becomes attractive only to the people who don't give a damn about what other people think.'

He had thumbed through to the final page and now picked up his coffee cup to drain the last dregs. Smacking his lips, he put his little finger in his ear and scratched before getting to his feet and closing the door.

'But what's more important than that at the moment,' he said sotto voce, 'is that this story has greater implications. If it's true.'

'What do you mean?'

'Default is like a wasp in the autumn. A real bloody nuisance, but not particularly dangerous. What is far worse is ...'

He plumped down on his chair and groaned quietly.

'The real scandal in all of this is that the Russians are interfering in the Norwegian way of life. Under a cloak of secrecy. I just can't understand ...'

Once again he began to leaf through the document.

'Apparently this has also come via …'

Shaking his head, he struggled to find the page he was looking for.

'Via Eivind Kåre Storheim,' Lars told him. 'He's the fourteenth-richest man in Norway, according to the last list published in *Kapital*. An investor. In other words, someone who makes a living from gambling.'

'Well, we depend on risk capital to—'

'To hell with that. Storheim is one of the people who kick-started Default.no. The other two withdrew after less than a year, when it got too defamatory to have your name associated with such a forum. Default turned into something different from what they thought it would be, they've both said since. But Eivind Kåre Storheim, he continued regardless. The guy has balls, I'll give him that. He's also picked fights in the established press, usually once every four years or so, every time he sticks his head out of his glass palace to say anything at all. An inaccessible guy. And capable. As far as money is concerned, anyway.'

'But what has this to do with the Russians?'

'Storheim is one of an increasing number of people here in Norway who believe we're conducting a policy that is far too hostile to Russia. Who basically think that the annexation of Crimea wasn't anything to get excited about. And that gays should just keep a low profile, since Putin is such a magnificent, smart guy. Storheim even invests in Russia, despite the risks. Corruption, changing frames of reference, and unpredictability keep many Western investors away, but not Eivind Kåre Storheim. In one of the rare interviews he's given, he called his Russian investments "toy money".'

Lars Winther drew big quote marks in the air.

'Money he can afford to lose. And the toy money has paid excellent dividends. This documents claims to be able to show …'

He leaned over the improbably untidy desk and placed the flat of his hand on the papers.

'... that half the money he gives to Default.no isn't his in the first place. It's Russian. Storheim has the contacts, he has the opportunity, and he definitely has the motive.'

The editor now had a deep furrow between his eyes.

'Why on earth would Storheim do something like that? After all, it's small change for a man with his wealth. How much are we talking about?'

'Petty cash, as you said yourself. For him. Four million a year. Two of them from him personally. According to the document, anyway.'

'Why would he take such a risk? In actual fact, he's laundering money. In a sense. It must be criminal!'

Lars shrugged.

'To be honest, I don't know off the top of my head. It'll have to be investigated further. It sounds fucking illegal for someone who claims to be part of the free, independent press to lie about where they get their money! But apart from the illegality, it would be a scandal for Storheim if it turns out that he is facilitating the Russian financing of the Norwegian "press".'

Once again he sketched the quote marks in the air, and added: 'And it would be a deathblow for Default.no.'

'I'm not so sure about the latter. Default has its adherents, no matter what. They don't feel bound by our norms about openness regarding such relationships. Nothing else either, for that matter. But without finance, of course they'd face an enormous challenge. Do they have other sources of income?'

'That's a bit hazy. Financial contributions from readers, perhaps, but it's difficult to imagine them amounting to large sums. Advertising probably brings in the most meaningful chunk of cash. They claim to have almost half a million unique readers each month. That's more than *Dagsavisen*.'

The editor pushed the papers across his desk. He narrowly missed knocking over a glass of something that looked like dead cola, and a pile of books fell on the floor.

'The problem is,' he began, letting a pause hang in the air between them for a few seconds, 'that I quite simply don't believe it.'

'What? Just like that?'

'No, on reflection.'

He rubbed his nose with a stumpy forefinger. 'It stinks of fake news.'

'Shouldn't you read the documentation more thoroughly before you make up your mind?'

'No. I don't think it's true. I can't imagine any reason whatsoever for Eivind Kåre Storheim to do anything so stupid.'

'But ...'

Lars Winther slid forward in his chair, and ended up barely touching the seat.

'You've got a week,' the editor said firmly. 'You can access data expertise within reasonable bounds. If this is really true, then it's a story. A cracking story. But, to be honest, I don't believe it. And we'll have to be totally and completely bomb proof on the truth content before we publish a single word of this.'

Lars jumped up quickly. His Tintin quiff was more prominent than usual. 'Fine. Thanks.'

'One week. OK? And if you should stumble upon something juicy about Pål Poulsen on the way, then well and good.'

This parting shot went unheard by Lars Winther: the door had already slammed behind him.

The Twitter Storm

A man sat in a basement room in Nordberg, tapping on a computer keyboard.

His name was Erling Hjort, he was forty-three and knew all that was worth knowing about computers. While his peers had wasted six months partying towards the end of their final year at high school, in 1993 he created and sold his first software program to the phone company that was still called Televerket in those days and had a complete monopoly of telecoms in Norway.

The young boy was a keen athlete, and after high school he had gained the qualifications to train as a paratrooper in the Norwegian Special Operations Forces. He completed the course as number two in his year. After twelve years on active service, he fell in love for the very first time. Maja was a captain in the army, and she was of the opinion that they could not possibly start a family if they both continued their military careers. It was difficult to argue against this. Erling volunteered to resign from the armed forces: his all-consuming interest in computers had not diminished. Quite the opposite. While Maja applied for a safer and more predictable posting in Oslo, Erling started up the telecoms and data company, Broadway. Six years, one wedding and three children later, Broadway was the third-largest company in that line of business in the entire country. Erling Hjort still owned 33 per cent of the shares.

He knew he was a well-respected man.

This was important. He had been purposeful ever since he was a toddler. His parents had died in an accident when he was only ten months old, and his grandmother and grandfather had brought him up. His grandfather was a kind man, but he placed high demands on himself and others. Especially on Erling.

Maja thought it had been his grandfather's influence that had made Erling so old-fashioned. So chivalrous, as she put it. Always with a smile in her voice. Her knight on a white charger, even though a captain in the army scarcely needed anything of the kind.

As a rule Erling Hjort voted for the Conservative Party, as both his grandparents had done. It was not something he spoke about, but neither was it something he tried to conceal if anyone asked. He was not particularly interested in politics, apart from his belief in a well-ordered society, in which the community looked after those who needed care, but where at the same time demands were made on individuals. He was irked about property tax, but all the same wanted a society in which everyone had the same access to the health service and free education.

There was only one area that riled him.

Defence policy.

Seventy-eight years ago, Norway had been caught short and virtually defenceless when the Germans arrived. Politicians in recent decades had learned little from that. Erling Hjort entertained a deep and steadily growing worry that their gargantuan neighbour in the east would be able to do whatever it liked with Norwegian territory. Membership of NATO, which had previously allowed both him and his friends in the defence services to sleep well at night, was no longer so reassuring. Europe's solidarity was wobbling, with Brexit in the west and the growth of nationalism in the east. The USA, with its new and totally unpredictable president, no longer provided the mainstay of security that it had done since the establishment of NATO in 1949.

Erling Hjort knew his defence history, and had immediately agreed when, at the age of twenty-eight, he had been contacted by a man and made an offer. It was not remunerative, but it was the right thing to do. So discreetly that he barely noticed any difference, he was enrolled in a kind of standing army. He knew nothing about how large it was, and little about what it did in peacetime. The man who made contact at that time had given him a set of codes and written instructions he had learned off by heart and then burnt. The only thing that meant anything to Erling was that the man was an honourable guy. A man who wished Norway well, who understood the military and was a freedom-loving pillar of society. A true democrat.

He had therefore followed the orders he received as he had been trained to do since he was a little boy.

It was the easiest thing in the world to set up false Twitter profiles. There was a bit more work involved in hiding the IP address. Of course, he could have used proxy servers, or even better, a VPN, but neither of these was safe enough. The accounts must not be able to be traced in any way. Erling Hjort was an expert, and it took him less than three hours to do what he had to. Tomorrow he would tackle the next task, which would be far more complicated.

But not impossible.

When he packed up and switched off the lights to go outside and mow the lawn, he had set the ball rolling for a whole campaign.

It would turn out to be astoundingly effective.

AUTUMN

Canis Familiaris

The wolf woke Selma. Its tongue was rough and its breath stank. In the far distance, something that did not exist could be heard.

The rumble of an engine. Like a car. There were no motor vehicles on the Hardangervidda.

Her Volvo had made it up here.

The noise grew louder, or maybe it was just that the wind had turned. It was a car. An ATV, perhaps. All-terrain vehicles were most likely to be found up here. Or a snow scooter. She had to get up. Follow the vehicle. Find someone. Summon help. If only the wolf would leave. The wolf stood between her and deliverance, and she could not get to her feet.

The noise continued, and she passed out again.

The wolf would not give up. Selma woke. The wolf whined. Selma felt her body and was aware that her heart was beating so fast that it was almost dangerous: very close to two hundred beats a minute.

The wolf sat down and offered a paw.

It did not look so frightening now. Selma concentrated on lowering her pulse. She breathed slowly, filling her lungs through her mouth, and letting it ooze out slowly through her nose.

The wolf cocked its head and whined.

Selma Falck knew little about animals. They did not interest her, and she was scared of most of them. Cats were elegant, elephants had beautiful eyes, and she understood that every creature on earth had a role to play in the ecosystem. Humans could eat sheep and cattle, and ride horses, but she could not comprehend the point of keeping dogs. Animals were far from Selma's area of expertise, but she had at least seen many pictures of wolves.

This was a wolf. It looked like one anyway. Large and grey, skinny and with long legs. Its fur was bedraggled and dirty. Its teeth were yellow and its eyes ice-cold.

'Hi, doggy,' she said, though her voice barely carried.

The animal's tail wagged more enthusiastically, forming a triangle in the wet snow.

An angel wing.

It must be a dog. In that case, it was the ugliest mutt Selma had ever seen. She was still terrified, a dog of this size was almost as frightening as a wolf, but she managed to sit up. The animal did not attack.

It lay down.

'Hello,' she whispered. 'Nice doggy. Very nice doggy.'

It had turned cold again. The huge animal's breath warmed part of her thigh. The blanket trousers had slid apart, and she was sitting with her bare skin on the snow.

Where there were dogs, there were people. This mutt must have come from somewhere. Dogs and humans had belonged together for thousands of years, and this dog must have a human owner somewhere.

She did not dare to move.

'Wuff,' said the dog and sat up. Its paw, with big black claws, scratched her thigh.

Wolves howled. They did not bark, Selma thought. This must be a husky, or maybe an Alaskan Malamut, like one of her neighbours had on Ormøya island. Fido was black and white and must weigh ten kilos more than this specimen.

This wolf-dog was just skin and bone, and it was completely grey.

It did not look as if it had a collar hidden in the scruffy fur of its neck. Nor a harness, like dogs in polar regions wore when they pulled sledges or pulkas. Now the animal was whimpering and scratching at her hand. Selma whipped her hand away. The dog had sat up again, and was wagging its tail even more furiously. It tilted its head and panted.

If this was a dog, then it had no owner. Maybe it had run away. It must have happened a while ago, but not so long ago that it had become feral.

'You're not wild. You're a tame dog. Canis familiaris.'

Her fear had wreaked havoc on the jigsaw puzzle inside her brain. Foreign words appeared. Latin words and expressions forced their way through. Selma gritted her teeth and refused to speak them aloud.

The dog craned its neck. It looked her straight in the eye before licking her cheek. Its gaze had reminded her of something just before she fainted, when she still knew that this four-legged monster was a wolf, and she was more certain she was going to die than she had been when she had stood in the middle of a snowstorm lacking clothing or shelter.

Her memory was in chaos again.

Most of what had come back to her piece by piece and fragment by fragment in the past few days was disappearing again.

'I'm not afraid of you,' she said, struggling slowly to her feet. 'I can't afford to be scared of you. Don't have time for this sort of thing. Go away.'

The headache, the pain in her back, the tenderness in every single fibre of her being, everything was as difficult to bear as it had been several days ago. Her feet had gone to sleep from the cold down inside her reindeer skin boots that were now sodden. The temperature had dropped. It would soon start snowing again. She began to walk, no longer sure of her direction.

'Away you go,' she said to the dog, which was staring at her with eyes she did not want to remember. 'Scat.'

Selma stumbled off. The dog followed.

'Off you go,' Selma mumbled as she placed one foot in front of the other.

The dog paid no attention. It padded after her, right on her heels, it whined and wagged its tail, desperate to come with her. Selma no longer had the strength to shout at it.

One foot in front. The other foot in front. Her eyes trained on the ground, she must not fall. She would not be able to get up again, she had to stay on her feet, keep moving forward on this interminable mountain plateau which might be the Hardangervidda and that never came to an end.

She needed to sleep. To rest. She wanted to lie down, just for a moment, a little nap before she trudged on towards the valley she must reach at some point, a gap in all this flatness that would lead down to someone who could help her. If only she could just close her eyes and gather her strength for a minute or two. Just five minutes, she needed to eat and drink, and there was nothing to be had here.

The dog barked loudly and then began to snarl.

Selma's body was still able to register fear. There was yet another dose of adrenaline inside her, and it spread through her body, making her heart hammer harder. Faster. There was still a final grain of strength in Selma Falck's body: she raised her eyes and lifted her right arm, ready to strike.

The wolf-dog was going to kill her.

It was standing in front of her now, barking angrily again. But not at her.

At a cabin, she now saw. A small red projection in the landscape, an anthropogenic point, something constructed by humans in the midst of this wilderness.

It began to snow.

The dog plodded away towards the cabin. Selma staggered after it. Every five metres, the dog stopped and looked back. Waited. Selma was aware of the dog's presence rather than saw it; her gaze was fixed on tussocks and stones and clumps of heather. She must not stumble, and there were only a hundred metres left to go.

The snow was falling more thickly.

Keep going, move forward, let your foot spring forward with every second step.

One more time. And yet another.

She simply could not do it.

Selma sank to her knees. The blanket trousers had fallen apart without her noticing. The part around her right leg had fallen off. The string that held the poncho in place around her waist was gone.

The dog approached her.

Selma smiled.

It looked at her with eyes that reminded her of a man. Tryggve Mejer was his name, and Selma was not afraid of him. She was afraid that something was going to happen to him.

The snow had taken on a host of colours. Mostly red, but also yellow and green and something that glowed. It was beautiful, and it gave off a pleasant warmth. Selma wrenched off the rest of the rags wrapped around her body, tossed them aside and felt the snow lie like little embers on her skin and then vanish. She had no need to worry about the dog: it would manage fine. She was worried about Tryggve Mejer. She felt anxious about him, and he was the one she must reach in time to deliver a warning.

The wolf-dog whined and Selma raised her head.

Through the myriad colours in the snowdrift, she saw the red cabin with a chimney on its roof.

A plume of smoke was rising from the pipe, and Selma wanted to laugh. She wanted to get up, struggle onwards, cover the last few metres, open a door and step inside a cabin with food and people and something to warm her other than glowing snow.

But it was simply not possible. Not without a brief rest.

'I must just have a little sleep,' Selma said to the dog as she lay down on the heather.

Four Days

'It's been four days. Why hasn't she been reported missing?'

'We don't know whether she has.'

'A woman like Selma Falck? If she'd been reported missing, it would be headline news in all the media outlets.'

'Maybe.'

'Not maybe, for absolute certain. What has happened?'

'I don't know. She lives on her own. And she has a job with no colleagues. It could take a few days.'

'But four have already gone by, I said! Someone with such a high profile and so many friends doesn't just disappear for such a long time without anyone sounding the alarm. What about social media?'

'No activity. She's dead, as I told you. Several times.'

'Someone should at least have noticed that she's disappeared from the internet.'

'Well, she does take breaks from time to time, in fact.'

'What about that down-and-out pal of hers?'

'He lives quietly with his cat. He's so scared of phones that he only rings her in a case of dire emergency. From an ancient Nokia mobile. No activity registered on it for ages.'

'Go up there again.'

'Up again? As I said, the site of the fire must remain untouched until she's found.'

'Use the drone.'

'Again? Good God, can you—'

'Use the drone, I said. Tomorrow. You can leave.'

SUMMER

The Funeral

It was now Tuesday 31 July, and Sjalg Petterson was to be cre-mated today. The sky was still a pale-blue arch above Oslo. Summer had not grabbed hold; it had settled down over the southern part of Scandinavia and fallen into a coma.

As usual, Selma arrived at the last minute. She had been in Bakkehaugen church before, at baptisms and funerals. This time too it occurred to her that despite the decorations by artists such as Carl Nesjar and Kai Fjell, this was the ugliest place of worship in the country. A pointed, A-shaped concrete block hammered down into the ground on a beautiful hillside. The belfry stood beside it, shamefaced, looking like a misplaced diving board.

The turnout was less than impressive.

This surprised Selma. She had thought she ran the risk of not finding a seat by coming so late. For a second or two, she stood looking around when she entered the church. No photographers discreetly dotted along the walls. Nowhere else in view either. Of course, there could be journalists here without Selma noticing them, but it did not appear so.

She caught sight of Anine. In the first pew, with Jesso on her right-hand side, and her mother-in-law on the other. Anine was not only dressed in black, she was wearing a pillbox hat with a black veil that covered her whole face. Selma felt the familiar prick of irritation: Anine exploited every situation to create unnecessary histrionics.

The very back pew was empty. Selma sat on the outside edge, with the shortest route to the door. The organ music struck up and the pastor emerged from the sacristy.

Selma did not like attending funerals in churches. Especially not in the ugly Bakkehaugen church.

Deep down inside, she did not believe in God, and she had never been contemplatively inclined. All the same, there was something blessedly relaxing about having to wait until it was all over. When she paid one of her rare visits to the cinema, she usually left before the film had ended. At parties, she sneaked away as soon as she grew bored. Even at meetings, at the time when she was a lawyer and had been compelled to attend more of these than she could stand, she became expert at cutting through things and wrapping them up in the shortest possible time.

Or finding an excuse to leave.

Selma Falck was allergic to boredom, but no one with decent manners left a funeral before the service was concluded. The situation forced her into a sort of trance in which the music, the psalms, the pastor's incantation and the eulogies floated past without her really listening. The interior of the church was beautiful in its simplicity, and she stared in fascination at the three rectangular stained-glass windows that comprised a kind of triptych above the altar. The sunlight outside toyed with the colours in the leaded glass and scattered rays across the chancel where the coffin stood.

Anine was sobbing.

Others sobbed too. Disturbed by the sniffing and drying of tears, Selma began to pay attention. The congregation had to stand up constantly at the command of the pastor's magisterial hands, but fortunately it was all nearing an end.

For the first time it struck Selma that the Progress Party was conspicuous by its absence. The party leader, two deputy leaders, and two or three members of parliament in addition had all been guests at the wedding. She saw none of them in the church now, not even when she craned her neck to obtain a better view. Not even Kolbein Fagernes was to be seen, despite being the deceased's best man only eleven days earlier, and presumably his best friend.

Remarkable. Admittedly, the previous day the party had become one deputy down with an explanation that no one believed. This made it necessary to douse the flames both in the party and in meetings with the press. Nevertheless, this was a final farewell to the obviously most ideologically rooted and educated member of the Progress Party in the entire country. The shocking nature of his death, given both the man's relatively young age and the deeply tragic circumstance of dying at his own wedding, should have been reason enough for them to attend.

The service was drawing to a close. The pastor invited the mourners to a memorial gathering at the Månefisken restaurant: everyone was welcome.

Except for me, Selma thought, knowing she was right.

She would like to demonstrate her presence to the relatives. On the other hand, she had not the least wish to stand in the crowd of people outside the church, with bowed heads and in awkward silence, as they joined the immediate grieving family to watch as Sjalg Petterson's mortal remains were stowed in a car and driven away for all eternity.

The solution was to wait inside.

The coffin was carried down the aisle by people Selma did not recognize, but one of the men must be Njål. He resembled his brother, even though he was smaller and darker. At the very back of the coffin walked Anine, arm in arm with Runhild, sobbing loudly behind the pathetic veil of black lace. Jesso had his arm around her on the other side, and looked as if he had lost a dearly-beloved son. Selma resisted the urge to shout out that he had not been able to abide the idea of welcoming Sjalg into the family. She withdrew further along the very back pew, just enough to be seen, but far enough away not to have anyone say hello.

Christ. Even Jesso's new flame was present. The young girl was walking immediately behind him, beautiful and unusually tall, with an expression of great suffering and captivating dignity.

Four months, Selma thought, and a bright light spread slowly behind her eyes. Jesso and this long-legged female had been an item for four months, and the woman could hardly have met Sjalg more than a couple of times.

Selma tried to relax, to breathe. In through the mouth, out through the nose.

When the coffin approached the doors, with a growing tail of mourners from the first pews behind it, Selma drew further and further towards the wall. The church bells rang slowly. In the end the church was deserted.

She walked to the door. There were still a few people mingling in the vestibule, but most of them had gathered in a large half-moon around the waiting funeral car. Selma felt a vague sense of panic: it would be difficult to escape without having to speak to Anine and Jesso. The crush was greatest just outside the double timber doors, beneath a tent-shaped overhang, and that was where it was easiest not to be noticed. She took a swift decision, dipped her head and moved out of the church. As soon as she was out in the fresh air, she took a sharp turn to the left. She straightened her back and stretched her neck as soon as she had put the last of the crowd behind her.

She looked at her watch to emphasize that she was in a hurry. It had been a dignified and successful funeral in every way, and with a smile to no one in particular, she signalled that unfortunately she had to rush to an appointment.

She hurried onwards and turned the south-east corner.

Having made her escape, she dropped her speed, No one had called after her, that too would be inappropriate on such an occasion. She followed the footpath down to Ustedts vei. The lawns on either side were scorched brown, and the leaves on the trees surrounding the church were already turning yellow, at least one month too early.

She became aware of someone walking behind her. As she picked up speed, she cast a quick glance over her shoulder.

It was a man. He did not seem to have taken part in the funeral service. His shorts were dark-blue and came to just below the knee. His baseball shirt had a red body and long white raglan sleeves. The guy was wearing a baseball cap on his head, pulled well down over his eyes, and he was wearing socks with brown leather sandals.

Selma stopped.

She was curious, but not afraid. It was the middle of the day, in the centre of Oslo, and only a hundred metres away, there were crowds of people.

The man also stopped. He produced a mobile from his pocket and became preoccupied with something or other. Selma started to walk again. She had found it difficult to find a parking spot so close to the time of the funeral, and still had another couple of hundred metres to go.

The man with the sandals followed her.

Selma stopped yet again. Wheeled around and walked calmly back towards the church. The man did not look up.

'What do you want from me?' Selma asked cheerfully.

He looked up warily from beneath his baseball cap. 'Not here,' he said softly. 'Keep walking.'

She recognized him immediately.

What Pål Poulsen was doing outside Bakkehaugen church immediately after the funeral of one of his good friends, wearing shorts, sandals and a baseball cap, was so difficult to find an answer to that she momentarily just stood gawping at him.

'Walk,' he snarled. 'Keep going towards your car.'

Selma hesitated for yet another second before turning on her heel and continuing to walk towards Nygårds allé, where her red 1966 Volvo was parked. She never looked back, but noticed that Pål Poulsen was following her. When she reached her car, she still acted as if there was nothing untoward. She opened the door and sat inside. Leaned over to the passenger seat and opened that door too.

He clambered in awkwardly. 'Drive,' he said.

'What do you want from me?' she asked again.

Selma had not yet inserted the key in the ignition.

'Drive,' he said, with more of a plea in his voice this time. 'Please. To Maridalen. Or somewhere. A place where there aren't so many people.'

The engine was still dead.

'I'm not driving anywhere until you explain your behaviour. And tell me what you want of me.'

'You must help me,' he said, ducking down in the seat as a woman with a pram came walking along the side of the road. 'Please, I'm begging you. Just drive.'

'No.'

'I'm being blackmailed,' he said. 'You have to help me.'

'Right now I've got another case on the go. Sorry. I never take on more than one case at a time.'

Pål Poulsen sat up straight in the seat. Leaning forward, he took off the baseball cap and cradled his face in his hands.

'I can't go to the police,' he whispered. 'And the press are after me. Everywhere.'

'They're not here. There were none at the funeral either, as far as I could see. Despite how much the media love death.'

'Can you ... please drive!'

His desperation was so obvious that it persuaded Selma to change her mind. She inserted the key in the ignition and turned it. A low, finely tuned hum filled the car and she drove slowly out into the road. Turned left on Maridalsveien, continued over Ringveien and was approaching Marka after only a few minutes. Just before Skjerven farm, she drove into the huge car park where she had given the first driving lessons to her children as soon as they turned sixteen. It was almost deserted, only two SUVs with dog cages visible in the back were parked beside the barrier on the fringes of the forest. Selma drove all the way to the other side of the car park.

'What's this all about?' she asked, as she stopped and switched off the engine.

'I'm the victim of a crime.'

'Then you should contact the police.'

Pål Poulsen was at long last sitting properly in the seat. His baseball cap lay on his knee. His legs were chalk-white: probably this was the first time in ages that he had worn shorts. The man usually wore nothing but long trousers, an open-necked check shirt and a dark blazer. Everywhere he went, no matter whether it was suitable for the occasion or weather. Even to the gala evening at the palace, he was normally dressed in differently coloured trousers and jacket, even though wife number three had forced him into a white shirt and a dress tie around his bull neck when she was permitted to accompany him for the first time.

'I can't,' he said. 'Not the police.'

'As I said, I'm working on another assignment at the moment.'

'Are you bound by confidentiality?'

'Well, yes, self-imposed, at least.'

'Someone is out to get me.'

'Who?'

The man broke down in sobs. Feeling queasy, Selma leaned against the door on her side of the car.

'I don't know,' Pål Poulsen sniffed. 'But they've found out things about me that should be absolutely impossible to prove.'

Selma shut her eyes.

'Nothing is impossible to discover,' she muttered, now at the end of her tether. 'There are no secrets.' Except for mine, she thought, before she went on: 'What one person knows, nobody knows. What two people know, everybody knows. Are these secrets of the kind that ... eh ... involves two people?'

His nod was so faint that it was almost imperceptible.

'Has it to do with sex?'

Now he simply blinked and let his head fall forward. His flesh looked like a pile of sausages between his chin and his chest. The comb-over he usually plastered over his bald pate, as if he had not received tips on hair care since the seventies, had dropped to one side of his head. Like a sad, grey flag, his hair flopped against his shoulder. His greasy, pink skull was flaking, with big white patches where the pigment had completely vanished. His eyes disappeared into his puffy face. His lips trembled, and there were brown half-moons of snuff-tinged saliva at each corner of his mouth. He was no beauty, Pål Poulsen, and Selma did not care for his politics either. But she felt sorry for him. It was as if all the air was slowly seeping out of the inflated windbag that had been so prominent in national politics for two whole decades.

Selma had always sympathized with people who fell from grace.

Without exception.

She felt sorry for Pål Poulsen, but she could not help him.

179

'Remember that everything passes,' she said, firing up the engine. 'Everything passes. It's just a question of time. That guy of yours in parliament, the one from Østfold, sent hard porn to a fourteen-year-old and suggested three-way sex with a fifteen-year-old. He survived, as far as I can see. You probably will too.'

Faster than she would have thought possible of him, his hand shot out and he turned the ignition key. He grabbed it, closing his right fist around the key ring, and sat on his hands.

'No,' he whimpered as the tears flowed. 'This is far worse. You have to help me. You're the best private investigator in the country.'

'Why didn't you just call me?'

Her sympathy for the man was fast diminishing, and she held out the palm of her hand. 'Give me my keys. Now.'

Pål Poulsen tore open the passenger door. Releasing his seat belt, he rushed out of the car. He angrily skirted around the bonnet of the Volvo and knocked violently on her window. She rolled it down, almost equally furious. He thrust his head into the car. Selma pulled so far back that the gearstick hit her on the back.

'I couldn't phone you,' he said with suppressed rage. 'I assumed you would be at the funeral, and I was right. I had to contact you this way. They're listening in to me. My phone is bugged. My house too. Everything. I'm absolutely sure of that.'

'Only … only the police listen in to people in Norway. And criminal cartels, I presume. Do you have connections with a criminal cartel?'

'They killed Sjalg Petterson!' he growled.

A fine spray of saliva splashed over Selma's face. Her eyes narrowed and she closed her mouth.

'And they're planning to kill me.'

Selma stared straight into his eyes.

'Get in,' she said tersely, holding out her hand.

This time she got her car keys back.

The Argument

Mum was back from her week's holiday. She and Dad were arguing again.

It was not even seven o'clock in the evening, but they were behaving as if it was really bloody late and Mina had gone to sleep long ago. She had been sitting in her room all day, despite the good weather. Several of her friends had contacted her. Some were still in town now, in the middle of the school holidays, and had asked her to come with them to Sørenga for a swim. A small group was going to Villa Paradiso in Løkka afterwards for something to eat. Normally Mina would have jumped at the chance to join them ages ago.

But nothing was normal.

As a rule, she used to listen when they were quarrelling downstairs.

Now she had closed the door of her room and lain down on the bed with a pillow over her head. All the same, she heard their voices. Mum's like knives through the air, Dad's like booming protests against everything Mum said. As for Mina, she tried to drown it all out by singing children's songs she hadn't known she remembered.

They just wouldn't give up.

It was still bright as day outside. Mina had drawn the curtains, but they were so light and white that they didn't help in the least. She had had blackout roller blinds since they moved in here, but two of them were broken. Dad had promised a thousand times to fix them but it was eighteen months since they had fallen apart.

Someone was crying down there, Mina realized when she removed the pillow to take a drink of water from her bottle. Dad never cried. Only once had she seen him break down, and that was when he had come to tell her that Grandma was dead.

These were not Mum's sobs.

Mum broke down in tears at the drop of a hat. Mina was sometimes sick and tired of all her weeping and wailing and all the fuss she made. And her tears. Mum's sobbing was just like Dad's wretchedness. It could make an appearance at all times of the day and night, and eventually, as Mina grew older, she had learned not to pay too much attention to it.

She tossed the pillow out of the bed. Sat up and covered her ears. Then dropped her hands again.

It was Dad who was in tears.

Mina felt a completely unfamiliar kind of fear. This summer was already the worst of her life, and really she no longer cared about anything at all. Dad's sore crying from the kitchen was unbearable all the same. She knew that he would pull himself together before Mina was halfway down the stairs if he heard her, so she stood up as cautiously as she could and crossed to the door, scrupulously avoiding all the floorboards she knew creaked. Safely at the door, she grabbed the handle and pushed the door firmly but slowly into the doorframe before pressing down and opening. The hinges would start to squeak when the door was opened forty-five degrees, so she stopped as soon as there was space for her to squeeze out. She stood on the landing on the upper floor.

As if frozen to the spot.

The quarrel blasted through the house.

The voices were still indistinct, though. She caught the occasional word, and these made Mina even more afraid. They were being vile to each other, Mum and Dad. They weren't usually.

They quarrelled and said stupid things, especially Mum, but they were never really nasty. Now they were.

Mina wanted to turn round. Creep back to bed, pick up the pillow from the floor, lie down and squeeze as deep into the mattress as she could. The windows facing west, the ones that let in most light at this time of the evening, she could block with the bedspread if she hung it over the curtain poles. She could put on her headphones. Listen to loud music, or maybe yet another episode of *Friends*, that ancient TV series that Mum had got her hooked on one night a year ago, on the last really cosy evening she had spent on her own with Mum.

Of course she should have gone back to her room.

Instead she crept down the stairs. She knew every tread and every creak, and reached the middle landing without a sound. She sat down on the top step of the last flight of stairs and listened.

Mum and Dad were going to divorce, that much she understood after only a few seconds.

That was what Mina had wished for.

They were no longer friends, that had been clear for a long time, and all Mina wanted was peace and quiet. At least now, after all that had happened, and after everything that had become impossible to bear.

At least on her own.

Mum and Dad were going to divorce, and Mina was filled with remorse that she had wished for anything of the kind. This was something she absolutely did not want, she knew that now, and her breathing grew shallow and rapid, through her open mouth.

'... I don't believe you any longer. You keep making promises, but all the same you're going to run back to the party, to Erna if she calls on you, to ...'

Mum was almost shrieking.

'… promise!' Dad shouted back. 'I've already told quite a few other people, I'm going to resign in the autumn and …'

As usual, he didn't get to finish what he was saying.

Now Mum was crying too. Yelling and crying and sobbing and talking.

'You're a politician, Tryggve. It's in every bone of your body! You're never going to manage to resist it. If you resign in the autumn, it won't be long until you come crawling back to that fucking hornet's nest. With all its hatred and insults and shit and crap. I can't stand it! I can't take any more, Tryggve. Don't want any more of it. It's over.'

'But you can't …'

'Yes, I can. I'm leaving. To stay with Guri and Thorbjørn for a few days. Then we can take it from there.'

Mina heard footsteps. She leapt up and ran as silently as she could back to her room. Shut the door, crept under her quilt and pulled it over her head. She heard Mum tramp upstairs and go into the bedroom she and Dad shared. It took only a few seconds for her to come out again. Mina was filled with panic at the thought of Mum leaving just like that, and without further thought, she jumped up, opened the door and shouted: 'Mum!'

Mum was carrying a bag. It must have been already packed. She turned to face Mina, dropped the bag on the floor and came towards her. Mina had never seen her so tear-stained: her face was red and blotchy, and her make-up was gone. Her hair looked as if it had died. It lay flat on her head, and above her left ear it was a matted clump as if on a toddler who has fallen asleep.

'Mina,' Mum said as she put her arms around her.

'Mum,' Mina said, standing stiff as a board.

She was taller than Mum now. She breathed in the smell of her, of the shampoo Mina use to steal and of the expensive Acqua di Parma perfume she no longer dared to help herself to. Mum carried the scent of cuddly toys, especially of Muffin Mum, the one that Mina had well and truly sprayed with perfume when she was five years old.

'You're getting divorced,' Mina said dully.

Mum did not answer, just hugged her a bit harder. She began to sway slightly to and fro, as if Mina was still a little girl and could be comforted by closeness and warmth.

'It'll be OK, I guess,' Mina said.

Mum just cried and swayed and hugged.

'We can talk tomorrow,' she said finally, when Mina tried to extricate herself, and Mum let go at last.

'Whatever,' Mina said.

'Tomorrow,' Mum repeated, forced some kind of smile, grabbed her bag and headed downstairs.

Mina went on standing there, her pulse hammering on her ear-drums. She felt that she wanted to cry, but something was lodged in her throat. In her head. In her whole body, really. Completely stuck, all she could hear was buzzing and noise and pounding in her ears and she could hardly breathe. From below, she could hear Dad shouting. It had something to do with Mina, something about that they both should have sat down and talked quietly to her, but Mum just shrieked even more shrilly, and the front door slammed behind her with a bang.

The house became totally silent. Dad was totally silent. Only inside Mina's head was everything filled with confusion.

She went downstairs. 'Dad,' she said softly when she arrived in the kitchen.

He was sitting at the kitchen table. Sitting up straight with his arms hanging loosely by his sides. He was snot-nosed, and his whole face was wet. Almost unrecognizable. It was as if the father Mina had always known had become smaller. He had shrunk somehow, and the tenacity in his eyes had vanished.

'Mina,' he said finally without looking at her. 'I'm so sorry.'

Mina was not sure what he meant. He could be sorry because he and Mum were going to divorce. Because she had left with a bag that held enough for her to manage for quite a long time. It could also be that he was sorry because this was how Mina had learned about it.

Maybe he was sorry for all these things.

She approached him, and put a tentative hand on his shoulder. He did not respond. 'She'll probably come back,' she whispered.

'No, she won't do that.'

'Yes, she will. If you're going to resign in the autumn, then … It's not long till the autumn. When … when is autumn for you? She's sure to come back then. And everything will be fine again.'

Now he did not answer. Just tried to stay calm, she could feel a faint trembling in his body every time he exhaled. Maybe he was actually sobbing. Her hand moved slowly over his back. Up and down, up and down.

Mina had never had to comfort her father before. It felt strange and quite scary, and he was so warm that the moisture snagged her fingers on the fabric of his shirt.

Suddenly he froze. Forced a smile and looked up at her. 'We'll get this sorted, Mina. You and I. BFF, eh?'

He stood up so abruptly that the chair nearly toppled over. 'Let's do something. Just you and me, what do you say? Play a game? Maybe go somewhere to eat?'

'No,' Mina said, taking a step back.

'Sure?'

His smile was like the Joker's, far too broad, and the lines around his lips seemed to have been washed away. The wrinkles he forced out made it look as if someone had slashed his mouth open with a knife.

She nodded.

'OK,' he said. 'We'll sit down and talk properly about this, of course we will. Tomorrow, maybe. I'll phone Mum, and she'll come here once everything's calmed down a bit. You must remember too ...'

He raked both hands through his hair and took a deep breath. Once again that spooky smile, it was not his, it was not even a smile.

'You're big enough now to decide most things for yourself,' he said. 'You don't need to worry about that. Where you want to live, and that kind of thing, I mean. You're sixteen, and you can choose for yourself.'

Mina had not even considered the enormous consequences of a divorce. She had no idea whether Dad could afford to stay in the house in Lofthus terrasse. Or if Mum would want it. They had a mortgage, Mina knew, and maybe it was not too large so that one of them could manage to handle it alone. But then the other partner would have to receive half the value of the property. That could amount to an incredible amount of money. Ingeborg's parents had been given a valuation of nearly twenty million kroner, now that they could no longer stand to live in the house after Ingeborg had committed suicide in the attic. Mum had told her that, and Ingeborg's house was directly across the street.

'Do we have to move?' she blurted out.

'We can talk about that tomorrow, sweetheart. If you don't want to do something together tonight, then I'm going down to the basement to do some work.'

He was going to work. Immediately after this. After the worst argument in the world with Mum, and after finding out that she was going to leave him. Dad wanted to work, even though he must know how Mina was feeling. He used to see her, he must see her. He was her father and he loved her, and he should really understand that everything was falling apart. That she couldn't cry. That her whole world had shattered to pieces.

Something was still stuck in her throat, and the only thing she managed to do was to nod her head.

Just imagine, work. At a time like this.

'OK,' Dad said, and disappeared.

She was left standing there. Mina, alone in the kitchen while the world went on spinning on its axis, as it had done for almost five billion years. As for her, she was entangled in something she would never manage to find her way out of, and her life had just become even worse now that Dad had started to spend so much time down in the basement.

She glanced up at the huge wall clock above the sliding door into the utility room. The time was now eight p.m. In four hours, she would be seventeen years of age.

No one had remembered that it was her birthday tomorrow, even though they had talked about it that same morning.

Mum had just walked out. Dad was busy with something that Mum had not even noticed, even though it had been going on for a long time. A couple of months, maybe even longer. There could be a connection.

There must be an explanation for all this. This routine bickering of theirs – Dad had called it a 'habit' – had never been dangerous. Just unpleasant. Daft and unnecessary, and Mina had long ago promised herself that she would never be like that if she got married.

But it had never felt threatening.

All of a sudden, that summer, the arguments had turned poisonous. When Mina finally managed to move to the tap to let the water run until it was really cold, she knew just one thing.

She had to find out what Dad was up to.

The Laptop

'I come bearing gifts, Einar.'

Selma narrowly avoided tripping over the old newspapers and a grumpy cat when she entered Einar Falsen's apartment with a laptop tucked under her arm.

'What's this you've got?' he snarled, pointing at the machine as he drew back towards the kitchen.

'A laptop. For you.'

'Take it away! You know fine well that I don't want it! Get away!'

'It's secured,' Selma replied with a smile. 'I've been on the internet and found the method to safeguard it.'

'It's not possible.'

'Yes, it is. Look!'

She sat down in the armchair and placed the unusually chunky laptop on her knee.

'A housing,' she said. 'It's ingenious.'

'Get it out of here.'

'No, I won't,' Selma said, waving a sheet of paper. 'Read this.'

'Is it switched on?'

'Not yet. Read it.'

Einar refused to come any closer. Discouraged, Selma got to her feet and handed the sheet of paper to him.

'It's completely scientific,' she lied. 'Developed by an institute in Switzerland for people who are electro-allergic. Removes 98.3 per cent of all radiation. I've printed out an explanation from the ScienceSee website for you. A serious company. Supplies them worldwide.'

'Only 98.3 per cent,' Einar said, still too sceptical to accept the piece of paper she was trying to give him. 'That leaves 1.7 per cent.'

'You can solve that by taking a sheet of tin foil ...'

Selma went to the kitchen, opened a drawer and returned with a roll in her hand. She ripped off a strip almost double the size of the computer and folded it once.

'Come here now,' she said, sitting down in Pussycat's spot on the settee.

She patted the seat beside her. The cat jumped up on the table and stared at her, its tail swinging slowly from side to side. Einar was still hesitant, but now he had at least begun to read.

The computer, a cheap Dell machine that Selma had bought at the Elkjøp store, was enclosed in a plastic housing that resembled steel. It had been advertised for sale on Finn.no by a teenager who made laptop shields on the side, in addition to a professional career as a gamer. The cover, rough and heavy, had been customized with a luridly multicoloured *Star Wars* theme, but Selma had sprayed it steel-grey with aerosol paint after picking it up in a garage in Ris. The company name ScienceSee was one she had found on the internet, and they provided fairly genuine products to protect customers who claimed to be electro-allergic.

Of course, it might be that Einar would actually venture to try the machine, and Selma had a lengthy lifetime's experience of creating lies that were as close to the truth as possible. The scientific report he was now quite literally holding at arm's length was something she had concocted herself.

'Hm,' Einar said, taking a couple of paces towards her.

The cat had given up, and was now curled in the armchair where Selma normally had to sit.

'Convincing, isn't it?'

Selma gave a broad smile. 'Now I'm going to switch it on,' she said. 'You won't notice anything at all. I promise.'

She put the vaguely rectangular piece of foil on the table. Placed the laptop on it and folded up the edges of the silver paper a centimetre or so on either side. The laptop was already fully charged and she switched it on.

'Voila. Do you see?' She spread her arms. 'You don't feel anything, do you?'

Einar padded another couple of steps towards her.

'Hm, n ... yes,' he muttered, touching his head. 'Maybe not. Or ...'

All of a sudden he stopped. Threw the paper on the floor and placed two fingers on each temple. His eyes were tightly shut, and his mouth contorted into a grimace.

'You can't feel anything,' Selma insisted as calmly as she could manage. 'Absolutely nothing. This patent has been developed by a Nobel prizewinner in physics!'

Now she really had to ease off. 'But it doesn't matter,' she added quickly. 'The most important thing now is for you to come and sit down here beside me. You have to trust me, Einar.'

He was still standing in the middle of the room, looking as if his head were about to explode.

'Trust me,' Selma repeated, softly and slowly. 'Come here. It won't hurt you, I promise.'

Suddenly he opened his eyes wide. He stared at the Dell machine in astonishment.

'You're right! I can't feel anything!'

'I told you so.'

He sat down beside her, as far away as possible, on the settee. Slowly, inch by inch, he moved closer to the laptop while Selma sat quietly waiting.

'I've taken out subscriptions in your name for the major newspapers,' she said as he manouevred his way towards her. 'The national press, plus the largest regional newspapers. And *Morgenbladet. Klassekampen* too. You can stop stealing them now, Einar.'

'That'll be good,' he mumbled.

Now he was seated so close to her that she had to breathe through her mouth.

'This is a search field,' she said, pointing. 'Writing something in here is called Googling.'

'I'm not stupid. I read newspapers.'

'These touchpads are really pretty tiresome, so I bought ...'

She rummaged in her bag and pulled out a computer mouse and mouse mat.

'... these for you. Look.'

She called up DG.no. The headline story was about Default.no. Their website had been targeted by a Twitter campaign. Individual users had, using a pro forma provided by someone hiding behind the nickname @stopthehatred, begun to send messages to major advertisers. The communications were polite and obviously legal, and gently raised the question of whether the company really wanted to be associated with a reactionary news blog that was so hostile to immigration. When a couple of national politicians joined in, the whole thing had taken off and the campaign had borne fruit. Large companies saw the politically correct writing on the wall and cancelled their advertising. A furious argument was raging. There were loud protests about left-wing extremists, sabotage and freedom of speech from one side; freedom of choice, legal action and of course also freedom of speech on the other.

This was of no interest to Selma and so she continued to browse.

'You move the cursor here ...'

Click.

'And write what you're looking for.'

'*Persian cat*', she wrote.

Click.

'Pussycat!' Einar grinned with pleasure when Selma asked the laptop for pictures. 'But he's far better-looking than all these ones.'

Selma spent an hour and a half teaching Einar the most fundamental functions of a computer. The broadband in the apartment block, which Selma had used when she lived there, was fortunately still accessible. Einar grew increasingly enthusiastic. Some things he found easy: after all, he had used a computer until the beginning of the noughties. All the same, it struck Selma over and over again how rapid developments had been since then.

'Like that,' she said after an hour and a half. 'Now you can do whatever you need to. Enjoy yourself.'

She gingerly pushed the laptop across to him to avoid the foil coming loose.

'And since you're really working for me, you'll be allocated a task.'

Einar did not even look up. He was busy clicking his way deep into an American page about illegal, state-sanctioned surveillance. A moment of doubt crossed Selma's mind: the opportunities for Einar to find confirmation of all his delusions were now legion. She snatched up her bag and put her hand on his shoulder. At last he looked up.

His eyes were sparkling. His lips were moist. His breathing was fast and shallow.

'This is exceptional, Selma. Thanks a million.'

'Remember that a great deal of what's on there is not true, though.'

'Yes, of course.'

'Quite a lot of it is written by people who are just as crazy as you.'

'I'm sure.'

'You're going to have a task to do, did you hear me?'

'Yes, what is it?'

Selma was already slinking towards the hallway.

'You've to find out everything you can about Pål Poulsen,' she said, turning round. 'You'll come up with nearly two million results when you Google his name, so you'll have quite a lot to work through. Ninety-nine per cent of it will be of no interest to me. Maybe even more than that.'

'What is it you're looking for?'

'I don't know. Use your instincts.'

'Sex, money, infidelity? Some reason for him to resign?'

Selma smiled: 'Something along those lines.'

'Have you taken on another case? I thought you only took on one at a time.'

Instead of answering, Selma said: 'Unfortunately, I don't think your competence on the internet stretches quite as far as the kind of sex that Pål Poulsen must have left traces of in there.'

She adjusted the strap on her shoulder bag.

'You were once a policeman, Einar. Use that. The guy's being blackmailed. At least he was. Find the cause. You probably won't get very far, but it's worth a try.'

Pussycat had jumped up into his usual spot beside Einar, who now glanced up at Selma with his broadest grin on his face and shot two thumbs up in the air.

'Will do!'

Einar Falsen barely registered Selma's departure, but Pussycat purred and stared somewhat disdainfully after her as she disappeared out the door.

The Bedroom

Selma was reinvigorated.

Her poker account was almost eleven thousand kroner fatter than yesterday. Even though these gambling nights deprived her of sleep, they brought her a sense of calm. As a rule she gave up about five o'clock in the morning, depending on how things stood, and caught three hours of sleep in bed before the day began in earnest.

This morning she had slept until ten, and woke so brimming with energy that she had begun her workday with a run lasting an hour and a half.

It was evening now, and she was sitting up in bed with an enormous pillow at her back.

She was half-following the evening news on an iPad on her bedside table. The first quarter of an hour had dealt with a strident protest about an alleged Norwegian attack on Russian sovereignty. The editors of a small newspaper in Murmansk had been exposed to a massive cyber attack, and the Russian Ministry of Foreign Affairs was seething. The traces led to Norway. The Norwegian Minister of Foreign Affairs seemed extremely indignant when she was interviewed in front of the statue of King Haakon in 7, juni plass, the square commemorating the dissolution in 1905 of the union between Norway and Sweden. She dismissed the claims in very forthright terms.

Selma sat up in bed, punched the luxury pillow and replaced it more comfortably behind her back. The photographs that covered three of the walls in her bedroom had been reorganized. With the help of the list Runhild Petterson had given her, combined with exhaustive searches on social media, Selma could now name the majority of the wedding guests. With a fine-nibbed archival pen she had written the names on every single photograph, which had taken her most of the afternoon. She was still missing the identities of six people pictured, all members of the restaurant staff. Four young girls identically attired in blue summer dresses with old-fashioned pinafores and two men in black trousers and immaculate white shirts who had obviously attended to the pouring of wine.

Jesper Jørgensen was going to come at eight o'clock to identify them.

Things had gone as Jesper had predicted. The Ellevilt restaurant remained closed. The media attention in the first few days after Sjalg Petterson's death had made a visit to the otherwise so well renowned eating-place far less tempting for most people. The young chef had announced that Ellevilt was taking four weeks' summer holiday. After that, the restaurant would reopen with a new menu. The announcement had been the butt of both genuinely amusing comments and downright vulgar humour on social media, but Selma knew that the collective memory was relatively short.

In four weeks, it would all be forgotten.

She hoped so, at least, for Jesper's sake.

They had not met since he had given her the assignment. He had phoned her once, and she had called him three times, even though it had not been strictly necessary. Selma rarely rang anyone unless it had been insisted upon. Since she had spoken to him a couple of hours ago and asked him to drop in, she had felt an unfamiliar kind of pleasure at the idea of seeing him.

More of a kind of eager anticipation, it struck her, and it was not unfamiliar at all. She gave herself a little slap.

The guy was half her age.

She turned off the iPad and got up. She did another round of the pictures, scrutinizing them carefully once again. By now she knew them almost by heart and had rearranged them in a sort of timeline. At the far end of the wall to the left of her bed, she had pinned up the earliest photos, the ones at the Opera House roof and arrival at the restaurant. Thereafter followed happy images of the bridal couple as they stepped out of a veteran car, Anine's many poses, hugs and toasts in lukewarm champagne. Beyond the gable wall came pictures of the newlyweds on the stone steps leading up to the terrace: Anine almost tripped up in one of them but Jesso was quick to help her in the next photo.

The dinner photos were pinned up on the right-hand side.

These were obviously the most interesting ones, and if any clue at all was to be found in these 400 photographs about what had really happened when Sjalg had ingested nuts and died, then it must be in these.

Selma had paid a visit to the FotoKnudsen store and had A3 enlargements made of three of these. Now she doubted whether there had been any point in that, as the technical quality was so poor that the pictures had become grainy.

The doorbell rang.

Selma felt a stab of anticipation and swore under her breath. She ran her hands through her hair and moved out into the hallway, where she pressed the electronic door opener on the door telephone without checking that it actually was Jesper at the door.

'Shit,' she whispered, and closed her eyes.

The pictures were pinned up in the bedroom. She should have displayed them in the living room. Laid them out on the floor there, for that matter. In bundles would have been easiest, and quick as a flash she tried to work out how long it would take to tear them all down again without spoiling the order in which they had been arranged.

Someone was tapping lightly on the front door.

She opened it.

'Hi,' he said, sounding despondent.

Selma did not reply, and merely led the way into the apartment. He followed and sat down on the settee.

'Water?' she asked, calling from the kitchen. 'Tea? Coffee?'

'Pepsi Max, if you have any, please.'

She returned and put a bottle down in front of him. No glass. She opened a bottle for herself, took a gulp and hovered beside him.

'Pepsi Max,' she said. 'Isn't that an odd choice for a chef?'

'I don't like water. It's too sweet. I drink Farris with meals, right enough.'

'Come with me to the bedroom.'

He gave her a blank look.

'All the photos are in there,' Selma added. 'I've sorted them and pinned them up.'

Jesper got to his feet and followed her.

'My goodness,' he said, stopping in the doorway. 'How many pictures have you got – a thousand?'

'Four hundred. And they're arranged in order of time. Starting over there …'

Selma pointed from the right-hand bedside table.

'And ending here.'

Crossing to the window side of the room, she put her palm on the big picture of the moment when Anine grabbed Sjalg with a wine glass teetering in her hand.

'These photos are from the minutes and seconds before Sjalg collapsed,' she said. 'And there are a few names here I need you to help me with.'

Jesper came across to her side of the bed.

'You see here,' Selma began, pointing. 'In these last few photographs there are no waiters or any other members of your staff.'

'We have a list of speeches and we stick to that. When it comes to pauses in serving tables and that kind of thing: during the speeches, the staff members have to keep quiet and withdraw.'

Selma nodded without taking her eyes off the photos.

'But here,' she said, running her index finger along a series of postcard-size photographs, '… there are a number I haven't managed to identify.'

'Hedvig Måsøy,' Jesper said, pointing at one of the young women lifting a plate from the table with her right hand while balancing two others in her left. 'She works at Ellevilt.'

Selma took the pen from the bedside table and used her teeth to remove the lid.

'Hedvig with a 'g' or a 'k'?' she murmured indistinctly with the lid in her mouth. 'Måsøy with "å" or two "a"s?'

'Does it make any difference?'

He smelled good. Dark and delicious. Like the forest floor, she thought, something dark, safe and reassuring. He must have come straight from the shower, and Selma now noticed that his hair was not completely dry. He had left the baseball cap at home this time, and until now she had thought that the moisture was hair gel. She slipped the pen lid into her back pocket.

'Yes, I have to be able to Google their names.'

'Svein Gunnar Jacobsen,' he said, putting his finger on a picture in which a man in black trousers and white shirt was pouring white wine into Jesso's glass. 'No hyphen between his first names. Jacobsen with a "c" and one "s". He's my sommelier. At Ellevilt, I mean.'

His finger moved again. His hands were well cared for. Clean, short nails with a suggestion of dry skin on the knuckles.

'Petter Moberg. Waiter. Written as it sounds.'

The snake's head was staring at Selma from his bare forearm.

'Are you not going to write it down?' he asked, moving his hand away.

'Yes, yes, of course.'

'Svein Gunnar, Petter and Hedvig have worked for me since the very beginning,' Jesper said. 'But she ...'

He had to crouch down to point at one of the photos near the foot of the wall.

'... is called Elisabeth something or other. She began as a waiter in Ellevilt only a month ago. I can find out her surname for you. Her, her and her ...'

His finger crept up the wall.

'... I don't know. They were young, as I recall. They couldn't serve alcohol, because they hadn't turned eighteen. We simply didn't have enough people, so the restaurant let us hire in some of their casual workers. Do you want me to ask them for their names?'

'Yes, please do.'

The snake was still staring at her. It was so lifelike, and from the tip of its fang hung a drop of poison. The liquid was green, and a reflection of light drew a tiny, shimmering star in the very centre.

'It looks sinister,' Selma said.

Jesper smiled and stretched out his arm towards her.

'This?'

'Yes.'

The reptile had devil eyes that stared at her, large as life. Cat's eyes. Selma placed two fingers on the snake's back, and ran them delicately along its diamond-patterned body. Narrower right behind the head, painstakingly broader all the way up until it wound around his arm and vanished. She caught it with her other hand and stroked Jesper's arm in a circular motion all the way up to his elbow. He smiled.

'We have an audience,' he said softly, glancing at the wall where hundreds of photos were displayed of happy wedding guests and one of the moment of death.

'It's fine,' Selma said.

She would regret this. This was not going to go well at all, of that she was well aware, even at that fateful moment.

The Basement

Both her parents had remembered her birthday by the time morning came.

Although it did not really matter: it was impossible to think of a worse birthday. Mum had sent a text message, adding seventeen roses, a shedload of hearts and a promise to drop in at five o'clock. Dad had brought her coffee in bed, though he still thought her too young. It was almost undrinkable. He had used just as much milk as coffee. The milk had obviously come straight from the fridge, and made the lukewarm liquid look like dishwater. Moreover, he had offered her hot toast and cheese. As if Mina had ever in her life eaten anything of the kind for breakfast. She would not receive her presents until the afternoon, he had told her with a strained smile; they both knew he had never bought her presents. It was Mum who organized things like that.

The house was empty.

The summer was truly Norwegian again.

It was August now and had rained yesterday. A light, cool breeze wafted through the open window, catching hold of the curtains. Mina felt a bit cold, and got out of bed. It was only a few minutes since Dad had left, so she wanted to wait a while before heading down to the basement. Sometimes he realized he had forgotten something and got his driver to bring him back.

Pulling on a pair of joggers and a T-shirt, she drew her hair up into a ponytail and stuck her bare feet into a pair of Birkenstocks. When she tried to shut the window, there was something wrong with the hinges. They had been slack for a long time but now the window stubbornly refused to close. Mina became annoyed, almost angry. She opened it wide and then pulled it back with all her might. The wood slid into place in the frame, but the glass cracked.

'Shit,' she said, biting her lip.

She was going to have to live with that damage for a long time. Dad did nothing at home these days. Other than when he headed down to the basement. He did not stay there for very long, and Mum had never asked him what he was doing down there. Not as far as Mina had heard, anyway. She probably wasn't interested. This house had turned into a place where no one bothered about anything.

Not even about Mina.

She put her earphones in place and keyed into Spotify for a song her parents had sung to her at her confirmation. That had been two years ago, when everyone believed that Dad's stint as a cabinet minister would only last until the election the following year. Her parents had still been friends, and they had rehearsed this song without Mina having any idea about it. Dad was pretty good on the guitar, even though he almost never took it out nowadays.

And we'll follow your footsteps

Want to know what you do and how you get on

Her lips moved along with the words. The song was a promise to a newborn child that its parents would never let it down. They would see her and love her, no matter what. Dad often used to say, long before her confirmation, that the most important mission in his life was to look after her. Always.

I put my hand on your cheek

My lips on your brow

And whisper words you can't understand

But still I'll protect you just the same

Dad had obviously given up on that job.

Mina was entirely alone in the house. It was half an hour since the black limousine had been here, and she finally made her way down to the basement. As she approached the door, she felt excited. She practically had butterflies in her tummy, as if there was something wonderful in there. Something that could explain everything, that could be used to make life good again, some kind of magic that would bring Mum back, and also repair everything that was now topsy-turvy though Mina was the only one who noticed.

There was nothing in here that she did not already know about.

The fluorescent tubes on the ceiling flickered repeatedly before they lit up the first basement room with a bluish-white light. Harsh, like a mental hospital depicted in films. Mina pulled out a couple of wire baskets from the units that ran the whole length of one wall. Children's clothes and old writing materials in one, *Spot the Dog* books and a collection of fairy tales by Hans Christian Andersen in the other. The baskets bulged here and there; they were far too full. Mum had just stuffed things in as Mina grew older. Along one wall, there was a long rail fixed at head height, with probably fifty articles of outer clothing of various sizes and types, including her snowsuit, as if Mum and Dad might have been planning several more children and had never quite managed to shrug off the idea.

Even years ago, it had been too late.

The air in here had the usual musty smell. Clothes and shoes and books and four schoolbags in a corner that stank of stale lunch packs. Dusty and slightly damp, and something cloying that she had never been able to identify.

At the far end, a door led into the storeroom, inside which was the expensive wine cabinet with slots for three hundred bottles, but which was almost empty. Mum said it was a waste of space, but Dad insisted that he was going to start collecting wine. Soon. When he had time.

The ventilation fan buzzed and whirred.

The radon extractor was placed high on the wall. As a little girl, Mina had been afraid of it. The display, the brand name and the pipes were attached in such a way that the grey box resembled one of the fish that lived many thousands of metres below the sea and looked terrifyingly dangerous.

In here, the smell was simply of the basement. Exactly like before. Nothing had changed since the last time she was here, which had actually been quite a long time ago. The safe in the corner had been here when they moved in. It was strange, Mum thought. Although it was substantial and built into the wall, it was only equipped with a four-digit code. Just as odd as the fact that the front door had three security locks, when it was really only a matter of walking around the house and smashing the verandah door if you wanted to break in.

Mina stood there for several minutes, looking around.

Thinking.

There must be something in the safe. Dad almost certainly did not come down here to drink wine on his own. In one corner, there was a completely unused carpenter's bench. It was now a number of years old, but there was no sign of Dad having hung about down here doing joinery work. No tools anywhere, no trace of sawdust on the floor.

At work Dad received new codes every single day, for his computer and office and everything else. He moaned about it all the time. At home, he usually used 0108, Mina's date of birth. Easier to remember, he said, as if there was any point in locking his computer at all.

She crept towards the grey metal door.

Turned the wheels to the day she was born. Grabbed the heavy, cold handle and tried to push it down but it would not budge.

1503. Mum's numbers. That didn't help.

For a second she was seized with something resembling panic. On her phone, everything locked if she keyed in the wrong code three times in succession. This door might well have the same security feature. Maybe it even triggered a siren. This was a cupboard for the safekeeping of genuine valuables, and it could well be that it was not quite as simple as she had thought.

The cupboard was old. It was mechanical. A sudden brainwave made her look along the floor. There was no electrical intake. Of course, it might be hidden in the wall. Or the mechanism could be battery-operated.

Slowly she turned the wheels one more time.

She had to try.

1201. Dad's own date. The handle would still not move, but no alarm went off.

Ten minutes later she had tried all the number combinations she could think of. Grandma's birthday. Grandma's date of death. She had to Google for her Grandpa's; she did not remember him very well, but there was quite a screed about him on Wikipedia. The accompanying picture was from some time in the seventies, and he was the spitting image of Dad. Or the other way round, as Grandma always commented when anyone pointed out the likeness.

Mina tried the postcode and the last three figures of Dad's phone number. And the first. And of hers: the first, the last and the four in the middle. Of Mum's, both backwards and forwards.

None of these numbers opened the safe.

Four digits. There were ten thousand possible combinations, she quickly worked out. Everything from 0000 to 9999. By now she had tried so many codes that she knew it would take less than a second to turn one of the wheels one notch with her right hand and feel the handle with her left. Sometimes it would be necessary to turn several of them, so if she allowed for an average of a second and a half between each of the numbers, it would take her 15,000 seconds to try each and every one of them.

Divided by 60 that would be 250 minutes.

It would take Mina four hours and ten minutes to go through each and every one. In all likelihood it would be quicker to find the right combination, since he would scarcely have used 9999. To be on the safe side, she tried the three last numbers in the numerical series she had already embarked upon.

The door still did not budge.

She reached a decision. Walked through the basement and out into the downstairs sitting room, from which she fetched a footstool and carried it back. Closing all the doors behind her, she placed the stool in front of the safe.

'0000,' she said in an undertone, and began to turn the dial.

AUTUMN

The Red Room

Selma Falck woke on something hard.

A floor, she discovered when she managed to open her eyes. Half her body was on the wooden boards, the other half on a rag rug. She lay curled up with something woolly warming her back. The wolf, she realized and abruptly sat up.

The dog did the same. It whimpered and wagged its tail and tried to lick her face.

'Stop that,' Selma mumbled, moving away.

She closed her eyes and struggled to remember.

She had fallen asleep in the snow. In a snowstorm that had threatened to turn into a blizzard. The dog had bitten her.

Selma opened her eyes again. Blue flecks from the dog's teeth were obvious on either side of her forearm. The canine teeth had left distinct marks. She gingerly rubbed her bare, tender skin.

The dog had certainly not bitten her, she remembered now. He, or perhaps it was a she, had tried to drag her. Had even managed to, for a metre or so, when the pain in her arm had become so bad that she had woken with a start. With one last shred of will to live, she had struggled to her feet. Staggered towards the cabin, the red building with a chimney from which she thought she had seen a plume of smoke. The snow flurries grew steadily thicker, but she had succeeded in reaching all the way to the front door.

Which was locked.

She had knocked.

The dog had barked.

Selma screamed at the top of her lungs, standing outside in the snow, and could swear there was smoke coming from the chimney. Someone was inside. It was warm in there. Someone had to open up, and she hammered on the door and wailed in chorus with the shaggy, hideous wolf-dog.

No one came. Nobody was there.

The feeling of surrender had been pleasant. There was a certain comfort in the unavoidable, and she had been battling for too long. Her life was over, and she accepted this with a sense of blessed relief. Only a faint spark was left behind her heart somewhere, and she sank on to the steps. Leaning her back against the white-painted door, she drew up her legs and let her head rest between her knees. The remains of the poncho hung loosely around her; she did not even have the strength to tuck it in.

She wanted to close her eyes and die, but her final glance landed on a small box beside the steps. It looked as if it had crashed down from the wall. Some kind of mailbox, even though no one up here would need anything of the sort. All the same, it was green, with an old-fashioned post horn painted in faded yellow.

There were no postal deliveries on the mountain plateau.

She leaned over the edge of the large block of stone that formed the top step. The lid of the box was easy to open.

There was a key inside it.

More than that she could not recollect.

Woof, the dog said to Selma, who was still sitting on the floor.

'Woof yourself,' she muttered, attempting to stand up.

She must have unlocked and opened the door. She must have walked in. The front door was closed and the dog was inside, she had obviously been conscious when she found the key and realized that life might be worth another go.

It was just impossible to remember.

She had heard of people leaving cabin keys in easily accessible places so far up in the mountains. It was a detail that could save someone's life, as now. It could also prevent a break-in at the cabin: if someone had come all the way up on to the mountain plateau to steal, then it was just as well not to let them damage doors and windows into the bargain.

She levered herself up by holding on to a rocking chair.

This was a living room. Larger than the one in which she had first woken, naked and suffering from loss of memory, and not quite so primitive. The small seating area was newer. The brightly coloured woollen blankets felt soft on her skin when she picked one up and wrapped it around her. There was a central lamp hanging from the ceiling, not a chandelier made of elk antlers with stumps of candles in it, like the last one. There were electric sockets in the walls, but she could not see any panel heaters. No sources of heat at all, just the obligatory Norwegian fireplace.

Something was glowing in there. It was impossible to take in.

Lots of ash and a couple of charred logs lay inside the hearth, but beneath the black cinders something was definitely smouldering. Selma tottered over to the fireplace and leaned against the rough stone of the chimneybreast. It felt warm to her hand. At least not cold. She removed the large spark guard, grabbed a poker from a cast iron rack and rooted around in the pile of ash. A little shower of orange sparks flew up and died away before drizzling down again.

Someone must have been here. Very recently.

Selma had just missed an encounter with humans. They must have been what she had heard, but they were no longer here. They had left, but that could not have been very long ago. A couple of hours at most. She used her hands to cover her eyes, which miraculously enough were able to shed tears.

This was of more concern to her than the pain she was suffering. Crying was both unwelcome and unfamiliar. Stiffness had taken over her body and made it difficult for her to move, but all the pain had eventually become just part of her. A normal condition. Tying the blanket around her neck like a cape, she snatched up a newspaper that had been stuffed into the firewood basket, pulled the pages apart and screwed them up. Her hands were shaking so violently when she put the paper into the hearth that she dropped it and had to use the poker to push the newspaper down into the ashes.

It flared up. Two little pieces of kindling crisscrossed against the hearth wall caught fire straight away when she put them in and blew on the flames. Selma straightened her back.

The dog whimpered.

'Are you a boy or a girl?' Selma murmured.

The dog did not answer and Selma gave him a severe look.

'Boy. You look like a wolf. A canis lupus. Lupus, that can be your name. It's dark in here.'

It could not possibly be almost dusk again. She had set off from the stone shelter at first light, and she had not walked all day. She would never have been able to survive that. The snowstorm must be smothering the daylight.

Selma looked around yet again.

The room was only a little larger than the living room in the other cabin. A dark-blue seating area with a painted coffee table sat in one corner. Ludo, Monopoly and The Vanished Diamond lay on top of it, stacked in order of box size, from the largest to the smallest. Underneath the windows on one side of the room was a shelf crammed with books. On the other side there was a small dining table and four wooden chairs with rush seats. On the walls hung three paintings of the landscape around the cabin as it probably looked in fine weather, all equally amateur and ghastly.

The living room had two doors in addition to the one leading into the hallway, one on either side of the fireplace. Selma guessed that the dining table was placed outside the partially open kitchen door.

It was virtually impossible for her to walk. Her muscles refused to cooperate. Selma could no longer lift her feet and instead slid them forward with each alternate step while supporting herself on whatever she could find.

Her guess had been correct. The kitchen was tiny, but still bigger than the last one. A light switch was mounted beside the doorframe and Selma flicked it on, but nothing happened. There was an old cooker with a small oven and two hotplates.

'There must be electricity here,' Selma said to Lupus.

The dog stared at her from the doorway.

Selma shuffled across to the sink and turned on the tap, but nothing happened there either.

Beside the worktop, someone had recently fitted a tall cupboard. The wood was lighter than the rest of the fittings, and there was still a faint smell of newly sawn timber. Selma opened the cupboard door.

'Good God,' she whispered. 'Thank you.'

Lupus growled, but that no longer bothered her.

The cupboard was full of food. Joika hamburgers and tins of Trøndersodd stew, peas and four tins of asparagus soup. Swedish meatballs and a jar of something that looked like beetroot. There was crispbread too, three full packets of different kinds.

Stabburet's liver paté, the coarse kind in portion packs. Pickled cucumbers and mackerel in tomato sauce. Selma counted eighteen tins of food before she grabbed a packet of Jaffa cakes and tore it open. Three of them fell on the floor and the dog gobbled them up before Selma had time to react.

'I don't think chocolate is good for dogs,' she complained with her mouth full.

Maybe it was OK for wolves.

Selma felt giddy. The lump of cocoa, dry biscuit and sweet orange slop would not go down. It seemed to grow inside her mouth, sticking to her palate, she couldn't breathe, and she had to hold on to the worktop and look down to avoid fainting. Her gaze fell on the bottom shelf.

She began to laugh. She spat and laughed and swallowed. Coughed and gasped and retched until she had cramp in her diaphragm and vomited green bile streaked with chocolate into the sink. Lupus backed out slowly and lay down in the living room with his head between his paws.

Selma wiped her mouth. She was still laughing, a rasping laughter verging on hysteria.

On the bottom shelf of the newly built cupboard, five big bottles of Pepsi Max were lined up beside an unopened bag of dog food.

SUMMER

The Codes

The code was this year's date. 2018.

It had taken Mina an hour and a quarter to arrive at the correct combination of numbers. When the metal handle had unexpectedly slid down, she had felt a stab of anticipation and fear. The handle was stiff and had to be twisted to ninety degrees. Once it was perpendicular to the four little numbered wheels, the heavy door allowed itself to open: the safe, however, was almost empty.

Mina got up from the stool, inhaled deeply a few times and then held her breath for a few seconds. All she could hear was the faint drone of the ventilation system. There was still no one at home.

The cupboard was almost a metre and a half high and maybe half a metre in width and was divided into four sections with three shelves. The two spaces near the middle were empty. There was a folder of some kind on the top shelf which Mina took out and opened carefully.

Nothing but a sheaf of documents.

Her birth certificate. Exam certificates and diplomas. Papers that did not mean too much but were worth keeping in a fire-proof safe all the same. Mina riffled quickly through them all without noticing anything in particular. She tucked them all back into the folder and returned it to exactly the same place.

At the bottom of the safe she saw a wooden box and a laptop.

If Dad had been doing something down here, it must have some connection with the laptop. That was the only logical conclusion, but the box looked more alluring and she drew it out carefully. After a furtive glance around, she laid it down on the carpenter's bench.

It was more of a casket, really, and beautiful in an old-fashioned way. Something Grandma would have liked. There was monogram engraved on the lid, surrounded by various flowers that Mina immediately recognized. A little bouquet of scilla, that Dad called Siberian squill, and something that looked like coltsfoot. And a solitary, fragile plant she recognized as either a white or blue wood anemone.

The monogram was an H with a 7 braided through it. Since it also had a crown on top, it might well have belonged to a king. Harald, perhaps. Mina dismissed the idea, because Harald was fifth in the line of Haralds. His father's name had been Olav, and in her haste she couldn't think further back than that.

The casket was locked.

'Shit,' Mina said.

All of a sudden she remembered. During the war, the king had been called Haakon the seventh. Dad had taken her to the cinema to see *The King's Choice* a couple of years ago. She had wept buckets, especially over the three little royal children who had been forced to flee from everything they knew.

Mina's curiosity was piqued. She took her mobile out of the pocket in her baggy jogging trousers. One search was enough: the monogram on the casket did in fact belong to the man who had been king in wartime Norway.

What her father was doing with such a casket was something she could not fathom. Mina had never set eyes on it before, and no one had ever spoken of it. If it had really belonged to a king, it might well be valuable.

She studied the incredibly tiny lock. Years ago she had been given an old but unused diary by her grandmother. It was covered in pink, padded plastic and was something Grandma had found in the attic. Mina did not keep a diary, and did not care for the colour either. The padlock, however, had fascinated her. She was about eight years old at the time and had believed that a minuscule heart-shaped padlock with the smallest key in the world was a lovely thing to own.

The key for this lock must be almost as tiny.

On the floor, immediately below the radon pump, there was a toolbox. She opened it and peered down into the jumble of screws and nails mixed up with screwdrivers, a couple of hammers and all sorts of other junk. She rummaged around and took out a long screw, but it was too large. Instead she grabbed a little awl. She tentatively touched her index finger with the point. Before Mina had time to think twice, she had inserted the tip into the old keyhole. Half a centimetre or so, before she carefully turned it round. Exactly as she had had to do with a darning needle once years ago when she had lost the key for the heart-shaped padlock.

The click was barely audible.

The lock opened at the first attempt. Mina pushed aside the little catch and lifted the lid.

Some sort of book lay on top. A pamphlet, really, with a sloppily drawn map of Norway on the cover. It was not even a real cover, but more like the first page of a loosely bound booklet. Mina opened it and read.

She understood precious little of it, but it was about something called *Stay Behind*. Mina had never heard of *Stay Behind*, other than that it was an English expression. She leafed through the booklet, carefully so that it would not fall apart, but quickly laid it down again.

The two memory sticks were far more interesting. Each was in a separate plastic bag though they looked identical. She pushed the casket further along the workbench to make room for the cheap laptop: Mina had no idea why this had to be stored in a safe.

The computer would not switch on.

She tried several times. Lifted it up, peering and poking at the whole of the machine in her search for concealed switches. There were none. The laptop might have no charge left, of course. Mina checked the shelves in the safe for cables, but found none.

The mobile phone she found in the casket must be an old one. It was chunky and heavy, and the display was extremely simple. In fact it most resembled some kind of walkie-talkie, and she let it lie.

It was now nearly half past twelve. Dad never came home at this time of day and Mum had said she would pop in at five. After mulling this over for a few seconds, Mina decided to take a chance. She stuffed the two little bags in her pocket, replaced everything else in the casket, put it back inside and locked the safe.

She had never run up the two flights of stairs to her room as fast as she did then.

Slightly out of breath, she roused her own MacBook from sleep mode and, placing the plastic bags on her desk, she opened one.

There was also a note inside. Accounts, it said in simple hand-writing. Mina inserted the memory stick into her own machine. It contained only one document, a single sheet that was not particularly comprehensive. She counted eight lines consisting of letters and numbers: four letters at the beginning of each line, followed by two columns of figures.

They could be codes. Without anything to work on, there was no way of cracking them. The strings of numbers conveyed absolutely no meaning as they now stood, until it dawned on her that these might refer to bank accounts.

Maybe these were eight bank accounts, or even thirty-six, since there were two rows of numbers on each line. She flipped open her mobile phone case and took out her own bankcard. The number had eleven digits. First four figures, then two, and then five. She thought she had heard that the first four of these said something about which bank you used, but she was not entirely certain.

The numbers on the memory sticks were not written in groups of eleven.

Each number contained fifteen digits, written consecutively. She had no idea what the letters meant either. On further reflection, she might have guessed correctly. The document contained codes, which, once decoded, would yield bank account numbers.

She removed the memory stick and dropped it back in the bag before inserting the second stick.

On this one also there was only one document stored. On the other hand, it ran to many pages. The pages were not numbered, but she counted twelve, with a long list of names on every page, in groups that varied in size. Each group was listed in alphabetical order. After each of the names there were three letters and sixteen numbers. Yet another code, she assumed. The groups had strange names. One was called Varg. Another was Skuld. The very last of the six groups was named Manus.

Once again she picked up her mobile phone and started to Google. Some of the individual names on the list were fairly common, such as Bjørn Hansen. That gave 8,600,000 hits. Others, such as Sophus Trønes Færder, did not turn up a single one. No one was called by that name, at least according to the internet.

Mina was none the wiser.

Dad harboured many secrets, she was aware of that. Everyone in government did. Especially the Prime Minister and the Minister of Defence, and the Minister of Foreign Affairs, of course. But also her father. State secrets, but the government's lips were also probably sealed about a lot of other things that might not be so dangerous. The state budget, for example, was kept super secret until it was all made public, so strictly under wraps that the printing workshop was kept under police guard. At least so she had heard. Sometimes, when her Mum and Dad were still talking nicely to each other, Dad could sometimes just smile at one of Mum's questions and say that he could not utter a word. That he had a duty of confidentiality.

Both when he had been a lawyer and through all his years as a cabinet member.

What was so incomprehensible was not that Dad had secrets, but that they were kept in a safe in the basement of Lofthus terrasse. Even though they had never had a burglary, and the safe was built into the wall, it had not taken Mina too long to open it. It was far from secure. Admittedly, the Justice Department had moved to temporary premises in Nydalen after a terrorist had blown the government quarter sky high, but Mina had herself experienced the strict security you had to pass through in order to arrive at her father's office.

Maybe he was a member of a club. Or organization.

Possibly this had nothing to do with his job at all, and it was merely practical to keep it all in the safe. Like a normal cupboard, in a sense.

Mina sat looking at all the names on the screen.

Dad was a member of the Conservative Party. And of the parish council at Grefsen church. Of the Oslo Council for Religious Cooperation. Dad hardly ever spoke about God, and only attended church on special occasions, but sometimes she had seen him pray. Very old-fashioned, with hands joined, without being embarrassed in the slightest.

Mum was an atheist, and sometimes swore like a trooper. Mina thought that it all might have fared better with them if they had a shared outlook on life. In everything, so to speak. She felt a sudden urge to cry, and tugged hard at her hair.

'Get a grip,' she hissed under her breath.

Moreover, Dad was an honorary member of the Norwegian Guide and Scout Association. In the past, he and Mum had played bridge once a month at Thorbjørn and Guri's house, but that couldn't really be called a club or an organization.

Mina felt completely at a loss. Her excitement at discovering what Dad had hidden in the basement had, for the first time in ages, enabled her to push aside thoughts of everything that was so awful. The subject she had really wanted to talk to him about, but was impossible to tell anyone. At least not to anyone having such a hard time as he was.

Just as she was about to uncouple the memory stick, she had the sudden impulse to take a copy of the contents. She changed the memory sticks and did the same with the other one, taking care to replace them in the correct bags, and went back down to the basement. When she had put everything back in the king's casket in exactly the same order as when she had opened it, it struck her that the little booklet might well be the key to the entire mystery.

It lay on top, and she picked it up again.

It had been written on an old-fashioned typewriter, the kind that Grandma had owned. Big and heavy, with a kind of ball in the middle of the opening where you inserted the paper. The ball was embossed with reversed letters and symbols, and twirled around quickly to the right place when someone pressed on a key. A ribbon impregnated with printer's ink moved on a roll from one side to the other between the ball and the paper and it had been difficult to get hold of those coloured ribbons during the last few years of Grandma's life.

Grandma had explained that some letters became worn after such a long period of use. In the end someone had come to repair hers and had replaced the ball. Mina could see that the print on the 'e's in the booklet were fainter than the other letters, and 'e' was the most common sound in the Norwegian language. Also, the lines were not quite straight. Here and there, a letter was fractionally out of alignment. Especially the 'g's, which were too low.

She Googled *Stay Behind*.

Wow. Nearly two million hits. She rapidly understood that the reason for this was that these words were also a common word combination in English, but the top result was from Wikipedia. The heading was 'Norwegian occupation resilience in the post-war period'.

After the Second World War, no one had occupied Norway, was Mina's reaction.

Norway was a member of NATO, and even though Trump was a raving lunatic, the generals had him under control. No one wanted war. Norway was not going to be occupied, and so had no need for any resilience group to counter such a thing.

Nowadays the battle was about the climate. It was against racism and nationalism, and against anti-Semitism, hatred of Islam and contempt for humanity. Not against war in Norway. The Russians treated gays dreadfully and had taken possession of Crimea. Putin was a shady character, but Russia would never dare to take over Norway. Neither would anyone else.

This was ancient claptrap.

Just something that Dad had to look after. Something antiquarian. The casket itself was probably valuable, and that was why he kept it in the safe. It did not contain anything to explain why Mina's parents were going to separate, or why Dad was behaving so strangely. No answer, nothing of value. She was tempted to tear the booklet to shreds, but in the end she pulled herself together. Replaced it neatly before it crossed her mind that her father had only recently set up a separate Apple-ID for her. Until six months ago, they had shared iCloud, which ensured that he received all her pictures and screen dumps on his devices.

That was no longer their arrangement.

Like a shot, she took a photo of the pamphlet. Flicking through, she took several more. By the time she had reached halfway through the little book, she lost interest. She put everything back, locked the safe and returned the stool to the sitting room.

In all honesty this was the worst birthday in Mina's seventeen-year life.

The Photograph

Outside, first light was dawning. Selma woke and automatically glanced at her wrist, but she had taken off her watch the night before.

She had taken everything off that night and now knew that Jesper Jørgensen slept absolutely soundlessly. He lay there as if dead, on his stomach with his head resting on his forearm and the quilt only half covering him. The snake's head protruded from beneath his cheek, but the wide-open devil's eyes were no longer quite so scary. Jesper's eyelashes were so long that they had become tangled overnight.

He looked like a teenager.

The sun rose about five a.m. this early in August and Selma guessed that it was quarter to. Wide-awake, she felt a welcome, familiar sense of peace. About the same as after the best poker nights, or the way it had felt in the old days to win an important match in extra time.

Endorphins, she knew, and her body still felt full of them. Besides, she was thirsty, pretty hungry, and had an insistent urge to go to the toilet. As quietly as she could, she crept out of bed. Once, she nearly lost her balance and had to use the wall for support. One of the enlarged photographs became detached and fell to the floor. Selma picked it up. She could not see the drawing pin anywhere; it must have rolled under the bed.

The curtains were fluttering and a shaft of morning light landed on the picture she held in her hand.

Anine looked really happy. Beautiful, with that blonde hair of hers, so different from Selma's own dark-brown locks: loose, full tresses on a bridal gown she had gone all the way to New York to have tailor-made for her. The look she sent Sjalg was full of admiration and gratitude. Full of love. It was certainly an incredibly attractive picture of two young people on the greatest day of their lives so far. Sjalg's raised glass of water relayed reflections of the bright sunlight on Anine's tiara. It could not be real: all those diamonds would have cost millions.

A tiara, Selma thought, with a sudden stab of irritation.

What vanity.

The sight of the half-filled glass of water reminded her why she had got out of bed. Just as she was about to put the photo down on the bedside table, snuggle into her dressing down and go to the toilet, she froze. Held the picture closer to her eyes and tried to catch more light by moving all the way to the window.

There was something about Sjalg's glass. Something that made absolutely no sense.

Selma was no longer paying any attention to Jesper. She tore off six more photos, so recklessly that several more drawing pins fell on the floor. Unconcerned, she grabbed her dressing gown and headed out to the open-plan kitchen, leaving the door wide open behind her. Placing the photos on the worktop, she switched on the lights beneath the top cupboards and slipped into her dressing gown without taking her eyes off Sjalg's glass of water.

It had been so hot that day of the wedding. Really hot, more than thirty degrees Celsius and not a breath of air.

The restaurant had not stocked Pepsi Max and they had run out of ice cubes before the dinner started. People had become prematurely drunk on champagne and white wine to quench their thirst and Selma herself had been forced to make do with lukewarm, sweet Mozell. The photographing of the bridal couple had taken longer than anticipated, as one of the staff had explained with an apologetic smile.

There were ice cubes in Sjalg's glass.

Selma definitely thought so. It was the ice, not the water or the glass, that had refracted the light towards Anine.

Selma laid the photos side by side across the worktop, now concentrating for the first time on all the glasses of water, both the ones set in front of the bride and groom, and all the others it was possible to see.

Sjalg was the only one who had ice cubes.

Selma blinked. Maybe she was mistaken.

She should have had a magnifying glass. The only person she knew who possessed such a thing was Einar, and she did not want to go there. Unceremoniously, she rushed into the bedroom, where Jesper was still sleeping, in the same immovable pose. Selma snatched up her iPad from the bedside table and went out again, this time closing the door. She sat down on the settee, hoisted her feet on to the coffee table and opened the enormous file of wedding photographs she had received from Runhild Petterson. It took her ten minutes to find the picture whose printout she had just examined. It was sharp enough in the ordinary format and just as beautiful, bright and overflowing with summer happiness. Using her thumb and forefinger, she enlarged the water glass, and it grew gradually grainier.

She might be right, but realized she could not be certain.

'Jesper,' she called out.

Not a sound from the bedroom.

'Jesper!'

Still total silence. She got to her feet, picked up the copy from the worktop and returned to the bedroom again. Perching on the edge of her side of the bed, she stroked his hair.

'Jesper,' she said yet again.

He grunted. Pushed her hand away, cast around for the pillow and put it over his head. Turned his back on her and tucked the quilt in behind him like a shield against the unwelcome disturbance.

Exactly like Johannes, Selma thought.

Her son, on all the Sunday mornings when she had refused to let him waste a whole day off in bed. When he had been seventeen or thereabouts.

Her body suddenly drained of endorphins and she stood up again.

'Jesper,' she said, harshly now. 'Wake up. I need to ask you something.'

'What is it?' he mumbled, curling up even more.

'During the wedding,' she began, '… didn't you actually run out of ice cubes very early on?'

He failed to respond. From his regular breathing, she understood that he had already fallen asleep again. Just like Johannes.

'This is important,' she said in a loud voice. 'I remember asking for ice cubes, and someone said you had none left. Do you know anything about that?'

When he still failed to answer, she yanked the quilt off the bed. He whimpered and curled up into a ball, still with the pillow pressed against his head.

'Yes,' she heard from the depths of the mattress.

'When did that happen?'

Jesper reluctantly sat up, retrieved the quilt, put the pillow behind his back and rubbed his eyes demonstratively.

'What bloody time is it?'

'Just past five. But answer me, please.'

He yawned, smiled sleepily and stretched one hand lazily towards her.

'Lie down again, won't you?'

'No.'

'Yes, please do.'

Selma stood up.

'This is important, Jesper. I have to know if you ran out of ice cubes before the meal was served.'

He lethargically scratched the stubble on his chin.

'Yes, we did. We'd used so much that the ice machine couldn't keep up. Also, it was hot as hell, and the bridal couple never fucking turned up. They were nearly an hour late.'

'You could have sent someone out to buy more?'

'We did that too. One of the boys took my company car and was to go to the nearest shop and buy thirty bags of Mr Iceman.'

He patted the sheet beside him encouragingly and gave her a crooked smile. Selma ignored him.

'Lovely dressing gown,' he said. 'Please take it off.'

'When did he come back?'

'Never.'

'What?'

'The fucking car broke down. By the time the guy had arranged to have it towed away and came back, without any ice, the bride-groom was dead and the party was over.'

Selma stood looking at him. He stared back at her.

'What is it?'

'Look at this,' she said, passing the iPad to him. 'First of all at the original photograph.'

He grabbed the tablet and looked at the photo without much interest.

'The bridal couple,' he said. 'I suppose this is right before he died. I wasn't there, I was in the kitchen.'

'Enlarge the glass of water,' she said. 'The one he's holding in his hand.'

Jesper placed two fingers on the iPad and did as she said.

'Bloody hell. Aren't those ice cubes?'

'I think so. No one else had ice cubes, only him. You can see that here and here and here.'

She scattered the other pictures over the bed. He studied them and returned to the iPad.

'But ... what does this mean, in actual fact? How could he have had ice cubes when we had run out an hour earlier? And what's the meaning of that, do you think?'

'That's what I'm going to find out,' Selma said. 'And in record time, you can be sure of that. Just sleep on. I'll be back in a couple of hours.'

'But ... where are you going?'

'I'm going to visit Anine,' she said, heading for the bathroom.

'But it's only five o'clock in the morning!'

She did not even take the trouble to answer: she was too concerned with rushing to make it to the toilet.

Berit Ullern

There was no longer any doubt.

Tryggve had broken his promise. Rugged/Storm-scarred had been activated.

The Major had spent all night collating the information she had gathered during the past fortnight. Partly by following the news and searching on the internet and partly by using her contacts.

And they were extensive.

When, as a young lieutenant, she had been contacted by Ellev Trasop, Berit Ullern had felt honoured. Despite the already elderly man having spent his life in the service of the trade union movement and never having had a formal military career, his efforts during the Second World War had been formidable. She had great respect for him. Berit herself had begun in the Home Guard Youth as a sixteen-year-old and gone straight into the army as soon as she had finished high school.

When Ellev got in touch with her for the first time, she was twenty-seven. The year was 1987, and letters were still delivered by the postman. She was stationed in Bardufoss. Her family in Tønsberg rarely wrote. The envelope with her rank and name handwritten on thick, quality paper from the Alvøen paper mill was so welcome that she had waited until bedtime to open it. The contents were short and succinct: she was invited to an overnight stay at Ellev Trasop's cabin in Nordmarka at the first opportunity.

Which had been a fortnight later, from Thursday to Friday.

The first evening had been a test, as she had quickly appreciated. He interrogated her. About her political standpoint, her personal preferences and her family situation. She was not very interested in sharing the last of these with him: her parents had never entirely recovered from their only child refusing to study law and enter her father's well-established legal practice. She had devoted her life to the army, and on the love interest front she had painfully little to report.

He was obviously looking for something of the kind.

Her stay had lasted precisely twenty-four hours. The cabin was located in Mylla, an old Finnish settlement from the 1600s where many of the Labour Party's old guard lived. Ellev's red cabin was in a secluded spot near the lake. Despite the density of the cabins and the many cross-country skiers in the area, they talked undisturbed throughout her stay. The then sixty-nine-year-old man was a character who made a greater impression on her than she had anticipated. Before her trip, she had re-read his biography, and this turned out to be useful when she now and again, while he was in the kitchen or outside to fetch more firewood, had the opportunity to examine more closely the peculiar memorabilia with which the living room was crammed. Grenades and a home-made radio, a German helmet with four skulls etched on the back. A rifle with four notches on the stock. In a modest wooden box on the mantelpiece that she dared to open, lay Haakon VII's Freedom Cross. The blue ribbon was faded, and the original white enamel Maltese cross was almost yellow. Berit managed to close the box just in time before Ellev came back.

He did not get to the point on that occasion. Instead he lectured her, in between his questions. About the end of the war, the division of Europe and the growing fear of the Soviet Union in the initial years of peace. About cold war and hot weapons and his own scepticism that it was all really coming to an end. Glasnost and Perestroika were both well and good, but Mikhail Gorbachev moved forward far too fast. He was going to lose control. The fact that pure Gorbamania was all the rage in the West did not mean that he was equally loved by his own people.

'Russia is Russia,' he said time and again. 'And so it will always be. A vast, strong, proud and stubborn neighbour. Dangerous, in other words.'

Berit Ullern agreed with him at that time and she still believed that Ellev Trasop had been right.

Now more than ever.

She logged off from her computer. It was already half past five in the morning but she was not tired. She was afraid.

People were naïve. For many years after the fall of the Berlin Wall, surely and steadily, Russia had ramped up the tension between East and West. NATO of course had to ensure that balance was maintained. The Russians still rattled their sabres all the same. Unannounced exercises in the immediate vicinity of NATO. Movements of materials and troops, often cloaked in secrecy, and sometimes all the way to the borders.

Most Norwegians did not understand this. Not even the attack on Crimea and the undercover warfare in the Ukraine was taken seriously.

People could not do any better. Know any better. They didn't want to know. Even in Parliament there were people who were deadly serious in their belief that Norway should sign the UN treaty banning nuclear weapons. As if nuclear weapons could be removed unilaterally. As if any nation at any time had achieved anything whatsoever by holding their hands in the air.

It was losers who behaved like that. If you held your hands in the air, you were destined to lose.

She poured the now-lukewarm dregs of coffee from a thermos and tossed them down her throat. Stood up and stretched her back.

Berit Ullern was fifty-eight, unmarried, childless and in good shape. She seldom watched TV, but read a great deal. Registered her vote every second year, always Conservative, and had a talent for discretion that had already impressed Ellev Trasop when she was only twenty-seven years old.

Two years later, the day after the Berlin Wall fell, he had invited her again.

In November 1989 they had met at Mylla for the second time.

Nothing had changed, and she was given an outline of what was expected of her. In silence she accepted her orders, thereafter carried them out to the letter, and then followed from a distance as all the Stay Behind groups throughout the whole of Europe were disbanded within a short period of time.

Except this one. The one that Peder Mejer and Ellev Trasop had the foresight to spend the late eighties hiding from sight.

In 1991, the organization was ready, and Berit Ullern became a board member of what was subsequently called only the Council. A powerful organization, with capital, weapons and relevant personnel. A bulwark against what might still happen. It was self-evident that the police and the military still had their secret services: the problem was that they were too weak. Too open. Being subject to political control considerably hindered them from doing what was sometimes strictly necessary. A Stay Behind group could never be subject to the control of outsiders. It was part of the nature of the expression that they had to be able to act freely. And quickly, just as only four weeks after Ellev had requested that she apply for a job in the banking sector, her services were engaged by DnB, Norway's leading bank. With the explosive development of the international financial market, they needed someone on the inside.

Berit picked up the two memory sticks and dropped them into their respective bags.

Ellev had not trusted Tryggve. On 17 May he had asked her to visit him in his old, dilapidated villa in Hasle. He had looked so frail, but nevertheless determined, when he had given her the memory sticks and a satellite telephone. He made her repeat the passwords a number of times, until she knew them by heart. They would unlock the codes for her. Tryggve had already known them for many years. His father had taught him them and Ellev had entered into a pact with Peder Mejer that he could not break.

Tryggve had inherited the casket, as agreed.

Until a year or two ago, he had appeared the perfect leader for the Council. Now he had changed so much that the pact should really have been broken.

Berit would have to ensure he did not misuse the casket.

She was the Major, and it was the Major who would make sure that the Council and all its resources were safeguarded until the time came when there would really be use for them. To be on the safe side, Ellev had removed Harlequin's codes from the casket.

That was what had surprised Berit most.

Ellev had died the very next day, and the gravity of the situation had sunk in for Berit. She had done her level best, done as she had been ordered to do, and demanded a vote on Rugged/Storm-scarred. In addition she had insisted that Tryggve give her his word.

She quickly gathered up the papers from the printer drawer and went into the bedroom, where she opened the wardrobe door. Leaning inside, she pressed a button and an internal door opened almost soundlessly. She picked up the document Tryggve had called Rugged/Storm-scarred from its discreet hiding place. She had destroyed the other copies and memorized this one almost word for word.

Once she had stashed the papers from the printer in the wardrobe, she was sure.

This was how it had to be, she thought, as she studied the front page of the document.

Sjalg Petterson's death was the opening gambit of the operation, even though liquidation was only mentioned in general terms in Tryggve's plan. How he had managed to do this without access to Harlequin was difficult to comprehend. But it had been competently executed, Berit had to admit, and it was a gift that the man had been hyper-allergic. The police did not seem interested in the case at all. The recent arrest in Randaberg, when a Norwegian-Russian married couple had been charged with growing hash, was the result of a conspiracy painstakingly described in Tryggve's document. The pair had never been interested in hash, but were instead involved in extensive activity centred on disseminating Russian propaganda on social media. In perfect Norwegian, and distributed to a total of fifty-three different accounts. They often provided links to articles from Russian websites and news channels loyal to the state, willingly translated for interested Norwegian readers. The aim had been to goad increasing numbers of people to anger about the strict policy Norway had adopted towards Russia. The couple had particularly concentrated on the part of the population whose views located them on the far left or far right, and they had succeeded. Now they would be behind bars for a substantial period of time because someone had set up a whole little narcotics plantation in the crawl space under their house and then set the house on fire a week later. The panicking couple had been struggling to dismantle the hash farm of which they swore they had no knowledge when the fire brigade, and then the police, arrived.

The little 'editorial office' in Murmansk, on the other hand, was an out-and-out troll factory. A producer of lies and fake news, with particular focus on making the population of the most northerly regions of Norway better disposed towards the Russians. In Rugged/Storm-scarred, it emerged that the preference was to destroy the editorial headquarters through hacking, that is to say from Norway, but in the worst-case scenario a physical assault might prove necessary.

Sabotage on Russian territory.

Berit Ullern shook her head in exasperation. She had no idea which of the alternatives had been used, but in any case it had caused a very minor diplomatic crisis to blow up between Norway and Russia. That Putin's regime suspected Norway in particular was not in the least strange, taking into consideration the real mission of the little pack of Russian journalists up there in the north.

She leafed through the document.

Blackmail was also an important weapon. This could be based on the kompromat already in the possession of their intelligence groups, but the action also involved re-laying honey traps and other use of people's weaknesses and foibles. She assumed that Pål Poulsen's recent abrupt departure from his post as first deputy leader of the Progress Party was the result of many years spent amassing the dirty linen of participants both great and small in Norwegian public life.

On the whole, revelations were sharp weapons. Everyone had secrets.

Sabotage, especially directed at the internet, comprised a considerable part of Rugged/Storm-scarred. For example, monitoring and terminating bot factories and automatically generating profiles that produced an enormous number of messages in order to create trending topics on social media.

The Twitter campaign against Default.no, which had attracted a huge response and pretty dramatic consequences for the website, might also have been part of Tryggve Mejer's misuse of the country's most secret occupation resilience group.

Operation Rugged/Storm-scarred included most of these tactics.

Berit Ullern would not normally have shed a tear over what had happened, And was about to happen if Tryggve were allowed to continue. She was just as anxious and worried as he was about the climate of debate in both Norway and the rest of the Western world. A brutalization of verbal exchanges was taking place, something that made them less interesting. Which again was a threat to democracy. The more-or-less undisguised attempts to exacerbate all this on the Russian side meant the situation was going from bad to worse.

Not a single tear would she have shed.

And not a single thing would she have done to stop Tryggve, if it were not for the danger of compromising the entire apparatus.

The organization, which had been assured of power and means by Peder and Ellev throughout the eighties and had kept an eye on Norway's security since the beginning of the nineties, was intended to protect the populace from an actual occupation. Norway could again be conquered, in the real meaning of the word. In Berit Ullern's opinion, the risk of Russian invasion increased with every year that passed, in inverse proportion to the will of politicians to look that same risk straight in the eye and ensure the country could really defend itself. According to serious, professional calculations, North-Finnmark could be captured in twenty-four hours. Since any such attack would probably be parallelled by conflicts in other locations, it was far from certain that NATO would or could come to the rescue.

These were the situations Peder and Ellev had envisioned. It had been on that basis, with that kind of mandate, that she had obediently placed herself at the disposal of Ellev Trasop when he had judged her and found her to have sufficient gravitas for his liking.

It was to counter such an eventuality that she had sworn allegiance: Norway must be able to fight back when the Russian superpower called the shots.

She placed the document in the little cupboard inside the wardrobe. Pressed the button once again, and heard the click of the lock closing before she put back the clothes hangers so that the cupboard disappeared from view.

Tryggve was using up his legacy from Ellev and Peder.

Berit knew she would have to stop him. And do so at any price.

The Confrontation

Anine sat beside the window ledge cradling a half-empty mug of tea in her hands.

She had watched the morning slowly settle over Oslo. Autumn had only just begun to nibble at night temperatures, and the huge oak tree in the neighbouring garden was already completely yellow.

The city was still in holiday mood, and the new school term had not yet started. It was as if the intense, long and totally abnormal summer had exhausted both humans and the natural world.

It felt good to sit like this and just think. Probably she was too young to have really understood how important funeral rituals were for people, she realized. But now she was wiser. The service in Bakkehaugen church had been awful. All the same, it had been a worthwhile marker of the finality of death, and that life must be kick-started again. The days were already improving but the nights were still difficult, and last night had been really dreadful.

Long before the woman walking towards the house was close enough to recognize, Anine knew it was her mother.

Selma Falck walked like a teenager. Quickly, with a spring in her step, as if she was always about to break into a sprint. She was carrying her bag with the strap across her chest, leaning forward slightly, as she did no matter where she was going. She had always been like that. When Anine was little, their Sunday trips to Marka had been a nightmare, with her mother tearing along at breakneck speed a few hundred metres ahead of her father, Johannes and herself. As soon as the three of them had caught up with her mother, waiting impatiently, they had to move on. Never any breaks. Never any jelly babies or caramels on the hilltops, the way her friends told her they got 'petrol' on hiking trips. Fortunately these excursions were few and far between since, until Anine was ten, they had spent most of their weekends at handball tournaments. The intention had been for Selma's children to develop a love of handball. When Anine was finally old enough to refuse, her mother had shrugged grumpily and said that no one should be forced to do anything. For the next seven years, Anine had spent six evenings a week at the Norwegian Ballet School, but her mother had not turned up a single time to the dancing displays held each term. Selma had not even bothered to attend the public performances, in full costume, with guest soloists from Russia and the Ukraine.

Her father had come. Her father had paid the termly fees and all the equipment, ferried her to and fro, and even taught himself how to prep pointe shoes by studying videos on YouTube.

Jesso took pictures of his daughter and was terribly proud.

Anine's father was a proper dad, and had always been so.

She had no intention of letting her mother in. Out of the question. It was not even six o'clock in the morning, an ungodly time to come visiting.

Just as she made up her mind, her mother appeared. Now she was near enough for Anine to see her face, it too enviably youthful. Her eyes glinted when the two of them made eye contact. She motioned with her hand, presumably asking to come in. Anine shook her head. Her mother flung out her arms in a gesture of desperation, then pressed the palms of her hands together and raised them towards her, as if in prayer.

Anine sighed. Slid down from the window ledge, put down her mug and went to open the door. She tried to be as quiet as possible to avoid waking her neighbours on the ground floor. For the same reason, she opened the door immediately to prevent her mother from ringing the doorbell. She put her finger to her lips and walked just as quietly up again with her mother at her heels.

'What are you doing here?' Anine said as soon as they were back in her apartment.

'I have to ask you about something. Something important.'

'You could have phoned.'

'How are you doing?'

Anine stood in the middle of the room, shaking her head.

'How do you think I'm doing, Selma? What do you think it's like to be me after all that's happened in the last few weeks?'

'Selma?' her mother queried. 'Have you decided to call me Selma now?'

'Isn't that OK?'

'No. I don't think it is, actually. I'm your mum.'

'That's a question fairly open for discussion, really. What do you want?'

'Can I sit down?'

Anine did not want Selma to become settled. She was already regretting having let her in, as she had finally broken up with her mother, something that had been years overdue. When, one November evening the previous year, her father had sat sobbing in front of the fire at Ormøya, something had shattered for both him and Anine. Mum had lost everything through gambling, including her family. The only possibility Dad had to save the house, Anine's childhood home, was to let Grandma move in. With her money he could buy out Selma, and Selma would avoid going to jail.

Mum had hoodwinked her entire family.

Anine studied her as she stood there in the doorway. Selma was taller than her, probably by seven or eight centimetres, dark-haired, and her eyes turned black when she was passionate about something. Straight, broad shoulders, narrow hips and with a lightness in her body that failed to match the nearly fifty-two years she was carrying. Her wide mouth had an unusually large Cupid's bow, as if she had received careful surgery for a harelip. Her teeth were so white that they must be bleached, and it was impossible for a woman of her age not to have a single grey hair without resorting to hair dye. She stood there, with her shoulder resting on the doorframe, one ankle crossed over the other and her hands in her jeans pockets, like an arrogant twenty-something.

Mum pretended all the time.

For instance, she pretended she couldn't cry. Blamed it on an old injury she had sustained during an Olympics match, but that couldn't possibly be right. Anine had spoken to several doctors about it, and they had never heard of anything like it. Selma quite simply did not *want* to shed tears. Couldn't bring herself to. Had no need for it, either. She felt so unbelievably small.

There was something wrong with her.

Selma pretended to be a Mum, but only when it suited her. As if everything could be fine between them from time to time, even though they had never really liked each another. Gran had told Anine that when she was only fourteen: Selma had been a bad mother when they were babies; cold and uninterested, she said, and once, after a bit too much red wine, she had slurred something about Selma probably having suffered from postnatal depression.

It was difficult to imagine Selma Falck being depressed.

'What do you want?' Anine asked again.

Selma sat down without permission. On the settee. It felt strange to remain on her feet, so Anine sat down on the armchair opposite.

'I just wanted to ask you about something that happened at the wedding,' Selma said.

'OK, then.'

'It has to do with what you drank.'

'OK. We didn't have time to drink very much. Why are you asking?'

'Ice cubes,' Selma said.

'Ice cubes?'

'Yes. The restaurant ran out of ice cubes long before you and Sjalg arrived from the Opera House roof. I'm well aware of that, because I asked for some. I had to drink an insufferably sweet, really lukewarm Mozell.'

Selma made a face at the very thought.

'I'm sorry your drink supplies weren't to your satisfaction during my wedding,' Anine said dully. 'A wedding at which I managed to become a widow even before the main course was served.'

'I didn't mean it like that, Anine.'

'I see.'

'The point is that Sjalg had ice cubes long after there were none left.'

Anine felt an uncomfortable heat rise from somewhere in her stomach. She was still wearing the tracksuit she had thrown on when she had given up on sleep at about three a.m. Her hair was in a tangle, and the unwashed feeling made her put one thigh over the other.

Selma, however, looked as if she was on her way to a catwalk.

The leather jacket was from Tom Ford, the trousers Armani. For some reason Selma had no age wrinkles between her breasts, and succeeded in wearing the deep V-neck of her T-shirt in a way not even Anine had dared to attempt. Then again, she did not have breasts that would create even the suggestion of cleavage.

'I have some pictures,' Selma continued, as she began to rummage in her bag.

'I think you're sick,' Anine said.

'What?'

That smile. That disarming smile Mum used at all times. After Anine herself had started studying law, she had occasionally heard, usually late at night when malicious tongues were loosened and gathered more courage, that Selma Falck was a lawyer who got away with anything. That she was not really as formidable as rumour would have it and her high-profile cases would suggest. That you could come a long way in the profession with an irresistible smile, big tits and celebrity status.

It was a lie. Anine knew her mother was clever.

A capable lawyer, first and foremost because she was wily as a fox when it came to cutting deals and getting along with people. She was so incredibly good at pretending to care.

There was nothing wrong with that. On the contrary, rather. The best lawyers were the ones who succeeded in bringing people to agreement. Persuading them to listen to each other. To meeting each other halfway. The crazy thing was that Selma Falck lied so much. And so often.

'Have you ever been investigated?' Anine asked. 'Checked up on, I mean?'

'For what?'

Selma raised her eyebrows in a parody of astonishment.

'I don't know. With this gambling addiction of yours, and—'

'I'm not an addict,' she broke in tartly.

'I think you have ADHD. Or something like that. You never stand still. You're—'

'Exactly. A medical sensation, in other words. With an average of 5.9 at the high school leaving exams, and 2.34 in the legal exams at university. With the ...'

She waved the word contemptuously away as she pronounced it: '... *alphabetical grading system* used these days you probably don't know what 2.34 means, but let me tell you it's exceptionally good. Extremely good for someone suffering from a pathological lack of concentration, I have to say.'

'But Mum ...'

'Did Sjalg have ice cubes in his glass when he died?'

Her voice was sharp, her face tense. Her cheek muscles flickered, and Selma's eyes were so narrow that Anine felt nine years old again.

'I don't know,' she answered in bewilderment. 'Anyway, he had a bad habit of eating ice cubes, so it's difficult to say.'

'What do you mean?'

'What I said. If Sjalg got ice cubes, he had always eaten them by the time the glass was half empty. It was pretty annoying, and certainly not good for his teeth.'

Selma pulled out a bundle of photographs from her bag.

'Here,' she said, pushing one of them across the table. 'Look at this. It was taken just before Sjalg ...'

'Died,' Anine murmured as she picked up the photo.

It was so beautiful. She herself looked so fabulous. She radiated the happiness she had felt so intensely there and then, and the tiara Runhild had lent her glittered in the sunshine. Her hair looked golden in the bright light, and Sjalg was even almost better looking in this picture than he had been in real life. He had got to his feet to give his speech, with a sheet of paper in one hand and the glass of water in the other.

'Do you see that the glass is full of ice cubes?' Selma asked.

'No.'

'Don't cry, Anine.'

'I'll do whatever I like, Selma.'

This photo had been taken only seconds before Sjalg's death. Anine could hardly grasp that the transition between life and death could be so sudden. Between the most extreme contentment and devastating misfortune.

A tear landed on the paper. She wiped it away with the side of her hand and glanced up.

'Can I keep this?'

'Eh ... Yes. Yes, of course. But can't you see that there are ice cubes in the glass?'

Anine placed the picture on the table and ran a finger under both of her eyes.

'No. But if you say so.'

'Anine!'

No one's voice could be more piercing than Selma Falck's. Anine pushed her shoulders forward and dipped her head. Picked the photo up again and forced herself to look at the glass Sjalg held. She remembered his hands best of all. Those soft, well-groomed hands, so unusual in a man; he was holding the glass with three fingers and had raised it, like in a toast.

There were ice cubes in it. Her mother was right. Two of them. One caught the light from the sun and relayed it to Anine's tiara, a heavenly confirmation that this bridal couple truly belonged together.

'Yes, there are,' she mumbled. 'It looks as if there are two ice cubes in the glass.'

'Exactly!'

Selma raised a fist and smiled as broadly as only she could. Anine gave a loud sigh.

'But what's the point?'

'The point? It's obvious! Sjalg must have got hold of ice cubes that didn't exist. It means that someone had kept some on the sly. Did he ask for them?'

'What?'

'Did Sjalg ask for ice cubes?'

'No, not that I know of. He would never have asked for ice cubes for himself without making sure that I at least got some too. Besides ...'

Again she took a deep breath and exhaled in a rush of exasperation.

'If they'd run out for the rest of you, then they'd also run out for us.'

'That's precisely what I mean,' Selma said, delighted. 'Those ice cubes were not meant for the rest of us. They were meant only for him, for Sjalg.'

Anine struggled to gather her thoughts. There was no sense in what her mother was saying. Of course no one would have made ice cubes especially for Sjalg and given them to him more than an hour after there were none left for everybody else.

Absurd.

'But don't you see what this might mean?' Selma asked.

'No. And now you have to go, Selma.'

'Mum,' Selma corrected her. 'I'm still your mum.'

'I'm the one to decide on that. I'm also deciding that you should leave.'

Her mother gave no sign of shifting.

'You're sick,' Anine said. 'You have some kind of … some kind of mental … damage. You probably need help.'

Selma's only reaction was to narrow her eyes ever so slightly.

'Gran said …'

'Don't tell me what Gran said. Gran knew nothing about me.'

'But, Mum, of course she did! She always said …'

Anine restrained herself. Sank back into the chair. Selma sat motionless on the other side of the table. She might just as well have been in New Zealand.

'Gran told me stories about you,' she ventured all the same. 'From when you were little. About how independent you were, how strong and stubborn and … how good you were with your brother. Gran was always so proud of you, but she said that something happened when Herman died. You were so close to each other, Gran said, and I saw that too, of course. But I've never …'

As she searched for words, Selma leaned forward.

'You've no idea about any of this,' she said, with suppressed rage, her voice low and menacing. 'I suggest you drop the subject.'

She grabbed the photo from the other side of the table and stuffed it into her bag.

'I can order you a new copy,' she muttered, getting to her feet. 'One that's not covered in fingerprints.'

Anine wanted her to go, to simply disappear. To stay away, far away, for always, so that the decision not to have anything more to do with her was something she could live with. The way things had become increasingly easy as their meetings grew less frequent.

'Gran told me stories about you with great affection,' she said defiantly. 'Like the time when she and Grandad were at the Woodstock Festival, and you and Uncle Herman were parked with that strange lady ...'

Selma had reached halfway to the door. She turned all of a sudden. Anine felt afraid. Her mother's eyes were like marbles, hard, shiny and black. Both hands were clasped so tightly that her knuckles were white.

'Parked is the word,' she snarled. 'It was sheer madness. Keep your mouth shut, Anine. I'm going now.'

'You were only three years old, Mum! You don't remember anything about this, it was just an amusing story that you've heard so many times that ...'

Selma stamped towards her, her feet pounding across the floor, and she did not stop until she was standing right beside the armchair. Leaning forward, she held her face closer to Anine's than it had ever been since she was a toddler.

'I remember,' Selma whispered. 'I remember a green bathroom and a really desperate feeling of being abandoned. Of being far too little to look after my even younger brother. I remember a lady who smelled of pepper and who babbled away without me being able to understand a word of it. I could only understand a little Norwegian, and far less English. I thought Mum and Dad had gone for ever. That they didn't want us any longer. They say you can't remember things from the age of three, and I really wish they were right. Unfortunately they're not. Leaving us with a complete stranger of a woman on an isolated farm for a payment of ten dollars while they went to a concert for three days and three nights was maybe a funny story for Mum and Dad later in life, but for me it was a nightmare. An absolutely unbearable feeling of being abandoned and terrified out of my wits. I've felt it every year since then.'

Anine caught whiffs of toothpaste and Pepsi Max on her face. The tirade was not over: 'I haven't been a good mother to you, Anine. But I have at least been able to stay in the background in the knowledge that you have an amazingly good dad. That's more than I can say about my own mother.'

Just as suddenly as she had leant over her, she straightened her back. All at once, her face took on an expression that Anine could not quite read. Anxiety, perhaps, or confusion. Her mouth was half open, and her eyes flitted around the entire room, as if she could not remember what she was doing in her daughter's apartment at all. Her arms hung straight down, and her hands were again slack.

Selma was so many things.

She was the extrovert athlete who, in six weeks flat, had learned to dance the cha-cha better than anyone else in the country. The super celebrity who took part in talk shows like an international star, and who used social media to depict her life past all recognition. Selma Falck was the strong one, the competent one, the attractive one, and Anine had always been in her mother's shadow.

Always. Even when Selma had disappeared from sight. The periods when she was grumpy and abrupt and just wanted to be alone when she was not working. Later, after all that had happened last autumn, Anine had realized that the dark periods had some connection with her gambling. The madness clearly sometimes took the upper hand.

Selma had many Selmas inside her, but this was one Anine had never seen.

'OK,' Anine said meekly. 'But it made you strong. Olympic champion and all that. I'm sure you could even cross Greenland on skis, all on your own. In the middle of winter. Naked in a snowstorm, if necessary!'

Selma closed her eyes. Her head moved slowly from side to side.

'I'm not an Olympic champion,' she said finally. 'Silver, Anine. I have two silver medals from the Olympics. And I don't actually like skiing. I do it only because I want to master it. We *really* don't know each other.'

Once again she headed for the door. There was not so much of a spring in her step now, and her shoulders were slumped.

Anine stood up and followed her. 'Mum,' she said.

Selma did not turn round.

'Mum, what's the meaning of the ice cubes? And what on earth are you doing, digging into this case?'

Still she received no response. Selma padded down the stairs and opened the main door. Only then did she turn to face her daughter.

'I want to find out what your husband died of because I'm curious, Anine. Because I like to solve mysteries. And because ...'

Her hand moved almost helplessly across her hair, and she held her breath in the middle of the sentence.

'Because I'd like you to know what really happened,' she completed the sentence at last. 'We don't know each other well. But I think it would be good for you to know the truth.'

Anine's eyes held her gaze. She said nothing.

'And as far as the ice cubes are concerned,' Selma added, speaking to one side, '... I believe the nuts may have been in them. That someone made some ice cubes especially for Sjalg. With nuts in them. Ground nuts, most likely, and in such minute quantities that they could barely be detected. Frozen into the water, like a capsule.'

Anine could scarcely understand the implications of this. She tilted her head.

'Why would anyone do anything like that?'

'To take Sjalg Petterson's life,' Selma said. 'Deliberately.'

Jesus

Lars Winther, *Aftenposten*'s news journalist, had not moved one step further forward.

For four days he had tried to find confirmation of the details in the documents someone had sent him from an IP address that had proved impossible to trace. The guy at Intersecure, the ICT specialist that *Aftenavisen*'s journalists were allowed to splash money on when they had a really promising lead, had in the end shaken his head and concluded that professionals must be behind this.

Which Lars had already assumed anyway.

No matter where he inquired, whether banks, analysts, researchers of extremism or experts on Russia, he was soon standing at the end of a cul-de-sac. They could all confirm that the facts he presented to them, carefully provided in fragments so that no one would see the whole picture, could very well be correct. But there wasn't anyone to vouch for them. No one wanted to be quoted on anything at all.

Furthermore, it looked as if his work was a waste of time anyway.

After the contagion on Twitter, increasing numbers of advertisers had advised Google that they did not want to feature on the web pages of Default.no. It seemed as if the website was on its way out with serious financial problems as a consequence of it all. According to the document sent to Lars, half their operating assets had been donated by generous Russians and the financier Erling Kåre Storheim. The remainder was income from advertising, in addition to the chicken feed that donors on the extreme right were willing to give by way of support.

Lars Winther approached the apartment block in Bøler where the editor of Default.no lived. The address was secret – in fact,

Kjell Hope never let an occasion pass without emphasizing the necessity for this. Because of hatred and death threats, he constantly claimed, though the police were unable to confirm anything of the sort. The apartment had not been too difficult to locate: all it had taken was for Lars to ask a colleague in the political section and he got an immediate answer.

A confrontation with Kjell Hope was his last chance. The risk of being dismissed out of hand was overwhelming, but it was one worth taking before Lars had to eat humble pie and admit that this story was just impossible to crack.

At least for the present.

Kjell Hope was a remarkable person. In his late forties, he was well groomed and obviously educated. Nowadays, anyway. In his youth he had been active in Blitz circles, the radical left-wing loose grouping of activists, anarchists, homeless and offbeat artists in Oslo. At the age of sixteen, the police arrested Kjell Hope for the first and last time. He had come dangerously close to Margaret Thatcher during her visit to the city in 1986. The stone he threw had missed her motorcade by only a metre or so. The boy was left sitting for forty-eight hours in a bare cell, something that was unheard of, according to both the law and his furious parents. Hungry, thirsty and shamefaced, he had gone home with them, where after three weeks curled up in a foetal pose, he had cut his hair and re-emerged as a liberal.

Oddly for such a youth, he had trained as a nurse. Conventionally enough, taking his gender into consideration, he did not actually spend long caring for the sick. By the time he was twenty-seven, he was in charge of a department at Ullevål Hospital. Six years later, he owned and ran Omsorgspluss AS, a private company that hired out health-care staff to the public sector. Kjell Hope had become a prosperous man.

And he had joined the Progress Party.

The man's journey to the right wing of the political landscape continued from there. He was one of those who had shouted loudest in 2011 that Muslims must be behind the attacks on the government quarter and Utøya island. In that he was far from alone. When, later in the evening of that fateful day in Norway's history, it had emerged that a white Norwegian from the west end of Oslo and the extreme right wing of politics was behind the massacre, he continued his harangues on social media all the same and did not fall silent until five days later.

But unfortunately not for very long.

For a number of years, Kjell Hope had provided a quasi-academic alibi for the really rabid right-wingers, as Lars Winther saw it. Not entirely an apologist for Breivik, but not far from it. He was active on suspect websites. Occasionally he was also given space in the largest, established media outlets, in line with the media doctrine that had been a result of 22/7: everyone's voice must be heard.

Being so vociferous had turned out to be an expensive matter.

His company went bankrupt in 2016.

By that time, mainstream media was established as an expression, and indeed the MSM was blamed. For everything. Even for Kjell Hope's bankruptcy, and for the fact that he had to move from a villa in Godlia to a three-room apartment in a block a kilometre and a half away.

Lars Winther was almost there now.

The high-rise blocks, three in total, were reminiscent of sixties buildings in the Soviet Union. Despite this, there was something paradoxically attractive about them. Something cheerful and bright, perhaps as a result of having luxuriant trees behind them and only low-rise blocks in front, in serried ranks broken by large, green atriums.

His colleague had let Lars know that the doorbell had no name on it. More important, however, was that his colleague also knew which floor and apartment Lars should go to. He hung about outside the locked door, apparently engrossed in something on his mobile, and it only took a couple of minutes before a boy emerged from inside and ran off, enabling Lars Winther to stop the door from closing and sneak in.

Sixth floor. Unmarked door.

Here it was.

Lars pushed his shoulder bag behind his back before ringing the bell. The less he carried, the less threatening he thought he would appear.

He heard footsteps inside. A security chain rattled, the lock was turned and the door opened.

A young man, barely twenty, stood inside the apartment. He stared nonchalantly past Lars Winther and said nothing.

'Hi,' Lars said. 'I'm looking for Kjell Hope.'

'Oh.'

The voice was just as characterless as the boy's appearance. He would have evaded any kind of identification parade. His face was symmetrical, his nose just the right size, his eyes uninteresting, and his mouth looked as if it was painted on. It could be the image of a man or a woman, and whether he was newly shaved or had no beard growth was difficult to decide. His hair was dark blond. Short, but not recently cropped. He was wearing grey jeans and a light-grey sweater. Lars would not have recognized him again if only an hour went by before they encountered each other again.

The guy looked like an illustration of a Caucasian in a dubious textbook.

'Eh ... does he live here? Kjell Hope?'

'No.'

'No?'

'Not now.'

'But he used to live here, you mean?'

'Yes, but he's left.'

'Where's he gone?'

His eyes took on a glimmer of life.

'What's it to you?'

'No, I … I'm a journalist. Lars Winther. *Aftenavisen.*'

The boy ignored his outstretched hand.

'I've come across some information,' Lars said, letting his arm drop. 'About Default.no. There's a part of it I'd like Kjell Hope's reaction to. He has the right of reply for much of what I'm going to write.'

'Default.no has been shut down.'

The boy's eyes were back to normal now, that is to say they were greyish-blue and staring at a spot approximately in the middle of Lars' chest.

'Shut down?'

In confusion, Lars took out his mobile and searched for the web page.

Safari cannot find the server came up in dark-grey script on a paler grey background. *Safari cannot open the page Default.no. Cannot find the server Default.no.*

His thoughts crashed to a halt. This was incomprehensible. As recently as on the subway up to Bøler, he had been looking at the page.

'When did this happen?' he exclaimed.

'A few minutes ago. I was the one who did it.'

'And you are …'

The young man was still more interested in Lars' solar plexus than meeting his eye.

'I'm the man Kjell Hope asked to shut down Default.no.'

'And your name is?'

'That's of no consequence. Kjell has found Jesus.'

It must feel like this to get a slap on the face, was what Lars managed to think before he could no longer manage to think at all.

'Found … found … he's found Jesus?' he finally managed to stammer out.

'Yes, he's gone abroad. He's staying there.'

'Whereabouts?'

'As I said, he's found Jesus. Matthew chapter twenty-eight, verses eighteen to twenty.'

'Eh … what?'

'The Great Commission.'

Lars Winther tried to buy himself some time by coughing into the crook of his arm. Shifting his weight from one foot to the other, he ran his hand through his hair and dredged up the broadest smile he could muster before suddenly growing serious again. It did not help. All he could come out with was: 'What did you say?'

'The Great Commission, Matthew chapter twenty-eight—'

'I heard that,' Lars cut in, 'but what does it mean? That Kjell Hope has become a missionary?'

'Yes. Well, he has to be trained first. Take a course.'

'Where?'

'Abroad. Now I don't have any more time for you, I'm afraid.'

The door was about to be closed in his face when Lars instinctively shot his foot into the gap.

'Where abroad?' he asked. 'What organization has he gone to?'

'Move your foot.'

'Yes, in a minute. I really must insist that you tell me where he is.'

'Move your foot.'

Finally the young man could be bothered to lift his gaze.

'If you don't move your foot back right now,' he said loudly, raising his left hand to display a mobile phone, 'then I'm calling the police.'

Lars complied, and the door slammed shut.

'Jesus,' Lars mumbled. 'My God.'

If the boy in Kjell Hope's apartment was telling the truth, then the default editor had set out on a new stage of his ideological journey. He had started on the fringes of anarchy before moving on to a social democratic party, after which he ended up in the right-wing populism of the Progress Party. And then taking yet another couple of steps to the right, actually made an impact with Default.no.

And now he was following Jesus.

Kjell Hope had gone right round the board.

Lars started to descend the stairs.

The move from extreme left to ditto right was not entirely uncommon. Especially not in the last decade, when the political axis had grown far less linear. The horseshoe theory was already well established: in the battle against globalization and elites, and for nationalism and protectionism, many common traits had cropped up between extremists on both sides. Contempt for Islam was also equally shared out among the parties.

Bringing God into it all was nothing new, for that matter, but Lars Winther still had no idea what to think. Although Default.no had not existed for very long, the project had obviously been Kjell Hope's attempt to create a magnum opus. The website was garnering more and more readers and was the subject of increasing attention. They were irritating and provocative, and by being outside the agencies and regulations of the mainstream press, they could dare to challenge the boundaries of freedom of expression more heatedly and more brutally than anyone else. Default.no was quite simply on the way to being significant: a Norwegian version of the American *Breitbart*.

Before Jesus had botched it up.

Kjell Hope could not have done this of his own free will.

Lars Winther never took the elevator, unless he was in New York. Now he suddenly stopped on the stairs between the third and second floors. He could hear the echo of children playing further down, and a sharp female voice struggling to get some kids to go outside.

There was a pattern here. Lars could not quite catch sight of it. Despite the material he had received from an anonymous sender now being almost worthless, there was someone somewhere who had something in mind by giving it to him. The purpose could not be anything other than damaging default, and possibly attacking the financier Eivind Kåre Storheim.

Maybe even both.

For all Lars knew, the comprehensive document could have been sent to several editors. Someone else could have stolen a march on him, and scared Kjell Hope into the arms of the Saviour before Lars had arrived.

The Twitter campaign to stop Default.no's advertising income stream had also been remarkably successful.

Lars descended another two flights of stairs before pausing again.

Someone was out to get Default.no and had been extremely successful. That in itself was not so remarkable – he too had wished the website nothing but harm for a long time.

It was the coincidence of timing that made him wonder.

Default, Kjell Hope and Pål Poulsen had all been forced to their knees in the course of only a few days. Pål Poulsen was not as extreme as Hope and his small editorial team, but nevertheless he had been the greatest sword bearer in the right-wing, populist, hostile-to-Islam army they regarded themselves to be. He had been their leader throughout two whole decades, loose-tongued and until now seemingly immune to both his own blunders and the stinging criticism of others.

The children down there were proving difficult to shift from the stairwell. The woman had started to yell, and Lars heard footsteps rushing towards where he was standing. Leaning against the wall, he took out his mobile and began to surf as plausibly as he could. Three laughing ten-year-olds swept past without paying him any heed.

'Christ,' Lars said slowly to himself when he saw the headlines on medier.24, an online news service. 'Bloody hell.'

There really was a pattern here, and it was becoming increasingly clearer.

And more significant.

He stopped again once the youngsters had disappeared into somewhere one floor further up. He gulped, and felt hot. His ideas slowly fell into place, and he could not fathom why he had not seen it immediately.

It crossed his mind that Sjalg Petterson was also dead.

And now this.

Everything was connected, and he now needed to get in touch with Selma Falck.

AUTUMN

The Guest Book

Selma thought that around twenty-four hours had passed. Outside, the snow had turned to rain.

After eating some cold asparagus soup, two slices of crispbread with mackerel in tomato sauce, and guzzling half of a large bottle of Pepsi Max into the bargain, Selma had given Lupus food and water. He ate even faster than she had. Then she had made sure there were both matches and large quantities of firewood available before going to bed.

In a real bed. With bed linen.

When she fell asleep, it had been about midday. Now that she was awake, it was light. There must have been a night in between, she thought. Even though her body felt stiff and tender, she had slept well, a good, dreamless sleep. Lupus had at one point jumped up on the bottom of the bed, but she had kicked him off again. Now he lay in a corner beside the door, a grey, tousled coil that looked as if it was barely breathing.

Body odour, of which she had not been aware for several days, was now really annoying her. She had not managed much more than establishing that there was a full wardrobe in the other bedroom before she had fallen asleep. Something had told her she ought to try to get washed before she put on any clothes, so she had collapsed naked into bed.

She was stinking to high heaven now, of something unmentionable.

In addition she had wet herself, she noticed, and saw a large stain in the middle of the mattress. It smelled rank and nauseating.

There must be some kind of bathroom here. She got up and on to her feet. Lupus lifted his head and sent her an icy-blue look before dozing off again. Selma staggered out of the room to a narrow hallway about five metres in length. The door on the nearest gable wall led into the living room, she thought she remembered, even though she was still aware that her thought processes were unusually sluggish. It was as if she was not completely awake yet. For a moment it occurred to her that this might all be a dream, and she would soon wake up in the stone shelter, helpless and alone, at any second. This moment of fear got her brain moving, and from old habit she touched the gash on her scalp with her fingers. It had completely closed now. She could still feel a distinct edge of dried blood, and around the wound her hair had knotted into a lump about the size of a doughnut.

But it was no longer painful.

Her throat was a different matter. The pain was intense all the way up from her lungs.

She found three doors in addition to the one she had just come through. The first led into the bedroom where she had found clothes the day before. It had bunk beds, so she had chosen the room with the double bed.

A double bed in a simple cabin was a luxury. Yesterday she had seen plug points and light switches. Here in the hallway, only lit by the little window at one end, there were also signs that the cabin was equipped with electricity. She began to walk to the living room, but neither of the two light switches she flicked resulted in anything other than an unproductive click. The ceiling lights were still in darkness.

A generator, it suddenly dawned on her.

Of course there were no electric cables run as far as this into the mountains. There must be a generator somewhere, an electric power plant that ran on diesel or petrol. She sniffed the air, but the smell of her own body was so strong that it smothered everything else.

Generators were normally located outside cabins, often in an annex, mainly because of the noise, but it might also have something to do with the risk of fire.

She opened the third door.

A bathroom. A tiny space with a basin and mixer taps. A shower cabinet. On the wall beside the window hung a small hot water heater with a lower front opening where something obviously should be lit. Gas, she assumed. A gas water heater, no less.

Selma felt dizzy at the thought of a shower, and had to use the wall for support as she stepped in and attempted to turn on the water.

That was not connected either.

'Shit,' she said aloud, and turned the tap up and down again, as if there was a chance that it would work.

There was no generator for water, as far as Selma knew. You need energy to heat up the water, but not to get it out of the damned tap.

Or maybe you did. There could be a pump somewhere that collected rainwater in a cistern, which was then pushed out by some kind of electrical installation.

Her throat was burning. Selma coughed and her head felt really bad.

She was hungry too, and thirsty.

The generator, she reminded herself. She had to find the machine that might give her water and heat. Then she would have a shower, get dressed, eat and then sleep some more.

Her teeth were chattering, she noticed, even though it was cosier in here than anywhere she had been for many days. She coughed again, hacking and clearing her throat, and noticed that her mouth filled with disgustingly slimy, sticky stuff.

She spat into the basin. The lump of catarrh was yellowish-green and smelled as bad as she did.

'Shit,' she said again, as she heard Lupus padding along the hallway.

If she were to go outside, she should have some clothes on. It would not really matter if she spoiled the clothes by being so filthy: she would replace everything she had used when she got back down from the mountains. There were plenty here. Or maybe she could just wrap herself in the blankets she had already soiled.

Selma gave up in the bathroom and tottered out to the living room, where she snatched up the blankets draped over a chair beside the dining table. She was fumbling to fasten them around her body when her gaze fell on something she should have noticed the day before.

The guest book.

Of course there would be a guest book in a cabin like this.

It lay crosswise on the shelf below the windows, on top of a row of books by Jo Nesbø. Selma crossed the room and picked it up.

'Dear God. Please let this book tell me what date it is. Let it say that the owners are coming back today.'

Lupus was whining. Just like Selma: her throat was so congested that her voice was reduced to a rasping whisper. It felt as if someone had stuffed a chimney brush down into her lungs and drawn it brutally up and down her throat.

The leather-bound book had stitching round the edges and in the lower right-hand corner, a picture of two pairs of slippers with a stack of firewood beside them. 'Cabin Book' was written in gilt letters. With hands that trembled both from fever and excitement, she grabbed the red ribbon bookmark and opened the book at the last written entry.

Dear Cabin – Dad and I have been really clever and there's now a new cupboard in the kitchen! Since we were allowed for once to use an ATV, we've stocked up with lots of food too. We've left materials for a new bed in the annex, and we'll build that in ten days' time if the snow isn't too thick by then. Dad says there's never been snow up here as early as this before, and it was a real blizzard. Climate change. ☹☹☹. First THIS summer, and then that. Well, well.

Red Cabin, Hardangervidda, Norway, Europe, The World, The Solar System, The Milky Way, The Universe, 12 September 2018, Karianne (21)

Selma was confused by the peculiar sign-off, but when she leafed back through the thick book she saw that *Karianne (21)* had signed off in exactly the same style since she was *Karianne (5 an a haf)*.

Selma had been right all along. She was on the Hardangervidda mountain plateau. And now she knew it was possible that Karianne and her father had left the day before Selma arrived. But then they must have left quite a blazing fire in the hearth, something they almost certainly would not have dared to do. The rumble of the engine that Selma was so certain she had heard when she had unwittingly been on her way towards the Red Cabin, must have been the two amateur woodworkers leaving in their ATV.

Selma had slept for one night.

In other words, it must be 13 September, and she had only three days left to stop a veritable execution.

SUMMER

The Video

Einar looked crazier than ever.

His hair was sticking out in all directions, and at some time or other he must have taken it into his head to shave. After removing half his zigzag beard, he had changed his mind and now only the right side of his face was clean-shaven, after a fashion. His clothes were the same as when Selma had left him two days earlier, down to the thick red hand-knitted sock on his left foot and thin black cotton one on the right.

The cat's toilet smelled rank. Normally Einar was fastidious on Pussycat's behalf. Now the animal was stretched out on top of the pile of newspapers in the hallway and miaowed plaintively at the sight of Selma.

'What on earth are you up to?' she blurted out as she stopped abruptly at the living-room door when she caught sight of Einar.

His fingers were yellowish-orange and all round his lips the remains of yellow grease painted a burlesque clown's mouth. The laptop keyboard was also being ruined by the muck. A one-litre measuring jug made of transparent plastic, filled with something Selma presumed to be water, sat on the coffee table.

'Mariska,' he murmured distractedly with his eyes locked on the screen as he lifted the jug.

Two thirds of the litre of water was quaffed in thirsty gulps.

'Einar,' she began, without knowing what more she could say.

'Yes, Mariska.'

Using two fingers, he was hammering on the keyboard.

'The internet knows everything. Everything. Did you know, for example, that Osama bin Laden was never actually killed by the Americans? That it was just a ...'

Closing one eye in a grimace of concentration, he raised one orange index finger in a parody of a command for silence.

'... a scam!' he finally finished. 'All that filming from the house in Abbottabad was done in Hollywood. Under the direction of Obama Barack. Obama. Osama. Do you think the similarity between those two names is coincidental? Hardly.'

'Einar. Listen to me, you must ...'

'That al-Qaida confirmed bin Laden's death was only because they got a huge sum of money from the CIA,' Einar continued as he pounded the keyboard without interruption. 'He's still alive, hidden in a castle in the desert outside Riyadh, from where he can return in four years' time. Good God, Selma, I didn't know that.'

She moved towards the settee.

'I warned you,' she said crossly. 'You mustn't believe that kind of thing. The internet is full of conspiracy theories and false stories. This is just nonsense, Einar. You'll realize that if you think about it.'

At last he looked up, and Selma stopped with a jolt. His eyes were bloodshot and along the moist edges there was something she thought at first glance must be congealed matter from a bad bout of catarrh. After a moment or two, she was able to reassure herself that it was only powder from the cheese puffs.

'Stop,' she said sternly, as she sat down beside him and shut the laptop lid on his fingers.

'Ouch! Let me ...'

He tried to push her away, but she refused to give in and pulled the machine towards her to hide it behind her back. When he tried to grab it again she caught firm hold of his wrist.

'You don't have a snowball's chance against me. You know that.'

The tension in his arm abated and she let go.

'This was a bad idea,' she said. 'Anyway, you need a shower. What have you …'

She began to pick up all the empty bags. In addition to the six she had spotted from the door, there was a half-full one on the floor.

'What's been going on? What have you been doing?'

Clearly irritated, she stood up with all the foil bags in one hand and the laptop in the other.

'I've been on the internet,' he said softly. 'There's so much on there. Far too much. Knowledge and facts and … everything. You just put a word in … in the search field, a random word, or combination of words, and then an absolutely crazy amount of information pops up. It has to be in English, though, because—'

'Einar,' she interrupted him sharply. 'Have you been sitting here for …'

She shot a sidelong glance at the clock.

'… for forty-nine hours? Without a break? Without even sleeping?'

He looked at her in bewilderment.

'I've been down to the kiosk. Twice. They've run out of cheese puffs, but they'll get more in tomorrow. Or today. Or …'

He clutched his head with both hands.

'Today, maybe.'

Now he was muttering and had started to rock from side to side on the settee.

'You can search for the CIA. And for surveillance. And for implants. And chips. In the same search field. You can even …'

'Einar! Stop it! Have you taken your medicines?'

'Don't remember.'

The rocking grew increasingly frenetic. Selma went to the kitchen with the cheese puff wrappers and threw them in the bin. She put the laptop in her bag and set it down in the armchair. Then she sat very close to him on the settee and placed a hand on his back.

'Relax, Einar. OK?'

He was shaking very slightly, she could feel, as if he had cramp in his back. She rubbed his spine, slowly up and down.

'I gave you a task to do, didn't I?' she said in an undertone. 'You were to search for something for me. Don't get bogged down in all that conspiracy rubbish. We've talked about it so many times, Einar. That we shouldn't listen to bullshit. Haven't we?'

'Yes.'

The rocking at least had stopped.

'Now I'm going to fetch your medicines, OK? And then you're going to take a shower. Do you have clean clothes?'

'Yes.'

'And then you'll really have to get rid of the rest of your beard while you're in the bathroom. You look a bit weird like that.'

'I thought of something,' he whispered back at her. 'In the middle of shaving. I was really meaning to take a shower as well, but then I thought of something that ...'

'It's fine,' she whispered in return. 'Don't think about it now. When you're clean and wearing fresh clothes, then you and I will go to Noah's and eat some lunch. You can have a kebab.'

She got to her feet. 'Come on,' she said, holding out her hand.

He looked up. The white of one eye was a really deep red: he must have burst a large blood vessel.

'You gave me a task.'

'Yes, but forget that just now. Come on.'

'I found out about it. It didn't take very long, unfortunately. And then I discovered how much more there was in there ...'

He stared at Selma's bag, where the laptop was hidden.

'Found out about it? What do you mean?'

'What someone's using to blackmail Pål Poulsen. You said he was being blackmailed and wanted help. But that he wouldn't tell you what the blackmailers had on him. So you said no. You wouldn't help him if you didn't get access to everything. Even though he was bawling like a kid.'

'Eh ... yes. And you've ...'

'Found out about it. I think so, anyway.'

He was still staring hard at her bag on the armchair.

'Can I have my medicine?' he asked, drinking some more water from the litre jug.

Selma hesitated for a second before heading to the bathroom and collecting his multicoloured dosage box. When she returned, he had already stolen back the laptop. It was open in front of him on the coffee table, the way it had been when she arrived.

'Honestly,' she said in annoyance. 'You can't just go into my bag!'

'It was lying on top,' he mumbled. 'I didn't see anything else in there.'

He stretched out the palm of his hand without taking his eyes from the machine. Selma saw that he had not taken his medicine for two days, and wondered momentarily whether he should take a double dose. On reflection, she decided that might be dangerous.

'There are four pills here for you to take every day,' she said. 'Do you take all four of them at one time, or do you divide them up over a twenty-four-hour period?'

'All at once,' he said, waving his fingers.

She gave him the pills and he tossed them into his mouth, washing them down with the rest of the water.

'Facebook,' he said in a strained voice.

'Are you on … have you created a profile for yourself on Facebook?'

For a second she was petrified at the thought that she might have inadvertently included her own profile when she had set up the machine for him.

'Yes. I didn't need to use my own name. On here I'm called Darius F. Einar Pussycat.'

He was totally serious, and Selma noticed he was still trembling. She sat down beside him again.

'But you need an email address in order to …'

'I arranged that too,' he said tersely. 'It's free of charge. I didn't know that.'

The damaged eye was staring straight at her.

'Do you have any friends?' Selma asked.

'Four of them. And one follower. You'll have to help me add some photos. To make a proper kind of …'

He was struggling to snap his fingers, but they were too greasy.

'Profile,' Selma helped him. 'And profile pictures. I don't think that's a good idea, to be honest.'

'You have to use a disposable camera or something.'

All of a sudden, terror-stricken, he stared at Selma's bag still lying on the chair on the other side of the table.

'Your mobile's not on, is it? I've got such a terrible headache.'

'No, of course not. But what has Facebook to do with Pål Poulsen?'

'He's got one of those open pages.'

'Public,' Selma replied, with a nod. 'That's much of the point, for politicians.'

'Naturally. Just about every tenth post he pastes in here …'

He shifted from his own to Pål Poulsen's wall.

'… is personal. Ninety per cent is "no to toll charges" and "no to immigrants" and "no to most things". Except for red meat and tobacco. Some he's written himself, and others are sort of …'

He was growing more and more animated, talking far too fast until he stopped abruptly and took a loud gasp of breath.

'Links,' Selma suggested. 'But now you really must calm down, Einar.'

'Links,' he repeated. 'Links. Links. The sort of thing you click on, and then something else appears.'

'Now I think we should just put the laptop away and—'

'No!'

His voice rose to a falsetto before he jerked his shoulders and went on: 'Links, they're called. He had loads of them. And then he has some that are personal. Mostly from Thailand, mostly from Thailand. He signed up to Facebook in 2007. Eleven years ago.'

Another jerk of his right shoulder, more vigorous now. Like a tic. Selma had never seen this before.

'Eleven years,' he repeated. 'Was married. Got divorced. Got married. Got divorced. Got married yet again. But mostly links on his page. Links. The whole internet is full of links.'

Selma thrust out her hand and tried to close the lid on the machine. He slapped her away.

'He's in Thailand,' he said dully. 'Often. He has an apartment there.'

'I know that,' Selma said, unfazed. 'It's been mentioned in several places. In interviews. He goes to Thailand with his family.'

'Three wives,' Einar muttered, clicking the mouse.

'Yes. But one after the other. Not all at once.'

'Lots of pictures from Thailand here.'

'Come on,' Selma spoke gently into his ear. 'Come on, I'll take you to the bathroom.'

Taken aback, she suddenly stopped for a moment. Einar had called up five photos he had obviously downloaded from Pål Poulsen's Facebook page.

'Where did you learn to do that?'

'Search field,' he mumbled. 'It's an oracle, Mariska. It answers all your questions. Look.'

His rough, sticky finger touched the screen.

Three of the photographs were from a beach bar. Apparently all from the same establishment, but taken at different times. Pål Poulsen wore different T-shirts, but was seated at exactly the same table. Wife number two was smiling at the photographer in one, along with Pål Poulsen's son, who might be about fifteen and was in a considerably worse humour. The two other pictures from the bar were more romantic, showing Pål Poulsen sitting with an arm around his latest wife, accompanied by three men and a woman whose appearance suggested she might be a Thailander.

One of the photos showed the Progress Party stalwart in front of a black limousine. He stood on his own, leaning against the passenger door with his arms crossed over his beer belly and a satisfied smile on his face, his gaze directed straight at the camera. His grey hair was plastered to his head from the left ear to the right.

At the top of the screen was a picture of the MP on a boat trip with five or six other people Selma did not recognize. In the background could be seen the islands typical of the area. Pillar-shaped, as if they had sprouted from the sea like colossal potted plants.

Selma glanced at the clock as discreetly as she could.

'Fairly typical holiday snaps,' she said. 'And now I'm taking the laptop, Einar, I have to go and—'

'Look at that guy there.'

Einar's fingers moved from picture to picture. Selma had not even noticed the man. He was short, slim and dark. In two of the pictures he was smiling, and in three his face was neutral, almost expressionless. He was never really in focus. Not completely included, in a sense. He was lightly clad in all the photos, in a dark-blue polo shirt.

'I'm looking at him,' Selma confirmed slowly.

'He doesn't seem to be part of the group.'

'No. Well, maybe he's a guide.'

'Maybe.'

He pointed at a picture in which the chest of the blue shirt was visible in its entirety.

'A logo.'

At last Selma was permitted to drag the laptop towards her. She raised it closer to her eyes.

'The Dream Well? Is that what it says?'

'Yes. The symbol is an old-fashioned well. Stylized.'

'And?'

Einar snatched the machine back and hammered more letters into the search field.

'A luxury hotel,' he said, pointing at the website that came up. 'An insanely expensive, beautiful hotel. It's located in Hua Hin, where Pål Poulsen's holiday apartment is also situated.'

'OK?'

Einar pointed at one of the pictures from the beach bar. Selma squinted at the screen.

'A name tag,' Einar said. His voice was now monotonous and almost staccato. 'With the same well on it. The man is called Prayut Pitsuwan. He works at the Dream Well. Worked. Now the hotel is no longer, and Prayut is in prison.'

'What?'

'Prayut is a friend of Pål's,' Einar said. 'Or a guide. Or someone who offers him something.'

'They're probably friends,' Selma said. 'Now I have to go. And I'm taking this laptop with me. Sorry.'

Einar glanced up, looking straight at her.

'The Dream Well was closed down in the spring of last year. After a major raid. It turns out that the hotel ...'

His eyes were brimming with tears that then trickled down his face, leaving shiny tracks in the yellow grease smeared over his face. He took a deep breath and began again.

'A group of the staff there ran a shop of kinds on the side. The manager, for one, and Prayut here.'

Once again he pointed at the recurring figure in five of Pål Poulsen's holiday photos. A man slightly on the fringes of everything, partially on guard, but not so much that he avoided being photographed. In the picture in which Pål was posing beside a black limousine, Selma could now, on closer inspection, see that Prayut Pitsuwan was about to get into the driver's seat.

A corner of the hotel logo could be seen on the side of the vehicle, at the far edge of the picture.

'People don't usually stay in a hotel in the same town where they have a holiday place,' Selma said casually.

'We're talking about sex,' Einar said, as if he had not heard her. 'We're talking about real filth, Mariska. Youngsters. Very young youngsters. We're talking ...'

He broke into a sob, as if he could not breathe.

Selma sat down again and put her arm around his back.

'I'm so sorry,' she whispered. 'You should never have been able to see all this.'

Once upon a time, when Einar Falsen was a police officer, he had killed a man in custody. Broken his neck, in an attack so sudden and effective that a colleague present had not managed to do anything but gawp before the prisoner was dead. Two minutes prior to the attack, Einar had opened a suitcase full of child porn. The picture on the top had been of his own daughter at the age of about eight. Ten years and a serious mental illness later, she had taken her own life, without ever having told anyone about the assaults inflicted on her by a neighbour. Not even her dad who was in the police force. Einar was jailed, descended into madness, and became Selma's clear responsibility and only true friend.

'Sorry,' she whispered with her mouth at his ear. 'We'll just forget this, eh? Is there something we can do to help you just forget all this?'

Einar wiped both eyes with his sticky yellow hands.

'It's OK,' he said. 'First of all I searched for ...'

'Shshsh. Forget it. I mean it.'

He wriggled out of her arms. His shoulder gave another sudden jerk.

'No! First I searched for ...'

Selma wanted to take the laptop, but Einar beat her to it. He clicked on a file he had already found, turned the laptop towards Selma and got to his feet.

'I can't bear to do this again,' he said. 'But this is what I found when I retraced the steps of the Thai police raid.'

Selma looked. She swallowed hard and looked at the video for a few more seconds. Her throat contracted and a violent burst of nausea surged from her stomach and filled her mouth with thick phlegm. Closing her eyes, she shut the laptop with such a bang that the fake radiation shield broke. It did not matter.

Einar Falsen was too fragile for this.

Einar had to live alone, behind closed doors, with Pussycat, yogurt and cheese puffs. With his daily morning round of stealing newspapers, decently edited publications. He could take walks in the enclosed back yard with the cat on a lead, and the occasional trip to the kiosk fifty metres down the street. That was all he could tolerate. Selma was his filter from reality, and he could not be equipped with a periscope into his contemporary world. She had thought he would be helpless in his encounter with a computer, and had forgotten that behind all the twitches and delusions, a police officer lay hidden. In his day, an extremely efficient police officer who had managed to familiarize himself with the internet around the turn of the century before he had vanished into an imaginary allergy to electronics and a paranoid conviction that society was under total surveillance.

An illusion that his forty-eight consecutive hours on the net had undoubtedly confirmed.

'Idiot,' she mouthed soundlessly as she slapped herself on the thigh.

She grabbed the damaged machine, stowed it in her bag and took out her mobile. It dawned on her that she could not switch it on in here.

'Do you understand?' Einar asked, sending a blank look in the direction of her bag. 'If these alleged blackmailers have managed to overthrow Pål Poulsen from his throne, then they must have something really bad on him. I think it has something to do with that. He could well have been a customer in Prayut's shop.'

His finger stabbed in the air, pointing at the bag.

'He can't possibly have been caught in the undertow. Taken by the police, I mean. But after the raid at the Dream Well, Pål Poulsen has never been back to Thailand. He's been afraid.'

Selma was still feeling nauseous. She tried to forestall her vomiting reflex by swallowing, over and over again, but it did not help.

'Go and take a shower,' she said in a strained voice. 'Now.'

He obeyed. When the bathroom door closed behind him out in the hallway, she dashed to the kitchen, where she leaned over the sink and let the contents of her stomach pour down into the dirty, shabby sink. As soon as she straightened her back, the nausea forced her to throw up again. Brown, sour slime ran slowly down the plughole.

Turning on the cold water, she used a well-worn washing-up brush to hasten the unappetizing muck. When the sink was reasonably clean again, she rinsed her mouth and splashed water on her face.

The queasiness subsided.

Einar had come up with a theory.

That was all it was. A theory. But it could well be right. When Pål Poulsen visited her after Sjalg Petterson's funeral, he had wanted help. He was desperate. All the same, he refused to say what they were holding against him. On that point, he was immovable, despite Selma's refusal to help him unless he laid all his cards on the table. Even when she had thrown him out of the car in Bjølsen and told him to stay away from her, he had not given ground on that point. Selma had drawn the conclusion that he must have been guilty of something really bad, but this was worse than anything she could have imagined.

The pictures, imprinted on her retina, that she was struggling to exorcise, were so dreadful that she quite simply could not make herself believe that Pål Poulsen had been involved in anything of the kind.

On the other hand, she could not bring herself to believe that any human being could perform such acts as the ones of which she had watched only a few seconds.

Nevertheless they had been done. By a disheartening number of people.

She switched on her phone. Lars Winther had tried to call her three times, she saw, and had also sent a request for her to contact him as soon as possible. She felt a tinge of curiosity; it was a long time since she had spoken to him, but she dismissed the feeling and tapped in a message. Fortunately, she had acquaintances everywhere, even in Kripos, the national criminal investigation service.

Hi Karsten – hope all's well with you. Just want to let you know that twice in the past 50 hours, I've been on the net and watched a dreadful video from Thailand. Children. Horrific. The alarms may well be sounding from your filters, but it was me, and it was

part of an investigation. It won't happen again. Coffee some day?
Love from Selma F.

The last thing Einar needed was to have the police at his door. Selma took a breath, as deep as she could manage. Closed her eyes and let the cold water evaporate from her face without wiping it.

She couldn't care less about the guy. Pål Poulsen was not her problem. His problems were not Selma's. He could burn in hell as far as she was concerned. Through many years as a lawyer, she had become used to seeing the human side of every criminal. She had seen fragility in rapists and tenderness in the most cynical white-collar criminals. She had comforted, helped and done her best even for child molesters. Nothing human was foreign to her.

Except for this.

Fuck Pål Poulsen.

She thought, and something crossed her mind.

She shut her eyes and tried to picture the desperate man who had sat beside her in her ancient Volvo. Struggled to remember precisely what he had said.

It dawned on her that Pål Poulsen was being blackmailed. Still being blackmailed. The blackmail was not behind him, as she had immediately assumed.

Selma had been irritated because he would not tell her what dark secret someone had got hold of. He had seemed so repulsive as he had broken down completely in her car. Disgusting, almost inhuman. His belly was enormous, his white legs far too skinny. With his flapping comb-over and piggy eyes that disappeared into his skull in total despair, he had got in the way of his own message.

'Idiot,' she whispered to herself yet again.

Pål Poulsen had already resigned as deputy leader of the party when he sought her out. He had fallen from grace some time ago.

Selma had taken it for granted that it was all to do with being blackmailed to force him to resign, and had also for that reason only listened to his story with half an ear. But it was not all over for Pål Poulsen, she now realized. Something even worse lay ahead of him.

Outside, the traffic rumbled past. From the bathroom, she could hear the water spray in the shower cabinet. Pussycat wailed and people were shouting at each other in the back yard. Selma shut it all out.

They killed Sjalg Petterson. And now they're going to kill me.

That was exactly how his words had come out. The allegation had aroused her interest only long enough for her to let him get into her car again. Before they had reached as far as Sagene, her patience had run out.

As a lawyer, Selma never insisted that her clients should tell her the truth. She was not interested in guilt or innocence. She was interested in knowing the facts. In what would emerge in court.

Only that, but on that point she was inflexible.

The facts had to be on the table.

Pål Poulsen had refused to give her them, and she had shown him the door.

If Einar was right, Selma now knew what lay behind Pål's shocking departure from the elite series of Norwegian politics. If there really did exist someone with definite evidence to assert that Pål Poulsen had purchased services behind the darkest curtains in the Dream Well hotel in Hua Hin, then he really was in a terrible fix. If they could in addition prove something, then his life, on the whole, was over.

If he did not give in to the demands they were making.

They killed Sjalg Petterson, the man had said.

And they are going to kill me.

Selma had been hung up on how repellent and inattentive he had been. Instead she should have been paying attention.

She should have asked him who 'they' were.

What 'they' wanted him to do.

And not least: what on earth could be the connection between Pål Poulsen and Sjalg Petterson? Admittedly, they were both members of the same political party, but while Poulsen was vulgar, ill bred and lacking in theoretical education, Sjalg had been intelligent, eloquent, well dressed and knowledgeable.

Selma strode up to the bathroom door.

'Are you OK?' she shouted.

'Yes,' Einar replied from inside.

'Can I go now?' Selma asked.

He sounded hesitant, and then she heard: 'As long as you come back.'

Luckily she still had Pål Poulsen's phone number. He had insisted on giving it to her, in case she reconsidered her decision.

'I'll be back,' Selma said. 'You know that. I always come back to you, Einar.'

The Folder

Selma Falck was on her way to meet Pål Poulsen.

She had tried to ring him when she had left Einar in the shower the previous day, but the failed politician had not answered the call. Only when she sent him a text message did he respond.

Almost at once.

He was at his brother-in-law's cabin, as it turned out, all alone in a place where no one had yet thought of searching for him. In Bærum, outside his terraced house, both journalists and photographers had hung about at all times of the day and night. Even wife number three had started to get fed up with it, Selma guessed. Chiefly with the situation itself, but Selma had thought she could read from Pål Poulsen's whining that his third wife had also begun to get cold feet as far as her husband was concerned. A backbencher in the local authority committee was not exactly what she had had in mind when she married him.

The cabin was in Dovre.

Pål Poulsen was audibly delighted that Selma had changed her mind and was keen to meet him. He cried with joy on the phone. His desire to travel back to Oslo was not quite so unqualified. Admittedly, he had hired a car in his brother's name, but closer to Oslo than Hamar he definitely did not want to go. Not even to meet Selma Falck.

The compromise was a lay-by on the E6 motorway outside Brumunddal.

Selma was already regretting this.

She had lost more than twenty-three thousand kroner that same night. Not a catastrophe in itself, since she was flush with money for gambling. Now the lost money belonged to her, however, in contrast with last year. The problem was that the insufferable restlessness had not subsided as per usual after a night spent in front of the screen. Win or lose, there was always relief to be found in gambling. Last night she had kept at it for a long time, and what's more switched to Black Jack when the poker cards did not work out. But her luck had not improved at that table.

Black Jack was simply a game she had not mastered, and she should have known better.

Exactly as with Jesper.

He had tried to get hold of her since an hour after she had left him yesterday morning asleep in her double bed. The visit to Anine had been too upsetting for her to countenance going home as promised. He must have found the spare key in the chest of drawers in the hallway, because when she finally returned to Sagene, Jesper had gone and the door was locked.

She did not like the idea of him having a key. Nor that he had been bold enough to search for one, either. At the same time, there was something seductive in knowing that he could let himself in whenever he pleased. Just in case, she had used the security chain last night – the last thing she wanted was to be taken by surprise in the middle of a jackpot.

The thought of Jesper was like the first mosquito bite of summer. Slightly pleasant, fairly annoying and impossible to swat away. Going to bed with him had been thoughtless of her. Although she didn't exactly regret it, everything had now grown considerably more complicated. Even though they had no contract as such, since Selma had never drawn up written contracts with any of her clients, she could hardly deny she was investigating a case on his behalf.

The conversation with Anine was also bothering her. Added to which, she was worried about Einar's relapse. She had no idea what she should do about Jesper Jørgensen. Right now she did not care a jot for Sjalg Petterson, and the very idea that she was on her way to meet Pål Poulsen made her feel sick. On top of all that, the weather had taken a real turn for the worse.

The rain was bucketing down, and her car was so old that the windscreen wipers worked at only one speed. A couple of times she had been forced to pull over and wait until it had eased off so that she could see her hand in front of her face. After driving for around two hours, just beyond Hamar, she finally pulled into the layby where Pål Poulsen complained in a text message that he had been waiting for more than an hour.

The man was soaked to the skin just from crossing the fifty metres or so to Selma's car. He had explicitly forbidden her to park any closer; her Volvo was so well known that he had qualms about any possibility of them being connected. Selma felt that his fear was pretty paranoid, as the only others who had taken a break in this horrendous heavy rain were two articulated lorries registered in Poland. To all appearances, the drivers were fast asleep.

Pål had brought a red plastic folder with him, but he had carefully tucked it under his blazer when he came waddling towards her car. Once inside the Volvo, he extracted it, hugging it close as if someone was trying to snatch it away.

'No one has followed you?' was the first thing he said.

'No,' Selma assured him, raising her eyebrows. 'Who on earth would?'

'You never know. Thanks. Thanks a lot for making the trip.'

'As I said on the phone, I want to know everything.'

'Everything except what they're using to blackmail me.'

Selma nodded. 'Except for what they're using to blackmail you. But I want you to confirm the following: it involves—'

'Hey! Wait a minute!' Pål raised his palms. The red folder dropped on to his lap. 'That wasn't the deal! You said that—'

Now it was Selma who broke in: 'The arrangement has changed slightly. Only slightly.'

'But—'

'Wait a minute. You only need answer yes or no to the questions I ask. I'm not going to ask for any details. Nor for time or place. Just answer me. It would be a shame if we've both come all this way to ...'

She peered out at the miserable weather. The lay-by was really only a blister on the side of the motorway, with an information board, public toilet and two shabby sets of rustic picnic tables and benches. Now everything was wet and colourless: even the dense forest flanking the road had faded and looked like a leaden-grey, solid wall.

'... way to Brumunddal for nothing.'

Pål hesitated. Fiddled with the red plastic folder. Tried to find a more comfortable position on the seat. Gave up.

'OK,' he muttered.

'It's about sex,' Selma said.

He nodded, almost imperceptibly.

'About illegal sex. Terrible, contemptible assault.'

He opened the car door and was on his way out faster than she would ever have thought him capable of.

'Stop,' Selma said. 'Calm down. I won't ask any more questions about it.'

He reconsidered for a few seconds before the pouring rain forced him to slump back into the car seat and close the door.

'I just don't want to discuss that,' he said firmly.

Selma had achieved what she was after. People who were asked if they had been involved in illegal sexual practices would have protested if that had not been the case. Loudly. They would not have tried to do a runner.

Einar had hit the target. The mere thought made Selma want Pål Poulsen to leave. Want to kill him, really. She screwed up her eyes, then opened them wide and forced out a smile.

'OK. Let me hear.'

'I don't honestly know where to start.'

'Start with that folder there,' Selma said, nodding towards his lap.

'Eh … yes. I got … Ten days ago I received a letter in the post.'

He got no further. Half a minute passed. He opened his mouth a couple of times, but only single-syllable sounds came out.

'I see,' Selma tried to help him. 'And when you opened it, you found this folder.'

'Yes.'

'Can I take a look at it?'

He could not even get as far as answering the question.

'Listen,' Selma said. 'I don't have a lot of time. Now I've spent more than two hours coming here. Either you answer my questions or else we'll just have to go our separate ways again. This time for good. I promise you that.'

'I received this,' he began. 'As I said, I received this folder. You can look at it. But ...'

As if he immediately regretted his promise, he picked up the folder and held it to his chest again.

'This doesn't contain anything about me.'

'Eh ... No, I see.'

'There was something in it when it arrived. Something about me. But I burnt it. After I'd read it, it took only a couple of hours before someone phoned.'

'Male or female?'

'Male.'

'And what did he say?'

'That I should resign from all my positions within a week. Well, not from my elected office in parliament, that's impossible, we can't just resign from that no matter what we might have done. I thought that ...'

Selma waited impatiently for him to continue. She felt dirty just from sitting in the same car as this man.

'What did you think?' she asked sternly when she saw his lower lip start to quiver. 'Don't start snivelling!'

'That it would then be all over. If I resigned, they would leave me alone. At the same time I ... I didn't understand what was the point of all this. Why they ... or the man on the phone, what do I know, whether we're talking about one or two or more of them, anyway, I couldn't see why I had been sent all this. Not until I read the back page over again.'

'What is it? What is in this bloody folder?' Selma held her hand out invitingly.

Pål Poulsen finally gave in. Falteringly, as if he were handing his very life over into Selma Falck's hands, he passed her the folder. She took it and drew out a bundle of sheets of paper.

There was silence between them now as the rain drummed on the car roof. The rear lights on one of the Polish lorries suddenly lit up to become glittering prisms of red and orange through the wet windscreen.

Selma read. Leafed through it, read some more, and flicked back again.

'Is this a copy?' she asked in the end, without looking up.

'The original. I didn't dare to ...'

Selma took out her iPhone and began to photograph the sheets.

Pål Poulsen rubbed his back on the car seat, shuffled his feet and began to grope for a lever to move the seat further back.

'What happens now?' he moaned. 'You have to help me. You will help me, won't you?'

Selma did not reply until she had finished. All the pages were now stored on her mobile. She stacked the sheets together on her knee and pushed them back inside the red folder.

'Who are "they"?' she asked.

'What "they"?'

'When we last spoke, you said that "they" had killed Sjalg Petterson. And that "they" were going to kill you.'

'I was really talking metaphorically, it's obvious that ...' He hesitated. 'Well, that's what I want you to find out! Who "they" are! Whoever killed Sjalg, and whoever is taking my life in this way.'

'What makes you think they're the same people?'

He stared at her indignantly. 'It's obvious, of course! The same party, the same opinions and ...'

'Sjalg Petterson died of anaphylactic shock. You're being black-mailed because of the totally unacceptable things you've been doing in Thailand. You're not really so similar, to my mind.'

His face was now puce. He began to gasp for breath, and Selma was afraid he was about to have a heart attack. Not that it would be in the least undeserved, but it would considerably delay her return to Oslo to have to sort out the formalities involved in having the dead body of the former deputy leader of the Progress Party sitting in her old, bright-red Volvo.

'Here,' she said in a loud voice, handing him a half-full bottle of Pepsi Max that she had stowed in the door pocket. 'Snap out of it. Drink.'

He took the bottle, unscrewed the cap and drank. 'How ...' he panted, but he was unable to get any further.

'How did I know what you've been doing and where? You're never going to know that.'

The bottle was already empty, and his complexion was returning to what passed for a normal colour.

'The only thing you can know,' Selma said slowly, 'is that you're now going to take your folder with you and get out of this car. You knew that Sjalg Petterson was my son-in-law. You used his name when you realized I didn't want anything to do with you. I became curious, and couldn't afford to pass up on the opportunity to find out more about my daughter's husband's death. You tried to use me. I won't put up with that. Get lost.'

He made no move to go. She wanted to lean over him and open the passenger door, but could not bear to move any closer to him. Instead she stepped out, skirted around the bonnet and wrenched the door open on his side.

'Out,' she ordered.

'But I ...'

Selma was already drenched. It actually felt good. She lifted her face into the rain and repeated: 'Out! Get out of my car!'

Pål Poulsen lifted his legs out and planted his feet on the ground right in front of her. Selma let go of the door and drew back. The noise from passing vehicles on the E6 was intensified by the wet road surface and she had to shout.

'I never want to see you again. If you think you're being threatened, then contact the police. They are duty-bound to help everyone. Personally, I'm more discriminating.'

With great difficulty, he finally extricated himself. In only a few seconds he was as wet as she was. The red folder protruded slightly from his blazer when Selma moved to one side to let him pass. An almost irresistible urge to strike him made her take a second step back.

Without another word, he began to walk towards his dark-green hire car that almost seemed to merge into the forest behind the lay-by. Selma slammed the door and returned to the driver's side. For a moment she hesitated to sit in such a valuable veteran car in her present state of being soaked to the skin, but she had no choice. Turning the key, she turned on the heating full blast and switched on the windscreen wipers.

Pål Poulsen could not even be bothered to hurry. It was as if the red folder weighed him down quite literally as he staggered, bowed over and unsteady, towards the fringes of the forest. For one fleeting second Selma felt sorry for the man. It was hardly possible for anyone to be more solitary than he was.

She grabbed the mobile from the centre console.

Stared at it without turning it on.

Her journey had been far from wasted. The information in the red folder had shaken her more profoundly than she had shown. She lifted her eyes and saw that Pål Poulsen had reached his car. He settled inside and just sat there. The vehicle was still dark and silent.

The red folder had not been compiled by amateurs. The contents could change the lives of eleven named persons. Selma recognized some of the names, but not all.

It struck her that it looked like a military operation, a precisely aimed and potentially deadly strike against a select group of individuals. What they had in common was not easy to discern. Of the ones she recognized, five belonged to the right wing of politics, the other three to the extreme left.

Pål Poulsen's car was still shrouded in darkness.

Maybe she should check that everything was all right.

Obviously everything was not all right, and Selma put her car in gear so that she could demonstrate her indifference.

The red folder attacked both east and west. Right and left. It was unfathomable, and as she set off in a northerly direction, looking for the first opportunity to turn back towards Oslo, she made up her mind.

It was time to answer the countless messages from Lars Winther.

Concern

'He's met Selma Falck.'

'Selma Falck? *The* Selma Falck?'

'That's what I said.'

'Why?'

'Presumably to get help.'

'Where?'

'In a lay-by north of Hamar.'

'I see.'

Pause.

'Hello? Are you there?'

'Yes. We have a problem.'

'Possibly.'

'I don't like it. I don't like it at all. Keep an eye on her.'

'I'm supposed to keep an eye on Pål Poulsen.'

'Put someone else on that. We have the resources.'

'Has she to be monitored?'

Pause.

'No. But keep an eye on her. I'm concerned.'

'But how will—'

'Just do it.'

Click.

The Hacker Attack

Mina was at home on her own.

Mum had called in earlier, in the late afternoon, as she always did, visiting Mina after work. It was absurd. Before this, before Mum moved out, days could pass between the times they saw each other for more than a few silent minutes at breakfast or while brushing her teeth. Now they had to sit down with a cup of tea and talk about the weather and the next school term.

Every day.

Mum might as well just stop coming.

Dad did nothing but work.

Mina had seen so many films and TV series in the past few weeks that she felt drained. Nothing tempted her, not Viaplay, Netflix, Dplay or HBO. She had started on the first season of *Friends* for the third time, but even that was beginning to pall.

Prior to this catastrophic summer she had kept up to date. Read newspapers. Paper copies, which Mum considered environmentally unfriendly and Dad could not eat breakfast without, as well as online versions. Mina had been a politician, the leader of the school's Pupil Council and she was interested in current affairs. This summer she had hardly any idea of what the outside world looked like.

The world in here devoured everything.

She lay in bed as usual, her MacBook open beside her as always. Her fingers moved automatically over the keyboard, and completely unaware, she had clicked into Altibox and NRK's real-time transmission.

NRK had been her Grandma's favoured channel when she was alive. At her house, the remote control was only used to switch on and off and control the volume: she never watched anything other than the state-controlled television channel, which Mina did not like. They had made *Skam*, of course, which had gone on to be an international hit, but she had watched that on the series' own website. When she was little, the NRK Advent calendars had been the best of the bunch. Also, she sometimes watched *Dagsrevyen*, the evening news round-up, but then always online before she went to bed.

Only old folk watched television nowadays.

As she was doing, right now, even though it was on a laptop.

It was seven p.m., and the *Dagsrevyen* headline story was about a hacking attack on DG.no and two other online newspapers. Mina put on her earphones and turned up the sound.

The comments pages had been destroyed.

The attack was comprehensive and extremely professional, according to an independent expert who wore a serious expression. People who tried to write comments had themselves been infected with a destructive virus. It had taken several hours before the extensive harmful effects had been noticed, and there was no solution other than to close down the whole service. The comments pages would not be reopened for some considerable time.

It could take weeks, the man said, and he seemed on the brink of tears, even though he was supposed to be independent.

A group calling themselves #trashfighters had claimed responsibility. They had set up their own Facebook page, exactly like the well-known hacker group Anonymous. In the meantime, they had posted only some kind of manifesto, which a monotonous female voice read out on *Dagsrevyen* while the picture displayed the text.

They were an army in the service of freedom of speech and democracy, they claimed. That was also like Anonymous. The difference was that whereas Anonymous wanted to have a free flow of opinion and information, #trashfighters were preoccupied with what they called 'a healthy and productive climate of opinion'.

All points of view are allowed, but all points of view are not of equal worth. Hatred, witch-hunts, conspiracy theories and threats, disparagement and racism should not be allowed to get in the way of a solid democracy, the woman's voice read out.

Mina sat bolt upright in bed. The strange thing was that this was all in Norwegian.

'*We have every reason to believe that #trashfighters is a purely national phenomenon,*' said a woman from Kripos. '*None of our colleagues abroad report anything similar. The only thing that is clear as of now is that this is an extremely advanced IT intervention.*'

The interviewer asked whether the attack could be compared to anything previously seen here in Norway. The woman hesitated, but finally answered: '*There have definitely been very damaging and very professional IT attacks against industry and commerce. But not against the free press. This is deeply concerning.*'

The chief editor of *DG* agreed. He intoned about freedom of expression and unwarranted intervention in editorial evaluation.

Mina smiled. It was about time that something like this happened.

The hackers were almost certainly young, she thought. Just like her, and really fed up with all of it. Who just wanted to discuss things in a decent manner.

She was about to leave the evening news and Google #trash-fighters when Dad was suddenly onscreen. Mina turned the volume up another notch.

'*Justice Minister Tryggve Mejer,*' the presenter introduced, '*this attack came on the same day that you made public the establishment of a new commission to examine freedom of expression. Is that sheer coincidence?*'

Dad smiled faintly.

'*Of course,*' he said. '*But in many ways this story can be said to highlight the basis and necessity for such a commission. Freedom of expression has not been discussed in its entirety in this fashion since 1999. That will soon be twenty years ago. Society has gone through really radical changes since then. Our reality, to put it simply and precisely, is absolutely and fundamentally different from when the last official report was drawn up.*'

'*And this is primarily because of the internet?*'

'*Yes. The net is a gift as well as a burden. It opens up the potential for greater democracy, but at the same time it creates opportunities to reduce it. Social media is used by everyone, from the man in the street to the American President. A great danger lies in this. We speak before we think. We become emotionally incontinent. We hurt one another. A medium that to start with has the ability to bind people more closely together, also pulls us further apart. It creates fear and exclusion, and many are reluctant to take part in public debate. We can't have that. Democracy itself will disintegrate if we don't take these problems seriously. By taking this action, I am attempting to do just that.*'

'Hello, Dad,' Mina said softly.

Maybe it was this commission he had been working so hard on. It must certainly take a lot of time to draw up a mandate. And members had to be nominated. It was also a huge task. People had to be found who were equal to it. They had to be asked, and some probably said no. Maybe he had found it difficult to convince his colleagues in government that a new commission on freedom of expression was necessary.

It had taken time.

This must be what Dad had devoted his summer to. Mina felt suffused by a pleasant sense of relief. She grabbed the bedcover and tugged it so hard that her laptop toppled over.

Dad had been sitting in the basement working on a secret commission that was no longer secret. The casket in the safe was only a souvenir. An old curiosity that he had inherited, maybe from Ellev, who had died in the spring. It had nothing to do with Dad's exhaustion and distance. On the contrary – what he was doing was important and right. He should have told Mum, even though he had a duty of confidentiality: Mum would have understood and would never have left him if she had known.

Maybe Mum would come home again.

Dad was the same old person. Truly, and at long last.

Mina burst into tears. She did not know why. The tears ran down her face, and it felt lovely. She sobbed and gasped for breath, and did not even try to stop.

Maybe she would finally be able to talk to him.

For weeks she had yearned for her father of old, the way he had been before, before she had needed a dad so badly. Now she would get up, make some hot food for supper, and wait for him to come back to Lofthus terrasse. They would sit in the kitchen with the first fire of the season in the hearth, and Mina would light all the candles Mum used to light in the past. It was starting to grow darker in the evenings. They would sit there, she and Dad; he would smile and ask for forgiveness for being so unapproachable, and at last she would be able to tell him the worst thing of all.

This summer had been horrendous, but now Dad would sort

things out. He was a good dad, a wonderful Justice Minister, and the best lawyer in the world to boot.

At last Mina had her dad back. Now she could harbour a little flicker of hope that she would escape punishment. It was at least something to cling to.

Dad could manage everything.

AUTUMN

Onwards

The generator refused to start.

Selma must have done something wrong, but she had at least tried. There was plenty of diesel in the tank. The machine had a pull-cord starter, like on an outboard motor or a lawn-mower. Selma had tugged at it with all her might, which was less now than a few days ago, but all she got for her efforts was a dry splutter from the generator and a sore shoulder.

An even sorer shoulder.

She had studied the apparatus to find a choke. She had searched through the cabin for a user manual. She could find neither. In the end she gave up. If she had guessed right with respect to the water and it was drawn into the pipe system by an electric pump, then she could just go on dreaming about a shower. As an emergency solution she had filled the largest pot in the kitchen with water direct from the tank and heated it up in the fireplace.

It was enough for a cat's lick.

The clothes in the wardrobe in the room with bunk beds were clean. Sensible. Quality clothes, bought and stored by people who had a good knowledge of outdoor life and the mountains. She dressed for the worst weather imaginable, even though an old mercury thermometer attached to the kitchen window told her it was three degrees Celsius outside. The rain had stopped and the snow had melted again. The clouds, higher in the heavens now, scudded along and from time to time cracks appeared in the grey sky, showing streaks of blue.

Dressing felt euphoric.

Real trousers. Marvellous. There were a couple of bras in a chest of drawers in the double-bed room, but they were both too small. She would have to manage without. Over a tight-fitting dryfit vest, she pulled a thin woollen sweater from Kari Traa. A well-used, traditional-patterned Fana cardigan over that again. Long johns of wool and a pair of overtrousers, slightly too large, with pockets at the knees. Thin woollen socks with thick, home-knitted ones on top. She found an expensive red Bergans jacket that was a good fit hanging in the hallway and a pair of mountain boots that were one or too sizes too big. That did not matter: she tied the laces tightly around her foot until they were snug as a glove.

Her bag was already packed. Hat and mittens and a litre and a half of Pepsi Max. A bottle of water, mainly out of consideration for the dog. Food enough for a couple of days, both for her and Lupus. In the store where the generator was located, she had found a dog harness and something she thought was a long lead: a thin length of orange plastic rope she had seen people using when they let their dogs walk freely through the woods where there was really a restriction to short leads in force.

Lupus was cooperative when she put the harness on him.

His company was better than nothing, and Selma felt something akin to concern that he might leave her now he was replete and rested.

'We'll walk together,' she decided and got him ready.

To top it all, Selma had also found a map. The Red Cabin was marked with a cross, and as far as she could calculate, there was only a kilometre or so to the next cabin. Which probably would not help her in the least. She had to find permanent residents. People.

She had far to go and had not managed to find a compass.

That was of no concern, though, as Selma knew nothing of orienteering. There was more help to be had from a battery-operated alarm clock in the bedroom that apparently showed the right time. It was now just over half past eleven in the morning, and in the present improved weather conditions, the position of the sun right now would give her some sort of idea of the points of the compass.

She had put the clock in her bag and was ready to move off.

Lupus followed her obediently out on to the stone steps. Selma locked the cabin and returned the key to the green mailbox. It crossed her mind that she should leave a message. A note in the guest book, perhaps. For a moment she considered letting herself back in again, but she could not be bothered. Instead she went down the two steps until her feet were planted on the ground.

It was like standing on the deck of a ship.

The world was spinning round and round. A bird screeched somewhere high overhead, probably an eagle, and she closed her eyes to shut out the dizziness even though it did not help in the least. Sinking down on the bottom step, she froze to the spot.

Selma was dressed for far colder weather than this, but she was trembling with cold and fever. She put her hand on her burning forehead. It felt as if her throat was bleeding. Her lungs were stinging and it was so painful to swallow that saliva was dribbling from her mouth.

It was out of the question for her to cope with this.

But she must. Even though she felt a hair's breadth from death, her memory had almost completely returned. The only thing she was still unable to grasp was how she had ended up in the mountains. She had no idea whether she had come of her own accord or whether someone had brought her here. Along with her Volvo, which was now a burnt-out wreck.

'I'll tell you a story while we walk,' she said hoarsely to Lupus. 'Or maybe not. It's painful for me to talk.'

She rose stiffly, grabbed the coil of long rope and began to walk towards the south-east with the grey, shaggy mutt close by her knee.

Onwards, onwards.

Someone had once told her about an old proverb from Greenland: *When you've walked so far that you can't walk any further, then you've walked exactly half the distance you can manage.*

There were sixty-five hours until the deadline, and Selma could barely imagine how she would walk one hundred metres.

Placing her faith in the Inuit, she plodded on.

The Order

'At last she's been reported missing.'

'Good. How long will it take before they start searching?'

'Don't know. But it was the crazy guy who sounded the alarm. He phoned the police, despite being hysterically afraid of mobiles. Whether the police will put any faith in him is an open question, though.'

'He's an old policeman himself.'

'Yes. Let's hope that makes him more believable.'

'It's no longer snowing up there.'

'No.'

'It's all melted.'

'Yes.'

'You have to go up and check. I want to know that she is dead.'

'Up there? Now? That's highly inadvisable. As I've told you till I'm blue in the face, the scene of the fire must be untouched when they find her. And for the hundredth time: Selma Falck is dead.'

'I'm worried. Set off on a hiking trip, won't you? Pass the place by chance. You can sound the alarm.'

'That's in direct contravention of—'

'It will all unravel if she's managed to get away. Then we'll have to be prepared.'

'All the same it—'

'Go up there. As fast as you can. Be a tourist, find the body, sound the alarm.'

'OK then.'

'You can go.'

The Pattern

L ars Winther arrived three quarters of an hour late.

It was less than two hours before Jesper was due to drop in, and Selma Falck tried to hide her annoyance when she opened the door to *Aftenavisen*'s newly appointed journalist. He greeted her with a hand to his quiff, which had become noticeably thinner since the last time they'd met. Selma gave a resigned smile in return and let him in.

'We only have an hour,' she said, 'because you're so terribly late. What's this about?'

'Straight to the point, as usual.'

'Yes. Tea? Coffee? Something else?'

'If you have coffee, I'd love a cup.'

While she had waited impatiently for him, she had prepared a thermos flask. She poured some into a cup already on the coffee table, and sat down.

'If you want milk, there's some in the fridge.'

'This is fine,' he said with a smile as he raised the burning-hot coffee to his mouth. 'Oi. Hot. I'll wait a minute. It's about Sjalg Petterson.'

Selma's eyes narrowed slightly. She crossed one leg over the other and flicked an invisible crumb from her knee.

'Yes?'

'That is to say ... I've come up with a kind of theory. Or ...'

Once again he raised the cup, as if the liquid could possibly have cooled in the seconds that had elapsed since his last attempt. Yet again he put it down without tasting it.

'Or what?' Selma asked when he hesitated.

'Have you noticed that ...'

Again he faltered. Leaning forward, he rested his elbows on his sprawled knees and folded his hands. His blue eyes were eager, but he was still struggling to find some way to launch into his story.

'There's some kind of ethnic cleansing going on,' he said finally. 'I think.'

'What?' Selma could not restrain a smile. 'Here? Here in Norway?'

'Yes. Or ... not ethnic, then, but political. And maybe not exactly cleansing, because of course that implies that people are killed. I think Sjalg Petterson's death has something to do with it. So, he's dead, and the others are not, but that's not what I ...'

He was stumbling over his words.

'A political cleansing,' Selma said curtly. 'In our country, well, well. I see.'

'Can we sit down at the dining table?'

Selma shrugged. 'Of course. Is there anything else on your wish list?'

The sarcasm bounced off him.

'Yes, please! Paper and pen. If you have those big sheets of paper, A3 for example, that'd be super.'

Selma went into the bedroom and opened the wardrobe. At the bottom there was a cardboard box of office supplies. She took out a large sketchpad and marker pens in various colours, and headed back. Both when going in and out of the bedroom, she was careful to open the door as little as possible, without making it appear too obvious. Lars Winther must definitely not see how the walls in there were decorated.

'Here,' she said, as she laid everything out in front of him.

'Sit down,' he said, and patted the seat beside him.

Selma complied, but pushed the chair a bit further away from him. She sat half sideways and let her left arm rest on the table.

'Don't you want coffee?' he asked, finally managing to drink some of his.

'No. It's too late in the day.'

Her irritation about his tardiness had not yet subsided and she darted a demonstrative look at the clock.

Lars Winther took the hint. 'Sjalg Petterson died suddenly,' he said quickly, writing his name at the top of the large sheet of paper. 'On the twenty-first July.'

Beside the name he drew a cross and wrote down the date.

Selma watched in silence.

'He was the great guru of the far right. The intellectual leader for thousands, if not tens of thousands, of angry young men. And middle-aged. And elderly. And a few women.'

He drew a nut beside his name. It looked like a turd.

'He died of hyper-allergy to nuts. Anaphylactic shock.'

Lars lifted his eyes. Selma nodded very slightly.

'Then …'

He wrote down another date.

'… a Twitter campaign started up, targeting Default.no. A campaign that very soon proved effective. Major advertisers such as Equinor, Telenor and Choice hotels informed Google that they no longer wanted their adverts to be displayed on the default web pages. Their income dwindled.'

Once again he looked at her.

Now she kept a straight face.

'Immediately afterwards,' he ploughed on, 'came the shocking news that Pål Poulsen was resigning from all his main posts in the Progress Party. In actual fact, all he's left with is his seat in parliament. And wife number three, for as long as that lasts.'

Selma coughed quietly into her fist, but did not blink.

'Are we in confidence mode now?' he asked, putting down the pen without replacing the lid.

'What do you mean?'

'Selma,' he said, looking a bit exasperated, 'we've done this before. Something for something. Are we at the stage where we can share information in complete confidence, and are ready to share whatever info we have?'

'How do you know I'm interested in whatever you might have to tell me? And that I have something to give in exchange?'

'You're interested. You want to know whether your son-in-law was killed because of—'

'He wasn't killed. He died. Because he was hyper-allergic.'

'Yes, of course. But bear with me here. This death is at least pretty remarkable. And let's say there's some kind of action being taken against … far-right agitators. Cut out the coyness, Selma. You always have something to offer. Even if nothing more than your powers of analysis. Come on. Quid pro quo?'

Selma stood up and crossed to the balcony door that had stood wide open all summer. The apartment had seemed more spacious with all the light and the faint summer breeze always wafting through the rooms, especially when she also kept the bedroom window ajar to create a through draught.

Now that the evenings were getting darker and light rain drew slanting trails of water on the glass, she felt shut in. Jesper was about to arrive, and Selma really did not know whether she wanted that. The thought that he would be here in an hour and a half stirred her in a way she could not explain. She could not quite recognize the feeling. She did not know whether it was good or bad, not even when she tried to check it out.

'Fair enough,' she said crisply with her back to him. 'But one thing I can say right away is that this sounds like a raving mad conspiracy theory. Who in that case would be behind such a … purge?'

'Just wait a minute,' Lars said enthusiastically. 'Sit down again, please.'

She turned around but remained on her feet.

'I'll take a chance,' he said, with a lopsided smile. 'That we can speak in confidence. On the same day that the Progress Party held a press conference to announce Pål Poulsen's departure, I received a letter. An old-fashioned letter. In the post, I mean.'

Selma looked at him impassively: 'I understand the concept of a letter.'

'It contained a document,' he added quickly. 'Which in brief terms stated that Default.no is partly financed by the Russians. Through—'

'By the Russians?'

Selma approached the table and stood with her arms crossed, staring at Lars's sheet of paper, which was still quite blank.

'Yes,' he said, nodding.

'That would be really sensational.'

'Absolutely! An outright scandal that would blow up in the faces of Default, its editor Kjell Hope and also Eivind Kåre Storheim.'

'Storheim? The financier? What has he got to do with this?'

'Sit down, and I'll explain.'

She sat down. Lars began to talk. It took him twenty minutes to tell his story, but by that time he had at least aroused Selma's interest in deadly seriousness. She noted that she could see the same outlines of a pattern as he did. Especially when she considered the document in Pål Poulsen's red folder in the context of the eventually comprehensive picture Lars painted for her. The temptation to show him what she had photographed in a rainy lay-by beside the E6 was insistent.

'So Kjell Hope has found Jesus,' she said slowly. 'Bizarre.'

'Well, maybe,' Lars replied. 'It does sometimes happen that people are born again, but the timing is significant, to put it mildly. Talk about leaving with your tail between your legs. To … the mission fields, of all places!'

'And this young guy who was in his apartment, what do you think of him?'

Lars Winther pulled a long face. 'Just a computer geek. For the moment I don't give a toss about him. This is far more interesting.'

He used the marker pen to point to the sheet of paper in front of him. In the course of his story it had filled up with scribbles. Names, dates and comments.

'Sylvester Berland,' she read out.

'Yes. The article about his problems was published when I was at Bøler. It made me think. Very seriously.'

'Wasn't he the leader of the Norwegian Communists or something? In the eighties, when the whole movement was on the brink of falling apart?'

'No, not the leader, but he was fairly prominent. He'd been involved since the very beginning in the early seventies, but during the eighties he took a gradually more nationalistic direction. He was an ardent opponent of Norwegian membership of the EU. For a time after the referendum in 1994 it seemed as if he might go after a career in the Centre Party. He bought a smallholding. Moved to the countryside and championed rural causes. Became a racist, too, for that matter. And passionately anti-Semitic, something he had already been for a while. Naturally the Centre Party wanted none of that, so the guy started a blog instead. When the internet became mainstream.

A fancy business, in fact it looks like a professional newspaper. The content, on the other hand, is totally off the wall. Conspiracy paranoia, all of it. I was standing in the stairwell in the apartment block in Bøler when I found ...'

He fiddled with his phone, located what he was looking for and placed it in front of her.

'... this article. He's being prosecuted. For contravention of the criminal code paragraph ...'

He searched through his memory for the correct regulation.

'... 185,' Selma offered by way of assistance, rather absent-mindedly. 'The racism paragraph. Or to be more specific, the paragraph protecting minorities. It needs to be a horrendous infringement to be caught out by that. The laws on freedom of speech are pretty far-reaching.'

'Yes. The article took me really by surprise, though. These people are fairly good at knowing exactly how far they can go to avoid having the authorities on their backs. They're often reported, but it seldom or never ends in criminal proceedings.'

'Just as well,' Selma muttered. She was still finding it difficult to concentrate properly on what Lars was saying.

'Of course,' he nodded. 'But now he's really gone over the limit. What he wrote is faaaar ...'

His hand swept across the dining table and pointed in the end through the window.

'... beyond anything that might reasonably be protected by freedom of expression. The Mosaic Faith Society has reported him, and the police have really got moving on it.'

'But the man claims he was hacked, doesn't he?'

'Yes. Persistently, but it doesn't seem as if many people are interested in listening to him. He's been given an interim injunction ... is that what it's called?'

Selma nodded. Her attention was deepening.

'The police have seized all of his equipment,' Lars continued. 'His computer, broadband gear, printer, everything!'

'What? That's incredible, to put it mildly. Interim injunctions for hate speech are a complex judicial area, and it usually takes an amazing amount to obtain support for such demands. As a starting point, you can almost say that it has to be a matter of life and limb. The decision is being appealed, I assume?'

'Think so.'

'It'll be overturned, for sure.'

'I guess so. But the damage has already been done! The rats are deserting the sinking ship in all directions!'

'What do you mean?'

'He doesn't write all by himself!' he said excitedly. 'Quite the opposite, he depends entirely on other people with the same twisted opinions. There are many of them, Selma. Scarily many. But when the police come rattling their handcuffs, they clear off. If you go into the most obscure websites now, you'll see that when poverty comes in the door, love jumps out the window, as the old saying goes. They're fighting like cats in a sack. Most of them usually write under a pseudonym. That kind of thing protects you from the general public, but not from the police. They know that. Even though these people might believe Sylvester when he alleges he was hacked, it will take time before they dare to find their way back to him. People generally are getting nervous.'

'People,' Selma reiterated. 'Those people there.'

'Yes,' Lars replied. '"Those people there".'

He raised two fingers and drew quote marks in the air.

'The extremists,' Selma murmured. 'On either side of the scale.'

She pointed to Marlene Halse's name.

'The cake baker,' she said. 'A fucking benefits swindler. She's set herself up with an Instagram account where she shows off the most fabulous baking. Sells them to order for thousands of kroner per item. The business is going full steam ahead. The problem is that the woman's on disability benefit. Really obese and unwell. Takes the cake money in cash. The police confiscated more than a hundred and twenty thousand kroner they found in a cake box in the lady's house during a raid. Following an anonymous tip-off. The story broke just the other day, didn't it?'

'Yes. If I know my old colleagues in *DG*, and I do, they'll have been given the whole story by some source within the police. The article is incredibly detailed.'

'She has around the same previous history as Sylvester Berland, hasn't she?'

'Yes, in a way. I wasn't born until '78, so what I know about the extreme left in that revolutionary decade is something I've only read about. But the circumstances were amazing. Lots of internal strife. Various groups were bitter enemies on the basis of conflicts that seem laughable today. Those two, Marlene and Sylvester, belonged to different factions and were never willing to work together. But they had definitely something in common that makes them interesting in this connection.'

With the marker pen held between two fingers, he tapped the large sheet of paper in front of him.

'They belong to the most extreme wing,' he concluded.

'Exactly like Pål Poulsen,' Selma said, looking askance at the scribbles. 'Only on opposite sides. Or in fact almost in the same area, if we're to believe the horseshoe theory. And I'm actually starting to believe in that.'

'Me too. So what do you think?'

Selma did not answer.

'Nothing?' Lars probed.

'You first.'

'Someone's after them.'

'After who?'

'You can see it for yourself. The extremists. The right-wing populists. The left-wing populists, whatever they might be these days. Sjalg Petterson, Kjell Hope and Pål Poulsen. Marlene Halse and Sylvester Berland. They've all been checkmated in the space of a very short time.'

Silence fell between them, and Selma felt a growing unease. She did not know whether this came from her distaste at acknowledging that Lars had a point, or worry that Jesper might appear while the journalist was still present.

'Who on earth could it be?'

'No idea.'

'Who would be interested in anything of the kind?'

Finally their eyes really met, for the first time since Lars had arrived. He had Norwegian eyes: round, mid-blue and with eyelashes that were slightly too pale. He looked the way she knew he was: persistent, smart, enthusiastic and a bit too honest. In addition, Lars Winther was capable of keeping a secret. He was one of very few people who knew of Selma's fondness for gambling. Nevertheless, he had never written a word about it, and not mentioned it to anyone else either, as far as she understood.

Probably he was gathering information to use when he needed it, as she herself did. Strictly speaking, he had a hold on her. All the same, Selma liked Lars Winther. She liked him a lot, and was not very far from trusting him. In all likelihood this was because she pretended less in his company than when she was with others.

They heard the snorting sound of the articulated bus in Arendalsgata, and a car alarm that had gone off not so far away.

'I think I must show you something,' Selma said.

The decision was easier to take than she had thought.

'I do have something to share. On condition you don't use any of it until I give you permission.'

'Promise,' he said, trying to conceal his eagerness.

To be fair, she owed Pål Poulsen discretion. On the other hand she had never accepted any kind of assignment from him. They had not entered into any sort of agreement. The man had voluntarily and without explicit terms shown the red folder to her, and he had no protested when she had photographed the whole document that had been sent to him, without asking.

From someone whose identity Selma was growing increasingly curious about.

'Word of honour?' she asked, even though this was unnecessary.

'I swear,' Lars replied.

'This concerns only five people,' she said, her hand swooping across the sheets of paper. 'What if I can tell you that there are eleven more of the same stripe whose lives may be turned upside down at any moment?'

'Eh?'

'Eleven more people. All either extreme populists or extremists, to be blunt, as far as I understand. Some of them I'm not really familiar with, but I do have the names.'

'What the hell ... what are you saying?'

'I'm saying this,' Selma went on, and began to tell the story.

It took her less time than Lars had taken. He listened with eyes that grew steadily wider, making notes on a fresh sheet of paper. The first one, now covered in notes, he had moved to the middle of the table. He interrupted her a couple of times, but otherwise was fully occupied by alternately looking at Selma's mobile and jotting down notes. A couple of times he had to explain to her who the people in Pål Poulsen's documents were.

'And that's that,' she said finally, as she put down her phone. 'The fates of eleven people. All belong to the extreme wings of Norwegian politics. Some will lose their footing entirely if this information is made public. Good that you recognized the ones I didn't know. I had never even heard of the Israeli organization.'

'Israel's Friends in Norway,' Lars said, with a nod. 'A far-right, pro-Israeli organization that is extremely hostile to Islam and makes *With Israel for Peace* appear moderate and balanced. Elling Madsen is the leader there.'

He used the marker pen to point at the name, then dropped it and asked again: 'And what action was Pål Poulsen to take with all this, did you say?'

'Call on a journalist in a serious media outlet. He got the choice of *DG, Aftenavisen* and NRK. He was to show them this, along with the documentation and everything, and also agree to stand up as a witness for the truth. He was given a deadline of one month, something that makes this even more malicious. The guy's going to die of anxiety in the meantime. He'll have a dreadful time, at least.'

'Christ on a bike, Selma.'

'You might well say that. Pål Poulsen moaned and groaned as he sat like a sack of potatoes in my car.'

Selma gave an exaggerated shudder.

'Tried to appear heroic by refusing. Pure, sheer self-interest, of course. People who live in glasshouses, and all that, and he won't be cast in a particularly good light if he does actually "out" all this gang.'

'I thought the guy had already fallen far enough.'

'Me too. That's why I wasn't especially interested to start with.'

A pregnant pause.

They sat looking out at the rain from the same side of the dining table, Lars completely motionless.

Selma heaved a silent sigh. She had to get Lars out of the apartment as soon as possible. At the same time, there was something about those two closely written sheets of paper that did not add up. She drew them towards her.

'Are these scoundrels the whole gang out there on the outer fringes?' Lars suddenly exclaimed. 'Do you become an extremist through breaking the law? Or do you break the law when you become an extremist?'

'Neither,' Selma replied without taking her eyes from the notes. 'A lot of this is not against the law. Nothing but muckraking. Incredibly unpleasant muck and dirty secrets. Most of us have those.'

She tried to ignore Lars's broad grin.

'If we've lived for a while,' she added without a blush. 'All human beings have secrets. Things we're ashamed of. Stories we don't even discuss with our very closest friends. If I asked you to tell me the very worst thing you've ever done, you would lie. For sure! What's interesting about all this is not that people have done things on the fringes of the law or generally accepted morality, but rather who might have the power and opportunity to gather all this in.'

'Could they ... could the conspiracy theorists be right?'

'About what?'

'About that ... the elite ... that the state or some other agency or ...'

He looked around for the thermos flask, and went to fetch it from the coffee table, filled his cup to the brim and sat down again. Selma's eyes followed him and stole a glance at the clock.

'It might look as if,' he began, no longer noticing her continual hints, 'as if ...'

'As if the centre is striking back,' Selma finished for him, with emphasis on her final words. 'In both directions.'

'Yes, but ... who actually comprises the centre?'

'You and I?' Selma asked. 'Isn't it people like us who actually stand in the centre?'

'The elite, do you mean? I don't belong to any damned elite.'

'Yes, you do. We all do. Norway has the largest elite in the world.'

'But can they be right to claim we're being monitored?' he went on. 'That Big Brother is gathering crap about us all? And that they have decided right now to attack the most intractable amongst us? That this—'

'Hold your horses,' Selma said, raising her voice and holding up both palms. 'Do you realize how demanding of resources such an apparatus would have to be? Of course we have state surveillance in Norway. Anything else would be a gross dereliction of duty. We have both the police security service and military intelligence. They work their fingers to the bone, and have to be selective about who comes under their radar. In the first place they have limited resources, as I said. Secondly they have regulations to follow. Thirdly they're under the control of other agencies. And fourthly—'

'But these people are sinister to start with, Selma!' Lars was almost shouting. 'Is it not precisely the extremists who are being watched? People like these? Has the PSS suddenly got really fed up and decided to destroy the whole damn lot of them?'

Now he was almost across the table. His arm covered both large sheets and he was trying to make eye contact with her from below.

'Idiot,' Selma said brusquely as she pushed away his arm. 'There's something odd here.'

Lars sat up and ran his hand in consternation through his Tintin quiff.

'Everything's odd about it,' he said.

'Sjalg is dead,' Selma said.

'Yes.'

'If, and I emphasize *if*...'

Now she was the one using the marker pen as a pointer. It quickly thumped on Sjalg Petterson's name at the top of the first sheet.

'... *if* Sjalg was also affected by this ... what should we call it?'

'Plot?'

'No. If Sjalg is also one of the ones in some strange way affected by this … group or whatever it might be behind it, then he is very different from the others.'

'Because he was smart and educated?'

'No, because he was killed.'

Lars was biting his bottom lip.

'Mm,' he mused, nodding. 'All the others have had their good name and reputation destroyed. Or threatened with it into silence and passivity. Sjalg died. Of natural causes, too. At least apparently so. Someone could well have tricked him into taking those nuts somehow.'

'The police are about to drop the case. The Food Safety Authority found no nuts. Neither did the pathologist.'

'No.'

He rubbed his face with both hands in a discouraged, childish gesture. Shaking his head vigorously, as if to waken himself up.

Selma could tell him about her ice cube theory. She could show him the pictures in her bedroom. The crucial photograph, taken just before the reaction began, with the sun's rays fractured in the frozen water so clearly that even Anine had to admit she could see two ice cubes in the victim's glass.

She did not.

Something for something, Lars used to say. It was best to hold back the currency of exchange until a later opportunity. Now he was overeager: 'It could also be that …'

Selma was no longer listening to what he was saying.

After she had discovered the ice cubes in Sjalg's glass and realized that they could have been responsible for his death, she had been completely stuck. In the pursuit of a perpetrator, she had to find means, motive and opportunity. The ice cubes fulfilled only the first of these. They were the weapon, if Selma was right. She still thought she was. How anyone could have tampered with

311

them so that they actually ended up in Sjalg's precise glass was however more difficult to grasp. Especially since they had run out of ice cubes for the other guests some time earlier. The serving staff of course had the opportunity, but they comprised Jesper's old colleagues and a couple of very young girls hired in for the occasion. Selma still kept open the possibility that it might have been one of them, but without complete comprehension of the motive, it was impossible to discover who was behind it. She needed a motive to find the right perpetrator, and the right perpetrator to find the motive.

'Catch 22,' she mumbled.

'What?'

'Nothing.'

A key was inserted in the door lock.

'Is it possible that ...' Lars began over again, glancing towards the hallway, 'that Sjalg Petterson's death was sheer chance? And that it has ...'

Jesper suddenly stood in the doorway.

'Oi,' Lars said, getting to his feet.

Selma grabbed the sheets of paper and folded them at lightning speed.

'Hi,' she said softly. 'You're a bit early. We've just finished.'

'Lars Winther,' Lars said, reaching out his hand.

'Jesper,' Jesper said lamely, dropping his bag on the floor and holding out his snake arm.

'The chef!' Lars said, grinning. 'Ellevilt restaurant, right?'

'You have to go now,' Selma said, crossing to the window.

Her mouth reeled off the longest line of curses she had ever strung together in her life, though not a sound passed her lips.

'Talk later,' Lars replied. 'ASAP!'

Selma could swear he was laughing when the front door slammed behind him.

Spotlight

Lars Winther had barely left Selma Falck's apartment block before he fished out his phone and tapped his way into his extensive contacts list.

Trine-Lise in *Spotlight* magazine would appreciate the tip-off. He felt a stab of conscience as he wrote the text message, but it soon subsided. Selma was footloose and fancy free, and could have her way with whomever she chose. Until now, her love life had been the most boring thing about the woman: no journalist in all these years had managed to link her with anyone other than her husband. Now her family life was dead and buried, and for the past six months a number of the girls at work had tried to pump him for information. Before now he had been able to offer neither gossip nor chit-chat, despite being the only person in the whole *DG* building who encountered Selma on a fairly regular basis.

Hi T-L – star chef Jesper Jørgensen just turned up to visit Selma Falck in Sagene. He had something that looked like an overnight bag with him. Smelled as if he'd just stepped out of the shower and was ready for some action. He's half her age! If you put a photographer outside her apartment early tomorrow morning, you might just get a photo. ☺ You owe me one after this. LW

As he clicked the send button, it dawned on him that Jesper Jørgensen had been responsible for the food at Sjalg Petterson's fateful wedding. It had completely escaped him in his astonishment at seeing the guy. The relationship between the chef and Selma, if there was one, could possibly be slightly more complicated than Lars had thought on the spur of the moment.

'Shit.'

It was too late. The message was on its way and could not be snatched back. For a moment he stood deep in thought. He could warn Selma. Ask her to make sure Jesper left tonight. He started writing a new message, but stopped halfway through, reconsidered, and deleted it.

He had no wish to damage Selma Falck, but love and celebrities in one and the same story couldn't be beaten. Even straightforward celebrity deaths generated a host of clicks, especially if they were unexpected. The age difference between Selma and the chef was spicy in itself, and it was never wrong to help colleagues get a juicy headline. That Selma Falck, soon to be fifty-two, was dating a celebrity chef in his twenties was so sensational that it would be headline news. Splashed on the front page, at least.

Lars Winther shook off his second thoughts as he unlocked his bike.

He had more important things to think about than who Selma Falck was sleeping with. If he pedalled at top speed to Kampen, he might also get the better of the feeling he had recognized the moment Jesper Jørgensen had slapped a black bag down on Selma's living-room floor.

The feeling was reminiscent of jealousy.

That was no good at all, and he cycled home to his wife and small children as fast as the pedals allowed.

AUTUMN

The Hunters

They were dressed as grouse hunters.

They even had a dog with them, an experienced Gordon setter that had scurried about in huge arcs in front of them all the way from the car park. If there were birds up here on the heights, they would probably be ptarmigan, different from the willow grouse that tended to remain on lower ground. The ptarmigan were more difficult for the dog: they used their legs instead of taking to their wings the moment they were scared off. Walked-up shooting was preferable up here in the high mountains, and more exciting too, flushing out the game birds, but neither of these two men knew that as, equipped with another man's dog, borrowed rifles and suitable hunting clothes included in the deal, they approached a marked point on the map they carried.

Even from several hundred metres away, they could see that the cabin was in ruins. That came as no surprise to either of them. They had been here before, when the building was still standing. Later they had seen pictures of it, taken by a state-of-the-art drone when the cabin had burnt to the ground.

They had not met anyone since they had left their vehicle three hours earlier. From time to time they had taken photographs with their mobile phones. One had posted a couple of them on Facebook, until there was no longer a signal to be had. When they sounded the alarm, as soon as they reached the site of the fire and found Selma Falck's body, it was important that they had ticked all the boxes.

That everything added up, from the trail walked to the shot fired.

They were together on a hunting trip, two old friends, even though they had only been out grouse shooting once before, and that had been nearly fifteen years ago, but such was life. They both had demanding jobs. Hans-Olav Storbergan was the regional director of NSB, the Norwegian state railways. Sture Jensen was a carpenter and building contractor.

They had little in common, if truth were told. Admittedly, they had both served in the Telemark battalion, but at different times. They had once been elite soldiers, and Ellev Trasop had recruited them both. In that they were alike, and for that reason they had tried to keep in contact to a certain degree. It might come in handy that they had a history as friends, or at least good acquaintances. Grouse shooting an eternity ago and a cycling trip in the Rhone valley five years' back, with their spouses. They were sensible, solid family men. Both had three children, and Hans-Olav's were almost grown up. Sture's kids were still of primary school age, and his daughters were the only reason he had entertained glimmers of doubt in the past fortnight.

The assignment had been far more complicated than they had envisioned.

The woman was really strong.

They had known that already, having done their homework before they had gone into action. Selma Falck could reach a bench press of seventy-five kilos and had run the Oslo Marathon in three hours and twenty minutes.

She had bitten them, to tell the truth. Quite literally. Sture still had a pain in his forearm, and the cut had only just begun to heal. He had had to tell lie after lie to explain the gaping wound to his wife.

The dog began to whine as they neared the charred ruins. Hans-Olav fired a shot at random: their story would have to hang together when they sounded the alarm that they had found a corpse in the burnt-out cabin.

The place still stank of fire. Wet ashes, mould and damp.

The chimney was still standing. A monolith soaring to the sky, supported on either side by the broad fireplace that the flames had not consumed either. The fire had been so fierce that the inner walls were completely absent, and only the granite perimeter wall was left to show that there had once been a building of around fifty square metres on this spot.

'We left her here,' Sture said.

He had tramped through all the black mess.

'Here,' he repeated, using his hunting boots to scrape back charcoal and ashes.

'Are you sure?'

'Idiot.'

'The woman was dead.'

'Yes, she was. But search.'

'Search? She was dead, bloody hell! Dead bodies don't move!'

Sture threw out his arms in consternation.

'I know that! But there's nobody here, for Christ's sake.'

'Maybe the heat was so intense that the body is ... completely obliterated.'

Sture crouched down and thrust his hands into the black wreckage.

'The skeleton wouldn't have been destroyed,' he mumbled, rubbing fine ash between his fingers.

'People get cremated, though. And the remains are put in an urn.'

'Yes, true enough. After the bones have been collected and pulverized. They become porous, but not completely destroyed. For that to happen, you'd have to use acid.'

Hans-Olav, who until now had stood outside the perimeter, stepped over the low, scorched stones.

'She broke her ankle in 2002,' he said. 'And had an almost ten-centimetre-long titanium plate drilled into her left fibula. That at least should be lying here somewhere. Titanium doesn't melt until nearly seventeen hundred degrees. In a fire like this, the temperature would reach only eight to nine hundred. Something like that.'

The Gordon Setter had begun to howl. She was tired after a long morning, and now ravenous. Neither of the two men showed any interest in feeding her. She had found water for herself all day long, in streams and puddles. After having put behind her more than five times the distance the two men had walked, she needed sustenance. She needed it now and pretty well right away, the way she was used to when her real owner hunted with her and took better care of his dog than he did of himself.

Her instinct took over and she began to search.

Only an acrid, repellent smell came from the site of the fire.

The setter's name was Gaia, something neither of the two men seemed to remember. They had hardly spoken to her on the whole journey. Gaia was from excellent stock and was even better trained, and as soon as they had let her out of the car, she had understood whom she should serve on that day. She had done so, and it was certainly not her fault that they had failed to understand her marking movements. She had worked hard. Now they had let her down anyway, and she began to walk in ever-increasing circles around the burnt-out cabin to take care of herself.

There was a strong scent from a pile of stones a short distance away.

Some of food, and a lot of human. Pee and shit and perhaps something to eat.

The smell was locked inside, behind a door, heavy and impossible to dig her way through.

Gaia yelped and whined before starting to bark ferociously.

At last the two men paid her some attention.

They came running, and maybe she would get fed at last. It turned out that this was hoping for too much.

'Did you see this stone shelter when we were here?' Hans-Olav said. 'It's not marked on the map, and it doesn't say anything about it on the website of the people who let out the cabin.'

'If I'd seen that,' Sture answered, 'I'd have mentioned it, of course.'

He opened the heavy door and recoiled from the stench of human excrement that belched out of the dark hole, but it did not prevent him from inhaling deeply, holding his breath and stepping inside.

Barely a minute later he was out again. Scratching his beard, he surveyed the magnificent open landscape. Evening was approaching, and in the west the mountain range was bathed in a pale pink glow behind the scudding clouds.

'She wasn't dead,' he said tersely. 'Somehow she escaped from the fire. Hunkered down in here. For how long I don't know, but there are two empty tomato soup tins lying in there. And a black stove has been recently fired up.'

'She was dead.'

'She can't have been. If she was, we're looking for a zombie.'

'We have to extend the search. In larger circles around the cabin. If she really was alive when we left her, she could have staggered out into the wilderness. She can't have managed for long, considering her condition.'

'It's only about a week since we brought her here,' Sture said. 'We've no idea when she left. We don't know if she's lying dead somewhere out here ...' He drew a wide arc with his arm. '... or if she's already reached safety.'

'If she had, she'd have let someone know. The police. We'd have heard about it. That old policeman, for sure. She hasn't done that; he reported her missing only yesterday. Was the stove in there still warm?'

He nodded in the direction of the stone shelter.

'No. But the charred remnants of what must have been a book were in the firebox. The pile of birch bark fragments on the floor suggests there was a lot of firewood in there, but it's all gone. I'd guess she stayed there for as long as she had enough to burn. The tomato soup tins were still a bit wet inside.'

'So she's managed to survive for five days on two tins of soup?'

Sture pulled a face.

'I don't know, but have the feeling she was here for a while. We thought she was dead, Hans-Olav. I've never had such a hard struggle as when she tried to get away. The way the weather's been this past week, the most sensible thing would be to stay here for a few days. To recover, if nothing else.'

'But she was naked.'

'There were clothes in there. Her own clothes were on top of her bag. If she rose from the dead before the fire really caught hold, she could have managed to take them with her.'

'That's what she must have done, then. After all, the woman couldn't wander around naked out here!'

Hans-Olav put a flat hand above his eyes and stared out over the mountain plateau.

Sture mulled it over for a long time.

'We have a problem,' he said in a monotone.

'Yes.'

'If she really has managed to get away from here, in the state she must have been in and with the weather as it was, then she's much tougher than we thought.'

'Where should we begin?'

'I wish I knew,' Sture said, hoisting his rifle on his back and starting to walk back the way they had come. 'All I know is that we have to find her. As soon as we possibly can.'

SUMMER

The Justice Minister's Daughter

S elma woke from a dream she forgot the very second she
opened her eyes.

She had been running, that was the only thing that came to
her. She felt afraid when she woke suddenly, and her pulse was
racing. A nightmare. Selma was used to them. Ever since she was
little, they had afflicted her several times a week. At that time
they had usually been about letting down her younger brother.
That Herman became ill, dangerously ill, and Selma had to go
out to find a doctor. Everything got in the way of her quest, the
shortcuts were too long, the obstacles too many, and she was too
young to really do anything. When she finally returned to his
sickbed, always still alone, he was dead and Selma woke with her
heart in her mouth, gasping for breath.

During her teenage years her nightmares had been apocalyptic.
The moon exploded, the earth fell out of its orbit, or a worldwide
nuclear war broke out. As an adult, the bad dreams were always
about running. Away from everything, in fact, and they never
passed quickly enough.

Jesper was sleeping like a log.

It was unbelievable that it was possible to sleep so soundly.
Selma could even switch on the light. She could go to the toilet,

flush the loo, wash her hands or take a shower without him moving a muscle. Not even Johannes, the nearest thing Selma knew to a sloth, slept as deeply as Jesper.

As for herself, a flutter of the curtains was enough to wake her.

He occupied almost the entire bed, lying on his stomach, as always, his head resting on the arm with the snake. Selma felt safer now in the presence of the huge reptile. Last night she had caught herself talking to it. Whispering, even though she could probably have given the snake a roasting without Jesper opening his eyes.

She had talked about how Jesper was a terrible idea.

He disturbed her. She got very little done. Her head had not been in quite the right place ever since he had turned up. It was not easy to see what she was actually doing. Where she was going. Not in life, and certainly not with this case, with which she could not seem to make any progress.

The snake had not answered her, but she had begun to like those eyes with the elliptical pupils. They gazed at her no matter where Jesper lay. Like the *Mona Lisa*, in a sense, and equally inscrutable.

Jesper was far too young. Selma noticed that, every minute of the day. He was devastated about the situation at Ellevilt. Several of the staff had started to look for other jobs, and although the reopening was imminent, there was no sign of interest from the public. Ellevilt and physical training were the only things Jesper took seriously, anyway. Otherwise he was as impulsive as a teenager: thoughtless and skittish and playful when the restaurant was not on his mind. He liked American action films and video games.

He could do nothing.

Of course he could. They were just totally different things from what Selma had learned throughout her life. Last night she

323

had insisted on watching *Dagsrevyen*, the news round-up. They had shown a brief interview with Gro Harlem Brundtland, the former Prime Minister, who was home in Norway on holiday.

Jesper had asked who she was.

'Good Lord,' Selma whispered to the snake. 'Is it even possible?'

Dawn was breaking and she guessed that it was around five a.m. She got up quietly and as she headed for the toilet, she nearly tripped over Jesper's clothes, lying on a heap on the floor. As she bent down to hang them up on the valet stand she used herself, a note fell out of the back pocket. Selma hung up the jeans, picked up the note and unfolded it.

Three names, written on three lines, with something that must be phone numbers beside each of them.

Female names. Selma frowned.

It suddenly occurred to her that these were the three girls from the restaurant. The three Jesper had not previously known, the ones who had been hired in on an hourly basis to help at the wedding. Selma had made a fuss about identifying them on more than one occasion, but Jesper had found it difficult to get hold of the guy who had hired them. He had gone on holiday two days after the wedding, and no one else at the restaurant in Ekebergåsen had known how to access the lists of extra helpers.

Typical Jesper.

He had finally got hold of the names and then forgotten to tell her. Selma took the note with her to the toilet and closed the door. Sat down on the loo.

Kristina Block Solstad.

Mathilde Johansen.

Hermina M. Selmer.

Three names that meant nothing whatsoever to Selma. She peed, washed her hands, shrugged on her dressing gown and padded out into the living room. In passing she cast a sidelong glance at Jesper, who now lay uncovered, apparently without having moved a muscle.

Selma took a cola from the fridge.

A real Coca-Cola, with loads of sugar and caffeine and everything she needed in order to wake up. As ever she drank it with a prick of conscience. As usual also with a joyful, almost euphoric feeling in her body when the black, ice-cold liquid reached her taste buds. She let it linger in her mouth, repeatedly running the fizz over her tongue, until the carbonic acid made it expand inside her mouth and forced her to swallow.

Cowboy-Cola. The very best taste Selma Falck knew in the entire world.

Taking out her iPad, she sat down on the settee, placed Jesper's note on the table and took another drink of the coke.

There was only one Kristina Block Solstad, according to Google. Born in 2001, she attended Foss High School and was involved in rhythmic gymnastics. Mathilde Johansen was a different matter: there were five of them, seemingly, but it took Selma only a couple of minutes to find the right one. She too was seventeen, lived in Lillestrøm and her leisure time was spent on youth theatre.

Hermina M. Selmer brought only three hits, with the top result on Wikipedia, no less.

Hermina (Mina) Mejer Selmer (born 2001) is a young Norwegian politician. She is the leader of the Nordre Aker AUF, the youth wing of the Labour Party. Mina Selmer is the daughter of the former (2001–2005) and current (2015–) Justice Minister Tryggve Mejer.

Tryggve Mejer.

Sjalg Petterson's long-time primary target, a man who must have secretly heaved a sigh of relief that the history professor could no longer plague him with regular, malicious diatribes.

His daughter had been a waitress at the wedding of her father's tormentor.

Mina Selmer. She Googled the name.

Her informal name triggered masses of results. Selma clicked into the images, and it struck her that there was something familiar about the young girl. This could be because she was pictured in several photos in Selma's bedroom, but the ones in there had been taken from a distance and were pretty indistinct as a result.

On the internet, she found portraits, some sharp close-ups, and there was something about them that Selma recognized.

Standing up, she returned to the bedroom, where she switched on the light on Jesper's side and turned the lamp towards the photos on the wall. Mina Selmer was in three of them. In one of these she was carrying something that must be hors d'oeuvres, one plate in each hand. Not like the more experienced waiter from Ellevilt immediately in front of her, who additionally balanced a couple of plates on his left forearm. In the second picture, Mina was carrying a jug of water.

It was not Sjalg's glass she poured the water into, but Jesso's.

Selma took out three drawing pins and brought the photographs back to the settee.

Means, motive and opportunity.

The ice cubes were the means. Mina Selmer's presence at the wedding reception gave her the opportunity. The groom's behaviour towards the young girl's father could be a motive.

Perhaps.

Or perhaps not. It was difficult to kill someone. Planning a murder was incredibly demanding. Not only from a purely technical point of view, but also emotionally. Most people had an inbuilt resistance to killing others, Selma was convinced of that. It was a matter of evolutionary utility, in addition to universal culture. Human beings needed to be able to kill when under threat or attack in order to protect themselves and those close to them. It was equally advantageous for us to shrink from planning to murder other people in cold blood.

It was impossible to imagine that a sixteen-to-seventeen-year-old might have done something like this, let alone a successful, clever teenager from a resource-rich home.

Out of the question.

It suddenly struck Selma where she had seen the girl before.

They followed each other on Instagram.

Selma received a maximum of twenty to thirty inquiries a week that were not in the category of nuisance. Someone wanted to make a video for his wife's thirtieth birthday, if only Selma could go to the bother of paying a tribute to this fantastic mother of young children in a video clip. Others wanted an autograph on expensive paper that they provided: there were still people who collected that sort of thing. Some of these, emails, direct messages and even the odd old-fashioned letter, were simply fan mail. They came in waves, depending on which series of programmes Selma was involved in at that particular time. During *Shall We Dance?* there had been so much post that she had given up entirely.

The only inquiries she always answered, if she went to the bother of opening the email or letter, were from young handball girls.

If there was anything that Selma truly loved unconditionally, apart from Einar, then it was handball. Her father had once said to her, she might have been thirteen or fourteen at that point, that all the time she spent on training and matches was wasted. A born athlete like Selma should have gone in for tennis. That was where the money was, and lots of it. At a pinch Selma could have chosen cross-country skiing, where the very best women at least could also earn a crust. She had not answered him. There was never any point in answering her father. For five years he had lived as a hippy and college student in the USA while he and his Norwegian girlfriend's penchant for peace and love produced two flower children. When they travelled home again, he had with him a wife, two serious little children and a patent for an alloy for use in bone prosthetics. This gave him the means to settle in Smestad and become middle class, something he quickly mastered entirely.

But he never succeeded in taking Selma away from handball.

She always answered them, these girls who played the sport.

She searched through her digital mailbox for 'Mina'.

An email exchange came up, from 2013, the year Mina turned twelve. The young girl had a Gmail address, and the email was competently written for a child. Selma had done unusually well in *Champion of Champions* the year before. Even though she had come fourth, she had only been beaten by three younger men. Mina was terribly impressed, and hoped to be just as fit when she was forty-six.

But first she wanted to be the best handball player in the world.

If only Selma Falck would be kind enough to give her some advice about that?

Selma answered. A long, comprehensive letter. A sincere thank-you came by return, including a heartfelt plea: Mina would really like for them to follow each other on Instagram. It was so cool to have an adult on such a platform – her parents knew nothing about social media.

That wish was easy to fulfil.

For a week or two Selma had followed her a little. After that, Mina had dropped into the long line of people who in the end numbered more than two hundred thousand followers on Selma's own account. It was true that she had been one of the first 'adults' to use Instagram. It had given her a useful lead. Secondly, and obviously most importantly, social media gave her full control over how everyone in the outside world perceived her situation.

Selma picked up her phone and took a look at Mina's account.

There was little sign of life there.

She had eight hundred followers, something that seemed fairly normal for a girl of her age. The last picture she had posted, however, was from early that summer. Selma browsed back in time. Until the beginning of April, Mina had been extremely active, often posting many times a day. She had not become the best handball player in the world, even though she still played for fun. Politics had obviously captured her. The photos and videos were a mixture of political appeals, selfies and close-ups of decorative food and drink. And a whole load of friends and nonsense.

Then someone had died. A friend, obviously, a close friend of the same age.

Her name was Ingeborg.

For a few weeks new pictures had been posted, but after the transition from April to May, they dwindled steadily.

Selma stopped at a video, taken in what might be a typical teenage girl's room. Mina was sitting on a bed with a white bedspread and three well-loved cuddly toys perched on the headboard. Behind her she could see a desk and a well-used schoolbag.

'I'm protesting against hatred,' Mina said gravely. *'Against smears and harassment, against shaming and rumours and fake news. Against ignorance and denial. I can't take any more. From today, my account is private. I have more than three thousand followers, but I'd rather be left with none than put up with all the crap about myself, my friends, my party and my father that streams in every day. I'm going to block everyone who doesn't behave properly. Fair criticism is acceptable, but only that.*

'Haters, back off!'

The camera tracking was shaky and ended up with nothing. The screen turned black.

Mina's public account had boasted more than three thousand followers. Now she had eight hundred in a private one. Once

Selma had read the most recent contributions more closely, she understood that the young girl had resigned as both local AUF leader and chair of the Pupil Council.

Something had happened. A death, obviously, that was certainly hard to bear, but there must be something more to it. The life of this mature teenager had clearly taken a turn for the far worse.

The very last post was published on 3 July. Long before the wedding.

Then there was total silence.

Means, motive and opportunity.

But it simply could not be.

Mina Selmer was a sweet, clever and enthusiastic teenager. Not a scheming killer. Not even on behalf of a father who had definitely been exposed to both smears and contempt by many people, but most of all, the professor at Blindern, who was now dead and gone.

Selma put down her mobile and iPad and tucked the note with the names of the three extra helpers into her dressing-gown pocket. When she got to her feet, she had to re-tie her belt.

She had lost weight. Not deliberately. Even though she weighed a few kilos more than the time when she had kept herself at match weight, quite literally, she had never felt any need to go on a diet. She was a tall woman, an athlete, and as long as she kept herself fit, she would never be really thin. Or fat, for that matter.

But of course she had to eat. And there had been very little food lately.

Jesper had only visited her four times since he had turned up in desperation to ask for her help. If it had been up to him, he would have moved in, but it was not up to him. Selma wanted to live alone. The food he served her should really be a good enough argument for moving in together without delay. Selma could rustle up everyday food without a problem, and had never been interested in spending an unnecessary length of time in the kitchen, but Jesper was amazing in that department too.

Yesterday he had thrown together a pasta dish with a kind of ham she had never heard of. And truffles. Selma had never tasted the eye-wateringly expensive fungi before, which had made him shave even more on to her tagliatelle in open-mouthed astonishment.

Selma had liked the pasta. And loved the ham. The truffles were wonderful, despite smelling of stuffy attics and tasting cloyingly sweet. All the same, she had not eaten very much – it was as if her appetite had vanished for the first time in her almost fifty-two-year-long life.

Opening the balcony door, she stepped barefoot out into the cool, almost chilly, morning air. The sounds of the city had already begun some time earlier, even though it was only just after half past five. In quarter of an hour or so the sun would rise. The spire on Sagene church punctured the dark sky in the west, but in the east, morning was on its way.

Selma finally realized why she had taken on this assignment for Jesper. It had to do with Anine.

It all had to do with Anine.

Browsing through Mina's Instagram pictures was like peeking into the life of the daughter she had always wished for. Admittedly, Mina had given up high-level handball, but most players gave up at the age of thirteen or fourteen. By then the teams were selected and many players got tired of sitting despondently on the sidelines. Besides, Mina was a girl who persisted. Who had opinions, and who could speak up for herself. Mina was a teenager who used words to let her voice be heard.

Anine had been so different, and was still so completely different, from Selma.

There was so much attitude with Anine, all through her upbringing. She had slammed doors, cried and showed her temper. Jumped for joy, laughed and expressed so many emotions, but Selma had never really understood where she positioned herself and what she actually thought. If she suddenly came home without saying hello and went straight to her room, Jesso could work out that she had quarrelled with her best friend. Picking at her food meant boy problems, Jesso knew. As far as Selma was concerned, picking at your food was being overly fastidious, something she could not bear.

A man stood with his back turned beside the rubbish bins on the other side of the street. He opened one of them and rummaged around. She guessed he was looking for empty bottles: there were plenty of people who could not be bothered to return their bottles to the shop to cash in the deposits. They relied instead on the Roma and other down-and-outs clearing up after them. The man had a bag at his feet, probably that day's haul. Now she could only see his back as he bent further down into the bin in his search for valuable pickings.

Loath to embarrass him, Selma turned her back, pulling her dressing gown more snugly yet again.

She had not taken on this case just because Jesper had an attractive backside. Or because he was so desperate. Or even because she was overly inquisitive. And not just to give her something to do either.

Nor was it because of the value of the bet she had taken that she was keen to help Jesper Jørgensen avoid acquiring a bad reputation. His food was good, but one extravagant restaurant visit a week for a whole year was something she could do really well without.

Selma Falck wanted first and foremost to help her daughter, she realized at last. That she had almost not been invited to the wedding had affected her far more than she had been willing to admit until now. The seating arrangements had hurt her deeply and made her angry, and she had left as soon as she could after the dramatic death. But really she had wanted to stay. She would have liked to be there for Anine, if only Anine had wanted to have her.

Selma had accepted the assignment of solving the mystery surrounding Sjalg Petterson's death because of Anine. She wanted to show her daughter that she cared about her. Always. That she was her mum. That Sjalg could not just go and die without Selma being able to find an explanation for what had really happened.

And who was to blame.

Selma was never going to be friends with Anine. It was far too late for that. All the same, she thought there was something worth saving in their relationship: Selma wanted to show her that she would like to be there for her.

This was the way she could be there for her.

By solving problems and uncovering the truth. Rushing through life at breakneck speed, but always being someone to rely upon when things needed to be sorted out.

It was now exactly half past five, and the sun broke through on the horizon. Within a couple of minutes the city was transformed before Selma's eyes. The light crept up over Torshovdalen and spilled out over Oslo. The city folk were waking up. Selma had put the hour of the wolf behind her yet again and was now able to breathe more easily.

She should do what she could for Anine.

This meant she had to speak to Mina Selmer, without having the faintest idea how she would manage that. Lifting her arms to the sky, she stretched her body and went back inside to shake some life into Jesper.

She had to get rid of this boy, but not quite yet.

Until then, he was far too good an asset.

Paparazzo

The man with the camera was named Andreas and he was nineteen.

He could scarcely call himself a photographer, but he did so all the same.

Until this point in his career Andreas had been paid for two assignments: his cousin's wedding photographs and a winning shot of last year's PRIDE parade that had been published by *Aftenposten*. His camera and equipment were certainly up to scratch, but he had no training. It was impossible to obtain an apprenticeship, and he had to work as a pizza delivery boy six days a week in order to make ends meet.

Photography was his life, though.

If he just took all the assignments he could get, then doors would open for him. He was convinced of that. Hard work was what it took. When Trine-Lise from *DG* had called him the previous evening, Andreas had become more excited than he had for ages. She had given him a brief outline of what the assignment entailed. Selma Falck was a super celebrity and Andreas knew very well what she looked like. She had apparently hooked up with a famous chef who, on the other hand, he had never heard of. Andreas had jotted down the name and Googled enough images to allow him to recognize him.

He had checked three times that he had the right address.

Trine-Lise had not been especially optimistic. Probably this Jesper guy would emerge on his own some time around the crack of dawn. Andreas was asked to rattle off a couple of photos of him, in case they got a nibble somewhere else with rumours about the two of them. Something to use right away was unlikely, and he would not be paid if the two lovebirds did not come out together.

Selma Falck was old. Older than Andreas's mother. Really old, in other words. The chef was only twenty-six. Admittedly, the

334

woman was pretty attractive, a MILF, really, but the age difference was so great that it was almost disgusting. A bit off, to say the least, and without a doubt it would make a good newspaper story.

For three hours Andreas had stood at his lookout post among the rubbish bins on the opposite side of the street. He was not cold – the roof overhang on the old apartment block afforded shelter from the morning drizzle – but he was starting to get seriously bored. He had rooted around in the waste paper bin to find something to read before it was even six a.m., but had not found anything. Now it was eight o'clock, and it was still too early to give up. But he could not be bothered hanging around much past nine. Anyway, his mobile was running out of battery; he had forgotten to charge it last night and had played games almost continuously.

Some of the passers-by in the last hour, rushing to work and school, had slowed down as they walked past. His camera was conspicuous, and an elderly man had almost tripped over the bulky bag Andreas always lugged around. A woman of around forty had asked sceptically if she could help him with something. He had flashed his broadest smile as he told her he was waiting for his girlfriend. The lady had reassured him that she was probably just delayed.

Andreas did not have a girlfriend, but he could see that something was happening at the door on the other side of the street. At lightning speed, he crouched down behind the recycling bin for paper and cardboard. He placed his camera on the lid and peered at the newly built block through the telephoto lens.

Jesper Jørgensen was easy to recognize. Despite the cool weather, he was wearing a tight-fitting, immaculate white T-shirt. Andreas could clearly see the large snake coiled around his arm, a tattoo that was also distinctive in most of his Google photos. Fortunately he had nothing on his head. Andreas reeled off a series of photos, but felt pretty disappointed that the chef seemed to be on his own. But all at once he almost leapt to his feet with excitement and forgetfulness. Selma Falck moved into sight through the glass door that Jesper was still holding open. She was bareheaded, dressed in a leather jacket, jeans and white trainers. As she came out, she raised her hand in nonchalant farewell to Jesper Jørgensen and turned left. She was clearly headed in the opposite direction.

'Come on, then!' Andreas whispered through gritted teeth.

As if Jesper had heard him, he grabbed Selma Falck's arm. She stood still, slightly reluctant, before looking around and trying to pull herself away. Jesper laughed. Andreas could hear the laughter from where he was crouched, and kept the shutter button pressed.

'Yes,' he hissed softly. 'Yessss!'

With a little jerk, the chef drew the woman towards him, leaning forward and kissing her while he put his other arm around her waist. Still resisting, she stood with her back arched as she held both hands on his shoulders. It did not matter, because when she broke free, she smiled and used her thumb to wipe his mouth.

The camera clicked and clicked before the couple across the street went their separate ways.

Andreas had sat down on the kerb by now. His hands were trembling with anticipation when he looked through the day's catch on the display.

Crystal-clear images. Kissing photos. Even an image of Selma Falck smilingly removing her own lipstick from the chef's mouth.

Or maybe it was only toothpaste.

What the hell, he was sitting on gold, and broke into a run to get the photos edited and sent to Trine-Lise as fast as he could.

Hard work, his grandfather had always said. Hard work and patience is what distinguishes the wheat from the chaff.

His grandfather was absolutely right, and Andreas ran at full pelt all the way home.

Hansakollen

The plane wreck still lay there, seventy-six years after a Luftwaffe pilot had met his fate on a mountain ridge in what was called the Maridal Alps, strangely enough. None of the hilltops – they lay like pearls on a string deep inside the Maridal valley – rose higher than 537 metres above sea level. The hike up, however, was fairly steep.

The nature reserve had been spared forestry and timber cutting. The two figures now standing in the shadows under the slopes of Hansakollen had therefore had to force their way through both fallen trees and dense vegetation to reach the area where the trail flattened out for the first time, directly facing east, on a marshy, dark tract.

'Odd that the wreck is still lying here,' said the man named Birger Hansem who was one of the five surviving members of the Council.

'A lot of it has disappeared over the years,' Berit Ullern said. 'Especially just after the war. Aluminium was valuable, and the wings were taken first.'

The forest was magical up here. Even so late in summer, long after the birds had stopped putting on airs and graces for one another, making a racket during the mating season, nature was filled with noises. Streams gurgled. Magpies screeched as they always did, and other birds warned one another of the humans and the black dog down below on the ground.

'Five years,' the man said, hunkering down in front of a black, twisted iron construction. 'They were here for five years, the Germans.'

'We have to stop him,' the Major said, staring at the St Bernard dog that lay prone in the marsh.

'I agree that Tryggve has to be stopped,' Birger replied. 'The question is how, though.'

The Major looked around and spied a toppled pine trunk. Sitting down, she opened a small rucksack and took out a thermos and two wooden cups. She came up here often. Lillomarka attracted far fewer walkers than the areas further west, and when out walking, as in other aspects of life, she preferred to be alone.

'Ellev told me he had removed Harlequin from the casket,' she said when Birger sat down beside her and accepted one of the cups. 'He left Skuld, Manus and the other groups, but he took out Harlequin.'

'The liquidation group.'

'Yes. Ellev didn't trust Tryggve. At least not in the last few years. There still remain in the casket keys to intelligence, hacking, sabotage ...'

She concentrated on pouring the coffee without spilling it.

'... you name it. But not liquidation.'

'But he managed it all the same.'

'Yes. Elegantly too, I'll give him that. I'd have liked to know how. The case is being dropped, isn't it?'

Birger Hansem was Deputy Chief of Police in Oslo police district. His background was in Interpol and the Justice Department, and he was the Major's closest confidant in the Council.

To the extent that she had confidants at all.

'Yes,' Birger answered, swiping away an insect. 'Even though it breaks my heart to let a straightforward murder pass, we can't risk Tryggve coming under the police spotlight. I had the case redirected to a newbie who doesn't know one end of a charge sheet from the other. She knows even less about investigation, and has been hooked up with the laziest officer in the force. In addition, I've called in on her, to welcome her. And drop more than a hint that Sjalg Petterson's death can be just punched out as "no criminal circumstances". Luckily, the family are not pushing.'

'Don't say that.'

'What do you mean?'

'Nothing,' she said lightly, shaking her head. 'I'm glad you've got it under control.'

He lifted his coffee cup.

'I don't like this, Berit. I really don't like it.'

The Major did not reply.

'There's peace in our country,' he went on. 'We're not supposed to go into action during peacetime.'

'We go into action all the time,' she said. 'Our intelligence service alone totals ...'

She broke off. Formerly it had been only Ellev who knew the capacity and size of the different groups. Now it was only Tryggve Mejer and herself.

'Every single day,' she began instead, 'some of us are active. Someone or other. Or several. Now and again they know of one another. Even more rarely several of them operate in tandem. We have soldiers and police, engineers and not least, a whole little army of IT experts. Teachers, doctors and the occasional bus driver. Nursery teachers and TV workers. Ordinary folk, Birger. We're an invisible army of ordinary people who understand the value of being able to defend ourselves. We gather information, we systematize it and we save it. Saving for a rainy day.'

'But that comes into the category of preparation,' Birger said, unexpectedly riled. 'Our entire raison d'être depends on being prepared for occupation! Not acting. Not springing into action in peacetime. Conduct intelligence gathering, by all means. But what Tryggve is doing is ... action.'

All of a sudden, he stood up.

'It's nonsense!' he roared, flinging out his arms in annoyance without a thought for the almost full cup in one hand.

A spurt of coffee splashed over a cluster of ferns.

'You're shouting at the wrong person,' the Major said, taken aback by Berger's unaccustomed vehemence. 'I agree with you. That's why I asked you to meet me. Of course we must do something. The question is, as you said yourself, what to do. I've tried to speak seriously to Tryggve. He even gave me his word of honour. I was naïve to believe him. Or ...'

She restrained herself and raised her cup.

In fact she had not taken Tryggve's word at face value. She had hoped, but not believed.

Something had come over Tryggve Mejer in the past year. Or maybe the last three years, when she came to think of it. It was as if the recent period as Justice Minister had changed him. She could follow him more closely than he could follow her: hardly a week went by without the Justice Minister appearing in the media. When he had taken over the department after three male members of the Progress Party had come to grief in less than two years, he had seemed to be Prime Minister Erna Solberg's saviour. Steady. Well-dressed and in top form. Tryggve had something agreeable about him, a conciliatory air that was nevertheless underpinned by tenacity and a fundamental conviction that he was on the side of the angels.

Slowly but surely he had grown more sombre. Tired, maybe. He had become more discouraged towards the end of his first year in government. On TV he seemed increasingly mechanical. Whereas earlier he had impressed even his most indignant opponents with his fresh ideas and unusually open mind for a party politician, he seemed after a while often to be operating on autopilot. Answered what he was asked. Stood firm on what he had done. Never beat around the bush and was still what people called 'good on TV'.

340

But it was as if a light had gone out inside him, at least in the past six months. During the meeting at which he had been keen to initiate Rugged/Storm-scarred, he had once again caught fire, but his energy had seemed to have something febrile about it.

'A penny for them?' Birger asked: he had sat down again.

'Tryggve has changed.'

'Yes, he certainly has.'

'What has happened, in actual fact?'

'Don't entirely know. But the world is different now from the last time he sat in that office. He gets more of a hiding now. With all these ... blogs. Social media. So-called online newspapers and God knows what else.'

'Yes. It's strange, really, that they go after him of all people, I mean. In many ways Tryggve is a ...'

She was searching for the right word.

'A decent man,' Birger suggested.

'Yes, he's decent. Friendly. Principled, but pragmatic when it counts. Consensus orientated. In many ways you could say he's more like Ellev than his own father. Peder was more short-tempered. Stubborn. For example, I can't understand why Sjalg Petterson should pick out Tryggve Mejer in particular as a target for his abuse and aggression.'

'No? I do.'

'Oh – why then?'

He helped himself to more coffee. Raised the cup to his mouth, blew on it and drank.

'In many ways Tryggve can be said to be the opposite of Sjalg,' he said quietly. 'Even though they were also alike. Both are intelligent, well-read men with a good education. Both have the gift of the gab. When it comes to the great schism between them, immigration, well, Tryggve's not exactly a rebel when it comes to that either.'

'No,' said the Major. 'He supports government policy, which is strict.'

Birger nodded.

'Personally he's probably more liberal, but he has always been loyal to the system. And he's not naïve. He understands that a society can't accept more foreigners than the population is willing to accept. Immigration and migrants have never been a matter of resources in this country. We have enough money. Instead it's about attitude: openness and courage and the ability to welcome other people. Which explains why folk in the large towns are less xenophobic than others. They are used to strangers. And so they cease to be strange.'

'You said the two of them were different, though?'

'Yes. Sjalg Petterson was in fact a pretty scared man. Behind the polished façade lurked anxiety and frustration, as I interpreted him, anyway. A man who insists that "niggers" and "mongols" are acceptable words because they're merely "well established terms whose meaning everyone understands", is a person who fears change. Who has stopped meeting people halfway. Stopped listening. Stopped paying attention to how other people perceive what you say.'

Bernhard came plodding across to them, gave a heavy sigh and lay down at his master's feet. Birger put his hand on the dog's large head.

'Sjalg Petterson was a thirty-six-year-old man who hankered back to the time before he was born,' he said. 'To an idea. Something he had never actually experienced for himself, but which obviously must have seemed idyllic to him. But Norway is no longer like that. We can never go back there again. Fortunately. Women don't want to stay at home. Homosexuals must have rights. Norway is no longer a totally homogenous society, even though we in this country are more alike than most people elsewhere.'

'And have a more peaceful existence.'

'Yes. But that dream of the sixties, of Sunday walks and old-fashioned meatballs, about mother, father and children all out picking berries in the autumn ...'

Birger smiled.

'In contrast to Sjalg Petterson, I lived through that time. I do *not* want to go back.'

The Major did not respond.

'People like Sjalg have a dream that can't be fulfilled,' he continued. 'A golden illusion ... no, *delusion*, about how things used to be. It makes them angry. They are triggered by the very *markers* of change, the milestones and symbols for what has become different. They are provoked by feminism, riled by hijabs and furious that Norway has inevitably become part of an increasingly shrinking world. And so they get angry with dark-skinned children wearing Norwegian national costume. With other nations' flags appearing in the procession on the seventeenth of May, our national day. These things constitute tangible symbols that everything that is Norwegian and safe is in transition. At risk, as they presumably see things.'

He became lost in thought. Drank some more coffee. Scratched the dog slowly and gently behind the ear.

'Tryggve is a mature man who is wise enough to appreciate that the world no longer belongs to us. At least he did until recently.'

'What do you mean?'

'The world is spinning so fast,' Birger said. 'I have to admit I can't always manage to follow it. But that doesn't matter too much. It doesn't threaten me. Young people have never been so well educated. They're smart. They care, and they'll manage. The world will get by with their help. I don't need to understand everything. People like Tryggve and me ...'

He looked askance at the Major and smiled.

'... and you, for that matter, still have a great deal to contribute. We're the ones who have to keep things on a tight leash. Try to restrain things as well as we can, but also know when to give them some slack when the time is right. The problem for Tryggve in recent years is probably that he ...'

Birger smacked his lips as if he wanted to taste his way to the right words.

'Overload,' he exclaimed. 'Tryggve has become overloaded. Not by having too much to do, but by his belief in how life should be lived being met by so much opposition. So much ...'

He fished out a snuff box from his jacket pocket. He used his thumb and forefinger to form a generous pinch and inserted it under his lip.

'So much fucking bias,' he concluded, spitting out a few flakes. 'A man like Tryggve is not formatted for the age of the internet. He's an educated man. Thoroughly educated and liberal. When someone is unprofessional towards him, he answers professionally. When he is met with spite and claptrap, he answers with facts. And he stands firm, and stands tall. Tryggve is in many ways an old-fashioned man with a modern attitude to change. Sjalg is a young man with an old-fashioned attitude to life. That was what sparked Sjalg Petterson to be so malicious towards Tryggve.'

'And now Tryggve has had enough,' the Major said sotto voce.

'That's what I fear. That he's on the verge of a breakdown. This whole Rugged/Storm-scarred operation is insane.'

Berit Ullern nodded. Although she had known Birger Hansem for twenty-five years, they had never had a conversation like this. During the meetings of the Council, he was a taciturn man. An observer, she had often thought. Silent mostly, and to the point on the rare occasions when he had something to say. She had been right. The Deputy Police Chief was a skilful observer.

They went on sitting on the tree trunk in silence. Bernhard, the big dog, had moved off again and was waddling around the area with his nose glued to the ground. The scents of forest, animals, marsh, weather and decay were so strong that even the humans could pick them up. For Bernhard, this was a veritable paradise.

An aircraft engine cut through the soughing of the trees. They both looked up, but the forest was too dense for them to see anything. Birger Hansem put his coffee cup on the ground, took out a packet of Smil chocolate, opened it and offered it to Berit. She politely turned it down.

'A picture is starting to take shape,' he said in a noticeably louder voice, as if he wanted to mark a change of scene.

He spat out the snuff and put a piece of chocolate in his mouth before he ploughed on.

'And I don't like it. Journalists and other parties could begin to catch sight of what's happening at any moment. There's a pattern to all this, Berit. The ranks of the loudest voices on the outer fringes of politics are being thinned out. That Pål Poulsen withdrew from everything in such a hopelessly unbelievable fashion is one thing. Everyone understands that there must be more behind it than his claim that he wants to spend more time with his grown-up children. If he cared a jot for his kids, he would have jumped ship earlier.'

He took another piece of chocolate and stuffed the rest of the pack into his pocket.

'Sjalg's death is a different matter. At least the general public has an explanation for that. But when this business of Default.no happens as well, and all these hysterical people are suddenly exposed and silenced and …'

'You're right,' the Major said when Birger broke off. 'At some time or other someone's going to see the pattern. Especially because Tryggve has only just started. He has the capacity to …'

This time she was the one who held back.

'Rumours in the police have it that the case in Randaberg was different from how it appeared,' Birger said, picking up a dead twig and starting to strip off the bark. 'Their computer was extremely interesting. They were agents provocateurs, without a doubt, but seemingly it's impossible to prove. Anyone can speak out, as we know, and the payment they received is apparently saved in an account in Russia. The couple go there twice a year.'

'Are they being hauled in for the hash plantation at least?'

'It seems so. But ...'

He tossed the twig away and rubbed his neck.

'Was this action of ours his doing?' he asked. 'Tryggve's, I mean? In the service of Skuld, to be more precise?'

'I assume so,' the Major replied. 'And the action against the so-called news desk in Murmansk was even described in the Rugged/Storm-scarred document. This could have ended up with a diplomatic catastrophe if the Russians had known how it was actually stopped.'

'I also recognize this hacker group from Tryggve's plans,' Birger Hansem said. 'Trashfighters, eh? He is moving into increasingly dangerous waters. A special team has been set up with us to take care of the case. I won't be able to stop that as simply as the Petterson investigation. To go for the jugular of the free press is ... unheard of. And incredibly stupid, from a purely tactical point of view.'

He gazed at her with his head raised, as if he expected a response. Instead she grabbed his cup from the ground without asking and stuffed both it and hers into her rucksack, got to her feet and looked down at him.

'You and I must have an eye for an eye,' she said in an undertone. 'The safeguarding of the Council and all the Council's resources.

346

That's absolutely the most important thing. Our groups are more important than anything else. Tryggve is putting everything at risk right now, and we know of course that he has only just started. Admittedly, I'm watching out. My people are following what his people are doing. All the same, it's not enough. Tryggve has to stop.'

'You've tried before to convince him.'

'You have to make another attempt now.'

'Why would he listen to me any more than to you?'

A peacock butterfly fluttered by. Berit followed it with her eyes. The large, black spots on the wings looked as if they were staring back when it landed on a pine trunk. A few seconds later, it danced on up the hillside. Bernhard lifted his snout to the north and sniffed.

'He simply must,' the Major insisted. 'You have to make him realize what the consequences of refusing will be. You have to fight fire with fire.'

She saw Birger swallow hard. His eyes evaded hers when she tried to make eye contact. Straightening her back, she repeated: 'I'm not ordering you to do this; I'm not in a position to do that. I'm begging you. I'm truly begging you. You know what's at stake.'

Birger got to his feet.

'You're the one in possession of Harlequin,' he said. 'How did Tryggve manage to kill Sjalg Petterson?'

'I don't know,' she said bluntly and began to walk. 'The point is that he did. He must have done. You have to stop Rugged/Storm-scarred. You must give Tryggve a reality check before too much damage has been done. He must learn how far we're willing to go to take care of what we were set up to protect.'

She felt a firm grasp on her arm and turned round sharply.

Birger was standing uncomfortably close to her. She could see black pores in his skin on the sides of his nose and caught a whiff of coffee on her face as he said: 'Using Harlequin in peacetime is a crime, Berit.'

'So is leaving Norway defenceless,' she said, pulling away from his firm grip. 'That would be the worst crime of all.'

AUTUMN

The Search

The hunters had been back to their car. Gaia had been taken care of at last, fed and put into a cage in the vehicle for a rest.

When Sture Jensen and Hans-Olav Storbergan had set out on another hike, this time without dog or rifles, they were far quieter than they had been earlier in the day. Now no photos were taken at all.

No one on Facebook would learn of what they were doing.

Including the gimbal, camera and batteries, the drone weighed nearly four kilos. Hans-Olav had carried it all the way. Not until they were a couple of kilometres from the burnt-out cabin could they set the drone to work. There were barely five hours of daylight left.

They were running short of time.

Selma Falck must have walked towards the south-east. The two men had to take the chance that she had reasoned this out correctly on her journey towards civilization.

It was the only option they had.

Hans-Olav launched the drone into the air. It had a range of seven kilometres and could reach a speed of more than one hundred kilometres per hour. The remote-control display showed a detailed map on the left-hand side, where the drone's position was marked with a bright red dot, and the right side was an aerial photo. Maximum operating time was less than half an hour, but fortunately they had several sets of batteries in the car from the last time they were up here.

The two men began to walk methodically towards the south-east and let the drone hover in wide circles above and ahead of them.

'Where there's life, there's hope,' Sture said under his breath, but he did not really believe it himself.

SUMMER

Toy Boy

It was now Friday evening, and Selma was alone at home.

Oslo bore signs of next week's new school term. An everyday solemnity had settled over the city, despite the start of the weekend. People were behaving differently, as Selma had noticed when she had come home from Einar's an hour earlier. They no longer ambled along nor were they laughing as they walked. Light clothing and uplifted eyes were absent. A sense of purpose had come over everyone, even those who had already taken a few drinks and were on their way out to sample some nightlife. The heat would still sneak out on occasional days in the weeks that lay ahead, but the sweltering, frivolous summer of 2018 was definitely over.

Selma's inbox contained an endless series of blue dots. She had hardly bothered to read her emails for the past few weeks. Now there were more than two hundred unopened messages awaiting her attention. Some were advertising, and she decided to sort through them all and delete these before she tried to take the others seriously.

This took time, and she felt restless.

Jesper had offered to come, but Selma had turned him down. She could not get anything done when he was there.

Nor when he wasn't, for that matter.

Apart from online gambling, and she was now indulging in that far too often. Although it did not help one iota. It was as if the effect had dissipated in the course of these late summer days. As if Jesper had introduced a constant disquiet into her life that demanded more drastic measures than a few rounds of Texas Hold'em to dispel.

Groaning inwardly, she headed for the fridge. There was still a can of real cola there, but she had already consumed the one can she allowed herself each week. In the door shelf, there was a half-full bottle of white wine that Jesper had left. Selma grabbed it, yanked out the cork and put the neck to her nose.

The white wine smelled sour. A little of stomach acid, and a lot of cheap perfume.

Red wine smelled of mould, which was even worse. Beer was bitter, Selma recalled from the one time when her sixteen-year-old self had been persuaded to taste it.

She re-corked the bottle and put it back again. Picked up the coke can and decided to bring forward next week's quota all the same. Opened it and took time to savour the soft hiss when the ring pull was removed and the beige fizz forced its way out of the can.

'Pull yourself together,' she whispered. 'Do something. Don't screw things up.'

She had at least tried to get in touch with Mina, having sent a DM on Instagram and still hoped for the best. The recipient had still not read the message, she could see, despite having sent it at around ten a.m. that same morning. The lie she had dreamt up was one of Selma's better ones, she thought: the Handball Association had asked her to contribute to an investigation into the dropout rate from the sport. Selma would like to speak to Mina in the light of the approach she had made five years earlier.

She had followed Mina's exciting development, she added with enthusiasm, and thought her exactly the kind of articulate and reflective girl Selma needed to talk to.

With her coke in one hand and a lighter in the other, she moved around lighting the candles she had ferreted out yesterday. The sun set by nine p.m., and twilight ended before ten.

It was cosier in here now, but her inclination to work was still almost non-existent.

With a sigh, she picked up the MacBook from the settee and set it down on the dining table. She had to sit up straight to avoid falling asleep. This simply had to be done. She began to delete the emails that were obviously of zero interest.

The phone rang. Glancing at the display, she saw it was Jesper and let it ring out. Continued to delete emails. Opened the occasional one she was not entirely sure of, and tried to move them across to the different subgroups she had organized when she had decided to strike out on her own prior to Christmas. Without a secretary, she had to learn to keep some kind of order in her affairs.

She saw that they wanted her to take part in *Celebrity Farm 2019*. The filming did not begin until May, but they were keen to put out feelers early to guarantee her participation. The man who sent the letter was in charge of casting for the production company, but Selma knew him better as a former beach volleyball player. A pleasant guy, she had met him several times, and now he was absolutely convinced that Selma Falck's participation would raise the popular TV programme to new and undreamt-of heights.

She moved the email into the folder marked IMPORTANT UNANSWERED.

Actually, it sounded tempting. She had scarcely seen a single episode, but to judge by the massive media interest, it might well be exciting. She would probably even win. She was not addicted to tobacco, and neither did she drink, and in the food department she was so easygoing that she sometimes, without thinking about it, lived on slices of bread for two days on the trot. She was strong enough to beat all comers, of that she was fairly certain.

The animals, of course, would be a problem. A big problem, to be honest. Selma could never bring herself to milk cows. She was terrified of the huge animals.

As she dismissed the idea of taking part, her mobile chimed again.

Jesper was persistent.

Irritated, she turned off the sound.

Runhild Petterson had sent her more wedding photos. This was the third time since their meeting. Selma had taken a closer look at the two previous messages in the hope that they might contain something of interest. However, they had not, and she moved this email to UNIMPORTANT UNANSWERED.

The display on her mobile lit up. A text message, she saw, and opened it.

Selma, call me! A journalist from DG has been in touch. They know we're an item (are we?) and want a comment from me. Christ, they're saying they have pictures of us! Where would that be from????? What should I say? Call me. Jesper.

Selma sat open-mouthed and read the message over again. And over again. In the end she knew it by heart, including the number of question marks and everything. Finally she put the phone down carefully.

This was a catastrophe.

Anine was Selma's first thought. Anine would never forgive her.

Her heart was hammering so hard that she could feel the strong, fast beats when she used both hands to touch her neck.

This was totally unfathomable. She had not told a soul about Jesper. She had been at several summer parties and other social gatherings in the past few weeks, but always on her own. Not even Einar had any idea that she had acquired a toy boy, as malicious tongues would almost certainly describe him. It was possible that Jesper had been a touch indiscreet at work, what did Selma know, but the two of them had not shown themselves outdoors at any point.

Except for this morning, it suddenly struck her.

For a few seconds, outside the main door downstairs, when Jesper had pulled her to him and kissed her. There must have been a photographer hanging about somewhere.

Maybe someone who had been rummaging around in her neighbours' trash earlier that morning rubbish, Selma had even turned away to avoid embarrassing him. The person in question must have received a tip-off. From someone who knew. Or who had worked it out.

Everything came to a standstill inside Selma's head. Until the penny dropped.

'Lars Winther,' she articulated slowly. 'May you roast in hell for this!'

The Logbook

Mina Selmer was lying in bed, feeling old.

She had looked through her messages on Snapchat. She could not even bring herself to venture into Instagram, it just reminded her of how much she had missed out on that summer. How fucking awful it all was.

When her father had been on TV, explaining to the whole of Norway why he had been working all summer, Mina had been so happy. She had received the answers she was looking for, and courage finally to take him into her confidence. She had been so sure that now, since the new Freedom of Expression Commission was no longer a secret, her old dad would come back. She had waited for him after the TV broadcast, with smoked salmon and scrambled eggs, well-cooked eggs the way he liked them best. She had even gone into the garage for a bag of firewood, even though there were only sixty-litre bags left. They were terribly heavy, and in the end she had had to cut the bag open in the courtyard outside and carry in five logs at a time. All the candles were lit when he came home, but he merely stood in the kitchen doorway looking sad.

'How kind of you,' he had said, with a sigh. 'Food and everything. But I'm afraid I'm not hungry. I had to have a bite to eat before the TV programme. But scrambled eggs will keep in the fridge.'

That was not entirely true. Hot scrambled egg was much better than cold. She had toasted bread too, and the slices would be dry and disgusting in the morning.

It was a mystery why Dad still felt compelled to spend time in the basement. There wasn't even a desk down there. It was probably OK to make use of the workbench, but it would be easier and handier to sit in the home office upstairs that he and Mum shared.

Mina felt dreadful.

Her whole body ached, as if she had exercised a lot for the first time in ages. Stiff, sore and slightly nauseated. In addition she had a guilty conscience about having lied to Dad.

Now he was in Trondheim.

Mina was old enough to be left alone at home for a night or two, but Dad did not like it. Last autumn, just after the start of term, she had been given permission to host a real party and it had got completely out of hand. Dad had forbidden alcohol and

356

insisted on an absolute limit of thirty guests, but there were already more than eighty when Mina lost count. In the end she had locked herself into her room with Ingeborg, both in floods of tears. Their neighbour had sounded the alarm after calling round to ask them to tone down the noise. The police turned up, Mum and Dad came home after being called and Mum had estimated the damage at almost twenty thousand kroner. Ingeborg and Mina had tried to gather up the empty bottles throughout the evening and hide them in the garage. Not a particularly good idea, since Dad had found the two huge bin bags of squashed beer cans, empty vodka bottles and filthy Red Bull cans that stank of booze early the next morning.

Her parents' fury had lasted for several days, even though Mina had offered to replace the damaged items with some of her confirmation money. Mum lost her temper at the drop of a hat, but it had been awful to see Dad so livid.

Since then he had always hesitated to leave her alone at home overnight.

I trust you but not the others, was what he always said.

At breakfast she had told him she intended to spend the night at Ida's. Only a few weeks ago he would have questioned her more closely: how many of them there would be, whether Ida's parents would be at home, and whether they were going to a party first. Along those lines. Now he had simply nodded and seemed relieved before he drove off in the black government car.

Mina struggled to sit up in bed.

Maybe she was coming down with something. She had not taken any exercise all summer, and her diet had not been particularly healthy either.

After her last visit to the basement, when she had finally cracked the code for the safe, it had dawned on her that she had made a major blunder. When she had copied the contents of the memory stick on to her own laptop, she had left electronic traces behind. All documents on such storage devices gave the date they had last been opened. She had been nervous for a few days, but typically enough, Dad had not noticed. He could not have done. He was just as distracted and distant as usual, and if he had seen it, Mina would surely be the only suspect.

Maybe it did not matter too much.

Maybe she had been right in thinking that the casket and its contents were merely some kind of souvenir. A memento of Ellev: Dad had been so fond of him, and he had been a presence in Mina's life for as long as she could remember.

If the secret lay in the laptop downstairs, it had to be about something other than the Freedom of Expression Commission.

Mina yawned.

She was nearly always tired these days; it was as if she never felt fully rested no matter how much she slept. Previously, she had not even been able to remember going to the toilet during the night. Now she kept waking up. Because of bad dreams or simply because she was lying in an uncomfortable position.

Mina was exhausted, but she could not sleep. She already knew that, as it was too early in the evening. She would just drop off into a doze and be jerked out of it after only ten minutes had passed. For once she felt a bit hungry too. Dad had said there was a salad from Lille Persille in the fridge. You would never catch him going to the Storo shopping centre to buy it, but the woman next door kept calling in with food. She was fit enough and very nice, but nearly eighty years old. She obviously thought men were simply incapable of looking after themselves when their wives left them. Just out of the blue, as Mina had heard her say to another neighbour over the garden fence one evening when the weather was still balmy and all the windows were open.

The whole street knew that Mum had walked out.

Mina was on the verge of tears. She would not cry, though, because she was too worn out. Instead she got up.

Once she had reached the ground floor and was about to head into the kitchen, it felt as if her feet continued on down entirely of their own accord. As if her will had split in two, and the worse half drove her downstairs and into the basement and then on into the technical store.

She was no longer either hungry or tired.

On the contrary – she felt a pleasant jab of excitement when she bent down in front of the large safe and crossed her fingers that her dad had not changed the code.

He had not: 2018 still worked.

Mina paid no attention to the casket with the royal monogram. She had Googled 'Stay Behind groups' twice more after her last visit to the safe, and had dismissed it all as old junk. Something that Ellev must have been involved in after the war. Mina had received the biography of resistance fighter and defence minister Jens Christian Hauge as a present from her old great-uncle a couple of years ago. The two of them had been long-time friends and party comrades, Ellev had told her, and seemed almost proud. Even though Mina had never heard of the man. She had read twenty pages of the book before giving up. History was enthralling but not a million pages about old men full of secrets.

It was the laptop that interested her.

The last time she had not switched it on.

It must have been out of charge that time, she realized, because now when she pressed the on-button, it began to light up. She scanned the room for something to sit on, and caught sight of a bundle of black cables beside the party glasses from Nille, on the top wall shelf. Dad had obviously just forgotten to put the cables in the safe.

She hesitated for a moment, but then ran to the living room and fetched the stool she had used last time. Setting it up in front of the workbench, she took a closer look at the screen.

Dad had not even used a password – typical!

The machine was not connected to the internet either.

It did not even ask her if she wanted to do that.

She did: there was really little point in a computer if it had no access to the web. Just as she was about to click into the settings to link up to the network, she had second thoughts.

There were machines that were isolated from the rest of the world. Air-gapped, she thought they were called, and they were usually used in banks, government departments and other places where information was stored that must not go adrift under any circumstances. Those, however, were huge systems with enormous data capacity, whereas this was a measly, cheap Dell laptop.

All the same, Dad must have chosen to have it like this. When you set up a computer, the internet connection was among the very first things the machine asked about. He usually had to ask Mina for help every time he got a new computer, one that did not belong to the Justice Department, but despite that he was not completely illiterate.

Mina decided to leave the machine as it was.

There was not very much on it.

Microsoft Office was installed, at least. She could not quite understand how he could have managed to do that without downloading the software through the internet connection. Maybe it was possible to use a memory stick or something. Naturally there was no search engine and no email box either. No photos were stored, and it felt strange to navigate around in a machine that clearly had never been on the web. No history.

And only one single Word document.

Mina began to understand why her dad chose to sit down here with this laptop, If, suddenly and contrary to all expectation, someone should turn up, she would have plenty of time to turn off the computer, put it back and lock the safe before they managed to come all the way down here. Then you could just pretend to be looking for something. Checking something, the fan for example, that hummed and whirred and was giving her a headache. This was yet another indication that he did not want anyone to have oversight of what he was doing.

She opened the document, a very ordinary docx file.

But it was huge.

LOGBOOK was written in capital letters on the first page.

Mina pulled the stool up to the workbench and began to read.

AUTUMN

Journey's End

'She doesn't want anything more to do with me,' she whispered to Lupus.

Selma Falck was finished with walking.

Once her memory had fully returned, she was completely drained of energy. She had sat down under a boulder, so massive that a whole little forest of dwarf birch trees had rooted on top of it. Facing south-west, where the mountain ridge sloped slightly towards the ground to afford shelter from the light rain, she had keeled over when one leg had stopped cooperating. She had tried to open her bag. Selma was no longer hungry, but the thirst was unbearable.

Her fingers would simply not work properly. She could not do it.

'Anine doesn't want to have my name. She doesn't want me as her mother.'

Lupus whimpered and snuggled closer.

'I'm no longer allowed.'

Selma's voice was gone. Her lungs were on fire. The words only just crossed her lips, on laboured exhalations, so softly that even Lupus might not have been able to catch them.

'Lupus,' she groaned, trying to pull him closer.

Her limbs had stopped working. Her eyes too, she realized, when she was unable to open them at will. Sometimes they slid open, all by themselves, and Selma could see that it was still light. Soon the day would disappear behind the mountains in the far distance. Then it would not take long until she died.

It meant nothing, not really.

'Never again,' she said, her lips still managing at least to form words. 'My daughter never wants to see me again.'

Lupus was a wolf. He would be able to survive, although in fact he was a dog.

'You can eat me,' Selma said.

She smiled, she knew, only just, at the thought.

The summer of 2018 had finally come back to her. She perceived the connections and patterns, and knew she would never get there in time. It no longer mattered. Of everything that had happened and everything that should never have happened, it was only her child's final rejection that dominated her thoughts now that she was about to die.

Johannes had just sent a text message.

The email from Anine had been formal. She had addressed her by her full name. She had attached a copy of her application to the Justice Department to have Falck officially removed as part of her surname. Along with a declaration of disclaimer of all rights to Selma's inheritance.

'Hereditatem,' Selma whispered. 'And something about repulsa, I think.'

Unwilling to think about Jesper, she pushed the memory away. She did not want to remember the warmth of his body, his hands, his touch, and the beautiful snake that stayed awake with her during the night. Don't think of Jesper's nonsense and games, the bottom lip that made him look like a child when he was in a bad mood. As when she told him he was never to come back. That her daughter hated her. That it was all his fault.

She had to tell him it was his fault to make him stay away.

363

It was not true.

Selma herself was to blame, but that was not what she should think about now.

Anine was in the midst of suing Jesper, she had stated in the email. Anine and Jesso had brought a civil action against Jesper. Jesso Mork, Selma's ex-husband, Anine's father. The one who had been a proper parent, a dad to depend upon, and Anine never wanted to set eyes on Selma Falck again. Jesper Jørgensen had killed her husband, and of all the people on earth, her mother had to jump into bed with him. Without saying a word, even when she had the chance, so that Anine had to read about it in the newspapers.

A betrayal. It was unforgivable.

'Lupus,' Selma struggled to say.

She tried to sit up more comfortably, but it was impossible.

Jesper had not killed Sjalg Petterson.

'I found out all about it,' Selma endeavoured to tell the dog. 'I was meant to tell Anine that Jesper was innocent. She would have forgiven me.'

Her throat contracted and there was a gurgling noise each time she drew breath. It was not even possible to cough. She wanted to open the zip of her all-weather jacket but could not manage that either.

She could manage nothing, and that made Selma smile.

A plane was approaching. A tiny little angry plane. Or a gigantic fly, an enormous mosquito that wanted to suck the last minuscule remnants of life out of her as she lay there under the boulder, dying.

Lupus stood up.

He growled, but did not leave her side.

Selma forced her eyes open one last time.

God came down from heaven, she heard. He had sent a plane to fetch her, even though she had never believed in Him. It was invisible, even though the noise grew louder and louder. Her eyes wanted to close, but Selma forced them to see.

The plane suddenly came into sight above her, and slowly sank towards the ground. Then it hovered silently in the air like a colossal dragonfly, staring at her and the wolf dog with a single big eye.

Lupus barked. God flew closer.

'I'm coming,' Selma said inaudibly, and passed away peacefully into a liberating, all-embracing nothingness.

SUMMER

The Ice Cubes

The weekend had been almost impossible to survive.

Selma Falck was not ashamed of a relationship with a man half her age. Nor of the whole of Norway knowing about it. Her love life was her own business, her own choice, and Jesper was a great guy with no other ties. The unfamiliar feeling of sorrow and the even more unexpected sense of shame were because she had children who did not want to have anything to do with her.

The article and images in *Dagens Gang* had made both her children finally break off with their mother.

Johannes had been brief. As usual. That was what he was like. His reaction to most things in life was a shrug of the shoulder, but his text message was brutal. In only 187 characters he had let her know that he never wanted to clap eyes on her again. That he supported his sister, and that it felt liberating to finally make a definitive break with Selma Falck. Someone he was not very bothered about to begin with, in fact.

The email from Anine had been far more expansive.

And Jesper was devastated.

But not as desperate as Selma, who had hardly slept since Friday. Now it was Sunday evening, and there would soon be grooves in the parquet floor along the path she had trod. From her bedroom, where in her rage she had torn down all the wedding photos and where drawing pins now lay strewn across the floor, to the living room, round the coffee table and dining table and into the open-plan kitchen arrangement where she rounded things off by banging her head on the fridge.

And then back to the bedroom, where each time she pricked the soles of her feet on the floor.

Over and over again, the selfsame lap.

By Saturday morning she had called things off with Jesper. By text message. He had phoned forty-one times before she finally gave up and accepted the call. She forced herself to be stern and angry and cold, but it was to no avail. In the end she had switched off her phone, even though she usually never dared to cut Einar off from all possibility of getting in touch with her. Twice before in extremis he had defied his anxiety, grabbed the old Nokia and rung his only benefactor.

All the same, there was nothing else for it but to shut off the outside world.

Half an hour later Jesper had let himself in.

Selma was strong, but she knew it was impossible for her to physically and forcibly eject a man like him. She used words instead. He was in tears when he left, leaving the key on the chest of drawers. Since then things had been quiet.

From his quarter.

Her mobile had nevertheless rung uninterrupted since DG.no had published the story at seven o'clock on Saturday morning. They had not succeeded in obtaining a comment from Selma Falck, said the text beneath one large and two smaller photos, but felt they had received all the confirmation they needed from Jesper Jørgensen about the racy affair.

He had not even had the wit to deny it.

Idiot. DG would not have dared to publish anything without confirmation from at least one of them.

In the beginning, Selma had attempted to keep track of who was trying to get in touch with her, but after the text message from Johannes had arrived, she gave up. The email from Anine did not arrive until around two on Saturday afternoon. Selma came across it by chance: it had been several hours since she had stopped looking at the internet when, in a burst of good sense, she had realized that she should really check what was actually going on out there.

Anine had been right. Selma certainly could shed tears.

The weekend would soon be over, and she could not remember ever having felt so exhausted. The face that greeted her in the mirror each time she went to the toilet was unrecognizable. Her eyes squinted through the swelling and lack of make-up. Her lips were dry and red and the sides of her nose were so sore that she had started smearing her skin with Lypsyl.

Thump. Thump.

She had to stop.

Her forehead was tender, and a dent had appeared in the fridge.

Most of all she wanted to go out and run. At speed and for a long distance. Sprint through the city, and for once break through the barriers into Marka. Continue as far as she was able, deep into the forest, racing for as long as there was life left in her. However, she did not dare leave her apartment. There might be someone out there.

Someone out there, with a camera.

The doorbell rang for the fifth time since Jesper's departure.

It could be him.

She hesitated. She had never been nastier to anyone. Apart, perhaps, from Anine.

She should not open the door. The security chain was on, and she felt trapped. Locked in, but nevertheless not safe. She didn't even dare step out on to the balcony, even though darkness had finally descended.

'Snap out of it,' she sobbed, banging her head extra hard on the metal.

She was a coward, and could hardly breathe.

The sense of loss of control was extremely alarming. Even last year, when a client had caught her red-handed following the misappropriation of countless millions, she had managed to remain calm. She had thought constructively, realized she only had herself to blame, and seized the life she had now made for herself.

A heart attack was imminent.

There was something tight around her chest, pain was stabbing her right side, she could not breathe and felt so dizzy that she staggered across to the dining table to sit down. Black flecks danced in front of her eyes, and she had tunnel vision. When she raised her hands to look at them, they were crawling with ants devouring them from the inside out, and it was as if they no longer belonged to her.

She formed her mouth into a big O. Took a deep breath, and let the air out slowly. Over and over again.

She managed to stand up. Walked to the kitchen and turned on the tap. As soon as the water was cold enough, she let it run over her wrists. Rinsed out the dishcloth without caring how rank it smelled. She draped it round her neck, still soaking wet. The water ran down her back beneath her blouse, reached the waistband of her jeans and soaked into the fabric. Selma tore off a long strip of kitchen roll and wet it too before applying it to her eyes.

'Snap out of it,' she told herself again. 'Right now.'

Her pulse rate dropped. Her breathing grew more regular.

This was what they called a panic attack, she realized, as she breathed more easily. She wet the cloths again. Using the edge of the worktop for support, she forced her heart into its usual, normal rhythm.

She no longer recognized herself. Really did not. This scared her more than anything else. The children had never been particularly close to her. By the time Anine was born, Selma had understood that her reason for having children was because it was the natural thing to do. Not because she had wanted them. The little bundle sucked all the strength out of her, quite literally, and hampered her ability to do all the things she had loved to fill her life with up till then. Also, the children had been uncommonly difficult to deal with. During a spell of colic lasting four weeks without a break, Selma had moved in with her friend Vanja after a few days and only gone home to use a breast pump. With her nights already plagued by nightmares, there was quite simply no room for a squalling infant.

For Jesso it had been completely different. He walked the floor, carrying Anine and hushing her to sleep, singing lullabies and loving the screaming tyrant from the very first squeak. When he promised to take on all the work with baby number two, Selma had agreed to have another child. Then she had been sterilized, since Jesso refused to have the snip.

She had it done in all secrecy to avoid yet another argument.

Selma was fond of children, she had always thought and almost felt, but she could never see herself in other parents' panegyric descriptions of love for their offspring. For a long time she had thought they were simply telling lies. Exaggerating. Selma went along with it, fibbing with the best of them, just as she had mastered participating in every conversation as long as she could be bothered.

Eventually, when Anine was about seven, Selma had acknowledged that she was different from other people. People truly loved their children more than life itself. There was something fundamentally wrong with her emotional life, she conceded, and she adapted to that. Children needed love, predictability and closeness. Jesso could give them all this, and Selma withdrew. After all, her two children had each other.

When everything had fallen apart before Christmas and her marriage with Jesso was over, both Anine and Johannes had been furious on their father's behalf. This had affected Selma, but in a sense she had known that everything would settle down.

Which is what they had been doing, partly with the help of Sjalg Petterson.

Now they were on the warpath again. She tried to tell herself that it would pass. These things did always pass, as most things in the world had a tendency to be forgotten with the assistance of time.

It was futile. Selma was going to pieces. The thought of never seeing her children again was choking her and there was no point in trying to calm herself with the thought of how angry they had often been in the past. There was something new in Anine's attitude this time. Her email had been matter-of-fact and dry rather than actually incensed. Far more ice-cold fury than red-hot anger. That Anine had resorted to the closest thing in Norway that could come to a divorce from your parents, change of name and repudiation of inheritance, made this final break-up so much worse than all the other ones put together.

Selma Falck was not going to lose her children.

She had already lost them.

That had struck her with a force she could never have anticipated, and she began to cry again.

Something had to be done. She had to do something. Fill her time. Steady her nerves.

Still with the dishcloth round her neck, she went through and sat down at the dining table. Opened her MacBook and switched it on.

One hour later she had lost almost thirty thousand kroner. She chose the wrong cards and went in far too hard. Slipshod and forgetful, she could not stop thinking about Anine and Johannes.

And of Jesper. This was unbearable, and she simply had to continue playing. Her next hand would be better. Another website, maybe, or a few rounds of Black Jack to balance the books.

'No,' she said sharply as she logged off.

But she had to do something.

It occurred to her that she could sort through her email, the task she had started on Friday evening and only just embarked upon when Jesper had sent his desperate message. A mechanical and undemanding exercise that would force time to pass.

Selma had only one aim: to make time pass, and pass, and pass.

She opened her mailbox and flicked as rapidly as she could through the mail from the past twenty-four hours. She would attend to all that another time, and she narrowed her eyes to avoid looking at the senders' names before she had navigated safely past the last twenty incoming emails.

Half blind, Selma pressed the wrong button, and the box of UNIMPORTANT UNANSWERED emails opened up. The top email was still unread, despite having already been moved. Selma opened it.

The text was brief and insignificant.

Runhild hoped she was well. She was not much better herself. She hoped Selma was making progress with the wedding album, and wondered if she could also have a copy when it was ready.

Selma could not be bothered reading it all. Instead, she opened the file of pictures Runhild had attached.

Four photographs.

One of the bridal couple in the veteran car on their way uphill to Ekeberg. Two pictures of the bridegroom with his brother and his parents.

The very last one had been taken in a different location.

The photographer must have been standing on the slope on the south side of the restaurant. The guests were all seated, but the way the photo was taken, neither they nor the bride and groom were in focus. In front of them all, beside a luxuriant hedge below the terrace, three little boys stood in a row, peeing. They could hardly be more than six or seven years old, and one of them had just spotted the photographer. He had an exaggerated look of alarm on his face under his blond fringe. The sun was refracted in rainbow-hued beams down from the left-hand corner: an original and amusing image of a wedding reception with guests of absolutely every age.

It would have to be edited to be really good. On the right, the brick wall was too dominant, and the back of the building lay in shadow. There was a figure standing there, a woman dressed in a blue summer dress with an old-fashioned pinafore on top. She was not part of the happy moment as she stood in the lee of all the others, out of sight, holding something that looked like a thermos in her hands. In front of her, on a little table, sat a jug of water.

Selma lifted her hands from the mouse and keyboard and held them up in front of her eyes. They had become hers again, but she was shaking so badly that for a second she thought another attack was imminent. Once again she concentrated on breathing properly, and as soon as she regained control, she downloaded the image into her Photos.

The quality was good. Even in the shaded area it was bright enough, and Selma zoomed all the way in on the woman who stood hidden behind the south-east corner of the restaurant in the middle of Anine and Sjalg's wedding reception.

When Selma recognized her, she got to her feet. With her eyes still firmly fixed on the screen, she walked backwards. Clasped her hands behind her neck and squeezed her elbows together into her head until it became painful.

There were more than two hundred guests at the wedding. If they had all taken an average of twenty photographs, there would be four thousand pictures of an occasion that had not even lasted three hours.

Two of them told of how Sjalg Petterson had died. One of these lay in a chaotic pile on Selma's bedroom floor, demonstrating that Sjalg had ice cubes in his glass at a time when ice cubes had all already been used up some time earlier. The other was this one, and it showed who was responsible for Sjalg's death.

Mina Mejer Selmer was holding a thermos in her hands. It was open and the little container was filled with ice cubes and water. The young girl looked as if she had just glanced up, and as the photo was taken, she looked across at the three little lads who stood alongside the hedge with their trousers round their knees. She seemed to be concentrating, and did not seem to be enjoying herself in the least.

Neither was Selma, of course.

Perhaps she could win back her daughter and almost certainly prove Jesper's innocence. Ellevilt would be saved. Sjalg Petterson's death had nothing to do with carelessness in the Michelin-starred restaurant's kitchen.

Selma could retrieve much of what she had been convinced all through this evening had been lost for ever. The price was shattering the existence of a girl who had just turned seventeen.

She stored the image and switched off the laptop. Crossing to the balcony door, she opened it and stepped out into the night, where Monday was only a few minutes off.

No photographers to be seen.

The city still lay before her. Time still ticked by. The air was cool and fresh, but it was certainly no easier to breathe.

The Threat

Deputy Police Chief Birger Hansem drained the last of the mineral water in a single gulp. He raised one hand deprecatingly when Justice Minister Tryggve Mejer pushed the fruit bowl towards him.

'No, thanks. It's been an excellent meeting. As I said, all the relevant statistics are contained in the folder. The prospects look good with respect to crimes for profit. And juvenile crime is waning. Although you wouldn't think so from what the media try to tell us.'

'Good,' the Justice Minister said. 'Thanks for coming.'

They had known each other for a couple of decades, these two men who sat in the Justice Minister's office following a meeting that had lasted barely half an hour. In the Council, they sometimes met frequently, but as a rule there were lengthy gaps between the times they met. In their lives outside Ellev Trasop's secret realm, they encountered each other far more often. Not a single time, not even when they were alone together, had they allowed these two worlds to collide.

Never, and that was how it had to be.

Until now.

Birger Hansem produced a sheet of paper from his inside pocket. He assumed that the cabinet member's office was not bugged, but he was a man devoid of illusions. His wife called him a cynic, an opinion with which he disagreed. It was simply that he took precautions. Throughout a long life, it had been shown to be prudent.

'No holiday for you, I understand!' He smiled as he unfolded the paper. 'What does your young girl have to say about that, then? They're very demanding at that age, I believe. Nothing less than a holiday abroad in the sun.'

He placed the paper on the desk and turned it over so that the text was facing the man on the opposite side.

'My children have been grown up for a long time now,' Birger continued jovially. 'But even when they were teenagers, some ten or twelve years ago, there was always a bloody fuss.'

Tryggve Mejer raised his eyebrows, took out a pair of reading glasses and put them on his nose.

'Of course it depends where you live,' Birger ploughed on without letting go of the paper. 'What friends are doing and are allowed to do, I mean. In some parts of the city it's probably still acceptable to take a trip to see grandparents.'

Birger watched Tryggve as he read.

The text was not long. It was handwritten, and Birger had gone through a whole series of sheets of paper before he had found the right wording. He had immediately burnt all the earlier drafts.

'That was what I had as a child,' he continued to babble, with a smile in his voice. 'We were dumped at Gran and Grandpa's in Stavern at the end of the school term, and weren't picked up again until two months later.'

Tryggve had grown noticeably paler, and beneath one eye, a slight twitch was visible. He licked his lips nervously. Finally he spoke: 'That was probably great fun. In Stavern for the summer.'

'Yes, of course. A paradise, you know. We didn't complain at all.'

Tryggve looked up, removed his glasses and laid them down on the desk. The twitch did not ease off, and he rubbed his finger angrily back and forth under his eye.

'I'll assess these statistics carefully,' he said.

He nodded at the loose sheet, not at the folders the Deputy Police Chief had given him.

'But I ask you to respect that I am the one, when push comes to shove, who makes the decisions. I am the one with the final say.'

When their eyes met, Birger Hansem gave a start. Previously, the politician had shown no obvious effects of the beautiful summer that was behind them, but now he looked really ill. Even paler than only a few seconds ago, and his forehead was damp. Birger slowly folded the sheet of paper again and returned it to his inside pocket. He rose from his seat and fastened his uniform buttons without looking up. When he had finished, Tryggve was already standing with one hand on the doorknob. He had taken off his jacket by the time Birger had arrived, and now he stood with one finger behind the knot on his tie, tugging and tearing at it as he opened the door.

As Birger passed him on his way from the room, the door quickly closed halfway again.

'If you all think you can threaten me, you're making a big mistake.'

Tryggve's voice hissed into Birger's ear. The policeman automatically pulled his head to one side. An undersecretary came walking along the corridor, and Birger smiled broadly and raised his hand in greeting. The woman returned his smile and hurried on.

'The Major has Harlequin in her possession,' Birger said softly. 'As you have probably realized by now. And as you just read, she's willing to—'

'Go,' the Justice Minister said dully. 'Now.'

Birger Hansem adjusted his jacket, tucked his uniform cap under his arm and walked off, to be escorted through the many security doors out to his waiting driver. Not until he was in the elevator did he dare to close his eyes and breathe freely.

This had gone far worse than he had feared.

Far, far worse, and it was unthinkable, what must necessarily transpire now.

The Truth

The first school day was over.

On her way to the city this morning Mina had felt somehow uplifted. At least, she felt some degree of expectation that things could be different, that the start of the school term would provide a break in this endless summer, a chance perhaps to forget everything. To bury both her summer and Dad's, far inside the innermost, hidden recesses of her brain.

Forgetting was the only thing she wished for, but it seemed impossible.

She had taken an earlier tram than the one her friends usually took: she had to be alone. She wanted to feel whether daily life had returned, whether daily life any longer even existed. Whether it might be possible to bind herself to her existence as a fairly ordinary student in the second grade at Elvebakken and let the calendar drag her from day to day until everything improved.

Her hopes had vanished by the time she alighted from the tram.

Groups of fellow students, large and small, streamed towards the school from every direction. They were all suntanned, and most had lighter hair than when the holidays had begun. Mina was almost winter-pale after having mostly stayed indoors for the past month. She felt branded. It was as if the dreadful events of the summer were visibly marked on her external appearance. In silence, she met her old life with eyes downcast. As early as the first break, it seemed the others had given up on her. Their laughter passed her by and there was nowhere for her to hide.

The first day of term was always mostly about fun and confusion and the joy of meeting up again, and by half past eleven that morning, she felt exhausted by feeling excluded from everything. So she went home.

If the system were already in place so early in the school year, then Dad would receive a text message about unauthorized absence. Mum too, but that was nothing to worry about. Mina lacked the energy to think about either of them, and snuggled under the quilt as soon as she let herself into the house in Lofthus terrasse.

She woke abruptly more than eight hours later. Her mobile showed that it was half past eight in the evening. She sat up and nudged the quilt aside. She was still fully clothed, her blouse was soaking wet, and she felt really parched.

Feeling woozy, she struggled to make her memory fall back into place. It took just seconds. This was the only time of day when life was still worth living: those short, empty moments when she woke and had not yet recalled everything that had happened.

Dad came home from Trondheim late last night.

Unable to face speaking to him, Mina had feigned sleep.

Everything had become too huge and unmanageable. So unfathomable, so far beyond anything she could sort out or process. The logbook on the laptop in the basement had revealed an incomprehensible story. She still harboured a faint hope that her dad was writing a novel. That was the first thing that had struck her when she had read a few pages into the logbook. Dad was writing a thriller.

In that case, it was the story of a very strange crime.

There were no main protagonists, for example, and nor was there much suspense in the action. The incidents simply took place, one by one, and it seemed as if the entire narrative simply had to do with damaging people. No one died, but they were all exposed in some way or another. Threatened and forced to submit. Hoodwinked by the police and thrown into prison for crimes they hadn't committed.

This was no novel; she quickly had to admit to herself. What it was she still did not know, but she grew afraid when she recognized some of the names. It involved important people, or at least some of them were. The names mentioned included Pål Poulsen, that horrible guy from the Progress Party who was among the few people Mina had ever heard her dad vilify.

Even though they had been in government together.

Mina did not want to understand the contents of the logbook. After reading two thirds of the document, she had scrolled down to the end to see how it ended.

There was no real conclusion, and that made her even more afraid.

She reached out for her glass of water. The lukewarm liquid had been poured the night before, but she drank it all down.

Dad was coming up the stairs.

His footsteps made her feel nervous. Dad's mood could so easily be read from how he walked, and these were footfalls she had not heard since the catastrophic party almost exactly a year ago.

Except that they were even angrier.

He did not even knock on the door.

'Have you opened the safe?' he roared furiously.

'Yes,' Mina gasped, crawling further back into her bed; the lie she should really have automatically come up with had stuck in her throat.

Dad went completely bananas. On the inside of the door, Mina had a coat hook loaded with carrier bags from high-end department stores. Urban Outfitters and Abercrombie & Fitch. An Armani bag from Italy and three cool string bags from her trip to New York at the Easter of 2017.

Dad yanked them so hard that the coat hook came with them. He was practically foaming at the mouth as he ripped them to shreds and scattered the pieces all around.

'Have you been in the safe?' he repeated over and over again. 'Have you been in my safe?'

Mina burst into tears, but her Dad did not even seem to notice. She grabbed Dumpling, the old rabbit that had lost one eye and smelled a bit too much of Mum. Hugged it close. It was too small to still provide comfort and protection, and she snatched up a pillow instead. Now she had retreated all the way to the corner of the bed, wedged in between the headboard and the room divider that hid the desk on the other side.

Her Dad was standing in the midst of all the scraps of paper, legs apart, and hands on his head. His hair was sticking out in every direction, and Mina felt an absurd urge to laugh. She was terrified, and needed to pee. Clasping the pillow even closer, she tried to hide her face.

'You've opened the laptop,' he screamed, his voice rising to hit top C. 'The logbook says it was last saved on Friday night. When I was in Trondheim!'

Mina nodded.

Her dad gasped for breath with his mouth open. When he spoke, saliva sprayed out in a cloud from his lips.

'What on earth is going on with you, Mina? Surely you know better than to mess about with other people's belongings? Have you read the logbook? Have you ...'

'I thought it had to do with you and Mum,' Mina sobbed. 'I thought that since everything with you and Mum had started falling apart, really falling apart, when you began to hang out in the basement, that there must be something down there that ...'

She broke down and could hardly speak.

'... and then I thought that I could do something, and ... I was so happy when the news about the commission came through, about freedom of expression, I thought that ... But then you didn't change one bit even though I needed for you to change, and for me to ...'

Her father was deflated. He looked like a rag doll hanging on an invisible stand. His head hung down on his chest. His shoulders seemed to shrivel, and his arms looked paralysed and just hung, dangling at the sides of his body.

'Have you opened the casket?' he asked hoarsely.

'No,' Mina rushed to answer.

A stab of hot nausea coursed through her body when it crossed her mind that the memory sticks also revealed when they had last been opened. Dad must not have noticed it. Or maybe he had not yet looked at them since then. She still had no idea what the numbers and names might mean, but they were clearly connected to the logbook in some sinister way. Like in a horror film, when you finally realized that someone was a crazy mass murderer, but could not grasp how he could have been a friendly bus driver earlier on. You understood that it was true, but could not work out how.

'No,' she repeated to be on the safe side. 'The casket was locked.'

'So was the safe!' her Dad bellowed, and he no longer looked like a rag doll. 'And that obviously didn't stop you!'

He took a couple of paces towards her.

'What have you done?' he groaned, touching his head again.

'I killed Sjalg Petterson,' Mina said. 'But I didn't mean to.'

The words came of their own volition. Mina had not only opened the casket. Not only taken the memory sticks up to her room and downloaded the contents on to her own computer. Not only had she taken photos of the first half of that strange, home-made book, but also on Friday she had secured a copy of her Dad's logbook on a memory stick that belonged to her. On that same device she had transferred the photos from her iPhone and the peculiar lists of personnel and accounts, before clearing up and deleting until in the end she just had everything collected on the memory stick that lay on her bedside table.

Her mobile and laptop were now clean. In case Mum, on one of her visits, might take it into her head to check Mina's devices, as she had occasionally insisted on doing because she had read an article about naïve parents.

Mina had just attempted to understand. To try to crack all the codes and put everything into the right context. She still thought that all the incomprehensible things in the safe had something to do with the relationship between her mum and dad. A little, at least, and she could not keep going down to the basement all the time. It was better to have her own complete copy.

Everything had been done in order to help.

Mum was gone, and Dad was having problems, and Mina wanted to make everything better for them all.

She had just made everything worse, she now realized.

Much worse. And she had to tell her Dad the worst thing of all.

'I didn't mean to,' she repeated in a whisper.

'What did you say?' Dad asked.

His eyes were wide and his mouth was open.

'He wasn't supposed to die!' Mina told him. 'I just wanted to make him ill. To spoil his wedding. He's so nasty ... he's been horrible to you for years, and you said that ...'

Her dad sat down on the edge of the bed, so slowly and gingerly that it seemed as if he was afraid it might collapse under his weight.

'I only used a really tiny amount of nuts,' she whispered, pressing the thumb and forefinger of each hand together, hard, until the opening in the middle became a diamond the size a pinhead. 'I've seen it on YouTube, you can take cayenne pepper or something and ... first of all you make a little ice cube, and then a bigger one on top and an even bigger ... it becomes a kind of time bomb, you see, but I just wanted to spoil the wedding.'

She gasped for breath. 'Dad,' she sobbed, 'help me, Dad.'

Mina stretched out her hand, but he did not react. Mina grabbed his hand, and he did not pull away, but his fingers lay slack and clammy in hers.

'What were you thinking?' he said, looking her in the eye. 'What on earth were you thinking, my love? You've turned seventeen and you're the smartest girl in the world, and then ...'

Now he broke down in tears. Absolutely silently, but with little sniffs from time to time that made it difficult for him to go on speaking.

'I won't go to prison, will I, Dad? I didn't mean it, word of honour, it was an accident, and I'm only seventeen and ... Dad. Dad!'

He cowered, pulling his legs up on the bed and curling into a big ball, with his arms wrapped around his legs and his head between his knees. He sat with his back to her.

Her whole dad was shaking.

Mina put her hand on his back.

Never in her life had she been so afraid. Not even during the wedding when, terror-stricken, she had realized that Sjalg Petterson was dead, and she had sneaked away to rinse out the restaurant's jug and her own thermos in hot water a thousand times in all the chaos that ensued. Not even on the bus home, when the enormity of what she had done sank in.

Every single day since then, she had been scared.

She was absolutely exhausted by terror, but this was worse.

Dad was going completely to pieces. He was howling, like a wounded animal or something, and was almost being suffocated by biting his own knees. His trousers were getting so tight from sitting like that, but all of a sudden his teeth took hold of the fabric and tore a huge hole.

'Dad,' Mina sobbed. 'Don't be like that, Dad. Please ...'

It didn't seem as if he could hear her at all.

The Speech

Lars Winther had been bedevilled by a guilty conscience ever since he had tipped off his old colleague in *DG* about Selma Falck's new flame.

All through the weekend, he had tried to get in touch with her.

He had called many times, sent text messages and written emails to both the addresses he knew she used. Twice in the course of Saturday he had also rung her doorbell, but no one let him in. He had even sneaked down into the garage complex to check if her old Volvo was gone, but found it parked there. All the same, it was not certain she would be at home.

Some time before midnight on Sunday, when both his wife and the children had fallen asleep, he had slipped out of his apartment. He was worried, and felt guilty. If only he knew that Selma was OK, then he would be able to leave her in peace. He was well aware that he was not exactly in her good books. A woman like Selma Falck had probably added two and two together and arrived at four; he would certainly be the prime suspect as far as the person who had spilled the beans to *DG* was concerned.

He had cycled to Sagene and stood in the shade of a chestnut tree the builders of Selma's apartment block had miraculously enough left standing. He had peered up at the wall, where only one of the apartments boasted a balcony. It protruded like a fungus on a fat pine tree, but he knew that Selma was happy to be one of the few people in the block to possess an outside space. Even though it was so tiny.

A light was on in her apartment. Which need not mean that she was there. He stood for a few minutes, unsure whether he should try to ring the doorbell yet again. When he had almost made up his mind, the balcony door had opened.

Selma came out.

She just stood there gazing out over the city. For maybe a couple of minutes, while she looked as if all she was doing was thinking. Then she went inside again and shut the door.

Lars had cycled home without revealing his presence.

On Monday he had had to take half a day off work. His eldest son was to start in the first year of primary school, and so much fuss was being made by the entire extended family that it had become a bit embarrassing. All four grandparents, two of them with new marriage partners, had met to cheer Leon on as, dressed in brand new clothes and trainers big enough to grow into, he had fought back tears and struggled with an overlarge satchel on his way into the very first classroom of his short life.

Now it was Tuesday, but Lars Winther still had Selma Falck on his mind. He had phoned again, sent three more texts and one email. Still no response. It was as if she had deleted him from her existence.

Until now he had been concerned, but he was no longer worried. Instead he felt his irritation grow. He was depending on her to get more meat on the bones of the juicy story they had together begun to close in on. Admittedly, Lars was a news journalist, but he was heading straight for the politics department as soon as an opening occurred. Selma's story would considerably strengthen his candidacy.

So it was annoying that he had not been given the green light to take part in the press conference announced by the Prime Minister's office at astoundingly short notice. He was ordered to cover an extensive chlorine leak into the Akerselva river. It would be conspicuous if he ignored a direct request, but Lars had managed anyway to postpone his meeting with the manager of the water and sewage service by an hour. The press conference was starting now, and he would manage to catch the first half hour online.

The major news outlets, including TV2 and NRK, were broadcasting direct. Lars felt duty bound to choose his own newspaper, even though he really thought that NRK's political commentators were better.

The Prime Minister was on her way to the rostrum.

Large and assured, with an equanimity unique to her in the kingdom. She had mastered the difficult balancing act of holding her tripartite coalition government together, and everything indicated that in the course of only a few months she would be able to bring the minuscule Christian Democratic Party into the fold and thus lead a majority government. She wore a dark-blue dress and low-heeled pumps, and had just been to the hairdresser's.

She took things calmly, and did what suited her. Giving a self-confident smile, and looking almost absent-minded, she threaded her way to the rostrum. She had no script, and simply adjusted the snaking microphone as she smiled again and cleared her throat.

'Welcome,' she began. 'Justice Minister Tryggve Mejer has today requested permission to resign with immediate effect.'

A buzz ran through the crowded audience. Someone called for hush.

'We have decided, Tryggve and I, that he be allowed to explain in person. I will therefore content myself with thanking him. He is my dear friend and my trusted colleague and I am extremely sorry that he now has to leave. But he has my greatest understanding for the reasons behind his resignation. Tryggve?'

She glanced at the side door, which opened.

Lars Winther realized that his mouth had dropped open, and snapped it shut again.

Tryggve Mejer walked into the room. The government's strongest card, perhaps, after the Prime Minister herself, and certainly her closest confidant in the eclectic, to put it mildly, and strangely composed Norwegian government.

He looked dreadful.

Pale and wan. While he had noticeably gained weight month by month in the past year to the delight of caricaturists, his suit was now too loose. His hair, enviably thick for a man in his fifties, looked soaking wet. Either it had not been washed for a couple of weeks, or he had been guilty of a serious overdose of hair gel that morning. It was as if even his gait had changed. Usually he moved confidently, with a straight back and his chest almost exaggeratedly thrust forward. Now he seemed to drag his feet, and he narrowly avoided a stumble as he walked up the two steps to the rostrum.

Tryggve Mejer had no script either.

The producer of the broadcast zoomed in for a close-up.

It struck Lars Winther that this was a man in crisis, just before Tryggve Mejer lifted his chin and looked up. Probably he would have preferred to do this in a press release. That, however, would have led to a posse of journalists hounding him from here to eternity, so this was something he had to endure.

He had to look the public in the eye.

Everything changed the moment he looked up. His eyes glittered with steel and conviction. The man had aged ten years over the summer months, but his eyes contained a steadiness that captured everyone's attention. When he began to speak, Lars noticed that his voice was deeper than before.

'Thank you all very much for taking the time to come here,' he began, a fairly original opening remark.

He swallowed audibly, and a small, almost shy, smile began to cross his face.

'I love having the top political responsibility for the justice sector in Norway,' he continued. *'During my three years in this government, I have waltzed my way to work. Figuratively speaking, of course; in actual fact I'm picked up by official car.'*

Lars heard widespread laughter.

'But all good things must come to an end, and for me now is the right time to choose a different path. As you all know, I'm a very private person. I avoid public attention directed at my family, and my wife and daughter have always wanted to lead independent lives. In order to explain my somewhat ...'

He glanced down for a second, as if he suddenly regretted not having written anything down in advance. He ran one hand slowly over his greasy hair.

'... my somewhat unexpected exit, I assume, I must ask for your indulgence. I must ask for forgiveness for encumbering you all with my personal problems for a moment.'

'Are you watching it, eh? Bloody hell, what's happened to him, d'you think?'

A colleague from the sports section poked Lars on the shoulder, grabbed a chair and sat down beside him.

'Shh!' Lars said.

'My wife and I have separated. That is our business, and I would ask you to respect that this is the last I'm going to say on that particular subject. When families split up like this, as many families do, unfortunately, many people are affected. The couple themselves, of course, but also the extended family, friends and colleagues. Principally, such situations are difficult for the children.'

Once again he paused, but this time he did not look down. Instead he let his gaze sweep around the audience, who were now completely mesmerized. For a fleeting moment, Tryggve Mejer looked straight into the camera.

'Christ,' the sports journalist said, nudging Lars again. 'Tough guy, don't you think? But the second cabinet member to leave in a matter of weeks, eh? Erna isn't having an easy time of it.'

'Shut up.'

'We have a long-standing tradition of giving parents the opportunity to take good care of small children in this country. By good fortune. It is not so very many years since parental leave for cabinet members, for example, would have been unthinkable. Not to mention the idea of male members of government taking paternal leave to spend time with their newborn children. We should be very happy about that: Norway has been and continues to be a leading country as far as arrangements for combining work and family are concerned. However, it is not true to say that children only need us when they are little.'

A crouching TV technician entered the picture, adjusted one of the microphones in front of Mejer and disappeared out again.

'Quite the reverse. We have full responsibility for our children until they are adults. In many ways a divorce can hit teenagers harder than toddlers. For older children, life can honestly be a trial. Admittedly, older children can also be a trial for their parents.'

Widespread laughter again.

'... but after all, that's life. My daughter's name is Hermina. We call her Mina, and she is the most important person in my life. She has just turned seventeen, and for her, this summer has been difficult. Extremely difficult, and she is still struggling. As her dad, I can't just sit still and watch. My estranged wife and I have inflicted pain on her, and that is why she and I must do all we can to make life easier for Mina. We have therefore put our heads together and decided that I should take some time off. Completely. Mina and I are going to travel abroad. We are going to spend time together, a long time. Just the two of us for most of the time, though Mina's Mum will visit us on occasion.'

He paused. Took a deep breath, placed his hands on the rostrum, and leaned closer to all the microphones.

'Don't look for us, please. Let me do this for my child. Leave my family in peace from the moment I walk out that door.'

He nodded in the direction of the Prime Minister, who stood beside the entrance. Taking another deep breath, for the first time he looked hesitant: *'If I can make one last wish after all these years in the service of Norway, it has to be this: be kind to one another. Show respect. Try to give people the benefit of the doubt, and we'll all get along a lot better. Managing to establish the new Commission for Freedom of Expression prior to my resignation is the one thing I look back on with a touch of pride. We have to clean up the way we talk to one another. As far as the rest of my achievements are concerned, both in the last period I sat in government and this one, I am simply grateful to have been allowed to make a contribution. Thank you to each and every one of you here today – you do an incredibly important job, and to all of you out there watching, for giving me the opportunity to serve my country.'*

Releasing the rostrum, he adjusted his tie and added as he turned towards the Prime Minister: *'And many thanks to you, Erna. You are a kind and considerate friend.'*

He had finished. As he moved down from the rostrum, someone began to clap. Sparse and faint to begin with, the applause then took off until they were all practically stamping their feet.

'That's ...'

The wide-eyed sports journalist pointed at the monitor.

'That's certainly never bloody happened before,' Lars Winther completed for him. 'The press clapping for a government minister.'

The Handover

It was night, and the Major was delayed.

That was not like her.

Tryggve Mejer had stopped at Solemskogen. Another three vehicles were spread out on the vast car park, but it looked as if they had been parked for a long time. Two bikes had been securely fastened to a mighty tree; at least five metres of solid chain had been threaded in and out of the frames and wheels and anchored with a substantial padlock. Some people drove up here to avoid all the hills, and then cycled on into Marka.

Tryggve was exhausted: it felt as if he had cycled up here himself. At record speed. However, he was calmer now. He had decided to forget last night, and he had already actively begun to suppress his major breakdown in Mina's room. He would probably remember it for the rest of his life, but from here on everything would just move onwards and upwards. When he had finally managed to pull himself together last night, he had been gripped by a firm sense of resolution that had kept him awake all night.

The tickets were booked, and also a hotel for the first fortnight. Everything had been sorted out via internet banking. Each month, a suitable sum would be transferred from his savings account to his current account, and all direct debits were already automatic.

They would start their adventure in the Seychelles.

Just after half past six this morning, he had contacted Cathrine. She had come immediately and been surprisingly responsive. Of course he had not been able to tell her about Mina's ghastly confession. Anyway, she could see with her own eyes that their daughter was far from well. He did not look really well either, she thought, and when Mina had assured her that there was nothing she would rather do than go away with her dad for a few months, she had said yes.

A car drove into the car park. Tryggve flashed his lights. The car turned towards him and did not stop until they were parallel parked.

The Major stepped out and Tryggve followed suit.

They did not exchange greetings, and said nothing until Tryggve opened the boot of his car, took out the cedar-wood casket that some unknown prisoner had made in the Grini prison camp just before the Germans capitulated, and handed it to her.

'Is everything in place?' she asked as she took it from him, and he nodded.

'Have you taken copies of anything?'

Tryggve shook his head.

'You must have had a computer to look at the contents of the memory sticks.'

He leaned over the boot once again and took out the simple Dell laptop purchased in Elkjøp.

'I've deleted everything,' he said, handing it to her. 'But you can have it anyway.'

She gave it a fleeting glance before opening the rear door of her own car and placing the casket carefully on the back seat. Then she took the laptop and set it down beside it. She slammed the door shut with a bang.

'Was it you or Ellev who tried to remove Harlequin from the memory sticks in the casket?' he asked.

'It was Ellev. He didn't trust you. Time has shown that he was right not to. Is there anything at all in your possession to link you to the Council?'

'Did Ellev give you exactly the same things he gave me?' he asked instead of answering. 'The lists, the satellite phone—'

'I received more than you did,' she cut in. 'I had Harlequin at my disposal.'

'But you didn't receive the casket.'

'No, not the casket. But I have that now. Is there anything at all that can connect you to the Council?' she repeated.

'No, you have everything.'

He glanced towards the rear window of her car. Sighed almost inaudibly as he took out a folded sheet of paper from his back pocket and handed it to her.

'Here,' he said. 'It's a list of the operations you have to abort. For example, you must let Pål Poulsen off the hook. As you see, I've written this by hand. There is no copy.'

'We'll certainly put out your fires,' she said after giving the paper a brief glance. 'It's not strictly necessary to give me this overview.'

'You've been watching, then,' he said, sounding discouraged.

'Of course we've followed what you've been doing,' she replied sharply. 'As you must finally have understood, we couldn't simply let you go rogue.'

Tryggve stepped back and opened the driver's door.

'Are you listening in to me?'

She looked at him, and let her eyes linger on his.

'No, Tryggve. We haven't bugged your home or your phone. You have my word on that. We don't monitor government ministers. Word of honour.'

She paused without relinquishing eye contact.

'And my word of honour is still worth something.'

Tryggve let out an almost imperceptible sigh. The Major was speaking the truth. She had to be. If she had knowledge of Mina's admission in her bedroom last night, she would have used it for all it was worth, and squeezed his balls even tighter. For the moment she knew nothing of that. There was great danger, however, that she would find out all about it. The owner of the casket would be able to have a handle on everything. As an extra insurance, he had therefore taken some precautions. The lists, codes and satellite phone no longer belonged to Tryggve. But before he had handed them over he had used the casket one last time.

If it ever became necessary to protect Mina further, he only had to dial a number on an ordinary phone.

'Good luck,' he said, without quite knowing what exactly this referred to.

He settled behind the wheel again. She did the same, and when he saw her car roll slowly towards the road leading down to the city, he fired up his own.

They had shared one of the country's best-kept secrets, Tryggve Mejer and the Major. For several decades. Their paths would never cross again, but the Major had not even said goodbye.

In a way that felt like a relief.

The Hypothesis

For nearly forty-eight hours, Selma had been lost in thought and doubt and had lived on crispbread.

Still she refused to open the door to anyone or answer the phone. She lived in the hope that the two photographs now taped to the dining table, surrounded by loads of yellow Post-its covered in closely written notes, would give her the final answer to what had transpired during the wedding.

For forty-eight hours she had not made much progress.

Selma herself was still convinced about the actual course of events. The point was that she had to convince others. Primarily the police.

She would have given anything to find just one more photograph. The missing link, one in which Mina was caught pouring water into Sjalg's glass from the same jug that had been on the little table behind the restaurant when the thermos was emptied into it. All logic suggested that the ice cubes had not been manufactured in the kitchen, where they had run out an hour and a half earlier. The ice did not come from the restaurant freezer or from an ice cube machine that had broken down through over-exertion during the intense heat. Instead they had been poured into a water jug from a small thermos belonging to Mina Selmer. At least, she had been the one who had handled it. The picture of the three boys peeing in the sunshine also showed that the young girl had tried to hide when she ensured that cool water could be served to the bridegroom just before he gave the most important speech of his life.

For Selma, the case was crystal clear.

Nevertheless, any lawyer would quickly pick apart the circumstantial evidence. She herself would have succeeded in two minutes flat if Mina had been her client.

On Sunday evening, in her elated relief at having found the crucial picture, Selma had decided to go to the police with what she had. With the photographs and her theories: hypotheses so strong that the authorities would be compelled to investigate them more closely. When Selma then began to think of the young prosecutor she had visited at police headquarters, she began to have doubts. The woman's uncertainty and obvious incompetence might suggest that the case of Sjalg Petterson's demise had not exactly been accorded the highest priority. At least, Selma had left her office at Grønlandsleiret 44 a couple of weeks ago with the uncomfortable feeling that things were not as they should be. Both Lars Winther and Selma herself had entertained the idea that Sjalg's death was part of a larger plot against the extremist wings of Norwegian politics. They had subsequently dismissed this: a possible murder did not fit into the pattern that emerged from the other cases.

In the end Selma was unsure what to believe. Her uncertainty about the police force's role in such a well-thought-out, systematic attack on parts of the population was too great to draw definite conclusions. That Mina Selmer might be part of such a plot seemed absurd, and for that reason alone, Selma should pay a visit to the police without delay. A police officer she knew, for example. Someone who, from experience, she was sure she could trust.

There was not a single soul in the world that Selma really trusted.

Not even Einar. Not in all areas. He was too crazy for that.

It was now Tuesday morning, and she had run out of Pepsi Max and crispbread. At some point or other, she would have to face the world. She would have to respond to people out there, and find a way to move on. If she was ever to have the chance to prove that Mina Selmer was behind Sjalg Petterson's death, she could not sit here for ever. She had two photographs and a good theory, but in order to reinforce it and somehow entertain any hope of having her children and Jesper back in her life, she had to venture out.

The mere thought made her feel ill.

However, it was time to snap out of it. She showered, washed her hair, got dressed and brewed a cup of coffee that was strong as dynamite. Without milk, even though she could not really stand it black. Whether this was to punish herself or to wake herself up properly she was not entirely sure. She cleared the photos and yellow notes off the dining table and switched on her laptop for the first time in several days.

The idea of clicking into DG.no felt repulsive, but there was no way round it. She was so tense that her neck prickled as the newspaper site came up. She did not exhale until half a minute later when she could see that the story about her and Jesper had been considerably downgraded.

In fact, she could not find it at all.

Instead the six top stories dealt with Tryggve Mejer's departure as Justice Minister.

Selma read on, drinking coffee and clicking into the video of the press conference. Read some more, and watched Tryggve Mejer's speech yet again. Then she moved on to the websites of NRK, *Aftenavisen* and *Dagbladet* and skimmed through every single article on the story she found there.

The comment articles were interesting.

Her coffee cup was emptied twice.

Her brain, on the other hand, was moving in top gear. Conclusions were drawn and discarded. Hypotheses mushroomed and then died. For more than an hour she sat staring at a screen that after only five minutes had gone to sleep and turned black.

Finally Selma was able to get to her feet, her mind firmly made up that she was now ready to stake absolutely everything on one single dangerous card. She simply had to wait until Mina Selmer and her father were well and truly out of the country.

What's more, she would have to prepare herself.

Thoroughly.

The Report

The date was now Tuesday 28 August.

Norway's Prime Minister was sitting alone in her office reading a report that had still not been made public. It had been written by an independent investigation committee and opened up a possibility that she had never dreamt of. Her plan was to continue as Prime Minister until the parliamentary election in 2021, and then take life onwards from there. If the Conservatives lost, it might be time to find something else entirely. She would be sixty that year, but was of the firm opinion that she had many good working years left ahead of her.

Time would tell. She took it calmly, as she had taken most of the many twists and turns of politics with an attitude that everything would turn out well. In the end.

Nothing was actually worth getting too agitated about.

There was, however, one possibility that made her a bit breathless. A slightly hectic flush had come over her cheeks as she read. When the Foreign Minister had contacted her that same night and told her what was about to happen, she had chosen not to place much credence in it all. There were always so many rumours. Names were constantly being tossed around as soon as an important international post was to be filled. As a rule, it ended up with something completely different from what they had all predicted. There were so many aspects to be taken into consideration. So many strings that had to be pulled.

She was well aware of that, but this was exciting news all the same.

The report was about the UN, or more precisely about UNEP, the UN's environmental programme. In the autumn of 2016, the leader of the programme, the former Swedish Minister of International Development, Harshad Kapoor, had been compelled to leave his post. The reason was an internal report that slammed Kapoor's leadership style, travel habits and spending. That the leader of an environmental programme did not do much more than fly around the world was not a particularly good look in the opinion of many of the member countries. Also, Harshad Kapoor had loudly demanded that the entire UN apparatus should undergo comprehensive reform. Their systems were ineffective, old-fashioned and unwieldy, and certainly unsuitable for a new, globalized world in which everything moved at an increasingly fast pace. In order to reach their climate targets, and not least to achieve the millennium targets on poverty, it would practically take a revolution.

As Harshad Kapoor had constantly complained to anyone who would lend him an ear.

And everyone else.

The criticism had caused many hearts to sink. The Americans in particular had been upset, and after only eighteen months in post, the Swede had been forced to resign. His homeland, however, had chosen to be loyal to their own man. Within an impressively short period of time, they had gathered enough support to appoint and finance an independent committee tasked with finding out whether Harshad Kapoor had been correct in his criticism.

And he had, according to PricewaterhouseCoopers.

Throughout a three-hundred-page report, they indicated point by point where the shoe pinched. Kapoor, who had certainly not been alone in his criticism, as the UN leadership had tried to suggest, received unconditional backing in the report. For many reasons, it was out of the question for him to try to be reinstated to his former post. Anyway, it was unnecessary, as the new leader of UNEP, an Italian woman, was on the same wavelength as her predecessor and appeared to be a reliable pair of hands.

The problem was more acute for the General Secretary himself.

It was no secret that he was the one who, when push came to shove, had forced Kapoor to resign. Despite vigorous diplomacy from the Americans as well as the Portuguese, it now looked as if the UN's General Secretary was beginning to symbolize everything that was wrong and out of date about the organization.

According to the Foreign Minister's nocturnal confidences, it appeared that he was going to resign. With almost immediate effect, in fact.

And this was where the Norwegian Prime Minister entered the picture.

The Americans wanted to have her in the Portuguese representative's seat if things went as badly as they feared. She would also receive broad support from the African countries, apparently. In Germany, the Benelux countries and the rest of Europe, there were murmurs that it was about time they had a North European leader again.

In all probability, Erna Solberg was about to be appointed the new General Secretary of the UN. Events behind the scenes were in full flow. It could be days before anything became clearer, or even weeks. Perhaps even months. But in all likelihood things would move extremely fast once the ball had started to roll. No one benefited from the General Secretary continuing in post as a kind of lame duck. Formally, the decision had to be taken by the General Assembly following a recommendation from the Security Council, but in reality it was in the backroom that the decision would be taken.

Erna Solberg was well liked by the Americans, to tell the truth.

She was female into the bargain. If there was something the UN needed, it was a powerful symbol of renewal such as that.

It might actually become a reality.

She closed the report. An ever so tiny sense of excitement was beginning to take hold, and she had a great deal to do. The bowl of Twist chocolates on her desk was empty, but that did not faze her.

The fact that her natural, and what's more, decidedly preferential, successor as party leader had withdrawn from politics and set out on an interminably long holiday abroad was a considerably thornier problem.

New Orders

Something had radically changed further up in the system. Erling Hjort, former paratrooper and founder of the TV company Broadway, was convinced of that.

Firstly, he had been ordered to stop one part of the projects that had already been set in motion. Secondly, the codes suggested that someone else was now issuing the orders. According to the protocol, he should then make contact with his former line manager and check that the line of command had really changed. No answer had been forthcoming within the prescribed twenty-four hours. The rules also set out guidelines for such instances: he should follow the new instructions he had received without hesitation.

The last instruction went against the grain, however.

It did not matter, he should do as he was told, but it was deeply unpleasant. The order to hack into a former Justice Minister's communications ran counter to most of what he stood for. The idea that the man could be more of a legal quarry now than when he had been in charge of the Justice and Public Security Department only a few days ago was difficult to swallow.

On the other hand, he could not know what had transpired in the interim.

Politicians seldom gave true reasons when they suddenly and unexpectedly resigned their posts. For all Erling Hjort knew, Tryggve Mejer might be mixed up in something that threatened the security of the realm. In any case, it was not his role to scrutinize the orders he received.

It had taken him a number of days, but now it was done. The former Justice Minister would not be able to conduct a conversation on either Skype or telephone without it being registered. A copy of every email would be sent to the same server, where Erling's superior would be able to listen in to conversations and read correspondence. Even text messages that Mejer might take it into his head to send would be copied and forwarded without the guy having any inkling whatsoever.

Erling logged off, packed up his equipment and locked the basement door.

Everything was as before, apart from the length of time it took before he felt the familiar satisfaction of success.

But such was life for an old soldier. He shrugged off his discomfort in the knowledge that he was serving his fatherland, and went to pick up his youngest son from the child-minder.

Lofthus terrasse

'Selma Falck?' asked the woman who opened the door.

'Yes,' Selma replied, proffering her hand, but the gesture was not reciprocated.

'I'm really sorry to disturb you.'

She smiled as only she could. Warm, sympathetic and inspiring confidence.

'At your work they said you were on sick leave. And that you had ... moved home again after Tryggve and Mina left.'

Cathrine Selmer nodded.

In truth, she looked in quite a sorry state. The woman was not as tall as Selma, but she was much slimmer. Skinny, really, which was remarkable considering her involvement in combat sports at a relatively high level. She was wearing a tracksuit with an Asian emblem on the right breast and held a steaming cup of liquid that smelled of flowers and lemons.

'Then I shouldn't have disturbed you,' Selma said, adding the apology to all the ingredients of her smile. 'Stupid of me. Hope you get well soon.'

She lifted her palms to underline the mea culpa, and turned to leave.

'No,' Cathrine said. 'It's OK. Do come in.'

'Sure?' Selma asked.

The woman opened the door wide and stepped back.

It worked every time, Selma thought with satisfaction, as she followed the woman into the kitchen. The sight of Selma Falck made people curious. If she had just gone away, Cathrine Selmer would have wondered for days on end what on earth she had wanted of her.

It succeeded every single time.

'It's so lovely in here,' Selma lied, looking around.

The kitchen would have looked attractive enough on a better day. It was spacious, had an open fireplace and a small TV set for casual viewing. Metres of worktop, a range cooker and the unlit candles scattered around all suggested that this was a room that usually looked more inviting. Now it was grimy and the sink was overflowing with dirty dishes. Five potted herbs at the window had died and should be thrown out. The grate was heaped with ashes and the kitchen table decorated with rings left by red wine glasses and coffee cups.

'I've read you only drink Pepsi Max,' Cathrine said. 'I don't have any, sorry. Would you like some tea?'

'That would be great,' Selma answered. 'Yours smells gorgeous. I'd love some of that.'

Cathrine Selmer filled a kettle with water without saying anything. She put it on the cooker, opened a corner cupboard and took out a box of teabags. She found a mug in another cupboard, still without uttering a word.

'You're probably wondering why I've come,' Selma said.

Not even that comment received an answer. Cathrine tore open the sachet, dropped the teabag in the mug and waited for the kettle to boil.

'I can honestly leave it till another day,' Selma said. 'Or send you an email. I shouldn't have come. Sorry yet again.'

'No, not at all. Why are you here, then?'

'I'm working on a project for the Norwegian Handball Association,' Selma began. 'A pretty extensive affair in which we take a closer look at what needs to be done to retain young players. You see, handball is a sport players usually start later than, for example, football, so it takes longer to spot emerging talent. You can often, though certainly not always, see the contours of a good footballer at the age of five or six. Someone who will go on to be a good handball player, on the other hand, will often ...'

'So it's really Mina you want to get hold of,' Cathrine interrupted her. 'She gave up serious commitment more than a year ago. Now she only plays for fun once a week. Played. It's been summer, and now she's gone travelling.'

'Yes,' Selma said. 'And yes to your other point too. She stopped. That's why she's of interest to me.'

Cathrine was still staring at the kettle. The induction hob hummed softly.

'It says in the newspapers that you're a detective these days,' she said.

'Private investigator. That scarcely takes up all my time. I do other things in between.'

Selma was losing Cathrine, she noticed. Now that she knew Selma was not interested in her, but in her daughter, it obviously made no odds to her.

The kettle began to whistle. Selma waited until Cathrine had poured the water, placed the mug in front of her and sat down.

'You see,' she said, smiling as she fiddled with her phone, 'your daughter got in touch with me five years ago, in 2013. When she was ...'

'Twelve,' Cathrine said, slightly more interested now. 'Did she really?'

'Yes, here it is!'

Selma pushed the phone across the table. 'Read from the bottom.'

Cathrine read. After a few seconds, her mouth stretched into something resembling a smile. She swiped on, and when she appeared to be finished, she read the email exchange once again.

Slid the phone back.

'Typical Mina,' she said softly, almost fondly. 'She's always been a one-off. So self-sufficient.'

'A great girl,' Selma nodded.

'She had a picture of you on her bedroom wall.'

'That's lovely.'

'In one of those competition programmes, I don't quite remember what it ...'

'Champion of Champions,' Selma suggested.

'Exactly.'

Once again they were quiet.

Selma lifted out the teabag and looked around for somewhere to dispose of it.

'Just put it on the table,' Cathrine said listlessly. 'I need to scrub it down anyway. Afterwards. Later. It's a mess in here, I know.'

'You should see my place sometimes,' Selma said cheerfully, placing the soaking wet bag in the centre of the table.

A little sea of brown liquid spread around it.

'Would you like me to give you a hand?' she asked.

Cathrine looked at her in surprise. 'With what?'

'Anything at all, really. You're not well. Do you need anything from the shops, for instance?'

'Eh ... no, thanks. Or yes, in fact, but I'll go shopping myself. Later. Could I read those emails again?'

'Of course.'

Selma located them and handed her the mobile.

Cathrine dissolved into tears as she read.

'Sorry,' she said under her breath, drying her eyes with the sleeve of her red tracksuit. 'I start crying over nothing these days.'

'I can well understand,' Selma said calmly, leaning across the table. 'This must be a very difficult time for you. For you all, of course, but Mina and Tryggve have each other just now.'

When Cathrine failed to respond, Selma continued: 'I've often thought what a strain politics must be. For politicians, but maybe even more so for their nearest and dearest. You haven't chosen this existence. Mina certainly hasn't, at least. With all these new social media, all the hatred, the bias and the witch-hunts ...'

Cathrine still sat quietly, weeping. But she was listening, Selma noted.

'You've maybe not picked up on it,' she went on, 'but a few days ago, *DG* ran a big story about me and my ... former boyfriend. It was absolutely awful. My children ...'

She left a carefully calculated pause.

'They became so terribly upset,' she then said. 'Our relationship was so new that I hadn't yet told them about it. You know how it is. They actually got a bit angry with me. And Jesper ... my boyfriend, got so furious that he called things off. This is small beer compared to what you've had to put up with, but I do understand at least partially ...'

'I got shit in the post.'

'What?'

'Shit in the post!'

Now she burst into a flood of tears, shoving the mug of tea away and cradling her head in her hands on the table.

Selma stood up, pulled her chair closer and placed a tentative hand on the exhausted woman's back. It was not shaken off. Selma was not nudged away.

'It's unbearable,' Cathrine said, her words half-smothered by her sobs. 'Tryggve can't keep away from politics, though we got on far better when he was just a lawyer. It's exactly as if ...'

She straightened her back with a jerk.

'People have gone mad,' she said loudly. 'They think they have the right to say anything they like. And they do. It affects Mina. It crushes Mina. It makes Mina ... Tryggve keeps saying that we mustn't pay any attention to it, that people just like to mouth off and they would never do anything serious about all these threats, but human excrement in a food container in the mailbox is surely doing something serious about it, don't you think?'

Selma had almost imperceptibly pulled her chair back a little.

'The police usually get to the bottom of these things,' she said, unfazed. 'They'll get their punishment. Not that it makes it any easier to accept, but ...'

'I haven't reported it.'

'No?'

'I don't even mention it to Tryggve when they get too aggressive. The ones out there. Not to him, and certainly not to the police.'

She waved distractedly towards the kitchen window, as if there were a police officer standing outside.

'On social media. In the comments. I say nothing. He gets so terribly upset if I show him things. He says that ... But he ...'

Now she was gasping for breath.

Selma got to her feet, turned on the tap and opened a couple of cupboards until she found a tumbler. Filled it with water and put it down in front of Cathrine.

'Try to drink some,' she said gently.

'Sorry,' Cathrine bleated.

'Nothing to apologize for. I understand totally. As well as anyone can understand things like that, anyway. Without having experienced quite the same myself.'

The other woman took the tumbler and drank all the water in one gulp. Put down the tumbler and straightened up with a visibly superhuman effort.

'I was raped once,' she said in a loud voice.

Selma sat quiet as a mouse.

'I've never told that to a living soul.'

From the direction of her gaze, she appeared to be speaking to the fireplace.

'I was nineteen and on my way home from a party, far too late. Well and truly drunk. I thought afterwards that if I didn't tell anyone, then the whole thing would just disappear. That with the passage of time I would forget all about it. It doesn't work like that. That's what it's like with all this other stuff too. I've kept thinking that if I don't say anything about it, if I don't tell Tryggve about everything he himself chooses to ignore, it will just sort of cease to exist. But it's not like that. This last while, this past six months, maybe, I've hassled and hassled and hassled him to resign. I should have ...'

Now she turned her head and looked at Selma.

Her eyes belonged to a woman who was slowly grasping that she had lost everything, Selma thought. If she played her cards right now, she would get what she was looking for. Seemingly on impulse, she leaned forward and grabbed Cathrine's hand.

Kept her eyes fixed on hers.

'Now he's resigned at last,' Cathrine continued, 'but I'm left sitting here. Everything has fallen apart. My marriage, my relationship with my child ... I'm falling apart. And my child is ...'

She took a long, trembling, deep breath.

Selma observed her, adopting a serious expression, as she ran her thumb over the back of Cathrine's dry hand.

'I can't comfort you,' she said softly and slowly. 'There are no words to assuage your sorrow. But I can stay here for a while, if you like. And even though you don't think so now, everything will get better. That's what life is like. Things will be OK.'

All at once, as if she had suddenly woken up, Cathrine let go of Selma's hand and exclaimed: 'What was it you wanted, actually? Why are you here when you knew Mina is abroad?'

'That doesn't matter,' Selma said. 'We can talk about it later. Another time. But, please, do you think I could use your toilet?'

Cathrine nodded. 'We're redecorating the guest bathroom, but you can go upstairs. First door on the left.'

Selma left the kitchen and went upstairs. The air in the house was stuffy and unpleasant, and a grey layer of dust had settled everywhere. When she reached the bathroom on the upper floor, it occurred to her that this bathroom too could do with some renovation. The silicon seals between the tiles and cornices were cracked and yellow, and there was a noticeable crack in the granite worktop. The tap was dripping, one drop per second, and the inspection hatch on the bathtub was missing.

Selma pulled down her jeans and sat on the toilet seat.

She really just needed a moment to think.

Cathrine had been incredibly close to total breakdown. Selma could not quite understand what it was that had suddenly made her sit bolt upright and ask her what she was really after. She felt dreadfully sorry for the woman, but Selma was there for a reason. Getting in touch with Tryggve Mejer was the only meaningful outcome for her. For days she had tried to find his contact information, with no luck. She had even contacted Lars Winther, despite how furious she still was with him – by text message, admittedly, as she could not yet bring herself to speak face to face with him. He had answered with endless excuses about tipping off *DG* about Jesper, and in the end added a PS in which he explained that Tryggve Mejer had been furnished with brand new, top secret telephone numbers and electronic addresses. There was not a newspaper in the country that had managed to locate the guy as yet, so sadly Lars could not help her with that.

Sorry, sorry yet again.

Selma had not replied.

Under the bathroom basin, there were four drawers, two sets of two. The bottom one on the right was Mina's. Wobbly capital letters written in permanent marker: MINA. She must have been about five. A sticker of a faded Smurf had obviously been impossible to remove over the years. Selma stood up and hoisted her jeans without looking down. She tore off a strip of toilet paper and placed it between her fingers and the handle before she pulled out the drawer.

Only women's handbags told more about them than their bathroom drawers. In both lay secrets, knick-knacks and necessities, all at sixes and sevens. Good taste and a penchant for quality were revealed. They disclosed whether the owner had a sense of tidiness or couldn't care less, spent money on herself or was tight-fisted when it came to personal hygiene.

Selma had opened more of them than she cared to remember.

MINA, the shaky lettering declared, and Selma pulled out the drawer carefully.

Tampons and night-time sanitary towels. Two hairbrushes and a saucer of scrunchies. Deodorant of the kind you bought at the local Rema 1000 supermarket for fifty kroner apiece. Four bottles of perfume, two of which were lying flat because the drawer was not deep enough. A little box that apparently contained cheap jewellery. Selma stood with the toilet paper in her hand, wondering whether to open the lid. The little kick she derived from rooting around in other people's private possessions felt good, almost intoxicating, and she was about to open the box when she noticed a tiny piece of sticky tape on the wall at the very back of the drawer. The lock mechanism prevented her from sliding it all the way out, so she crouched down and peered in instead.

The tape attached a black gizmo to the back wall. Completely ordinary masking tape, beige and easy to remove. She thrust in her right hand and caught hold of the little piece of plastic.

And tore it off.

A memory stick. That Mina had hidden away. That she, in other words, didn't want anyone else to see.

And which therefore might well contain something of interest to Selma.

She stuffed the storage device into her pocket, depressed the handle to flush the toilet, and washed her hands thoroughly after firmly shutting the drawer again.

'Sorry for all the mess up there,' Cathrine said when Selma came back downstairs. 'Everywhere, for that matter. As I said, they've taken out the whole bathroom downstairs, and when everything gets so dusty, you lose the urge to make any effort to keep everything clean. You know how it is.'

Nodding, Selma assumed that Cathrine's presence in the hallway was a hint that it was time for the uninvited guest to leave.

'I really hope you'll feel better soon,' she said.

'Thanks.'

Cathrine was holding her mug of tea in her hand. It was no longer steaming, and it looked as if she just needed something to hold on to.

'Can't you tell me why you came?'

Selma gulped. She tucked her hair behind her ear and tilted her head.

'A lot of my work is wasted if I can't get a chance to speak to Mina. It'll take only five minutes, but it's important. In a way, I've sort of built a kind of narrative around her, and then ...'

Now she would have to be careful, really careful.

'Forget it,' she said quickly. 'Mina's probably forgotten all about the project, the way her summer has been.'

'Mina doesn't have any new devices,' Cathrine said. 'She wasn't even allowed to take her phone or her iPad. Not her laptop either. Tryggve doesn't entirely trust her, and he doesn't want to be found by journalists for a while at least. A seventeen-year-old is hardly capable of having access to social media without using it.'

'No, I see. Just forget it. Thanks for the tea.'

Her mug sat untouched in the kitchen.

'Of course, I could mention to Tryggve that you'd like to talk to Mina,' Cathrine said without moving as Selma made to approach the door. 'I speak to them both on Skype once a week. Using his machine.'

This was about to go awry. The USB stick was burning in her pocket, and Selma was keen to make her escape as fast as possible.

'They're doing better,' Cathrine said, looking down into the tea in her mug. 'We Skyped yesterday.'

'That's nice. Now I have to go. And as I said, just forget it. Tryggve has far more important things to think about. Mina too.'

'Wait a minute,' Cathrine said, moving into the kitchen.

Selma heard her rummaging through a drawer. A few seconds later, she re-emerged and handed her a note.

'Tryggve's Skype address,' she said sotto voce: she had started to cry again. 'Please, I beg you, don't pass it on to anyone. Thank you so much for coming. You're a good person, Selma Falck. Come back any time.'

'I will do,' she replied, and gave Cathrine a long, friendly hug before leaving her in the full knowledge that she would never venture anywhere near Lofthus terrasse again.

The Warning

'I don't like this, Selma. I really don't like it at all.'

Einar was calling her Selma again, something that could be both a good sign and a bad sign. Either he was in fine fettle, or else terrified out of his wits. Selma was worried that he might in fact be both.

'But what *is* this?'

Selma had gone straight home after her visit to Cathrine Selmer. For some reason she had drawn the curtains when she checked the contents of the stolen memory stick. She had really

413

overstepped the mark even by opening the drawer, and could not quite explain why she had done it.

Desperation, perhaps.

A forlorn hope of finding some hint of the whereabouts of Tryggve Mejer and his daughter was probably the most important reason.

On reflection, it amounted to the same thing.

When she had excused herself to go to the loo despite not needing to, her intention had been to collect her thoughts. She had been in the process of hounding Cathrine Selmer in the direction she wanted her to go, but something had made the poor woman pull herself together before breaking down completely so that Selma could extract from her what she was looking for.

The earlier adrenaline kick had turned into a sliver of guilty conscience, a feeling of which Selma had very little experience.

An hour and a half later, that feeling had long vanished into thin air, and she sat with a stack of printouts, totalling one hundred pages.

'But what on earth *is* this?'

Selma had brought a Big Mac and cola for Einar. He had eaten the hamburger immediately and her papers were smeared with grease and ketchup. Pussycat sat on the coffee table, licking the polystyrene container clean.

'This is something you should give a really wide berth,' Einar said, getting to his feet.

'I can't,' Selma told him as she sorted out the twelve sheets of paper that basically comprised a long list of names divided into subgroups. 'To judge from the names, most of these people are ethnic Norwegians. But not all. Each has a series of numbers after it. They're not phone numbers, because they have far too many digits.'

'Codes,' Einar said succinctly. 'The phone numbers are hidden within them. The same applies to addresses and other personal details.'

'How do you know that?'

'I don't know for certain. I'm guessing.'

'But what about this, then?'

Selma pointed at a sheet of paper that contained only eighteen lines of letters and numbers. Four letters at the start of each line, then two columns of figures.

'No idea. No idea at all.'

He made a sudden move and Pussycat, startled, jumped down from the table. The polystyrene box was totally clean, and the cat lay down on a pile of newspapers and began to give himself a wash.

'No idea,' Einar repeated, as he stood with his back to the wall beside the kitchen.

'Have you taken your medicines?' Selma asked.

'Yes, every morning. I'm fine. Absolutely tip top.'

He was pressing his body so hard against the textured wallpaper that he was standing on tiptoe.

'But you have to stay away from all that stuff,' he added. 'Burn it. Forget it.'

'I can't just forget it,' Selma said calmly, waving the largest sheaf of papers. 'If this isn't a really screwed-up novel, it documents something outrageous. Injustice. You don't need to be a lawyer to see that ...'

Einar breathed out from his lungs accompanied by a piercingly loud noise that made Selma glance at him in apprehension.

'Everything's fine,' Einar said, waving his hands dismissively. 'I just need to pull myself together a bit.'

He let himself drop on to his heels. Rubbed his face vigorously. His mouth cracked into an exaggerated smile. He moved towards the cat, lifted it up carefully and sat down for once in the armchair. With the animal on his knee. The cat was happy to be hugged, and started licking his hands.

'Everything's fine,' he repeated. 'Now that I've composed myself. I've absolutely composed myself.'

Selma did not quite recognize him.

Einar Falsen had some good spells, and unbelievably many bad ones. The latter came in fits and starts that she could never really predict, and it was practically impossible for her to monitor him every single day. All the same, down through the years she had learned to be a short step ahead of him. There were small signs and warnings each time he was on his way to a really bad period. Stopping eating anything other than cheese puffs was one of them. A little indication was also whether he called her Mariska or Selma. Most clear of all, however, was this physical restlessness. This was new, and had first started after she had persuaded him to come inside and renounce his homeless existence.

Outdoors, he was forced to save energy. He had remained quiet on most of the occasions she had visited him when he lived under the Sinsenkrysset intersection. No matter how bad he was. Here, indoors in the warmth, she noticed that his downturns were usually preceded by progressive agitation. It normally ended in tirades of tics, twitches and fretful pacing from room to room. When he became like this, Selma knew that she must, as calmly as possible, accompany him in the journey down into Einar's bottomless pit. As a rule, there was little she could do other than make sure that he survived.

Now he was moving full speed ahead into one of these downturns.

Three minutes later, he was sitting quietly in a chair with Pussycat on his lap.

'Are you sure you're OK?' she asked.

'We're fine, Pussycat and me.'

His hands ran slowly over the cat's fur.

'Did you already know anything about this?' she asked.

'My Pussycat,' Einar whispered, lifting the cat up to his chest.

Selma gave up. She had come to see Einar for want of a better idea. On good days he could certainly contribute a great many things, and this Stay Behind stuff was something she herself had only heard whispers about in the past. Einar, on the other hand, had been visibly moved when Selma gave him the bundle of photographs from an old-fashioned book on the subject. It was more of a pamphlet, actually, and looked as if it had been written on an ancient typewriter. If she thought back, this was when his agitation had gathered momentum. When he began to read the copy of the little book. She had tried to get him interested in the lists of names and rows of numbers, but he had been so engrossed that he had not even seemed interested in the remarkable, to put it mildly, logbook.

There was some kind of group who called themselves the Council.

Selma had recognized three of the six names in the logbook. The Justice Minister, Ellev Trasop and Birger Hansem, the Deputy Police Chief in Oslo. She had Googled the three others, and if she had succeeded in putting the correct faces to the names, they were also people with prominent positions in Norwegian public life. Only one of them was female. After Trasop's death he did not appear to have been replaced from outside, and Tryggve Mejer had simply stepped up in the hierarchy to become a kind of leader.

The Council was clandestine, that was obvious. A sort of organization, it looked like, with terrifyingly extensive resources. From what little Selma previously knew about Stay Behind groups, it might even appear that one of them had survived the major reorganization of defence policy in the late eighties.

Or maybe sneaked out of sight. It just could not be possible.

The logbook gave detailed information about actions that were not only illegal but also scandalous. In direct contravention of the Constitution.

Absolutely, totally unheard of.

The papers included a full description of Pål Poulsen's blackmail, in cool, technical, and forensic detail. The prelude to a diplomatic spat between Norway and Russia after a news outlet in Murmansk had become the target of comprehensive sabotage might well be far more serious than had emerged in the media. The hackers had been sitting in an adjacent room in the building where the news outfit was housed. They had arrived in the town on a tourist bus under cover of being fishermen from Finnmark.

The damage had been done on Russian territory.

To be honest, Selma did not know whom to believe. Where she should turn.

And most crucial of all: how this could be used to best possible effect so that she could get her children and Jesper back.

The theory Lars Winther and Selma had almost not dared to discuss, the possibility that someone was attacking the political fringes in Norway, appeared to be true.

But the Police Security Service were not the ones behind it. Nor the military intelligence service either. As it appeared to Selma at the moment, she was in possession of documents proving that there was indeed a deep state. It was just so deep that it was not even the state.

It was the middle, as Lars had called it.

Respectable, moderate Norwegians at the centre of the country's political landscape in 2018.

'Bloody hell,' she whispered.

Einar was hiding his face in Pussycat's fur. The cat miaowed.

Lars Winther could undoubtedly have been of more help to her than Einar, but she refused to speak to him. At least not yet. This story was so bonkers, so serious, and with the accompanying documentation so close to having full evidential weight that he would have wanted to wade straight into it. Written about it.

That was not how it should be used.

These were documents that would force Mina Selmer's confession. Or more to the point, her father's.

'Something for something,' Lars was in the habit of saying, and there was scarcely anything on earth that he could give her in exchange for all this.

'You know who Ellev Trasop is?' Einar asked suddenly, putting the cat down on the floor.

'Yes,' Selma replied. 'Former LO leader. He died a while ago. Just after the seventeenth of May, wasn't it?'

Einar leaned forward, closer to the coffee table. This time he left the photographs of the old-fashioned booklet and instead picked up the printout of the logbook.

'He might be dead, but this here obviously lives on.'

'What do you mean?'

'In 1988 I spoke to Ellev Trasop.'

'Oh?'

'That is to say, he spoke to me. Twice, in fact.'

Einar stood up. The click of his knees was very obvious now and seemed almost a parody. He disappeared into the kitchen and soon returned with an apple.

My goodness, Selma thought, but she did not say anything.

'He wanted to recruit me into something.'

'What was that?'

'I don't actually know. I dismissed the idea as soon as I knew what direction we were taking.'

'What do you mean?'

'In contrast to you, I'm a child of the Cold War, Mariska.'

'I was born in 1966, Einar. A cold time in relationships between east and west.'

'In other words, you're a baby of the Cold War. You hardly know what a Stay Behind group was.'

'True enough,' Selma said, and a frown appeared above her nose.

'Ellev Trasop wanted to recruit me into something shady. Something similar to that there.'

He pointed at the papers with the apple and chewed a chunk that was far too big, as if he were a man possessed.

'I had a couple of colleagues who were also sceptical, ' he snuffled with his mouth full of fruit.

'Didn't you sound the alarm?'

'There was nothing to sound the alarm about. Nothing tangible. Those boys there know how to word things.'

'Did you hear from him after that?'

Einar took another bite of the apple without finishing the first piece. Something got stuck in his throat and he began to cough. Selma stood up and skirted around the table.

The coughing fit made his face darken dangerously.

'Spit it out, won't you!'

Selma gave him a hard thump on the back. He let the chewed apple drop from his mouth on to the floor.

'Fruit,' he said contemptuously. 'Hazardous stuff.'

'Idiot,' Selma said, handing him the beaker of cola from McDonald's.

Grabbing it, he sucked down the rest of the contents and kept swallowing. He turned to face Selma and put a hand on her shoulder.

He had never done that before.

'Selma Falck,' he said with such gravity that his voice quivered.
'Yes?'

'You need to stay well away from these people. Burn it all, and forget all about it. This time you really must listen to your old friend Einar Falsen.'

His eyes were different. New life had sparked into them. Selma caught a glimpse of the otherwise so dull, yellowish-brown irises. Something sharp and present. It was as if, in a matter of seconds, he had become the man he used to be, the man she had known for a very short time before, in a rage, he had killed a prisoner and descended into psychosis and anxiety.

'Maybe,' Selma said. 'We'll see.'

The Seychelles

Mina Mejer Selmer was bored to death.

She sat on a kind of verandah in front of the house with a view into a dense forest. Or jungle, really. There were lizards everywhere here, so just in case, she had drawn her feet up on to the chair.

The exhausting journey from Oslo to Victoria had taken three days and nights. There had been intermediate landings and changes of aircraft in Moscow and Dubai and three other places she couldn't even be bothered to remember the names of. In that respect it had been wonderful to arrive at last.

Dad had not even told her where they were going.

When, on the final stretch by air, she had understood that their destination was the Seychelles, she had felt a little happy. Not truly happy, of course, but she imagined it would be beautiful there. Warm, anyhow, but it was lashing with rain when they landed. Despite the rainy period apparently not beginning until Christmas. At least it said so in a brochure she had picked up at the airport, and then the bad weather did not last terribly long. As things turned out, they were headed for a different island from the one where the capital and airport were situated, which took even longer.

A hotel was what Mina had had in mind.

The Seychelles was a travel destination for tourists from all over the world, and Mina and her father would most likely stay at a hotel. It would be better than school in any case, the way school had ended up after the summer holidays.

Instead Dad had rented a house. Someone had rented it for him, at least, she assumed, since he kept stressing that there were only a very few people they could trust.

They had ended up in the middle of a fucking wilderness.

The island was called La Digue, and they lived in a small isolated bungalow. Everything was old-fashioned, apart from the internet connection, but that didn't help Mina in the least.

Dad watched her all the time. Supervised her, really.

He had promised that they might, in a couple of weeks or so, be able to go to one of the hotels on the other side of the island for a meal. Now more than a fortnight had passed without her seeing anyone other than the old man who came on a bicycle to bring them water and food.

Before they left, Dad had taken possession of her iPad, phone and laptop. He had placed them all in the safe in the basement after forcing her to delete all the content from her devices. Software and everything. When they arrived she would receive new ones, he swore, but that must have been just to get her to go along with it without protest. Here on this shitty island, Mina lived a life without telephones, computers or internet, and this was the last straw.

Mina had never believed her dad could be as angry as he had been that night. As upset. As out of his mind with fury, before being convulsed by sobs for another half-hour. In the end he had started to make plans. He had called Mum and she had arrived in the middle of the night. In the early hours of morning at least. Fortunately Dad had not told her what Mina had done, but Mum had agreed that they should go travelling all the same.

Mina understood her father's wrath. She had done something unforgivable. It had tormented her all summer long, turned her holidays into a living hell, but nevertheless she thought her dad should appreciate that she had not intended to kill anyone. He was behaving as if she had done it all intentionally. Shrieking that her future was destroyed and that she was going to be punished, and all sorts of things until in the end it became totally impossible to listen.

So she had not dared to tell him about the memory stick.

He would only have been even more furious.

If anything of the kind was even possible.

Mina had thought of deleting the contents. With her dad hovering over her as she emptied all her devices, it was simply out of the question to tell him that she had yet another copy of the contents of the safe. Afterwards, when he had taken her belongings down to the basement and undoubtedly changed the code for the safe, she was left with no computer to allow her to open the memory stick in order to wipe it.

Just after the crack of dawn, when Mum and Dad had sent her to her room while they talked in unusually subdued voices behind closed doors in the kitchen, she decided to get rid of the damn memory stick. She just did not know where to put it. Smashing it was also an alternative, stamping on it or something. Mum, who always made such a fuss about data security and electronic traces, used to say that nothing could really be removed from the internet. Nor from computers, as there were experts who could retrieve stored material even after they had been destroyed by fire.

The safest thing would be to hide it until she came home and could wipe it properly.

Not in her room. Mum sometimes snooped around in there.

She left her bathroom drawer in peace, though.

It could lie in there until she came home again. They must return at some point, after all. Dad insisted it was necessary to put everything at a distance, as far away as possible. Sjalg Petterson's death, for instance. The case must be dropped by the police first. Reporters must stop showing an interest in the Mejer-Selmer family, as journalists were constantly in pursuit of new stories, the latest news.

A lizard skittered across the verandah and Mina tucked her legs up even more snugly.

The summer had been filled with anxiety and remorse over what she had done. Her parents' separation and Dad's obvious sorrow and bewilderment had made her dreadfully distressed. Now she was bored to tears, more than anything else, and also felt mean and ungrateful. All the same, she was no longer so afraid, and Dad had offered up his career for her sake.

It was just so unbearable to be denied access to the internet.

From inside the bungalow, where Dad sat doing something incomprehensible, she heard the bubbly, easily recognizable ringtone that meant someone wanted to get hold of them on Dad's new Skype account.

'Mum?' she murmured as she went inside.

Skype

Selma had spent twenty-four hours preparing for this.

She would have liked even more time, but the danger that Cathrine Selmer would contact her little family was so inescapable that she did not dare postpone any longer. If Mina's mother

424

mentioned that Selma Falck had called round, and the alleged reason for the visit, then Selma's cover would be blown. She would still have the photos of Mina from the wedding, and she would still have the information and documentation about the Council and its activities, but she would have lost the element of surprise.

Everything hinged on him taking her call.

She had decided to set up a Skype account in a different name, but soon dismissed the idea. Selma's own identity was probably the best magic spell. She had understood that the little family in Lofthus terrasse held her in high regard, and though Tryggve Mejer was exercising extreme care at present, everyone knew that Selma was not a journalist. Tryggve and Selma were also both former members of the legal profession and had met on a number of previous occasions.

Good acquaintances, you might say, and Selma offered up a silent prayer that curiosity would once again open doors for her.

She had sat down at the dining table with her back to the window. For once she had poured her Pepsi Max into a glass, and she placed it beyond range of the laptop camera. Newly showered, wearing discreet make-up, she had spent a couple of minutes rehearsing the smile she had decided to flash by way of introduction. Friendly, but measured. Obliging, but far from servile.

She placed Cathrine's note in front of her and opened Skype on her laptop. Keyed in Tryggve Mejer's address. This was what she had prepared for, this was the decisive card, win or lose. Her heart was thumping but not too fast. She was alert, but not overly nervous.

This was Selma Falck's game. She clicked on the video icon and waited.

No answer. For a long time. And not even then.

Selma aborted the attempt before trying again.

Suddenly Tryggve Mejer was staring at her.

'Hello,' Selma said quickly. 'Selma Falck here. I don't know where you and your daughter are, and I'm not interested in finding out either. What I'm going to tell you is of extreme importance for you and Mina, and so I beg you earnestly not to disconnect the call. I have a great deal of information, and it will be really damaging for both of you if you don't listen to everything I'm about to say.'

He was sitting far too close to the camera. His head was cut off at the hairline and it was barely possible to see anything of his surroundings. To judge by the light, he was indoors. The image was grainy and dark, but on his right side daylight seemed to be spilling in from a window or an open door.

He said nothing. Ran his finger over the bridge of his nose and licked his lips, but he remained silent.

'Did you hear what I just said?' Selma asked.

He nodded haltingly in the slow video transmission.

'The connection's not too good,' Selma said in a loud voice. 'Can you hear me?'

'Yes. Where did you get my Skype details from?'

'I'll tell you that later,' Selma said, calmer now. 'The most important thing is that you can hear me, that you continue to listen, and that you do not cut me off under any circumstances. If the call disconnects for any technical reason, you must answer when I call you back. Do you understand all that?'

She caught herself leaning as close to the camera as he was.

'I'm not interested,' he said.

The sudden jerky movements on the picture might indicate that he was about to end the conversation despite her warnings. Selma was prepared for that.

'Mina killed Sjalg Petterson,' she said loudly and just fast enough to stop the movement in the onscreen image. 'And I have proof. Photographic evidence.'

Now he was leaning back. All of a sudden his hands covered the camera and remained there for a few seconds. When the picture returned, Selma could see a dark wall with a painting of a white, deserted beach.

It could be anywhere, but apparently it was in a hot climate. He was bare-chested. In advance Selma had given thought to time differences; if the father and daughter had for example travelled to Hawaii, it would now be in the middle of the night for them.

It was obvious that was not where they were, as the unsteady strip of light on the wall must be sunshine filtering in through a fluttering, light curtain.

'You can't have,' he said impassively. 'Because it's simply not true.'

'You know that it is,' Selma said, equally unflappable. 'And as I said, I have photographic evidence.'

'That shows what? The man died of anaphylactic shock. There's absolutely nothing to suggest any kind of crime. The case is being dropped by the police as we speak, as far as I understand.'

Selma picked up the two photos she was now able to describe in the tiniest detail.

'I could show you these photos here and now,' she said, 'but the quality of the Skype link is so poor that it would be better if you gave me an email address. Then I could send them to you, with a brief explanation of what I think they prove.'

'Not interested,' he said, with a protracted yawn. 'And I now consider this conversation over and done with.'

Once again his movements suggested he intended to carry out his threat of disconnecting the call.

'The Council,' Selma yelled. 'I know all about the Council. I have read your logbook. I know ...'

He broke off. The picture died.

'Shit. Shit, shit, shit!'

Selma hammered her fists on the table.

He could not have heard what she had said.

The cards were not working. She had been so sure they were a royal flush. So much preparation had gone into it. All conceivable scenarios had been rehearsed. She had formulated a plan for each and every one of them, painstakingly learned by heart, and nothing was really meant to go wrong.

A new Skype call was notified on her machine.

Selma closed her eyes. Raising her hands, she joined them together and took a couple of deep breaths before accepting the call.

'Now you're the one who's going to listen to me,' Tryggve Mejer said.

'Yes,' Selma replied.

'You're going to answer my questions.'

'I'll answer what I can, but get a grip, for heaven's sake.'

'What is this Council and what is it you know about it?'

'It's a clandestine organization with immense power. Power to exert authority that in a democracy should lie with politically controlled agencies.'

'How do you know this?'

'I refuse to answer that.'

Tryggve gave a deep sigh and bowed his head. He jerked it up again and leaned so close to the camera that she could only see the top part of his face. The picture was distorted by the wide angle and his nose grew enormous.

'What is the name of this alleged logbook you mentioned?'

'Its name? What do you mean?'

'If there is a logbook, as you claim, surely it has a name?'

Selma smiled. Picking up her glass, she drank the remainder of the cola very slowly. She licked her lips, folded her hands and smiled again. More broadly this time.

'Rugged/Storm-scarred,' she said slowly, with exaggerated enunciation.

He stared at her. Said nothing. Selma cursed the appalling connection; it would have been useful to be able to see the details of how his expression changed. Even on the grainy image, it was as if his face collapsed. The bags under his eyes became darker and his eyes sank further into his skull. Around his mouth she definitely thought she could make out a slight tremble.

'I have everything,' she said when the hiatus had lasted exactly as long as it should. 'And the minute I make it all public, you won't be able to hide away any longer. Then it won't only be journalists who are after you. The very second I let the cat out of this bag that for the moment only I have in my possession, you'll be a wanted man internationally. Wanted by the police.'

Still he said nothing. He had covered his face with his hands. All of a sudden he stood up and disappeared out of the picture, but without breaking the connection.

Selma waited. And waited. This was also something she had prepared for. Now he was as far down as he could go.

At last it was time to offer him some hope.

He returned with a bottle of water. Opened it, drank, and was about to say something when Selma beat him to the punch.

'I'm not out to get you, Tryggve Mejer. I'm after justice for Sjalg Petterson. My son-in-law, even if only for a few hours. If you come home and let Mina take responsibility for what she has done, I'll bury the Council. The logbook. The lists of what seem to be personnel, codes and probably bank accounts. You'll get it all back. But Mina must tell the police how she used ice cubes with what I assume to be ground nuts in them to kill Sjalg Petterson.'

Tryggve Mejer gawped at her. He looked as if he could not quite fathom what she had just said. As if she had suggested travelling down there to marry him or something equally absurd.

'As I said,' Selma began, 'the choice is—'

'Do you have children, Selma Falck?'

He sounded dumbfounded. Indignant, bordering on furious.

This was a development Selma had not included in her calculations.

'Eh ... yes.'

'And yet you make such a demand? Are you completely off your rocker?'

Selma did not respond. The performance was no longer following the script.

He laughed. Almost hysterically. Tipped his head back and roared. Slapped his hands on the table, grabbed the bottle of water and drank nearly all of it before suddenly becoming deadly earnest and peering into the camera.

'What is it you want to achieve?' he demanded. 'What is the most important thing for you here?'

'That Mina takes the blame for Sjalg Petterson's death,' Selma answered slowly. 'As I told you.'

'No,' he replied grimly. 'You're looking for *someone* to take the blame. Not necessarily Mina.'

Selma could not comprehend where he was going with this, and so did not respond.

'I'll give you an alternative,' he said.

The man had gone through so many changes in the course of this conversation that Selma felt dizzy. Now he had become a lawyer again. The Justice Minister. The dispassionate, determined politician he had always been: he could just as easily have been sitting there in a well-fitting shirt and tie.

'And this is the only thing I'll go along with,' he continued. 'Let Rugged/Storm-scarred, and therefore me, take responsibility for Sjalg Petterson's death. I'll arrange for the evidence myself. Bury whatever you have on Mina. Let my daughter go

430

free. She didn't mean to kill Sjalg. She just wanted to spoil the wedding. Let me take the brunt of it. Of everything. Of what lies within Rugged/Storm-scarred, and everything connected to your son-in-law's death.'

Still Selma did not answer. This was so beyond everything she had envisaged that she was terrified of making a misstep.

'I've just spoken to Erna Solberg,' he continued, equally composed. 'For reasons I can't go into now, she intends to resign as Prime Minister and Party Leader within a very short time. In connection with that, an extraordinary national meeting of the Conservative Party will be held on the sixteenth September.'

'Eh ... really?'

'It will all be officially announced in the next twenty-four hours. I promise to return home for that meeting. I promise to use all the means at my disposal to create a media storm about my crimes. I will not shirk either the condemnation of the people or the courts. In return you are going to give me one, overriding promise: Mina is to be left in peace, able to continue with the life she deserves.'

Selma struggled to think. Quickly. It was impossible – her thoughts collided and became tangled. She could not work out whether this was a good or bad outcome.

For her.

'Yeee ...'

'Surely it makes no difference to you, Selma Falck. Not so for me.'

Something appealing, almost pleading, had come over his entire demeanour. His chin hung low, as if he no longer had the strength to hold it up. His voice tailed off.

Selma Falck had not considered the possibility of such a solution.

The man was offering himself in place of his daughter.

And Selma got what she wanted all the same.

'OK,' she said finally, nodding her head. 'We'll do things that way.'

'I'll contact you with the details,' he said, and rang off.

Harlequin

The warning sounded, as warnings were programmed to do. Berit Ullern was deeply concerned.

Private investigator Selma Falck had made contact with the recently resigned Justice Minister Tryggve Mejer.

The conversation on Skype, or to be more precise, their two subsequent conversations, had lasted exactly eight minutes and four seconds from the time Selma had first called until they hung up for the last time. Brief enough for the Major to listen to it three times over.

The last time, she took notes.

When she was finished, she read through them. She sorted out what she had written and thought through what had happened. Struggled to understand, but could not quite succeed.

She already knew that Selma had visited Cathrine Selmer. She had precise transcripts of what the two women had discussed. The Major had told the truth when she had sworn that Tryggve Mejer had never been under surveillance while Justice Minister. However, he no longer held that position. Two men from the Action Group Manus had bugged the residence in Lofthus terrasse as soon as Tryggve Mejer's hotly discussed press conference was over. When he had left the government's premises for good, he was reduced to the status of a loose cannon on the deck with no kind of defence.

Other rules then came into play.

Selma Falck's visit to Cathrine Selmer had aroused deep suspicion in the Major. She had been on the alert for the former lawyer as soon as it became clear that she had spoken to Pål Poulsen. Following the meeting in the layby near Brumunddal, her nervousness about what

Selma Falck might actually know increased, but later it seemed as if she had lost interest in both Poulsen and everything else to do with Tryggve Mejer's activities. Especially after she was targeted in lurid stories about a spicy love affair, and had remained indoors for days on end without contacting a living soul.

The Major was about to let the former lawyer drop out of sight when she again cropped up in the case. One of the Major's many problems now was that there was nothing in the conversation between Cathrine and Selma to explain how the latter had obtained intimate knowledge of both the Council and Tryggve Mejer's activities in recent weeks.

The two women had talked about hatred and witch-hunts and human excrement in a blue food container. About a rape that held no interest for the Major, and that life was a place where most things passed. In the end.

Nothing about the Council. Nothing about an operation called Rugged/Storm-scarred which Cathrine's husband had set in motion off his own bat in contravention of the law, justice and the Council's explicit prohibition.

Berit Ullern really could not fathom where Selma Falck had obtained this knowledge. She got up from her desk and fetched the casket. It sat as an ornament in her living room, just as Ellev Trasop had always displayed it on his mantelpiece.

She placed it on the desk, but did not open it. Not yet. First she gathered all her notes and fed them into a small shredder in the corner of her home office. She retained only one sheet.

It was handwritten, and described what action she now had to take.

Placing it on the right-hand side of the casket, she opened the exquisite lid decorated with King Haakon's monogram.

Sadly it was now necessary to breathe life into Harlequin.

The Discovery

S elma heard voices.

Singing, dancing voices: several of them, and they could be angels she heard.

Lupus had come with her to heaven. He lay beside her, almost on top of her body. He was warm. Selma was freezing. She wanted to open her eyes, but her body refused to function.

Someone touched her neck. She had a mask over her face. She didn't want it, was desperate to pull it off but her hands would not obey.

Lupus growled. She could feel the vibration in his throat. He was going to scare them away. She wanted to be left alone to finish dying in peace.

That was the only thing she wanted. To finish dying.

They were denying her that, and she tried to hit out at them.

Her eyes, Selma thought. She had to be able to see.

These people thought she was alive, but actually she was dead. Last time they had thought she was dead, but they had been wrong. She was still alive, and could hear everything they said.

It was impossible to see them this time.

'Lupus,' she said, without being able to hear her own voice.

Her lips were so dry. She was so terribly thirsty.

'We'll take care of your dog,' she heard a woman say. 'Don't be afraid. Did you say Lupus? Is his name Lupus? I have him on a lead already. He loves you, that dog. He's probably saved your life.'

'I'm Bjørn,' a man spoke into her ear. 'The others here are Mathilde and Eirik. We come from Geilo Red Cross Rescue Team. You were reported missing, and the police found out that you had gone into the mountains. Now all you have to do is lie absolutely still. We're going to get you out of here.'

Selma was lifted up.

It was painful. She was light and heavy at the same time. The angels smelled good. Their hands were warm. Their voices sang. Selma wanted to fight, she would not let them kill her, she wanted to resist as she had done the last time.

She wanted to see them, but could not.

Selma wanted some water. Someone gave her an injection in her arm. It felt fine, she could feel it: a needle prick that showed she was still alive and had arms, at least one. She was lying on a bed. A hard bed, a bench, a bunk, they tied her to it, gave her blankets, and she felt warm.

They thought she was dead, the men who had taken her.

These were different people. They thought she was alive.

Selma herself was not entirely sure.

Someone carried her across the mountain plateau. They cheered and slapped her cheek, it was a woman who was shouting, telling her she would soon be there, a voice that annoyed Selma even though it was of no consequence.

Not at all: she fell asleep. A deep sleep, completely devoid of nightmares.

Too Late

Two men stood with binoculars, watching the rescue operation.

'Fuck,' one of them said under his breath.

The other one said nothing at all.

Instead he keyed in a number on a satellite phone before putting it to his ear. When there was an answer at the other end, he said: 'Too late. The Red Cross beat us to it by quarter of an hour or so. The drone found her, we were on our way, but didn't get there in time.'

He listened for a few seconds, gave a confirmatory reply and stuffed the phone back into his pocket. He lifted the four-kilo drone from the ground.

'Come on,' he said, heading back in the direction they had come. 'We've got a lot to do.'

The Ambulance Helicopter

Selma was flying.

She was inside the mosquito, inside the dragonfly that must have been a drone.

There was no room for a human being inside a dragonfly. Not in a drone either, but she was certainly flying.

If she opened her hands, she would let go of her life.

Selma's knuckles whitened, and a red man put a hand around her fist. His clothes were red. His hair and beard were red. He said something; her eyes were open at last. His mouth was moving, he was smiling, but the engine noise drowned out everything. Lupus was not there. Neither was Lars Winther. Selma had to get in touch with Lars Winther.

The man could not hear her.

If she opened her hands she would die, so she clenched the palms of her own hands as hard as she possibly could.

Plan B

'She'll never survive.'

'How do you know that?'

'We're listening in to their radio communication. She's in shock. Her heart has already stopped twice. They're transporting her to the National Hospital, but it's too far. Her organs will break down, one by one. No one can survive what she's been through.'

'You said that last time too.'

Hans-Olav Storbergan swallowed audibly. He moved the phone from his right to his left hand, and pulled the car over to the side of the road.

'She's dying,' he said firmly. 'In any case, that's the best we can hope for. We've no way of reaching her now. There's nothing more we can do.'

'What about the documentation?'

'Her mobile and laptop were in the ruins. Completely destroyed, as we planned. In her apartment in Sagene we found a bundle of printouts, and we took care of them before we came up into the mountains. We were thorough. We even found a hidden cupboard in her wardrobe, full of loads of photos from what looked like a wedding. To make doubly sure, we destroyed them too. Only Selma herself is a threat now, and soon she will be eliminated.'

Berit Ullern disconnected the call. She replaced the clumsy yellow-and-black phone in the casket. Closed the lid, and let her fingers slide over the elaborately carved wild flowers.

Selma Falck was dying. Her documents had been taken care of. It could only be a matter of hours or minutes until she no longer posed a problem.

That was how it had to be.

Tryggve Mejer and his daughter were on their way home from the Seychelles. The Major was reluctantly impressed that

437

Sjalg Petterson had died so elegantly, without any assistance from Harlequin.

So the young girl had been responsible for that.

Even more admirable, in fact.

Tryggve and Mina would land at Gardermoen airport an hour after the start of the Conservative Party's extraordinary general meeting at the Radisson Blu Airport Hotel. Norway had no idea that the pair were on their way home. The authorities did not know either that the former Justice Minister planned to deliver a speech at the hastily convened gathering. Only Erna Solberg herself knew of his return, and she was ready to pass a note to the chairperson when the time was right. The stage would be cleared for Tryggve Mejer, the popular politician who would lend his support to the Prime Minister's candidate for new party leader.

In the party, he had been a well-loved figure even before his resignation, and the farewell speech he had given about parents' responsibilities to older children had sparked a wide-ranging, interesting debate about the role of the modern parent. If he wished the post for himself, he would be chosen by acclamation.

Instead he had been invited in all secrecy to give an election speech for someone else. With his weight on the scales, the short and fairly brutal election campaign would be over.

What not even the Prime Minister knew was that Tryggve did not plan to give a speech in support of the Defence Minister.

However, Berit Ullern knew, and the man therefore had to be stopped. Tryggve Mejer no longer had any evidence. He had no documents, no codes or yellowing papers that would uncover an illegal organization. All he had was his own story and personal credibility on which no one would cast doubt.

Unfortunately, that would be enough.

He would use his speech to confess. To expose the Council and its members, the organization's activity and purpose.

Out of the question, really.

Berit Ullern had entertained the notion of threatening him, forcing him to continue his silence. She knew the truth about Sjalg Petterson's death. Mina would no longer be safe if Berit tipped off the police.

The problem was that she had no access to Selma Falck's photographs. Since the Major never gave out more information than what she felt was strictly necessary, the two men who had ransacked Selma's apartment had destroyed the huge pile of wedding photos. That was a serious blunder, but she had only herself to blame for that. Without the photos, an accusation that the historian's death had been caused by a teenager's foolish trick with ice cubes would fall on completely stony ground.

Before he reached that rostrum, Tryggve Mejer had to die.

It had been taken care of. It was going to happen, Berit Ullern mused, as she went to pack her suitcase. Even though everything was sure to go according to plan, it was necessary to keep open the possibility of an alternative outcome.

According to plan, Selma Falck should have been dead long ago. Her life should also have been taken care of. All the same, she was still alive.

Or maybe not.

In any case, the Major needed a Plan B.

At least she had personal control over that.

The Password

Lars Winther was out of breath when he finally stood in front of an entrance door in one of the most run-down apartment blocks in Oslo. The door was smeared with two diagonal stripes of some unidentifiable sticky substance, and he pulled his sleeve over his hand before knocking loudly.

He heard shuffling footsteps from inside the apartment. A security chain rattled but to judge from the sounds it was being hooked on, not off. Lars waited impatiently.

Selma had seemed completely out of it. Drugged, almost.

Maybe she was: it was a doctor who had phoned Lars. He was a surgeon at the National Hospital, he said, and had a patient who really should not talk to anyone. Between the lines he could detect total astonishment that Selma was in a condition to explain anything. Lars was worried, and his concern did not diminish when he had Selma on the line. She slurred, and was using strange words. Her sentences were disjointed, but before someone took the phone from her and disconnected the call, he had understood two things.

Firstly he must get hold of someone with backbone at the Conservative Party's extraordinary general meeting at Gardermoen. Tryggve Mejer must be stopped before he stepped up to the rostrum, and be taken to a secure place with a police presence.

Lars Winther had called four people: three colleagues in the press, and a Conservative mayor from Vestfold who owned a cabin beside Lars's parents. They had all protested. Tryggve Mejer was not here, they claimed obstinately, and there was still no one who had any idea where the man had gone after his dramatic departure as a government minister.

With increasing anxiety, Lars had then jumped on his bike to fulfil Selma's other command.

The rattling finally stopped on the other side of the door, and it was opened a five-centimetre crack.

'What do you want?' asked the peculiar man Selma Falck called her best friend.

'Mariska says hi,' Lars announced in a loud, clear voice, the other thing that Selma had ordered him to do.

'Oh, she does, does she!' the voice responded enthusiastically.

The chain was unhooked and the door opened wide.

'Come in,' the man said, padding through to the living room with an ugly cat at his heels. 'So she's been found. That's good. I was so worried. I told the police. Sometimes a few days pass between her visits, but ...'

The rest disappeared when the guy stuck his head under the kitchen sink.

'Here,' he said, turning to face Lars. 'Mariska asked me to give you this if you knew the code word. And you certainly did.'

Hesitating, Lars took the thick folder, a green cardboard cover with an elastic band around it.

'What's this?' he asked.

'I don't know,' Einar replied. 'I don't snoop in other people's belongings.'

Lars's phone began to ring. Einar shrieked and rushed off to the corner of the living room. Lars, remembering what Selma had told him earlier about the man's attitude to electronics, ended the call quickly and turned off the sound. Four messages, he noticed, and yet another missed call visible on the display.

'Sorry,' Lars said loudly. 'It's turned off now.'

'Go away,' Einar whimpered hoarsely. 'Go and take that thing with you.'

Lars did as asked and by the time he was out on the street again, he had missed three more calls.

The National Meeting

Mina's mother collected her. Miraculously, no one had noticed her when she had walked on ahead, following her father's orders, as they disembarked from the plane. They did not even sit together on the last leg of the journey. She picked up her luggage on her own, and trundled her case out into the arrivals hall, where Cathrine Selmer stood on the fringes of the crowds craning their necks as they waited for the passengers. Mother and daughter greeted each other casually, also as agreed, and walked together out to the short-stay car park. Five minutes later they were on their way to Skeikampen, where a friend of Cathrine's sister had a cabin they could borrow for a few days.

Tryggve Mejer was met with a far greater flurry of publicity.

Someone had already noticed him on the plane from Paris. An elderly woman and a middle-aged man in a pinstripe suit had taken the liberty of speaking to him during the flight. Tryggve had responded with a strained smile and then closed his eyes. After that, he feigned sleep until the aircraft touched down.

The Prime Minister's office had arranged everything. Tryggve was met by two men in suits at the door of the aircraft, and escorted through corridors he had never seen before. His luggage would be attended to, he was told, and before Tryggve knew anything about it, he was sitting in a car that drove him the short distance to the Radisson Blu Hotel.

He was wound up. Not actually nervous, but extremely tense. He knew these would be his last hours of freedom; he would be arrested as soon as anyone managed to collect their thoughts sufficiently to contact the appropriate authorities. He hoped things would progress rapidly. It would be more secure that way. He had spent the last few days in the bungalow in La Digue arranging his affairs.

Now everything had been settled, and he was prepared.

He did not have a script this time either. He did not need one. The speech was carefully rehearsed and well memorized. There would be time for the details in subsequent interviews. All that was necessary on this occasion was to detonate a bomb so explosively that Mina escaped attention.

Mina now had only one enemy: the Major.

Berit Ullern very probably knew that Tryggve's daughter had accidentally killed Sjalg Petterson. The Major most likely knew everything now, as she always ensured she learned everything she wanted to know. Even though she might not possess the same photographs as Selma, she would never hold back such a trump card when the police reached her. Maybe tomorrow. Maybe as early as this evening.

The Major could point to Mina, but Tryggve had also taken steps to prevent that.

He was totally ready.

At the hotel, he was whisked past the main entrance. The two men led him down to a smaller door fifty metres away. A woman inside let them in, and Tryggve was escorted along a corridor and into a small, windowless room.

'Wait here,' was the instruction from one of the guards.

Tryggve sat down on a yellow settee.

He was aware that his hands were clammy, but they were not shaking.

Life as he had known it would suddenly end, but he would have time to explain himself. Plenty of time. First in the police interrogations, then the interviews he would probably be able to give as soon as the preliminary investigation was over. As soon as the rest of the Council members were arrested. As soon as the very last Stay Behind group in Norway was dismantled and destroyed.

It was time. In the distance he could hear applause, amplified when the door opened. With one guard in front and the other immediately behind, he strode towards the conference hall.

Tryggve raised his arms in a final gesture of triumph.

Thunderous applause. He fixed his eyes on the rostrum in the distance.

Someone shouted his name. Out of the corner of his eye he saw a woman come running. He recognized her immediately; she was head of *Aftenposten*'s political section. She was struggling to say something, she was screaming, but was restrained by security guards who had now appeared out of nowhere. To his left, Tryggve caught sight of Hermod Fredriksen, the jovial mayor from Færder. His face looked different from everyone around him. He seemed dumbstruck. Afraid, in fact, and he said something that failed to reach Tryggve. Everywhere else there were smiles and enthusiastic cheers, a warm welcome for a man they all admired and were delighted to see. Up at the rostrum stood Erna Solberg herself, holding out her hand in an imperious, welcoming gesture.

Tryggve scarcely noticed he had been shot.

He felt no pain.

Only a little jolt to his chest. Close to his heart. Tryggve managed to look down in surprise at himself, a man in the prime of life and at the height of his powers who would never live to be more than fifty years and eleven months old. Only one thought passed through the convolutions of his brain before it short-circuited: Mina was safe.

Both the men from Harlequin and Selma Falck would make sure of that.

Frogner

The Major sat in her spacious apartment in Frogner, Oslo, fully aware that she had succeeded. Harlequin had done what they had to do.

Tryggve Mejer was dead, she read in the dramatic coverage in the online newspapers. Shot through the heart on his way to the rostrum during a national meeting at which Erna Solberg's rumoured intention was to resign after a long life in the service of the nation, and welcome a new party leader and Prime Minister.

Two hours later, there was still great uncertainty about what had taken place. The assassin had not been caught, and no gun had been found. The news was surprising to the Major, but no less gratifying. The killer was terminally ill with pancreatic cancer and would not have lived long enough to be tried for his crime anyway. A professional soldier, he was trained to keep his mouth shut. His family would be well taken care of in the years ahead. If, against all the odds, he had managed to escape after the assassination, Harlequin would still look after the man's wife and children. In addition to him, for the short time he had left on this earth.

The Council always kept its word.

Police officers from all over Østland district were on their way to the airport, along with a large number of ambulances and paramedics. Around ten people had been injured in the panic that ensued after the shot was fired, but at present there was no report of any deaths.

Apart from Tryggve's.

Selma, on the other hand, had not been mentioned by any journalist.

This unsettled the Major.

She had started to pace around her far-too-large apartment, moving from room to room. She stopped only each time she entered her home office, where she pressed 'refresh' over and over again.

Still nothing about Selma Falck's death.

There was silence from the National Hospital, and the police had battened down the hatches. None of her sources could provide any information.

Selma was an A-list celebrity, but maybe not prominent enough all the same to supersede the spectacular news from the Radisson

Blu hotel. Only the king would be able to do that, the Major tried to reassure herself. Anyway, it would take time from the moment of Selma's death until the family had composed themselves sufficiently to make an announcement about her demise.

That's how it must be.

It must be so, but Berit Ullern continued to walk the floor.

Until she could no longer bear it, and sat down at her desk for good.

The men who had entered soundlessly, through the old back door that serving girls had used in the old days, overpowered her swiftly. However, she resisted long enough to remember that Tryggve had expressed himself rather oddly. In Solemskogen he had given her the casket and asked: *'Was it you or Ellev who tried to remove Harlequin?'*

'Tried to remove' were the words he had used, and Berit Ullern died with ironic knowledge of who had actually killed her.

Let down in the end by her own side.

SATURDAY 29 SEPTEMBER 2018

The National Hospital

S elma had slept.

That was mostly what she had done. She remembered nothing of her first few days in hospital, even though the doctors could assure her that she had not fallen into a coma at any time. The couple of heavy blows to the head during her fight with the two kidnappers had apparently not inflicted any permanent brain damage. At least not as serious as had been feared.

The damage to the rest of her body was far worse.

When Selma finally summoned the strength to ask a doctor about the injuries she had sustained, he had given her a lopsided smile and answered that it was easier to give her a list of what she was not suffering from. He thought at least she could comfort herself with the knowledge that virtually all her teeth were intact.

And also her nose was not broken.

In every other respect, she had been in a dreadful state when she had been flown in thirteen days earlier. It was nothing short of miraculous that she was still alive, according to the doctor, who smacked his lips expressively. Cardiac arrest twice. Two fractured fingers. Kidney and liver damage, pneumonia, frostbite, and feet so badly battered that for a time there was real danger that one leg would have to be amputated just below the knee.

Through three surgical interventions, the doctors had battled to save her foot, and they had succeeded.

'Nothing short of a miracle,' the older consultant repeated, patting her on the hand before continuing on his morning rounds.

Selma could see now. Sometimes she had double vision, especially when she was overtired. An eye doctor thought it would be temporary. Every day an optometrist turned up to force her through a half-hour of extremely boring eye exercises.

Selma herself was more preoccupied by physiotherapy. To be fair, a young man arrived three times a day with a ridiculous exercise programme for oldies that she had to complete in bed, but Selma was desperate to get up and stand on her own two feet. She was completely convinced that she would be able to return to her old, athletic self.

However, her mood was definitely improving.

She was allowed her first visitor. Family members had been able to come earlier, but neither Anine nor Johannes had been in touch. This was not unexpected. Jesper had not made contact either, which was probably not so strange, in light of how she had thrown him out of her life.

It disappointed her all the same.

But the bet had been won, and at some time or other she would claim her winnings. There was some kind of hope in that.

Einar, the closest she came to having a big brother, would scarcely have been given permission to set foot in an intensive care unit. Fortunately, he had not tried to come. Instead he had defied his dread of his old Nokia and called her on the new iPhone a young nurse had obtained and set up for her. He had taken ten seconds to assure himself that she was going to survive, before giving her a dressing down for not paying heed to his warnings about the Council. Both parts, Selma thought, felt good.

A bouquet of flowers came in the door.

From behind the colossal floral arrangement, Lars Winther peeped out.

He stood with the gigantic bunch of flowers in his arms, uncertain of where to put it. A care assistant rushed to relieve him of it.

'Selma,' he said warmly.

'Lars,' she replied. 'I'm still furious with you for that story in *DG* about Jesper and me. Have you made sure that Lupus is being looked after until I get out?'

'You can't be *so* very angry,' he said with a broad smile, 'since I'm the one you send messages to about all sorts of things. The mutt is with my cousin in Jessheim and is doing great. And besides … that package you left with Einar, it's the biggest thing that's ever happened to me.'

Now he was grinning from ear to ear before he hastily added: 'From a purely professional point of view, of course. After all, I've got children.'

'But you didn't manage to save Tryggve Mejer.'

'No.'

Glancing around the room, he found a tubular chair that he dragged across to Selma's bedside.

'Maybe I should have alerted the police,' he said softly as he sat down. 'But I thought that would just lead to a whole lot of fuss and delay. Bureaucracy, I mean. So I contacted three colleagues and a mayor I know, but none of them managed to do anything.'

'And there's still a killer on the loose?'

'Yes. There were CCTV cameras in several locations in the hotel, but he was able to map them out and avoid most of them. On the two where he can actually be spotted, he's walking with his head bowed, wearing a cap. The only thing known for sure is that he's slim, in fact pretty skinny, and around five feet eleven.

In the complete chaos that ensued, he quite simply managed to sneak out.'

'A pro,' Selma said succinctly. 'He was from Harlequin.'

'Yes, I'm sure he was.'

There was silence between them. It took Selma by surprise to feel how good it was to see him. When a carer came to tell her that a young man wanted to visit her, she had really hoped for Jesper. In that sense, Lars had been a disappointment.

He was not even particularly young.

'Bit of a story, then,' she said, reaching out for his hand.

He looked taken aback, but let her hold it.

'I've had seven front-page stories in less than a fortnight,' he said. 'Sixteen articles under my byline. The political pundits have also had a field day, and virtually the whole news desk has been working at full capacity. On just this one story. What a scandal. What a gargantuan scandal.'

He looked overjoyed.

'There's material here for a few weeks yet. Years, in fact, because after us will come the writers. Researchers. There are already demands for a full-scale independent inquiry into the whole shebang, and in Parliament they're fighting tooth and nail over how such a committee should be set up. The idea that an independent, powerful state within the state exists here in Norway, beyond all political control, it is just so ...'

'A kind of deep state,' Selma said. 'Just very, very deep.'

She was tiring already.

'I'm not allowed to read very much,' she said. 'But I think I've been able to follow the most important bits. This Major, Berit Ullern, did she really commit suicide?'

'It looks like it. The time of death has been established as a few hours after the drama at Gardermoen. That gives a kind of logic to a suicide, since she would know for certain that the assassination would be thoroughly investigated. She was in deep shit. The lack of a suicide note and a couple of technical details at the crime scene, though, mean the police have hesitated to draw conclusions. My sources say they'll do so as soon as possible.'

'Would there not have been a beautiful symmetry, in a way ...' Selma gave a wan smile, 'if the two of them had each other killed?'

Lars looked at her with eyes like slits. 'What do you mean?'

'They began as allies, a number of years ago. They believed in the same things and guarded a secret together. What if they both had control of Harlequin? And so it all ended with the only people the Council ever really engaged in mortal combat being those two. Tryggve Mejer and Berit Ullern, old allies who in the course of a few months became deadly enemies. And in the end had each other killed.'

'Well, I'm not sure about beautiful,' Lars muttered. 'I wouldn't exactly have used that word myself. At least ... the only thing that ...'

He let go of her hand and drew his chair nearer to the bed.

'The only thing that's still unclear to most of us,' he said in an undertone, 'is what actually happened to you.'

'I've spoken to the police. I don't know if I've got the strength to go through the story again.'

'OK,' Lars said quickly.

The police interview had been painful enough. When it was over, Selma had made up her mind never again to speak about her involuntary stay on the Hardangervidda. At least not for a very long time.

Lars Winther's visit did something to her, however. He brought the outside world with him into the white, sterile room with all the machines that clicked and hummed and that had for several days been necessary to keep her alive. He came to symbolize that everything at some point would return to the old way of life.

Her relationship to Lars had begun less than a year ago, when he had threatened to report her to the police for the theft of a wildlife camera. Gradually he had become a useful collaborator. The man who had brought a bouquet costing many thousands of kroner and who now sat with his elbows on his knees looking at her with concern in his eyes had in the end become a friend.

A real friend. Someone who saw her as she was, and for whom she did not need to put on an act. Someone who even knew that she gambled crazily on occasion.

'They abducted me from my apartment,' she whispered. 'I was lying asleep. They must have knocked me out somehow, because the time from when they overpowered me until I woke on the back seat of my car is still a complete blank. I was tied up. Gagged. But not yet beaten up.'

Lars sat totally still. Selma wanted him to leave. She had no wish to talk about this all over again.

'I must have woken too early,' she said all the same. 'Long before they had expected the sedative to wear off. For some reason I had enough presence of mind not to make a sound. The man driving my car was actually speaking to the other one on the phone. They must have needed a vehicle to drive back to the city, of course, so they had split up. I managed to hear what they were planning. What they were going to do to Tryggve as soon as he came back to Norway. And what they were going to do to me.'

She had started to cry, she realized. It was as if she had several decades' worth of accumulated tears that had to be released. She was not crying because she was upset, because she was not. Neither was it to gain Lars's sympathy, because she had that already.

She was crying because there was nothing else to do.

'When we arrived at the cabin, I pretended to be unconscious. They carried me in and stripped me naked. I could not fathom why they had not killed me at home. A dead body would be easier to shift. The police told me it was a safety precaution. The time of death, which pathologists are so good at establishing, could not occur too early. That was probably why I woke before I was supposed to. They did not use too much sedative to make sure there would be no traces of it in my body when I died.'

She stretched out for the glass on her bedside table.

She had still not drunk anything other than water since her arrival at the hospital. She had begun to get used to the insipid, sweet taste of fresh water without carbon dioxide. She drank and then replaced the glass.

'They put me in the lower bunk in the bedroom. They had found me naked at home, and would probably have wanted to make it look as ...'

She sniffed and tried to catch a hair on her tongue.

'... as if you'd gone to bed yourself?' Lars completed the sentence for her.

'Yes, I assume so. But I would never have gone to bed without pyjamas in a basic cabin in the mountains, of course.'

She finally caught hold of the hair, pulled it out, glanced at it and dropped it on the floor.

'You're exhausted,' Lars said. 'I'll leave. We can talk about it another time.'

'When they started to build things up for a bonfire, I got really scared,' Selma said. 'I got up. I was terrified by what I had heard, and wanted to search for a way out. Away from that place before they set it on fire. They found out, and ...'

She clasped her hands to her face.

'We'll stop now, Selma. Honestly.'

Now Lars was on his feet. A nurse came in, probably because the machines Selma was connected up to were warning of both suddenly rising blood pressure and racing pulse.

'It's time for you to go,' the woman said firmly to Lars, who was already backing out towards the door with his palms raised.

'They beat me senseless,' Selma said in a louder voice, following him with her eyes. 'I tried to fight back. I hit out and kicked and bit and pulled their hair. I used everything I had, but it wasn't enough.'

'There, there, there.' The nurse pressed her carefully but firmly back down on the pillows.

Lars disappeared out the door. Selma closed her eyes. She was breathing with her mouth open, as it was still difficult at times to fill her lungs after the serious infection she had suffered. Gasping for oxygen, she greedily snatched the mask the nurse handed to her.

Selma had fought tenaciously, but the battle was really decided in advance. After one of the men had used a log to deliver a violent blow to Selma's head, she had keeled over. Swearing and cursing, they had left her lying there, on the floor in front of the massive fireplace. One of them had compressed her throat tightly with two fingers that stank of fire and blood.

And declared her dead.

She had died, too, in a sense.

But she had woken up again. Only just.

She was still alive. And she was going to survive.

Now she was dozing off. Maybe the nurse had given her something, because the ceiling above her was rising up towards the sky and the machines were hushed. It felt as if she grew lighter: she floated up from the bed, and her eyes slid shut.

'Mum?' she heard faintly in her ear. 'It's Anine.'

Something soft touched her cheek.

Someone.

Selma smiled, and allowed herself to fall asleep.

AUTHOR'S NOTE

This book is fiction, so I have invented the plot. Living persons are named by their own names, and treated respectfully to the best of my ability. The fictional characters are products of my own imagination.

It is always difficult for a novelist to say exactly where she has found her inspiration. I can't say anything other than that I read newspapers and follow daily events as well as I can.

Nevertheless I would like to mention a few publications I have read that gave me direct help. The first one is the thesis 'Cold War, Secret Army: Stay Behind in Norway' by Frode Fanebust, whose master's degree was awarded by the University of Stavanger in 2016. I would also like to thank the author for his willing help with checking facts in one of the sections of this book. Another inspirational thesis was 'Russian Action to Influence: Is Norwegian Crisis Management Ready for "Active Measures 2.0"', of autumn 2017, written by Paul Fjellmo Grostad at the Norwegian Defence University College. Both these theses make interesting reading and are accessible to the public on Bibsys.no.

During the writing of the final draft of the book, I read an opinion piece in *Aftenposten* by a political adviser in the Norwegian Labour Party, Thomas Boe Hornburg: 'Polarization in Norwegian'. It contained so much fascinating material that I have placed some of the content, lightly reworked, into the mouth of this book's fictional character, Tryggve Mejer.

In the midst of this process, in January 2019, a paper came out that discussed the very impetus for this novel. The pamphlet, called 'Democracy in Trouble', was written by the historian Bård Larsen, and published by the conservative-liberal think-tank Civita. Reading this paper was a solid nudge in the direction I was keen to travel and I have also quoted from it in my introduction to this novel.

Thanks go to my friend Kristin Clemet for a couple of good tips along the way.

Many thanks too to Doctor Frøydis Olafsen at the Molo Clinic, specialist in childhood illnesses and allergies, who patiently and pedagogically answered all my questions on nut allergy.

The little song quotation on page 202 is from Besvärjelse (Vi kommer älska dig då) by Oskar Danielson.

When I phoned my wife from a swelteringly hot Florence in July 2018 and told her that I wanted to write a crime novel about the dilemma facing liberal democracy, her response was rather cool. I thank her for that, since it forced me to go many more rounds of sharpening up the theme in order to convince her. She eventually gave me an enthusiastic thumbs-up, and has since then been exactly the stern critic, wise adviser and supporter, never letting me down, that she has been for more than twenty years. Thank you for that, dearest Tine.

Warm thanks also to our daughter, Ioahanne, who as I write will soon be finishing her first year at upper high school. She knows so much and looks so differently and in such exciting ways at everything. Thanks too to her many friends, they know who they are, who show me snippets of what it is like to be young, nearly fifty years after I was a teenager myself. That has been important for me in relation to this novel's young Mina Mejer Selmer.

Finally I would like to thank my patient and efficient editor Espen Dahl. A thrilling collaboration has only just begun!

Larvik, 12 June 2019
Anne Holt